9.4.19

KT-448-316

Windsor and Maidenhead

95800000049592

PRAISE FOR *EVERYBODY'S FOOL*

'A delightful return ... to a town where dishonesty abounds, everyone misapprehends everyone else and half the citizens are half-crazy. It's a great place for a reader to visit, and it seems to be Russo's spiritual home.' *New York Times*

'The *Fool* books represent an enormous achievement, creating a world as richly detailed as the one we step into each day of our lives.... Sully in particular emerges as one of the most credible and engaging heroes in recent American fiction.... Bath is real, Sully is real, and so is Hattie's and the White Horse Tavern and Miss Peoples's house on Main, and I can only hope we haven't seen the last of them. I'd love to see what Sully's going to be up to at 80.' T.C. Boyle, *New York Times Book Review*

'Elegiac but never sentimental ... Russo's compassionate heart is open to the sorrows, and yes, the foolishness of this lonely world, but also the humour, friendship and love that abide.' *San Francisco Chronicle*

'Buoyantly unsentimental ... You hold his books to your heart.' *Boston Globe*

'Rollicking and heartfelt.' *Seattle Times*

'For fans who've missed Sully and the gang, *Everybody's Fool* is like hopping on the last empty barstool surrounded by old friends.' *Entertainment Weekly*

'I was holding my breath for fear *Everybody's Fool* wouldn't live up to its predecessor, but I shouldn't have worried. As good as Russo was in 1993, he's even better now. And *Everybody's Fool* is a delight [with] enough bizarre events, startling revelations, unlikely heroes and touching moments to supply a dozen small towns ... He is also a master of plotting, from cliffhangers to twists that deftly link apparently unrelated threads. This book's tone is largely comic, but Russo writes with uncommon insight about love, families and friendship.' *Tampa Bay Times*

'A madcap romp, weaving mystery, suspense and comedy in a race to the final pages.' *Wall Street Journal*

'[A] sweeping comic novel ... Whether you loved *Nobody's Fool* or never heard of it, reasons abound to read its sequel.' *Providence Journal*

'A writer of great comedy and warmth, Russo's living proof that a book can be profound and wise without aiming straight into darkness. [His] voice can play in any register, any key, any style [in this] portrait of an entire community, in all its romance and all its grit.' *USA Today*

'How could twenty-three years have slipped by since *Nobody's Fool*? ... Russo is probably the best writer of physical comedy that we have.' *Washington Post*

'Everybody should read *Everybody's Fool*. Almost nobody in Richard Russo's novel is sure of anything, but I'm sure of that.... [He] has given readers all they should want.' *Pittsburgh Post-Gazette*

PRAISE FOR RICHARD RUSSO

'Russo is a master craftsman [and] the blue-collar heartache at the centre of his fiction has the sheen of Dickens but the epic levity of John Irving.' *Boston Globe*

'No novelist working today can better capture the rhythms of small-town life, from its comic idiosyncrasies to its wicked undercurrents of gossip and prejudice.' *Sunday Times*

'Richard Russo can write like Edith Wharton leavened with a touch of David Lodge.' *The Economist*

'What has made Russo's work so consistently compelling is the depth of character, the richness of life.' *Minneapolis Star Tribune*

'One of the best novelists around.' *New York Times*

'A masterful storyteller with a mission: to chronicle with insight and compassion the day-to-day life of small-town America ... Alternating episodes of boisterous humour with moments of heart-wrenching pathos, Russo captures with perfection the pulse of small-town life and the rhythm of dramatically changing seasons.' *Houston Chronicle*

ALSO BY RICHARD RUSSO

Mohawk

The Risk Pool

Nobody's Fool

Straight Man

Empire Falls

The Whore's Child

Bridge of Sighs

That Old Cape Magic

Interventions

On Helwig Street

Everybody's Fool

Everybody's Fool

RICHARD RUSSO

ALLEN&UNWIN

This is a work of fiction. Names, characters, places and incidents are products of the author's imagination and are used fictitiously. Any resemblance to actual events, locales, or persons, living or dead, is entirely coincidental.

First published in the United States of America in 2016 by Alfred A. Knopf, a division of Penguin Random House LLC, New York
First published in Great Britain in 2017 by Allen & Unwin
Copyright © Richard Russo, 2016

The moral right of Richard Russo to be identified as the author of this work has been asserted by him in accordance with the Copyright, Designs and Patents Act of 1988.

All rights reserved. No part of this book may be reproduced or transmitted in any form or by any means, electronic or mechanical, including photocopying, recording or by any information storage and retrieval system, without prior permission in writing from the publisher.

Every effort has been made to trace or contact all copyright holders. The publishers will be pleased to make good any omissions or rectify any mistakes brought to their attention at the earliest opportunity.

Allen & Unwin
c/o Atlantic Books
Ormond House
26–27 Boswell Street
London WC1N 3JZ

Phone: 020 7269 1610
Fax: 020 7430 0916
Email: UK@allenandunwin.com
Web: www.allenandunwin.co.uk

A CIP catalogue record of this book is available from the British Library.

Hardback ISBN 978 1 76029 480 9
Trade paperback ISBN 978 1 76029 533 2
E-book ISBN 978 1 95253 527 7

Printed in Great Britain by Clays Ltd, St Ives plc

10 9 8 7 6 5 4 3 2 1

For Howard Frank Mosher

Everybody's Fool

Triangle

HILLDALE CEMETERY IN North Bath was cleaved right down the middle, its Hill and Dale sections divided by a two-lane macadam road, originally a colonial cart path. Death was not a thing unknown to the town's first hearty residents, but they seemed to have badly misjudged how much of it there'd be, how much ground would be needed to accommodate those lost to harsh winters, violent encounters with savages and all manner of illness. Or was it life, their own fecundity, they'd miscalculated? Ironically, it amounted to the same thing. The plot of land set aside on the outskirts of town became crowded, then overcrowded, then chock-full, until finally the dead broke containment, spilling across the now-paved road onto the barren flats and reaching as far as the new highway spur that led to the interstate. Where they'd head next was anybody's guess.

Though blighted by Dutch elm disease in the '70s and more recently by a mold that attacked tree roots, causing them to weaken and constrict and allowing the ground, without warning, to collapse in pits, the original Hill section was still lovely, its mature plantings offering visitors shade and cool breezes. The gentle, rolling terrain and meandering gravel pathways felt natural and comfortable, even giving the impression that those resting beneath its picturesque hummocks—some interred before the Revolutionary War—had come there by choice rather than necessity. They seemed not so much deceased as peacefully drowsing beneath tilting headstones that resembled weathered comfy hats worn at rakish angles. Given the choice of waking into a world even more full of travail than the version they left, who could blame them for punching the snooze button and returning to their slumbers for another quarter century or so?

By contrast, the newer Dale was as flat as a Formica tabletop and every bit as aesthetically pleasing. Its paved pathways were laid out on a grid, the more contemporary grave sites baked and raw looking, its lawn, especially the stretch nearest the highway, a quilt of sickly yellows and fecal browns. The adjacent acreage, where the Ultimate Escape Fun Park had once been pictured, was boggy and foul. Lately, during periods of prolonged rain, its pestilential groundwater tunneled under the road, loosening the soil and tugging downhill the caskets of those most recently interred. After a good nor'easter there was no guarantee that the grave site you visited featured the same casket as the week before. To many the whole thing defied logic. With all that seeping water, the Dale should have been richly verdant, whereas everything planted there shriveled and died, as if in sympathy with its permanent, if shifty, inhabitants. There had to be contamination involved, people said. All those putrid acres had been used as an unofficial dump for as long as anybody could remember, which was why they'd been purchased so cheaply by the fun park's planners. Recently, during a prolonged drought, dozens of leaking metal drums decorated with skulls and crossbones had surfaced. Some were old and rusty, leaking God-only-knew-what; other newcomers were labeled "chrome," which cast a pall of suspicion on neighboring Mohawk, a town once rich in tanneries, but these accusations were emphatically and for the most part convincingly denied. Anybody wanting to know what those tanneries did with their dyes and carcinogenic chemicals only had to visit the local landfill, the stream that ran through town or the hospital's oncology ward. Still, didn't the drums of toxic slurry have to come from somewhere? Downstate most likely. On this point the history of New York was unambiguous. Shit— both liquid and solid, literal and metaphorical—ran uphill in defiance of physics, often into the Catskills, at times all the way to the Adirondacks.

No jaunty, charming grave markers in Dale. Here the stones were laid purposefully flat so they couldn't be tipped over by teenage hooligans. Bath's legendary eighth-grade English teacher, Beryl Peoples, whose dim view of human nature she occasionally shared in acerbic letters to the *North Bath Weekly Journal,* had warned what would happen. With all the stones lying flat, she cautioned, and without any trees or hedgerows to provide an obstacle, visitors would treat the cemetery like a supermarket parking lot and drive directly to whatever grave they had in mind. This warning had been dismissed as perverse and outrageous, a slander on the citizenry, but the old woman had been vindicated. Not a week went by without someone calling the police station to report tire tracks across Grandma's headstone, right where her survivors imagined her upturned, beatific face to be. "How'd you like it if somebody drove a pickup over your skull?" the angry caller would want to know.

Chief of Police Douglas Raymer, arriving at Hilldale late to witness the interment of Judge Barton Flatt, was always at a loss how to respond to such queries, which seemed to him so fundamentally flawed that you couldn't even tell if they were real questions. Were people inviting him to draw the obvious distinction between driving an automobile over an ancestor's grave—an insensitive, inconsiderate act, sure—and driving it over a living person's head, obviously a homicidal and criminal one? How was it helpful for him to imagine what either felt like? It was as if people expected him to make sense of both the physical world and its miscreants, the latter too numerous to count, too various to explicate, the former too deeply mysterious to fathom. When had either become part of the police chief's job description? Wasn't explaining the world's riddles and humans' behaviors what philosophers and psychiatrists and priests were paid to do? Most of the time Raymer had no idea why he himself did what he did, never mind other people.

Whatever his job was, most days—and today was certainly no exception—it sucked. As a patrolman he'd imagined that, as chief, his hours would be filled with genuine police work, or at least real public service, but after two terms he now knew better. Of course in North Bath most crimes didn't demand much detective work. A woman would turn up at the hospital looking like somebody'd beaten the shit out of her, claiming she tripped over her child's toy. When you visited her husband

and offered to shake, the hand he reluctantly extended looked more like a monstrous fruit, purple and swollen, the skin splitting and oozing interior juices. But even such dispiritingly mundane investigations were fascinating compared with Raymer's current duties as chief of police. When he wasn't attending the funerals of people he didn't even like or addressing groups of "concerned citizens" who seemed less interested in any solutions he might propose than how much churlish invective he could be forced to swallow, he was a glorified clerk, a mere functionary who spent his time filling out forms, reporting to selectmen, going over budgets. Some days he never got out from behind his desk. He was getting fat. Also, the pay really sucked. Okay, sure, he made more than he had as a patrolman, but not enough more to cover the endless aggravation. He supposed he could live with the fact that the job sucked if he was any good at it, but the truth was that *he* sucked. He had no idea what he'd have done without Charice—speaking of aggravation—and her incessant badgering. Because she was right, he *was* increasingly forgetful and unfocused and preoccupied. Since Becka . . .

But no, he wasn't going to think about her. He would not. He would concentrate on the here and now.

Which was hot as Uganda. By the time Raymer crossed the cemetery parking lot and walked the hundred or so yards to where a couple dozen mourners were clustered around Judge Flatt's open grave, he was drenched in sweat. Such punishing heat was unheard of in May. Here in the foothills of the Adirondacks, Memorial Day weekend, the unofficial beginning of summer, was almost always profoundly disappointing to the region's winter-ravaged populace, who seemed to believe they could will summer into being. They *would* have their backyard barbecues even when temperatures dipped into the high forties and they had to dig out their parkas. They *would* play softball, even after a week's worth of frigid rains made a soupy mess of the diamond. If a pale, weak sun came out they *would* go out to the reservoir to water-ski. But this year the town's fervent prayers had been answered, as they so often were, at least in Raymer's experience, with ironic vengeance. Midnineties for the past three days, no end in sight.

Raymer would've been more than content to suffer on the periphery of today's proceedings, but he mistakenly made eye contact with the mayor, who, before he could look away, motioned for him to join the other dignitaries, which he reluctantly did. Yesterday, he'd tried his best to weasel out of this funeral, even going so far as to volunteer Charice, who was growing increasingly desperate to get away from the station house, to attend in his place. He'd explained to Gus that he not only had no particular affection for Barton Flatt but also counted him among the many banes of his existence. But the mayor was having none of it. The judge had been an important man, and Gus expected Raymer not just to attend but to be decked out in his dress blues, heat or no heat.

So here he was under the punishing, unseasonable sun, honoring a man who'd disdained him for the better part of two decades. Not that Raymer was alone in this. Disdain was His Honor's default mode, and he made no secret that he considered all human beings venal (a term Raymer had to look up) and feckless (another). If he disliked criminals, he was even less fond of lawyers and policemen, who in his opinion were supposed to know better. The very first time Raymer had been summoned to the judge's chambers, after accidentally discharging his weapon, the judge had fixed him with his trademark baleful stare for what had felt like an eternity before turning his attention to Ollie North, the chief back then. "You know my thoughts on arming morons," he told Ollie. "You arm one, you have to arm them all. Otherwise it's not even good sport." Over the years Raymer had had numerous opportunities to improve the man's low estimation of him but had managed only to worsen it.

But of course there was another reason Raymer had tried to weasel out of this. He hadn't been back to Hilldale since Becka's funeral, and he wasn't at all sure how he'd react to her proximity. He was pretty sure she was out of his system, but what if the shock and pain of her loss came flooding back and he broke down and started sobbing over the memory of a woman who'd made a complete fool of him? What if legitimate mourners witnessed his blubbering? Wouldn't his unmanly sorrow make a mockery of their more heartfelt grief?

"You're late," Gus said out of the corner of his mouth, when Raymer joined him.

"Sorry," Raymer replied, out of the opposite corner of his own, though he wasn't and in this heat he hadn't the energy to pretend otherwise. "A call came in as I was leaving."

"And you couldn't let somebody else handle it?"

Raymer had a ready answer. "I thought you'd want me to handle it myself."

At this the mayor twitched visibly. "Alice?"

"She's fine. I brought her back home."

This was Gus's batshit wife, who, unless Raymer was mistaken, was off her meds again. Charice had radioed him apologetically, explaining the situation. "Really?" Raymer said, his heart sinking. "Not the phone again?"

"Yes indeed," Charice confirmed.

The new cellular telephones, rampant in New York and Albany for more than a year (and gaining traction up the road in Schuyler Springs), still hadn't really caught on in Bath. Gus had one and was threatening to get one for Raymer, with whom he wanted to be in more or less constant touch. Alice had apparently observed people talking on these and immediately understood their application to her own circumstance. Seeing no reason that the pink phone in her bedroom wouldn't serve her purposes nicely, she unhooked the receiver from its cord and put the neutered device in her bag. Then, out in public, when she felt the conversational urge, she took it out and began speaking in the manner of someone talking on an actual cell phone and, in the process, totally freaking people out.

"Why don't you let me take care of this?" Charice had said. "You'll be late for the funeral."

But Raymer was reluctant to allow anyone else to confront the poor woman. She was often frightened by uniforms, but she'd been a friend of Becka's and always recognized him, though his uniform did seem to confuse her.

"No, I'm glad to do it," Raymer said. He was actually fond of the woman. Most of Bath's crazies were belligerent, whereas Alice was docile as a lamb. More than anything, she seemed lonely. Becka's death had hit her hard.

"Maybe another woman—" Charice continued, not unreasonably.

"Thanks, but I need a cool head at HQ," he told her, his usual line. It happened to be true, though. Charice did have the best head in the station house, including his own.

"What. You think I'm gonna scare the mayor's wife? Me being black and all?"

"No, Charice," he assured her. "That thought never crossed my mind." Though it had, just for an instant, before decency could send it packing. "Where is she?"

"The park," she said. "I just hope you don't think you're fooling anybody."

"Charice, it really has nothing to do with—"

"You just don't want to go to that funeral," she said, wrong-footing him with this new tack.

"It won't take long," he said, though in truth he hoped it would.

"Because I could send Miller."

"Miller," he repeated. Could she be serious? Miller? "He's liable to shoot her."

"He's standing right here, Chief."

Raymer sighed, massaging his forehead. "Tell him I'm sorry. That was unkind."

"I'm kidding. He's not really standing here."

"Then I'm not sorry."

"He could've been, is my point. This is how you're always getting into trouble."

"I'm always in trouble?"

"I'm not happy until you're not happy?"

"I asked you not to bring that up, Charice."

"I'm just saying."

"I know, Charice. You're always just saying. I'm asking you to please stop just saying, okay?"

He found Alice sitting on a bench in front of the war memorial. Even in the shade it was blistering hot, though she appeared not to have noticed. She held the pink receiver to her ear. "I could never be so cruel to a friend," she said to whomever she imagined she was talking to.

"Hello, Mrs. Moynihan," Raymer said, sitting down next to her. At some point in her life Alice had apparently been a hippie, and now, in her late fifties, had become one again. She'd stuck a dandelion in her long, graying hair and wasn't, he noticed, wearing a bra. Charice had been right. Again. He should've let her handle this, just as she'd suggested. She'd nailed his motive, too. He *hadn't* wanted to go to the funeral. "How are you today?"

Alice regarded him strangely, as if stumped by the question, then smiled, having evidently decided that, despite his policeman disguise, he was someone she actually knew. Pressing the spot on the phone where the answer/hang-up button would've been if it really was a cellular phone, she slipped it in her bag. "Becka says hello," she told him, causing a chill to run up Raymer's spine even as a bead of sweat trickled down. This wasn't the first time she'd mentioned being in touch with his dead wife.

"Tell her I said hi back."

Alice sighed and looked away, as if embarrassed. "So many men."

It took Raymer a moment to realize they weren't talking about Becka anymore. She was looking at the columns of names on the memorial.

"Boys, most of them," he said.

"Yes, boys. My son is there."

Which was untrue. She and Gus were childless. She'd been married before, but his understanding was there'd been no offspring from that marriage either.

"War is a terrible thing."

"Yes," he agreed. Three names in the Vietnam grouping belonged to classmates of his.

"Becka wanted children."

"No," he said, remembering the only time they'd discussed it. Becka had been adamantly opposed, so he'd pretended he didn't want any, either. "I don't think she did, actually."

"I'll ask her next time."

"Can I give you a lift home, Alice?"

"Should I go home?"

"Gus said you should," Raymer told her. A lie, though it's what he *would* have said had he been aware she'd slipped her leash again.

"Gus loves me," she said, as if reporting a curious, little-known fact.

They rose and Raymer walked her over to his Jetta and helped her inside. They didn't speak again until he pulled in to the driveway of the old Victorian where she and Gus lived, the last house on Upper Main, across from the entrance to Sans Souci Park. Before getting out, she turned to face him. "I keep trying to remember who you are," she said.

"WHERE IN THE WORLD did they find this guy?" Raymer whispered to Gus.

The clergyman delivering the eulogy actually looked a bit like Alice. He had shoulder-length hair, and the intricate, multicolored stitching on his gauzy, flowing tunic suggested ... what? That he had a girl-friend? That he embroidered in his spare time instead of watching sports on TV? There was something viscerally repellent about him, Raymer decided, though it took him a minute to figure out what. With no shirt collar visible above the neckline of the tunic, neither cuffs at the wrist nor socks at the ankle, he gave the impression of being naked underneath his glorified shift, and Raymer was visited by an unwanted vision of the man's dark, swinging genitalia.

"For more than four decades," Reverend Tunic intoned, "Judge Bar-ton Flatt was the voice of justice and reason in our fair city. That was the phrase he used to describe this place we all hold dear. *Our fair city.*"

Raymer stifled a groan. He was reasonably confident that His Honor had never once uttered any such words. In fact Flatt had exhibited little affection of any kind, except for an abstract concept he called "small-town justice," which he claimed to dispense. How that differed from other kinds of justice Raymer never had the temerity to ask, but he suspected it meant "likely to be reversed in a higher court." Proud of his maverick reputation, the judge had rendered his verdicts with the resigned air of a man who knew all too well that other legal minds would in the full-ness of time see things differently. *Our fair city?* Raymer didn't think so.

Dear God was it hot. He could feel distinct rivulets of perspiration tracking down his chest, between his shoulder blades and from beneath his armpits, all this moisture puddling in his bunched-up jockeys. At the bottom of the open grave, which was a good six feet deep, was a patch of shade that Raymer found himself genuinely longing for. That far down it would be cool and fresh smelling. How pleasant it would be to just crawl in and curl up, to rest in such coolness. Okay, there were probably finer things for a man to desire, but in all honesty he couldn't bring any of them to mind. His encounter with poor Alice, and her referencing Becka out of the blue, had caused his spirits—already near low ebb—to plummet further. Since his wife's death a year ago—okay, fine, so he would *think* about her—he simply hadn't been himself. Most mornings, even after a good night's sleep, he woke up feeling so dull and lethargic that he had to talk himself into getting out of bed. Also, his appetites were on the fritz. His sex drive had disappeared completely, and down at the station Charice often had to remind him to eat. Grief, was how she explained it, but Raymer had his doubts. Sure, he'd loved Becka once, loved her with his whole heart, and the way she'd died was indescribably horrible, but now he was mostly just curious to know who she'd been about to run off with.

Gus nudged him, his voice barely audible. "How's your speech coming?"

"Almost done," Raymer assured him, though he hadn't written a word. Monday's big event, the capstone of the holiday weekend, the renaming of the middle school in honor of Beryl Peoples, was something else he'd tried unsuccessfully to weasel out of. Somehow Gus had found out he'd been Miss Beryl's student and had immediately dragooned him into the proceedings. Raymer explained he was a C-plus student at best and could hardly exemplify her teaching prowess. Why not ask somebody who'd at least gotten a good grade? Because the smart kids, Gus informed him, had all moved away, as you'd expect. No, Raymer would have to do it. Earlier in the week he'd sat down with a yellow legal pad and made a couple feeble attempts before giving up. This afternoon he'd try again. If he came up empty, he'd ask Charice to write something.

"Our . . . fair . . . city," Reverend Tunic repeated in mock wonder. Through rhetoric alone, the man had worked himself into a state approaching rapture, and he opened his arms wide, as if to embrace all of Bath, though at the moment his only constituency, apart from the handful of wilting mourners, were those in graves that extended in all directions as far as the eye could see. "As we lay this giant of a man to rest, perhaps we should pause to reflect on what he meant by those words."

Giant of a man? Five foot six, a hundred and forty pounds, tops. Raymer could've clean and jerked this particular giant and given him a good, long toss. In fact, on more than one occasion, he'd imagined doing that very thing.

"Did he mean that here in Schuyler County we're blessed with an abundance of natural beauty and an embarrassment of resources? Of mountains and lakes and streams and springs?"

Springs? Why bring them *up? In Bath they'd all run dry.*

"Of cool, dense forests where once trod swift, silent Iroquois in their soft, supple moccasins?"

Iroquois? Raymer's heart sank. If fucking Indians were creeping into the judge's eulogy, on what possible grounds might anything else be deemed irrelevant?

"I believe he did," declared Reverend Tunic. "But was this *all* he meant?"

Raymer was willing to stipulate that this was the sum total of the deceased's intention if that meant they could all go home, but no such luck.

"*I* for one believe that this was *not* all."

Was it conceivable that this doofus represented an actual church somewhere? He seemed more the start-your-own-religion sort of guy. Or was he some kind of interfaith minister on loan from the college in Schuyler Springs, where he was charged with soothing all the students' sensibilities in the unlikely event they sobered up long enough to have any. An academic affiliation might explain both his windy nonsense and the confidence with which he delivered it. Still, you had to wonder what sort of instructions he'd been given. Hadn't anyone informed him that Judge Flatt had been Bath's foremost atheist? That this was why there'd been no church service? Did he not understand that his appearance here today was a reluctant concession to the man's status as a public figure and the community's desire to pay its final respects? (Okay, Raymer himself felt no such need but conceded that others might.) Reverend Tunic, far from comprehending he'd been given an ass-backward task, seemed convinced it was his duty to deliver the same sermon he'd have preached from his own pulpit to honor the passing of his own beloved deacon. Or, at the very least, to ensure that these proceedings would require the same amount of time under the broiling sun as they'd have taken indoors with the AC blasting.

What would Miss Beryl have made of this dimwit? "When you write," she'd advised Raymer and his classmates, "imagine a rhetorical triangle." At the top of their essays she always drew two triangles, the first representing the essay the student had written and the second, a differently shaped one that would supposedly help improve it. As if bringing in geometry—another subject that had given Raymer fits—would clarify things. The sides of the old lady's triangle were *Subject, Audience* and *Speaker,* and most of the questions she scribbled in the margins of their papers had to do with the relationship between them. *What are you writing* ABOUT? she often wanted to know, drawing a squiggly line up the page to the *S* that marked the subject side. Even when they were writing on a topic she herself had assigned, she'd insist that the essay's subject was unclear. Other times she'd query: *Just who do you imagine your* AUDIENCE *to be?* (Well, *you,* Raymer always wanted to remind her, though she steadfastly denied this was the case.) *What are your readers doing right now? What leads you to believe they'll be interested in any of this?* (Well, if they weren't, why had she assigned this subject to begin with? Did she imagine *he* was interested?)

But her most mysterious and baffling questions always had to do with the speaker. That side of Raymer's triangle was always so tiny, and the other two so elongated, that the resulting geometric shape resembled a boat ramp. On each of his essays she wrote *Who are you?* as if *Douglas Raymer* weren't printed clearly at the top of the first page. When questioned about this, her explanation was equally baffling. There was always, she claimed, an "implied writer" lurking behind the writing itself. Not you, the actual author—not the person you saw when you looked in the mirror—but rather the "you" that you became when you picked up a pen with the intention to communicate. *Who is this Douglas*

Raymer? she liked to ask provocatively. (*Nobody,* he wanted to tell her, perfectly willing to be a nonperson if it meant she'd leave him alone.)

Because it seemed so important to her, Raymer had tried his best to comprehend the old lady's triangle, though it remained as deeply mysterious to him as the Holy Trinity's Father, Son and Holy Ghost. At least that was billed as a profound mystery that you were meant to contemplate, even while knowing that it was beyond human comprehension—a great comfort to Raymer, since it was certainly beyond his. Whereas Miss Beryl's rhetorical triangle was something he was *supposed* to understand.

Today, ironically, more than three decades later, Raymer finally grasped what she had been going on about: Reverend Tunic's triangle was missing two whole sides. He'd clearly given no thought whatsoever to his audience or its suffering in the punishing heat. Nor did his subject really matter. Judge Flatt himself, of whom the man clearly knew nothing, amounted to little more than a rhetorical opportunity. Worse, to fill the resulting void, the speaker side of the triangle, the one that truly flummoxed Raymer as a kid, was the part Reverend Tunic had down cold. If asked, *Who are you?* the clergyman would have replied that he was *somebody* and, to boot, somebody really special. Raymer doubted Miss Beryl would have shared his conviction, but so what? The Reverend Tunics of this world didn't care. Where did such breathtaking self-assurance come from? Though he loathed the man viscerally, Raymer couldn't help envying his dead certainty. Untroubled by a single misgiving, this Reverend Tunic obviously considered himself the right man for this job, probably for any job, even before the job was explained to him. He had everything figured out, couldn't wait to share and seemed to feel there was enough of him to go around.

By contrast, Raymer had always been tortured by self-doubt, allowing other people's opinions about him to trump his own so thoroughly that he was never sure he actually had any. As a kid he'd been particularly susceptible to name-calling, which not only wounded him deeply but turned him imbecilic. Call him stupid, and he suddenly was stupid. Call him a scaredy-cat, and he became a coward. More depressing, adulthood hadn't changed him much. Judge Flatt's remark about arming morons had hurt his feelings precisely because he'd been sized up correctly. Because, face it, his judgment *had* failed that day. He'd allowed Donald Sullivan—another bane of his existence—to get under his skin. That was who'd been driving his pickup on the sidewalk in a residential neighborhood, and Raymer had had every right to arrest him. But he shouldn't have unholstered his weapon, certainly shouldn't have aimed it, even in warning, at an unarmed civilian, and he certainly had no business flicking the pistol's safety off and thus compounding his first two errors. He couldn't remember pulling the trigger but must've—a warning shot was how he'd immediately rationalized it, the thought traveling faster than the bullet. Not much faster, though. A split second later came the distant sound of tinkling glass from—miraculously, Raymer still thought—a tiny octagonal bathroom window a block and a half away, beneath which an elderly woman had been seated on her commode. Had she been quicker about her business or more spry in rising when it was finished, she would've caught the bullet in the back of her head.

The incident had made a pacifist of him. For a good month, until Ollie North noticed something untoward about his bearing and asked to see his weapon, Raymer never even loaded it. Nor would he have thought to wear it if the handbook hadn't stated specifically that the uniform was incomplete without it. Ollie, even more mortified by Raymer's unloaded gun than he'd been by the accidental discharge of his loaded one, had explained that if anything was more dangerous than a civilian with a loaded gun it was a cop with an unloaded one. "Do you have a death wish?" he wanted to know. Even as a young patrolman Raymer knew that the correct answer to that was no, but instead of saying that he'd just shrugged, leaving the question hanging.

What made him so vulnerable to the judgments of others, he'd always wondered, when others got off scot-free? Okay, maybe the dead judge would've had little use for this Reverend Tunic. Were he alive to hear his preposterous eulogy, he'd likely have remanded him into custody for character defamation. But to Raymer the two men were more alike than different: neither seemed to worry about being wrong, nor were they inclined to revise their thinking. (*Revise, revise, revise,* Miss

Beryl always recommended. *Writing is thinking, and good, honest think-ing involves revision.*)

Not judging, though, apparently. Raymer had been summoned to Flatt's courtroom on numerous occasions, and to his knowledge the man never, ever amended his original verdict. Most recently Raymer had given testimony against a man named George Spanos, who lived on the outskirts of *our fair city* with his wife and children and a dozen mangy dogs, all of which he beat savagely until they, too, became sav-ages. When Raymer'd gone to arrest him, he'd been bitten three times, twice by dogs and once by a feral child. (The woman, blessedly, had been toothless.) The little boy's bite wound had become infected, requir-ing antibiotics, and the dog's had necessitated a tetanus shot, yet when Raymer limped to the witness stand, Flatt evinced not the slightest sym-pathy, even though, unlike the earlier incident, Raymer'd been clearly and unambiguously in the right. There, under the magistrate's stud-ied, theatrical gaze, Raymer couldn't help feeling that somehow he and the accused had swapped stations. It was *he,* the chief of police, who was being asked to explain himself. It was understandable, the judge allowed, that he'd been bitten by the dogs. But how in the world, he begged Raymer to explain, had he contrived to get nipped by a child as well? During the entire proceeding Spanos sat next to his lawyer wear-ing an expression of aggrieved innocence so convincing that Raymer almost believed it. Whereas he himself—and he didn't require any mir-ror to see the face he presented to the world—looked like he always looked: guilty as charged. Clearly, Judge Flatt considered him a fool, which left him no choice but to become one. It was appearances that mattered, and as usual they ran against him. Justice? How could there be any such thing when innocence looked like guilt and vice versa?

Even more galling than his repeated humiliations in that courtroom was the fact that the old goat had taken a shine to Becka. Not long after they married, she'd by chance been seated next to Flatt at a retirement dinner. The judge always had a keen eye for attractive young women, and after his own wife's death he'd evidently seen no reason that, as a geezer, he shouldn't indulge himself in the occasional flirtation with someone else's. That evening Becka had been provocatively attired, at least by North Bath standards, in a black dress with a plunging neck-line. Throughout the dinner she and the judge, who were seated at the far end of the banquet table, conspired like old cronies with a vast store of shared memories. At one point their heads came together, and Becka's eyes briefly met Raymer's before she burst out laughing. Naturally, he'd concluded that His Honor was recounting for her amusement the day her damn fool of a husband nearly shot an old lady off her toilet.

"What a sweetie," Becka enthused later, strapping herself into the RAV, the seat belt causing her dress to gap and one lovely breast to be fully exposed. Had Flatt been treated to this heartwarming spectacle over the ginger-carrot soup, Raymer wondered. "He couldn't have been nicer. Why'd you warn me about him?"

"Well, he did call me a moron," he reminded her. He'd told Becka about the gun incident early in their relationship, feeling it was prob-ably best that she hear about it from him rather than the Bath grape-vine where the story—like so many others where he was the butt of the joke—still had considerable currency. "In front of my boss. In front of the man I'd arrested."

"Well," his wife began, pausing long enough for him to wonder where this was going. (*That was ages ago?* . . . *I'm sure he didn't mean anything by it?* . . . *Can you blame him?*) What he hoped she'd say was *Actually, he spoke very highly of you,* but of course she didn't. Instead: "I know how much you were dreading the evening, but I had a good time."

In her considered opinion Raymer was far too self-conscious. "Not everything's about you," she liked to say, making him sound narcissistic. She was right, though. He *did* have a bad habit of internalizing things. Take, for instance, the judge's two dramatic resignations. Could it be coincidence that he'd tendered the first of these the very day Raymer was elected police chief? And that his second came exactly four years later when he was reelected? Yes, Becka assured him; it not only *could* be a coincidence, it most assuredly was. Over the last two decades, the poor man had battled three separate cancers, first a tumor on his lung, then some particularly aggressive cells in the prostate and finally a small but malevolent nodule attached to his brain stem, a malignancy that for a time seemed merely to focus his ferocious intellect, to sharpen his wit and tongue, neither of which in Raymer's view had required further honing. In fact, he had just about concluded that cancer wasn't the lethal killer it was cracked up to be when word came that the old man had lapsed into a coma and then, a few days later, that he was finally gone.

About which Raymer was surprised to have mixed feelings. On one hand, he'd never again be fixed by that scrotum-shrinking judicial gaze of disapproval. Nor, except in memory, would he be called names by this figure whose opinion carried such weight. But if the spirit lived on, as many people believed, didn't that mean Judge Flatt would consider Raymer an idiot for all eternity? How fair was that? Was he really so ungifted? True, he'd never made stellar grades in school. Though he'd been orderly and never caused trouble, his teachers all seemed relieved at the end of the school year when he moved up a grade with his peers and became someone else's burden. Only Miss Beryl, who kept drawing her triangles and asking him who he was in the margins of his compositions, had seemed to feel something like affection for him, though even here Raymer couldn't be sure. The old woman was forever shoving books at him, and while another boy might have considered these gifts encouragement, he had wondered if they might instead be punishment for some misdeed he hadn't noticed.

The cover of one book, he recalled, pictured a bunch of people hanging out of a hot-air balloon. To him the illustration had looked all wrong. The colors of the balloon were too bright, and the humans in its tiny dangling basket looked happy to be trapped there when common sense suggested they'd be scared shitless. Another book seemed to be about a group of explorers who'd entered the bowels of the earth through a volcano. What the hell was she trying to tell him? That he should consider going someplace far away? That up or down really didn't matter so long as he just went?

He'd thanked her for each book, of course, but at home he'd hidden them all on the top shelf of his closet where his tiny mother, unless she stood on a chair, couldn't spot them and brood about where they'd come from. Throughout his childhood she'd harbored a deep-seated fear that he'd end up a thief, like her own father, and whenever he came into possession of anything she herself hadn't given him, she immediately demanded to know where he got it. If his explanation struck her as suspicious or implausible there would be trouble—the same screaming and crying and crazy hair tearing that had finally driven his father away. The whole hair-pulling thing particularly frightened Raymer, because hers was already so thin you could see her pale scalp, and he didn't want to be the only kid in town with a bald mother.

"They're going to come and take you away," she warned him over and over, her eyes swollen and red rimmed and wild. "That's what they do with thieves, you know."

Then she'd fix him with that look of hers, waiting for him to absorb the truth she was telling him, after which she'd sigh mightily and stare into the distance, into memory, at the central event of her own childhood. "They took my father. Came right up on the porch and knocked on our door. I begged Mama not to open it, but she did and they came inside and just took him." She'd relive the awful moment for a long beat, then return to her son and the present for the inevitable postscript. "How he cried! How he begged them not to take him!" The clear implication was that, when the time came, Raymer would likewise blubber and beg the policemen not to cart him off to jail. Though he'd never stolen anything and had no desire to, he hadn't been able to entirely discount the possibility of what she foresaw so clearly. His plan, if you could call it that, was to keep from wanting anything bad enough for stealing it to become a serious temptation.

Many of the books Miss Beryl had given him were old and musty smelling, their pages dog-eared, the sort of books you wanted to give away, but others were in better condition, a few brand-new. Often the name *Clive Peoples Jr.* was inscribed on the flyleaf. When he asked Miss Beryl about these inscriptions, she told him this was her son, but he was all grown up now, a banker. Something about how she said this suggested that either Clive the boy or Clive the man had disappointed her. Had he, too, failed to master the rhetorical triangle? Raymer's heart went out to the kid. Imagine having her for a mother, your whole life a giant margin for her to ask her impossible questions in.

Still, he felt bad about only pretending to read the books she'd given him, and he wished he could've figured out how to get her to stop. He also wished she'd quit asking him about the ones he claimed to have read. Why couldn't she be more like his other teachers, who looked at him blankly the following fall when he said hello to them outside Woolworths, having in a matter of months forgotten his existence entirely? Old Lady Peoples, he feared, forgot exactly nothing, and she had no intention of forgetting him.

Like so many of his anxieties, this one proved well founded. Throughout high school, Miss Beryl persisted in tormenting him. "What are you reading, Douglas?" she asked whenever their paths crossed, and when he couldn't come up with a single title, she'd tell him to stop by her house because "I have several books I think will interest you." Each time he promised he would, though of course he never did. She'd retired from teaching by then, and it was possible she was just lonely, her husband, the high school's driver's ed teacher, having been killed in the line of duty a decade earlier, launched through the windshield by a nervous beginner. He was sorry if she was lonely, but that was no fault of his, and he sensed her firm intention to keep posting her queries in the margins of his psyche forever.

After graduating, he tried a year of community college downstate, but then his mother fell ill and there'd been no money, so he'd returned to Bath. Having lost touch with Miss Beryl, he discovered he was no longer so afraid of her and maybe even missed her a little. More than once he thought about paying her a visit, maybe asking her what she'd meant by giving him all those books. He might even confess that he had no more idea who Douglas Raymer was now than he did in eighth grade. But by this time she'd become Donald Sullivan's landlady, and he doubted it was possible for the same person to feel affection for two such different men. Fine, he told himself. Let the old woman write in Sully's margins. See how *he* likes it.

It was during this same period that he got a custodial job at the college in Schuyler Springs, and it was there he met an old campus cop who suggested he go to the Academy, which he'd eventually done. A uniform, he then discovered, was the next best thing to an identity, and even Miss Beryl seemed genuinely pleased, if a little surprised, when she saw him in it for the first time. "That outfit seems to have done wonders for your self-confidence," she told him. "Your mother must be proud." Actually, unless Raymer was mistaken, his mother was more relieved than proud. His becoming a policeman seemed to have eroded her conviction that he would end up in the clink. He didn't have the heart to tell her that the two career paths weren't mutually exclusive.

Then Becka had come along. Raymer pulled her over for doing fifty in a thirty-five. She had a Pennsylvania license and plates, having moved to Bath just a week earlier. She was an actress, she explained (she was certainly beautiful enough), and she was speeding because she was late for rehearsal in Schuyler Springs and the play's director was going to be furious. In fact, she might even lose her part. Was there any chance he could let her off with a warning? God, her smile.

He wanted to, but no. She'd been traveling at an unsafe speed, and it wasn't right to let her off just because she was beautiful and had smiled at him and because she managed in handing over her license to touch his wrist. His decision to write her a ticket seemed to genuinely astonish her, and she later admitted that she'd been stopped for speeding any number of times without ever having been given a citation. It had made her wonder what kind of man he was. Three months later when she said, "You know what? You should ask me to marry you," he couldn't believe his good fortune.

How swiftly that sense of good fortune had been undermined. He'd noticed when they left on their honeymoon that Becka's suitcase was suspiciously heavy, but he was pretty sure that asking her about why would be getting off on the wrong marital foot. When they arrived, though, and he hauled her bag up onto the king-size bed and she released the clasps, several plays and three or four thick novels tumbled out, causing the blood to drain from his face. There'd been lots of books in her apartment, of course, as well as groaning bookcases full of books about acting, as well as novels and plays. It was okay with him that she liked to read. She was a girl, after all, and many of them, like the scrawny ones at the college in Schuyler, were similarly afflicted. But their honeymoon was only for a week. What did she need with so *many* books? His first horrified thought was that they'd somehow gotten their signals crossed and she meant for the marriage to be platonic. That turned out not to be the case, though after they finished making love, Becka would often sigh contentedly and pick up a book and immediately become engrossed, which made Raymer feel like a short, possibly insignificant chapter. She also read by the pool and on the plane ride back, closing the last of her books just as the wheels touched down.

At the baggage claim, as they watched other people's luggage circle and waited for their own to emerge, he decided to ask straight out, "Why do you read so much?"

At first she didn't seem to understand the question, or maybe that its source was genuine, profound bewilderment. Shrugging, she replied, "Who knows? Same reason as anybody, I guess. To escape. There's mine!" she pointed, momentarily confusing Raymer, who thought maybe she'd spied an escape from their marriage, not just her suitcase. Still, she read to escape? Why? Not once during their glorious week of warm sun and fancy food and drink and knee-buckling sex had Raymer wanted to be anywhere other than right where he was.

"I suppose you know all about the rhetorical triangle," he said, feeling his eyes fill with unexpected tears. Because naturally she would. Worse, she probably understood it, that and the Holy Trinity and every other abstract concept that had stumped him during his long, tortured childhood and adolescence. Somehow he'd managed to marry someone who'd actually *enjoyed* school. He could picture his new wife as a kid, sitting there in the front row with her hand raised, practically waving in hopes of being called on, always confident she knew the answer. He could even imagine the expression on her young face—a combination of pity and exultation—when the teacher called not on her but some dullard trying his best to remain invisible in the back row, a boy who almost never knew the right answer and, on those rare occasions that he did, lacked the courage to risk volunteering it.

"What's a rhetorical triangle?" Becka asked him, hoisting her suitcase off the conveyor and studying him closely. "Are you . . . *crying*?"

In fact, he was. "I love you," he explained, which was true but hardly the reason for these tears. What had become powerfully obvious to him was how profoundly, impossibly different they were. He would be wise to enjoy her while he had her, though that wouldn't last long.

"Where's yours, I wonder?" she said, scanning the trundling bags,

or pretending to, perhaps annoyed by his unmanly public show of emotion. "They went on the plane at the same time. Wouldn't you think
they'd come off together?"

"It's probably lost," he said, suddenly sure of it.

"Lord, you're a pessimistic man," she said, standing on her toes for
a better view. Strange that she should be just as certain that his suitcase
would materialize any moment as he was that it was gone for good.

He'd been right, though. His suitcase was lost, and so was he.

BECKA, he thought, his eyes filling at the memory of that all-too-brief
period when they were still in love. Since none of the other mourners
were paying him any attention, he decided to risk glancing toward her
grave. He knew roughly where it was, but with the stones lying flat
here in Dale, he couldn't tell precisely. Someone had placed a bouquet
of long-stemmed red roses on one of the graves in her section, causing
Raymer, who'd let the first anniversary of her death go unmarked, to
feel a deep pang of belated guilt. Becka was an only child, her parents
having died in a car wreck when she was in high school, and her theater
friends were mostly too self-absorbed to miss or even remember her.
Which left only Raymer to do so, unless you counted Alice Moynihan.

Or unless you counted the man Becka'd been about to leave him for.

When Gus nudged him again, a perplexed expression on his face,
Raymer realized he'd pulled the garage-door remote out of his trouser
pocket and was unconsciously fondling it. Not long after her death, he'd
sold Becka's RAV back to the Toyota dealership where they'd bought it
two years earlier. He thought he'd cleaned the vehicle out pretty carefully, but the service department, preparing it for resale, discovered
the remote when they pushed the driver's seat all the way back on its
runners. "Bet you went crazy looking for this," the guy said when he
returned it to him at the station. "How it got wedged up under the seat
like that's beyond me."

At the time Raymer had naturally assumed the remote was for their
own garage. He'd put the town house on the market the day after her
funeral, making a mental note to give the remote to the new owners.

Then he'd put it in his desk drawer for safekeeping and promptly forgot all about it until a couple weeks ago. The house had sold pretty quickly, and he distinctly remembered handing over two garage-door remotes, along with the door keys, at the closing. So what was *this* remote?

"You okay?" Gus whispered.

"I'm fine," Raymer whispered back, returning the device to his pocket, though in truth he was feeling light-headed.

"Quit weaving."

Having not realized he *was* weaving, he quit.

It was possible, of course, that this weird little mystery had nothing to do with Becka. The RAV had been a demo model with several hundred miles on it when they bought it, so the remote might've belonged to a salesman at the dealership. Probably not, though. It hadn't been dropped. No, it had been hidden deliberately. One of the more serious obstacles to small-town adultery was the problem of what to do with your car. If you left it out at the curb, it would be noticed and maybe recognized. You could leave it a couple blocks away, but people would still conclude you were having an affair; they'd just be wrong about who you were having it with. Better to arrive under the cover of darkness, drive directly into your lover's garage and lower the door before either you or your car could be identified.

"What's that?" Charice had wanted to know when she entered the office unexpectedly and caught him examining the thing as if it were a fossil.

"A garage-door remote."

"I can *see* that," she told him, irritation her default mode, at least with him. "I mean, like, what's the story with this one?"

He explained where it had been found, in Becka's RAV, up under the driver's seat.

"Throw it away," she said, without the slightest hesitation.

"Why?" he asked. Because you could tell at a glance that she'd leaped to the same conclusion he had.

"I'll tell you why. Because it doesn't necessarily mean what you think it does."

What we *think it does,* she meant.

"Could be she let somebody borrow her car," Charice continued, "and this other person dropped that remote in there."

"But if somebody borrowed her car, why would that person have his garage-door opener on him? Wouldn't that be in *his* car? Do you carry your remote around in your purse?"

"I don't have one. I don't even have a garage. Also, it's none of your business what's in my purse."

"Okay," Raymer said, ignoring her. With Charice you did well to ignore a good portion of what she said. "Then how'd it get wedged up under the driver's seat?"

She shrugged. "Could be an innocent explanation, is all I'm saying." He raised an eyebrow at this.

"Admit it. You been thinkin' sideways since Becka passed." Selling the condo, she meant. Moving into the Morrison Arms. Selling the RAV instead of his piece-of-shit Jetta. All three decisions motivated by spite and self-loathing.

"And anyhow," Charice went on, standing over him now with her hands on her hips, "suppose you're right, which you aren't. You plan to do what, exactly? Go around to every house in Bath and point that thing at all the garages and see which door it opens?"

That was, in a nutshell, the very plan taking shape in Raymer's brain, though he was reluctant to admit it to someone so clearly determined to deride it. But *was* it such a bad idea? After all, Bath was a small place, and he could cover it neighborhood by neighborhood in his spare time. Wouldn't that just be good, methodical police work, eliminating the innocent from your inquiries?

"Thing about garage-door openers, Chief? They send out, like, a radio signal, except that one there—the one you're holding?—that's not the only remote with the same signal. It's like the key to your car. Say you own a Volkswagen Jetta."

"I *do* own a Volkswagen Jetta."

"There you go. And you got a key that starts your car."

"Charice—"

"Here's what you *don't* know 'cause you're not a criminal. Your key? The one to *your* car? Probably starts half-a-dozen other VWs, maybe even an Audi or two. Anything German. And that's just here in Schuyler County. Never mind Albany. Or the rest of New York State."

As was often the case, Raymer was puzzled by Charice's logic. "So you *are* a criminal, since you *do* know this?"

"I know because I know lots of criminals. 'Cept for me and Jerome"—this was her brother—"our family's mostly crooks. I got a cousin in Georgia did time for auto theft? He broke into this car and set off the alarm and got himself collared. Tragic part? Turned out he had a key that fit the ignition. Wasn't any need to break in, even."

"He was a car thief. He got caught and went to jail. This is tragic how?"

"Plus," Charice added, undeterred, "how's it gonna look, the chief of police standing outside citizens' houses, trying to open their garages? God's own fool is what you're gonna look like."

In this she'd been proven correct. Early the following morning Raymer had begun his investigation in his and Becka's old neighborhood, sort of as a control. After all, it was unlikely that she'd been having an affair with someone on their block, in which case she'd have walked, not driven. But he was curious to see if Charice was right and the device might open some innocent doors. He'd gone up one side of the street and back down the other without setting a single door aflutter. He'd even tried his and Becka's old condo on the off chance the remote was a spare he'd forgotten about. Returning to the Jetta, he found a man in a bathrobe waiting for him. "So what's this about, then?" he said, pointing at the remote, his brow knit with dark suspicion.

"Police business," Raymer told him, a feeble explanation people sometimes accepted.

"How's trying to open my garage door police business?"

Raymer repeated what Charice had told him about how these remotes work, implying that his interest was official, that he himself was concerned because "your remote could open *my* garage door and let you into my *house*."

"Except I wasn't pointing mine at your house. You were pointing yours at mine."

"I was speaking hypothetically," Raymer told him.

"I wasn't," the man said.

The following day he'd made the mistake of telling Charice about this encounter. "What'd I tell you?" She seemed unnaturally adamant on the subject, though with her it was hard to tell. Charice was pretty adamant about most subjects. "Throw the damn thing *away*. You want that garage-door remote to mean adultery. Which it doesn't. Plus you're ignoring the real problem."

His mental health, she meant. In Charice's oft-stated opinion, Raymer was clinically depressed. "I mean . . . look at where you live," she said, as if the apartment house he'd moved into after fire-saleing their condo settled the matter. Okay, sure, the Morrison Arms was crappy subsidized Section Eight housing in the equally crappy south end of town. The Moribund Arms, people called it. And yes, half the serious calls that came into the station involved the Arms via drug dealing, loud music playing in the middle of the afternoon, urgent reports of domestic violence, somebody off his meds shouting obscenities in the courtyard at no external referent, even the occasional gunshot. For all Raymer knew, actual arms were sold there. The way he figured it, though, living at the Morrison Arms saved time going to and fro. Wasn't it also possible that his very presence would reduce the number and seriousness of incidents there? He had to admit there'd been no quantifiable evidence of this so far. Neither the residents nor their guests seemed frightened of him or, for that matter, even inconvenienced by him. Worse, his own apartment had been burgled twice, both crimes still unsolved, though his tape player had turned up at a pawnshop in Schenectady so reasonably priced, Raymer thought, that he'd bought it back.

"Jerome's right," Charice insisted, still on the subject of Raymer's yearlong funk. Her brother had nearly as many opinions about what was wrong with Raymer as she herself did. "Ever since Becka died, you been punishing yourself. Like it was your fault, like it was *you* steppin' out on *her*. That's what all this is about—you punishing your own self."

"When I find out who the guy was," Raymer assured her, holding up the remote, "it's not me that's going to get punished."

"Right. You find out who it was—who you *think* it was, because his garage door goes up—and you shoot him and go to prison. You tell me who's the big loser in that scenario."

Well, Raymer thought, she did have a point, though it was hard to see how a man shot dead could be construed as the winner. Anyway, that wasn't how this thing would go down. Before there could be any thought of punishment, there'd be an extensive investigation, the painstaking gathering of evidence. The remote would be just one link in a sturdy chain of it, the last link being, he hoped, a confession. Then and only then would he decide on whose ashes would get hauled. He'd tried to explain all this to Charice, but of course she was having none of it. In the three years they'd worked together, he'd never won an argument with the woman and was unlikely to win this one, either.

On the other hand, maybe she was right. Feeling unsteady in the withering heat, with Becka's grave no more than fifty yards away, he could feel his purpose waver. It was true. Since losing Becka, he *had* come unmoored. Somewhere along the line he'd lost not only his wife but his faith in justice, in both this world and the next. Nor was it really about punishment. All he wanted was to know who the guy was. Who Becka had preferred to himself. And even he had to admit that this part was crazy, because the list of men Becka preferred over her husband was probably comprehensive. Charice was probably right about the Moribund Arms, where everything from the puke-green shag carpet to the rust-stained ceiling smelled of stale cooking oil and mold and backed-up plumbing. Poor Charice. She was afraid that if he wasn't careful he was going to become totally lost and completely befucked. Apparently she couldn't see that he already was.

Wishes

ON THE DIRT SHOULDER of the road that separated Hill from Dale, Rub Squeers sat in the shadow of the backhoe he'd used to dig the old judge's grave earlier that morning. Left to himself, Rub would've let the machine sit right there, but his boss, Mr. Delacroix, said mourners didn't like to see it beside a freshly dug grave, much less to reflect on the fact that the hole had been dug by such an ugly, unfeeling contraption, and they certainly didn't like to see someone like Rub Squeers sitting on it, looking impatient for the deceased to get planted so he could finish his work for the day. So Rub, who happened that day to actually *be* impatient, had driven the backhoe a good hundred yards away and taken a seat in the shade it cast.

"You know what I w-wisht?" he said out loud. As a boy he'd been afflicted by a terrible stammer. After puberty it had disappeared, but now, for some reason, it was back. Perhaps because the stammer wasn't quite so pronounced when there was no one around to hear it, he'd recently begun talking to himself or, rather, pretending to talk to his friend Sully.

What? What the hell do you w-wish now? Which was, he knew, exactly what Sully would've said if he'd actually been here. Rub would've changed very few things about his best friend—okay, his only friend—but sometimes he wished Sully wouldn't kid him quite so much. Especially about his stammer. Rub understood that kidding was just how

Sully dealt with everybody, that he didn't mean anything by it. Still, he was tired of it.

"I w-wisht that guy would stop talking." The man in the flowing white robe had been jawing for a long time, more than half an hour, Rub was pretty sure. Fridays were half days, and Mr. Delacroix had told him that as soon as he was finished with the judge and returned the backhoe to the shed and locked it, he could leave. "Then everyone would go home and we could finish up." As if it would be the two of them—him and Sully—pushing the mound of dirt on top of the casket, making short work of it like in the good old days.

Again Sully's voice was in his head. *Don't wish your life away, Dummy.*

Rub didn't mind Sully calling him Dummy, recognizing it as a sign of affection. He called most men Dummy and most women, despite their age, Dolly.

"You know what I really wisht?" Rub continued, ignoring Sully's advice.

Wish in one hand and shit in the other. Let me know which fills up first.

"I wisht you weren't so forgetful," Rub said, because lately Sully couldn't seem to remember twice around, and he wasn't sure he could bear the disappointment of being forgotten today.

I won't forget. I already put the ladder in the back of the truck.

He'd agreed to give Rub a hand with the tall tree that grew alongside his and his wife's house, one particular limb scratching at her bedroom window every time the wind blew and driving Bootsie crazy.

What do you mean, her *window?*

They'd been married for less than a year when Rub tired of the marital bed. To escape its rigors, he told Bootsie she snored—she didn't—and this allowed him to take up residence in the small, dusty, unheated spare room down the hall. There he slept on an old army cot, too narrow and rickety to support a woman of Bootsie's majestic girth. Rub had explained all this on numerous occasions, but Sully still liked to rib him about it. At any rate, with her husband in the spare room, Bootsie had quickly replaced him with lurid romance novels, one right after another, and it was these from which she was cruelly distracted whenever the wind blew. To her, the scraping of the tree branch on glass sounded like a child—the one she'd once hoped for and was never going to have?—trying to get in.

What would a child be doing thirty feet off the ground in a tree outside her bedroom window? Sully objected. Rub had wondered the same thing but knew better than to ask. It probably wouldn't take more than fifteen minutes to prune the offending limb, but these days Rub didn't see as much of Sully as he used to, and he hoped to parlay it into the entire afternoon, assuming Sully remembered in the first place.

"You know w-what else I wisht?" Rub said.

What?

"I wisht things would go back to like they were." This was a pipe dream, of course. Rub knew it was pointless to wish any such thing, but he couldn't help himself.

That's not how it works, Dummy. Things don't go backwards just because you want them to. If they did, we'd all be getting younger.

Which was true, naturally. Like it or not, Sully's luck had changed. He didn't have to work anymore, and it had been work, or economic necessity, more than friendship that had made them inseparable for so long. Rub could wish and want and even desperately need until the cows came home, but it didn't matter. *Anyway, don't be an idiot. You got a good job right here. Why would you want to go back to working for Carl Roebuck?*

He didn't, not really. Carl had always saved the coldest, wettest, foulest, most dangerous jobs for him and Sully. He'd paid them under the table, too, so they couldn't really complain. Bad as the work was, though, Rub had loved every minute of it. Standing for long hours knee deep in sewage, so cold he couldn't feel his fingers, he'd been happy because Sully was right there with him, showing him how things were supposed to go, how to endure and even, at times, prevail. There'd been comfort in the fact that whatever happened to Rub was also happening to Sully. It was like they were on a journey, and his friend knew the best route. If Rub himself was cold and hungry and discouraged and lost, so what? Sully was there to tell him what to do, to listen to his many misgivings, his dreams about how much better everything would be if life was different and cheeseburgers were free.

You liked it better back when my luck was rotten, is that what you're saying? When I had to put in twelve-hour days on a bum knee that swelled up like a grapefruit? That suited you better?

The other thing Rub would've changed about Sully was his knack for making Rub feel guilty about stuff. Like it was *his* fault Sully'd fallen off that ladder and busted his knee. Like *Rub* was to blame that his trifecta never won once for thirty years straight.

"No, I just wisht . . ." But he allowed the thought to trail off. Belatedly and with great reluctance, Rub was coming to understand that life could trick you into wishing for the very worst thing and then grant that wish. Sully was a prime example. Back when they were working for Carl Roebuck, Sully was forever wishing his rotten luck would change, and Rub, who never doubted his friend's wisdom, had just gone along and wished for it, too, apparently adding some needed torque. When Sully finally won that trifecta, Rub, slow to sense the hitch, simply thought, Good. They wouldn't have to work for Carl anymore. And had it stopped there, things would've been fine.

Things don't stop, though, do they? They keep going. Be careful what you wish for.

"You started it," Rub replied to this unfair injunction. "I only wished what you did."

And how'd that work out?

Not well, he had to admit. Incredibly, that first trifecta was just the beginning. What Sully had always accused Carl of—being lucky enough to shit in a swinging bucket—was suddenly true of himself, as well. It took several additional strokes of good fortune, but eventually an awful, unthinkable truth came into focus: Sully not only didn't have to work for Carl Roebuck anymore, he didn't have to work *at all.*

Nor was this the only thing Rub hadn't seen coming. That Sully could prosper without Rub prospering alongside him was another possibility he'd never really considered. Why would he? Every Friday afternoon for a good decade, he and Sully hunted Carl down—he had a knack for disappearing when he owed you money—to collect their pay. And right there, on the spot, Sully gave Rub his cut. Good weeks, they both did well; bad ones, poorly. It was like they were in a potato-sack race at a picnic, awkward and clumsy but inseparable, their financial destinies interlocked. When Sully's landlady died and left him her house, Rub half expected to come in for a share, but that didn't happen. And later, when the city paid Sully all that money for his old man's property on Bowdon Street, Sully hadn't offered him part of that windfall, either. Apparently they weren't for-richer-, for-poorer-type partners after all.

Hey, Dummy. Who got you the job here at Hilldale?

Rub shrugged, chastened. "You did," he admitted reluctantly.

All right, then. How about a little gratitude?

Rub sighed, his eyes filling with tears. He knew he should be more grateful. The cemetery job wasn't nearly as nasty and backbreaking as working for Carl had been, and it was steady, too. But—

You just don't like paying your taxes.

Coming from Sully (sort of), who had worked off the books his entire life, this criticism was particularly hard to swallow. Yet there was some truth in his charge. Rub did resent the strictures of legitimate employment. Working for the city meant Rub not only had to pay federal and state taxes but also local ones, as well as Social Security and who knew what else. Worse, the government, unaware of his existence for so long, now wanted to know where he'd been all those years, and what was he supposed to tell them? It wasn't bad enough he had to fork over money that otherwise might have been devoted to cheeseburgers, but the amount of the theft was recorded right there on the stub of his paycheck. Why couldn't they just let him believe he was taking home the money he'd earned? Why did they have to remind him of exactly how much they'd taken without his permission each and every week? Still, Rub felt compelled to object to Sully's characterization. "It's not the taxes," he said.

What then?

"I miss—"

What?

Rub swallowed hard.

What, Dummy?

"Y-y-you," Rub managed to choke out, the very thing he could never say when Sully was actually around.

What do you mean, me?

Unable to explain, Rub looked away. Down the hill, the man in the white robe was still talking. For how long now? Rub glanced at his watch, feeling his spirits plummet even further. Back when he and Sully were partners, he'd never needed to wear a watch. Sully was always right there to tell him what time it was and when they could knock off. On this new job, quitting time was five every afternoon except Friday, and he was supposed to know when that was so he could lock his tools in the shed. He'd been entrusted with several keys he didn't want, but there was no Sully to hand them to.

See?

"What?"

You're better off. Now you know what time it is without having to ask.

Sully was forever making this claim—that Rub was somehow better off without him—as if he expected him to agree one day, which he never would. "I liked it better when *you* knew."

Hey, Dummy. Look at me.

But Rub couldn't. How could he bear to look where his friend used to stand and no longer did? Or be told he was better off by the person whose absence made him so miserable?

Fine. Be that way.

He still remembered his awful first day on the new job, how lonely it had been, how slowly the hours had passed. When it was finally over, after locking the shed like he'd been taught—

With your own keys . . .

—he'd gone down to the cemetery's main gate to wait for Sully to pick him up so they could head to the Horse, like always. After forty-five minutes and no Sully, he'd hitched into town to look for him. Jocko was locking up the Rexall. "Hey, man," he said, when he noticed a forlorn-looking Rub loitering at the curb, "you look like you lost your best friend," intending the observation as a figure of speech, though for Rub it was anything but.

"You know where he is?" he asked.

Jocko consulted his watch. "Six-thirty? Well, if I were to hazard a guess, I'd say he's right where he always is this time of day. In fact, I bet I could guess which stool."

Rub was about to tell Jocko he was wrong, that Sully *couldn't* be out at the Horse for the simple reason that, if he was, then Rub would be there, too, which he wasn't. After all, they hadn't discussed Sully *not* picking him up. He'd just assumed he would, because otherwise how could their regular evenings proceed? But suddenly he saw he was wrong. Again. He'd been wrong about everything else, and now he was wrong about this. He'd concluded it was only the days that were going to be different now that Sully didn't have to work anymore, but it was even worse than that. Much worse. If he meant to join Sully at the Horse in the evening, he'd have to get himself there. And when he arrived, Sully would already be seated at the bar, showered and smelling of aftershave, like on the weekends. Before, nobody'd minded when they both showed up looking and smelling like men who worked for a living, but they *would* mind if Rub alone showed up in that state.

Standing there on the curb, Rub understood the full extent of his abandonment, which went beyond hours and days and weeks and also beyond physical proximity. Back when he and Sully had worked together, when they stood side by side, forty-plus hours a week, what Rub had enjoyed most was sharing his deepest, most intimate reflections about life and what would make it better on a minute-to-minute, real-time basis. Could he bear that loss? Possibly. But only if he believed Sully missed their friendship, too, even if maybe a little less. But what if Sully didn't miss him at all? No sooner did this possibility occur to him than he was visited by an even-darker thought. What if Sully had gotten him the cemetery job to be rid of him?

"I'm headed out there now if you want a lift," Jocko had offered, but Rub, feeling gutted, turned away so the other man wouldn't see his tears spill over. Here was the terrible truth he hadn't wanted to see: he was on his own.

We're all on our own, Dummy. No exceptions.

"But—" Rub began.

Besides, you're exaggerating. It's not like I abandoned you.

Not completely, no. When Sully's luck first changed, that had been Rub's worst fear—that Sully would just move away, to someplace nicer, warmer, where Rub couldn't follow. But so far he'd shown no such inclination. Sometimes out at Hilldale, Sully's truck would pull up outside the tool shed on Friday afternoons as Rub was closing up, and they'd head for beer at the Horse like they used to. Other times he'd drive out to where he and Bootsie lived, and together they'd drive back into town and eat breakfast at Hattie's and after that stop in at the OTB. But not often enough. Rub needed to know when Sully was coming, otherwise he'd wonder all day if he was. Only every night and every day would be often enough.

Noticing, finally, how dejected and listless Rub had become, Sully had tried to explain how he was staying home more now, not wasting so much time carousing. He wanted to set a better example for his grandson. It wasn't good for the boy to see him coming home shitfaced every night after the bars closed, getting his name in the police log for some damned foolishness or other. Rub wanted to believe him. He truly did. But from small things Sully let drop, it seemed he was still a regular at the Horse. Suspicious, Rub sometimes called and asked for him, but Birdie, the regular bartender, recognized his stammer. She always claimed Sully wasn't there, hadn't seen him for days, in fact. But then Rub had heard her say similar things to the wives of men sitting right in front of her, so he could easily imagine her raising an eyebrow in Sully's direction and him shaking his head no, just like these other men did.

"I just wisht you weren't always in such a hurry," Rub said weakly. He hated it when Sully went silent. It was bad enough when what he said was untrue or unfair, but silence was even worse, because to Rub that either meant he'd lost interest or didn't think what Rub was trying to explain merited any response. These days Sully always seemed to be in a hurry, anxious to be off to the next place, as if he was being pursued by something neither of them could name. Was that how things would be this afternoon? Not if Rub could help it. Pruning the offending tree limb wouldn't take more than half an hour, but he was determined to make an afternoon of it. With Bootsie safely at work and Sully's son and grandson away, they could pull up a couple of lawn chairs and Rub could tell him all the things he'd been storing up, each thought leading to the next and then the next, until he'd covered all of it. Whereas if he sensed Sully was in a hurry, the words would get all jammed up in the back of his throat.

That had been the worst thing about being Sully's friend: having to share him. At Hattie's, the OTB, the White Horse Tavern? It didn't matter. The cruel arithmetic of their friendship was such that while Sully was Rub's only friend, Rub was one of Sully's many. In addition to his son and grandson, both of whom Rub resented deeply, though he knew he wasn't supposed to, there was Carl Roebuck, whom he resented even more. As their former employer, he had exactly no claim on Sully's affection but seemed to have it anyway. And then there was Ruth, down at Hattie's. Sully claimed they weren't carrying on anymore, but if that was true, why was she still his friend? The list went on and on. Birdie out at the Horse and Jocko and all the other regulars. Also Sully's Upper Main Street ladies, elderly widows who lived in decaying Victorians and counted on Sully to bring them to the hairdresser and fix their faulty plumbing, though they never paid him. Why did any of these people come in for a share?

Since it seemed to be a real math problem, for a time Rub had put his faith in subtraction. When Sully's landlady died, Rub imagined he'd be first in line for the old woman's share of his friend's time and affection, but somehow that hadn't happened. And he'd allowed himself to get his hopes up a year later when Wirf, Sully's lawyer and boon drinking companion, had passed but again, no dice. Indeed, every time someone in his friend's inner circle died or moved away, it was as if Sully himself was proportionately diminished, so there was never a net gain. This fall Will would head off to college, and Peter claimed that when this happened he, too, would be leaving town, news that once upon a time would've buoyed Rub's spirits, but no longer.

You should've listened to your mother.

"You nuh-nuh-nuh—"

I nuh-nuh-nuh?

"You n-never even met her."

She told you what would happen, though. You just didn't believe her.

Even after all these years Rub didn't like to think about his mother, who'd tried her best for him. As a child he'd been slow to talk, going on three before he uttered his first word. He'd been named Robert, after his father, but she wanted to call him Rob, since her husband was Bob.

But Rub had struggled with the sound, indeed with many sounds, and before long it became clear that his speech would be seriously impeded. It took him so long to spit out the *R* sound that he was exhausted, and what followed sounded more like *ubb* than *obb,* so his mother had decided to just go with that. Later, seeing how lonely and friendless Rub was at school, where his stammer made him the butt of endless jokes, she'd recommended Jesus, who she claimed was the most important friend to have, though she couldn't have anticipated Sully. Sometimes she took Rub to the ramshackle church she visited on Sundays where they talked about Jesus and the rapture at the end of the world, but one week a man brought snakes, and Rub was so terrified that after that his mother left him home with his father. And Jesus became, for him, just the man on the calendar.

Every month there was a new one to contemplate—January Jesus, June Jesus, December Jesus—with all these as constant and reliable as the seasons, as ubiquitous as time itself. Though Rub's circumstances grew increasingly dire as the months unfolded, Calendar Jesus always bore the same beatific expression. Even carrying the heavy cross, his head crowned with jagged thorns, his palms punctured (a discrete drop of bright red blood on each), Jesus remained serene, and Rub, an anxious child, hoped that when he grew up, he, too, would find such grace in the face of hardship, that his more or less constant longing would yield to tranquil acceptance. Of course this wasn't to be, and twenty years later when he accidentally punctured his own left palm with a nail gun, he discovered that if you weren't the Son of God (or at least a distant cousin) serenity in the face of that kind of pain was not an option.

His poor mother. Most of the time she bore a kind, faraway expression that made Rub wonder if she could read the future and if that was why she worried about him so much. But maybe it was her own future, her own loneliness, she was contemplating, not his. Though he and his father were right there, to Rub she seemed every bit as forlorn as he was, and for this he blamed himself. While he knew he was just a boy and no proper companion for a grown woman, he felt guilty anyway. She never left the house except to go to church, for which his father religiously ridiculed her. You might as well believe in the Easter Bunny, he liked to tell her, which was how Rub had come to understand there wasn't one. Because he loved his mother and knew it was what she wanted, he tried praying to Calendar Jesus for a while. She'd taught him how, but obviously he wasn't doing it right, because when he finished saying the words he wasn't filled to overflowing with the Savior's love, like she said he'd be, but even more empty and alone than before. His father? Rub knew it was a sin, but he hated the man even as he loved him, for his nasty laugh and his refusal to ever have a kind word for anyone. In the end, though, he came around to his father's view with respect to Jesus, after which the Son of God assumed a status more or less equivalent to the Bunny with whom he shared a holiday.

Why, then, Rub had wondered many times since, had he grieved his father's passing? Because that's what boys were supposed to do when their fathers died? Because his mother, who had every reason to be happy that the man was gone, had sobbed so pitifully? How could she possibly miss a man who'd belittled her as naturally as he'd breathed? By the same token, how could Rub himself? One of his clearest memories was of one Sunday morning when his mother had gone off to church, leaving the two of them alone in the house. He could still see the old man sitting in the corduroy armchair that no one else could sit in and watching, with an expression of sneering wonderment, as Rub tried desperately to communicate something of importance, he no longer could remember exactly what. His stammer was always at its worst around his father, words turning to concrete shards in his mouth. Part of the reason he continued to struggle, he now recalled, was that he'd actually managed to get out part of what he wanted to say and mistook his father's curious expression to indicate interest. But then he saw it wasn't curiosity at all, simply disgust. "Why don't you just give up?" was what his father wanted him to explain.

"How *dare* you?" said a voice he didn't recognize. Neither Rub nor his father had heard his mother return. She'd just materialized there in the doorway, and her fury was so focused that she not only sounded but also looked like another woman entirely. He'd never known her to raise her voice to his father before, but here she was, glaring at him, shaking with rage, and in her hand a gleaming kitchen knife. At that moment his mother, who could often calm his stammer by simply resting a cool, dry hand on top of his, looked perfectly willing to kill the man whose verbal abuse she took, day after day, as if it were her due.

"*You,*" she went on, the usual quaver in her voice now absent as she pointed the tip of the blade at his father. "*You're* the reason he's like he is."

Rub's father, his mouth open, as if on a hinge, seemed less frightened by this knife-wielding specter than dumbstruck by her words. If so, he was no less stunned than Rub himself, who tried desperately to make sense of what she was saying. He knew all too well that his stammer was worse in his father's presence, but how could he be to blame for the affliction itself? If Rub's mouth didn't work properly, if he couldn't make it behave, how could it be anyone's fault but his? Hadn't his mother always told him it was *nobody's* fault? Hadn't the lady at the university she'd taken him to see—a speech therapist, she was called—concurred? Rub had wondered if they were just trying to make him feel better and, if so, fine. He didn't object to being let off the hook. But this was different. Had his mother lost her mind? How could his stupid mouth be his father's fault?

"You're a hateful, *hateful* man," she continued as Rub looked on in horror. "Your only joy is tormenting the people who love you."

His father started to say something, but no sound came out of his mouth, which was just as well because Rub's mother wasn't finished. She pointed the sharp end of the knife at Rub now.

"That boy actually looks up to you, you *hateful* man. He doesn't know there's no such thing as pleasing you. He doesn't understand that you *enjoy* watching him suffer. And you know what? Neither do I. So explain it to us. How can it feel *good* that this boy, *your* child, is so terrified every waking moment that he wets the bed at night?"

When Rub heard this, he could only stare at the floor in shame. He had no idea his father knew about the bed. His mother had told him it would be their secret, but clearly she hadn't kept her promise. *You're the reason he's like he is,* she'd said earlier, and what she must've meant by that now crystallized. She wasn't just talking about his stammer but rather about *everything* that was wrong with him, his totality as a disappointing boy.

He also understood something else. His mother's rage, her willingness not just to defend him but to shift the blame for his failures to his father, were in direct response to his father's question: *Why don't you just give up?* At first he'd assumed he was advising him to pause, calm down, collect himself and begin again from a more tranquil state. After all, that was what his mother and the speech therapist always encouraged him to do. Now, though, thanks to his mother's fury, he understood that what his father had actually wanted to know was why, given the entirety of his experience, Rub didn't give up altogether and stop believing in the possibility of good outcomes.

So again, why grieve the loss of such a man?

You tell me.

But Rub couldn't, any more than he could explain why now, so many years later, he wasted so much time indulging silly, impossible fantasies. Because Sully was right. You couldn't turn back the clock. Which meant he and Sully would never again be best friends. "Will we?" he said.

But again Sully was silent.

Maybe, Rub thought, there were some things in this world you just needed, against all reason. Maybe his need for Sully wasn't so very different from his mother's need for his father, a man who never tired of disparaging her. Because she *had* needed him, of that Rub was certain. Not long after his father's death, she stopped going to church and, without warning or explanation, Calendar Jesus disappeared from the kitchen wall, as if with only the two of them in the house they had no further need to mark the passing of days and months. By the time Rub was in middle school, she'd begun to wander off, and people would bring her home dazed and disoriented. Worse, she began to regard Rub, whom she'd been willing to defend with that gleaming knife, as if she couldn't quite place him. It was the same look Sully sometimes gave him lately. Would what happened to her also happen to Sully? Was his new forgetfulness, his inability to sit still, an omen of what waited ahead? Would Sully, like Rub's mother, become so abstracted that he'd start wandering off? If so, who would bring him home? Who would remind him who his friends were if he forgot? Would Rub himself be among them?

Hey, Dummy.

"What?"

Quit that.

It was true, Rub had begun to blubber, which Sully always hated. He'd made the mistake of looking over at the funeral gathering at exactly the wrong moment. The man in the flowing robe had made a sweeping gesture toward the gleaming casket, and in that instant the sun had reflected off its surface to blinding effect, and suddenly Rub knew for a certainty what had perplexed him only a moment before. His mother had still been relatively young when she began to lose her mind. Sully was old. He wasn't going to wander off. He was going to die. And the worst part was that when the day came it would fall to Rub to dig his best friend's grave.

You hear me? Quit.

"I can't help it," Rub blubbered.

Listen to me.

"What?"

Are you listening?

Rub nodded.

I'm not going anywhere for a while yet, okay?

"Promise?"

How about if I stick around until you're squared away? How would that suit you?

Rub nodded. That suited him fine. Because this much he was certain of, just as his mother had been—he was never going to be squared away.

Not ever.

Karma

A BANNER WAS STRUNG across Main Street for the Memorial Day weekend. THE NEW NORTH BATH: PARTNERING FOR TOMORROW. This was the brainstorm of Gus Moynihan, the town's new mayor, who'd been swept into power the previous year on a tidal wave of born-again optimism, more than a decade after the demise of the Ultimate Escape Fun Park, an economic catastrophe that had ushered in a golden age of self-loathing and fiscal pessimism deeply rooted in two centuries' worth of invidious comparison with Schuyler Springs, its better-looking twin and age-old rival. Schuyler had long possessed everything to which Bath aspired—a vibrant local economy, an educated citizenry, visionary leadership, throngs of seasonal downstate visitors, an NPR affiliate radio station.

Okay, sure, there'd been some shitty luck involved. Bath's mineral springs had mysteriously dried up over a century ago while Schuyler's continued to percolate up enthusiastically from its shale. Schuyler also had a famous thoroughbred racetrack, an acclaimed writers' retreat and a center for the performing arts, a high-toned liberal arts college (Bath had only a beleaguered two-year community college), as well as a dozen fancy restaurants that served exotic foods like ramps, whatever they were. On the restaurant front, all Bath could boast was its run-down roadhouse tavern, the White Horse, Hattie's Lunch, a donut shop and a new Applebee's out by the freeway exit. What all this amounted to, everyone agreed, was a complete economic and cultural rout. For a while the fun park had gotten people's hopes up, but when they were dashed the collective despair was so profound that the town had even stopped stringing the buoyantly optimistic Main Street banners that had become its dubious trademark, the last of which had read: THINGS ARE LOOKING ↑ IN BATH. The gloom had lasted until Gus Moynihan, a retired college professor who was renovating one of the grand old Victorians on Upper Main Street, wrote a guest newspaper editorial decrying the town's mordant defeatism and criticizing the current Republican administration's unspoken policies, which could be summed up, he claimed, in nine words: *No Spending. None. Ever. On Anything. Under Any Circumstances.* Why not string one last banner across the street, he suggested: LET'S EAT DIRT.

The editorial had struck a chord and made a mayoral candidate of its author. Even his opponents had to admit that Gus and his cronies, many of them "from away," had run a clever campaign. *Let's BE Schuyler Springs* was the gist of it. Instead of competing with their obnoxious neighbor, why not take advantage of its proximity? Half the people who came to the racetrack and performing arts center in the summer had no place to stay and ended up in hotels as far away as Schenectady. Why shouldn't they stay in Bath? Okay, the Sans Souci Hotel and Resort with its nearly three hundred rooms had run into legal difficulties fueled by local resentment when it became known that the new owners would be using downstate contractors and labor for almost everything. The old hotel's lavish renovations had cost far more and taken much longer than expected, causing it to miss much of the summer-tourist trade that first season, and the locals had steadfastly rebelled against the prices at its fancy restaurant.

But that didn't mean its basic concept was flawed, or so the Moynihan crowd had argued. Instead of throwing up roadblocks to entrepreneurship, the town should have offered tax breaks and other incentives. Same deal with restaurants. During the short summer season, desperate, hungry travelers even mobbed the Horse, so why not entice a young chef or two up from New York City. Find out what the hell ramps were and serve them, if that's what people really craved. It wasn't like Schuyler Springs had cornered the world ramps market and refused to share. Overnight, the new byword was "partnering." Whenever possible, Bath would partner not only with odious Schuyler Springs and moneyed downstaters but also with local entrepreneurs in projects of exceptional merit.

One of these locals was Carl Roebuck, who most people were surprised to learn *was* an entrepreneur, having known him all their lives as a con man and an asshole. Carl's father, Kenny, they'd liked. He'd built Tip Top Construction from nothing by working fourteen-hour days. Like so many men of his generation, he hoped his son wouldn't have to work quite so hard. On that score he had no legitimate worries. In college Carl learned to drink and seduce women and spend his father's money and loathe all things Carhartt, especially the brand's connotations of hard, honest labor. Returning home, he gave no indication that he meant to work at all if he could help it.

After his father's unexpected death, he couldn't help it, but he was lazy and did shoddy work and nearly lost the company when the Ultimate Escape Fun Park went belly-up. He hadn't been directly involved in that doomed venture, but he'd gotten wind of it early and purchased for virtually nothing a tract of adjacent land he figured would eventually be needed for parking. There, using federal dollars, he set about erecting a dozen low-income housing units and awaited the groundbreaking of the fun park, after which he intended to sell the parcel, improvements and all, at extortionary profit. But then, at the eleventh hour, financing for the park had fallen through, and Carl, who'd seen no reason to build his units to code, thinking nobody'd ever live in them, had been stranded with a dozen substandard duplexes whose brand-new roofs already leaked, whose porous basements sucked sulfurous moisture from the nearby wetlands every time it rained and whose moldy walls sported earthquake-sized fissures. It had taken most of the last decade to extricate Tip Top Construction from the resulting quagmire of litigation. To save it, Carl had to sell his house and half the heavy-construction equipment on his lot—the half, he privately lamented, that still worked. He hadn't minded losing the house because at the time his wife, Toby, was divorcing him and would have ended up with it anyway, but still. It had been a decade of painful misfortune from which Carl had learned, as far as anyone could tell, exactly nothing.

His current project, snakebit from the start, was the conversion of the long-abandoned shoe factory on Limerock Street. The concept of the Old Mill Lofts was so dumb—or so the conventional wisdom had it—that it took your breath away. Ever since it was announced, people had been writing in to the *North Bath Weekly Journal* pretty much non-stop, decrying its abject lunacy and its complete and utter waste of tax-payer ("partnered") dollars. Even assuming you could accomplish the planned renovations—a point no one conceded—and could also drive out the army of rats that reportedly had taken up residence in the building's nether regions, and then could fix the roof that'd been leaking for forty years, who in Bath could afford to live there? The cheapest units on the ground floor were supposed to start at around a quarter of a million dollars, the larger units on the top floor going for three times that. Those were Schuyler prices.

But according to Mayor Moynihan, who himself had a down payment on one of the units, the high price tag was precisely the point. The Old Mill Lofts signaled that Bath was back in the game, a town with much to offer. Sure, the project was ambitious, the new administration conceded, but it was hardly unprecedented. Decrepit, abandoned factories were being converted into living and retail spaces all over the country. In fact lofts, like ramps, were all the rage. Better yet, Schuyler Springs, which had never engaged in anything as grubby as manufacturing, had no decrepit old mills to retrofit, so in this respect Bath had a clear advantage. (Yes, the habit of invidious comparison was hard to surrender.)

The real problem with the Old Mill Lofts, according to others, wasn't so much the concept as Carl Roebuck himself. The units were being billed as upscale urban-style dwellings, but woven deeply into his character and experience was the desire to do things on the cheap and pocket the difference. Old-guard pessimists grumbled that the town wasn't so much partnering for tomorrow with a gifted entrepreneur as fronting for yesterday's known swindler. Some even wondered if Carl might be up to his old tricks, having purchased something seemingly worthless on insider information in hopes of flipping it when its true value became apparent. Maybe the work being done on the mill was just for show. Carl, who was widely rumored to be distracted by health problems, was seldom *at* the mill when important decisions needed to be made, and when he happened to be on hand, he didn't seem to care much whether they zigged or zagged. Even those who gave him the benefit of the doubt when it came to his motives still worried that Tip Top Construction, impaired by relentless court judgments and harsh penalties, simply lacked the working capital necessary for a project of this scope. What was left of Carl's heavy machinery sat rusting out at the yard, fritzed beyond repair. At present he employed only a dozen workers and kept most of them under forty hours a week so he wouldn't have to pay benefits. Every week rumors circulated that this would be the one where he failed to make payroll.

The other problem with the new Bath, at least at the moment, was that it stank. Literally. In the *Schuyler Springs Democrat*—known in Bath as the *Dumbocrat*—it had been dubbed "the Great Bath Stench," a phrase that had been picked up in the *Albany Times Union*. For the last two summers, whenever the thermometer hit eighty-five, a thick, putrid odor blanketed the town, everywhere at once, so you couldn't even tell where it was coming from. Bath, visitors remarked, wrinkling their noses and quickly getting back in their cars, needed a long one itself. Some argued that the stench originated in the fetid wetlands adjacent to Hilldale Cemetery and was borne into town on summer breezes. Except that the odor was less powerful out there. One local fundamentalist minister thought the problem might be moral in nature. Nearby Schuyler Springs had a substantial and growing gay community, and he wondered from the pulpit if God wasn't sending a message—an idea that failed to get much traction, begging as it did the fairly obvious question of why God wouldn't visit olfactory retribution on the actual offenders and not their innocent neighbors. This summer, as if Carl Roebuck didn't have enough problems, people who lived nearby claimed the stench was emanating from the old mill. But how could that be? The building had been boarded up for decades. There was nothing *in* it to stink.

Then yesterday, more bad news. After two straight days of drenching rain, the Tip Top crew discovered a foul, viscous, yellow goo oozing out of a crack in the basement's concrete floor. Carl, true to form, was for sealing up the crack and forgetting about it, but a Bath selectman insisted on consulting a state inspector, who demanded that Carl jackhammer out a section of concrete and find out what the hell was down there. The town's sewer line paralleled the front wall of the factory, and while the ooze didn't look or smell like raw sewage—it in fact was far, far worse—the inspector speculated that maybe the pipe had been invaded at the seam by tree roots. Once inside and fed a steady diet of sewage, roots could grow like tumors and cause the pipe to rupture. At which point whatever was in the line had to go somewhere. Who knew? Maybe there was a reservoir of really awful shit under the mill. Only after the concrete was ripped up would they know what they were dealing with, and how much of it. And whatever was down there would have to be mucked out.

It was this necessity that caused Carl to think of Rub Squeers, whose sense of smell had been compromised, people said, by adolescent glue-sniffing, as a consequence of which he could stand hip deep in ripe manure without complaint. Rub lived on the outskirts of Bath with his harridan of a wife, Bootsie, but this time of day he was likely out at Hilldale, where he served as the cemetery's caretaker. The person who would know was Donald Sullivan, Carl's friend and, since losing his house, his landlord. Since busting Sully's balls invariably improved Carl's spirits, which happened just then to be at low ebb, he decided to pay him a visit.

SULLY WAS PERCHED on his usual stool at the end of Hattie's lunch counter. He'd been there since six-thirty, as he was most mornings, helping Ruth through the breakfast rush, though today he'd been pretty much useless, his chest tight as a drum, his breathing shallow. Since then the place had emptied out. Come noon it would be busy again, but that was an hour away. On the counter next to Sully's empty coffee mug was this week's *North Bath Weekly Journal,* folded so that his former landlady's photo smiled up at him knowingly. *Legendary middle-school teacher Beryl Peoples,* read the caption. *To her many students, Miss Beryl.* The "Miss" had hurt the old woman's feelings, Sully knew. She might've been tiny and gnomelike, but she was also a married woman, whether or not her eighth graders could imagine her with a husband. Sully had mostly called her Mrs. Peoples, which she seemed to appreciate, and in return she'd called him Mr. Sullivan, which he didn't know how to feel about. "Does it ever trouble you," she once asked him, "that you haven't done more with the life God gave you?" "Not often," he replied at the time. "Now and then." Something about her expression in this newspaper photo suggested that even today, nearly a decade after her death, she was still waiting for a more honest answer. Sorry, old girl, he thought.

He couldn't help wondering what she'd think of the weekend's festivities. She'd always taken a dim view of pomp and circumstance, and he suspected she'd be ambivalent at best about the middle school being renamed in her honor. Nobody's fool, she would recognize the gesture as politically motivated, another of the new mayor's dubious initiatives—"Unsung Heroes," this one had been dubbed—calculated to instill pride in a community long accustomed to self-hatred. The idea was that each Memorial Day someone who'd made valuable contributions to the community would be celebrated. Apparently Miss Beryl had been a unanimous choice for this the inaugural award, which indicated to Sully—and he was confident his old landlady would agree—that the pickin's were slim. Who would they tab next year?

It was entirely possible he'd never learn. Two years, the VA cardiologist had given him. Probably closer to one. He'd suspected something was wrong for a while. The shortness of breath, at first on steep stairs, then on any sort of incline, and lately whenever he tried to move even a little fast. Why had he waited so long, the doctors wanted to know. Because, well . . . admit it, he had no satisfactory answer. Because in the beginning the symptoms came and went? Because he'd be fine for weeks at a stretch, during which he could tell himself it was nothing? Sure, but deep down he'd known, and when the symptoms returned he wasn't surprised. Even then he probably wouldn't have gone in if Ruth hadn't noticed him struggling and badgered him to get it checked out. After two minutes on the treadmill, they'd shut down the stress trial.

"So what's the deal?" she'd asked the minute he got back.

"They think I should quit smoking," he told her. Which was true, just not the whole truth and nothing but.

"Really?" she said. "Imagine that. Cigarettes aren't good for you? Who knew?" She seemed satisfied with the explanation, though. Didn't grill him like she usually did when she thought he was bullshitting her. Lately, though, he'd caught her staring at him quizzically, so maybe in the intervening two weeks she'd become suspicious.

The whole truth and nothing but the truth went more like this: A-Fib. Arrhythmia. A racing heart. Brought on by physical exertion. By stress. By nothing at all. Leading to: congestive heart failure. Solution: Open-heart surgery. Quadruple bypass. Not particularly recommended for men his age, whose condition was so far advanced and whose arteries were so obstructed from years of smoking. Any other possibility? A procedure to insert an internal defibrillator to tell the heart when to beat, when not to. Routine process, an hour tops. Small incision. A couple hours later you're up walking around. The next day you go home. Cured? No. Most likely you'll still die of congestive heart failure, just not so soon. The other possibility, given your age and physical condition, is that you die on the operating table. If you do nothing? *Two years, but probably closer to one.* "Your heart could fail at any time," the cardiologist admitted. "You could die in your sleep."

This scenario, Sully gathered, was supposed to scare him into the procedure, but it hadn't. "Wake up dead?" he said. "That doesn't sound so bad, actually."

Nor had the cardiologist disagreed. But given his age and condition, there was also a distinct chance he could have a major stroke and *not* die. Spend the rest of his days unable to talk, feed himself or shit of his own volition. Though this could also happen if he *didn't* have the surgery, the man had added.

"If you're telling me what I should do," Sully said, "I'm not hearing it."

The doctor shrugged. "Most people want the defibrillator. Or their kids do. Or their wives. Are you married, Mr. Sullivan?"

No. An ex-wife, Vera, no longer in the picture. No longer even in her own picture, really. Poor woman, her grip on sanity had always been relaxed. A couple years ago she'd slipped into dementia and now resided in the county home. Her second husband, Ralph, already lived there, having suffered a catastrophic nervous breakdown years earlier, so it would have been a reunion of sorts had Vera recognized him, but she swore she'd never laid eyes on the man before and certainly wouldn't have *married* anyone who looked like that. Afterward her decline had been swift. In a matter of months she no longer recognized Peter, her son, or Will, her grandson. Confident she wouldn't recognize him either, Sully'd paid her a visit, but when she saw him her eyes immediately narrowed, and she began muttering profanities under her breath, looking right at him the whole time. According to the nurses, this was a whole new madness, one he shouldn't take personally. "You probably just remind her of someone," one nurse speculated, to which Sully replied, "Yeah, but the person I remind her of is me."

So, no. No wife to please.

His son, then? His grandson? the cardiologist had inquired. Wouldn't they want him to do the procedure?

"You're going to tell them?"

"You're not?"

Probably not. He hadn't made up his mind completely, but no, he doubted he would. Definitely not Will. No reason to burden the boy, who was off to college in the fall. His son? No real reason to burden him either. If he told anyone it would be Ruth. He'd started to half-a-dozen times, then decided against it. Studying his landlady's newspaper photo, he wondered if he'd have told her if she were still around.

"Question," said a familiar voice at his elbow, making Sully just about jump out of his skin. Attired in his customary Ralph Lauren polo shirt—pink today—and light cotton slacks and cream-colored canvas shoes, Carl Roebuck looked, as always, like the owner of an automobile dealership who was late for his tee time. That Sully had been so deep in thought that a man like Carl could sneak up on him was unnerving, and he quickly scanned the room for other potential threats. Carl himself wasn't dangerous, but whenever he entered the room you did well to check if his appearance had tipped over the edge some otherwise rational person—a woman he'd recently jilted, perhaps, or that woman's husband, or somebody he owed money to, or maybe just somebody who'd gotten fed up with his never-ending bullshit. With this latter group Sully felt particular sympathy.

"On average," Carl said, fixing Sully seriously, "how often would you say you think about sex?"

Ruth was on her way down the counter now, coffeepot in hand. "I'm curious how he'll answer this myself," she admitted, putting a mug in front of Carl. She and Sully had been lovers on and off for more than twenty years, but for the last decade just friends, an arrangement Ruth seemed to resent, even though it had been her idea. His mistake, as near as Sully could make out, was that he hadn't put up enough of a fight at the time or expressed sufficient regret since. Though she was unlikely to scald him until he answered the question, Ruth, armed with a hot coffeepot, inspired caution, and he instinctively leaned back until she finished filling Carl's cup and set the pot down on the counter. Only then did he give the other man his complete attention. "He's not here," Sully said.

"Who's not here?" Carl said.

"Rub," Sully said. "The person you're looking for."

"Says who?"

"Fine," Sully said. "We'll change the subject. What's this yellow slime I'm hearing about over at the mill?"

"What yellow slime?" Carl said, and anyone who didn't know better would have testified his innocence was genuine.

Sully *did* know better. "The lake of gunk you found yesterday. On top of which all those rich assholes are going to be living."

At this Carl released a deep sigh. "You shouldn't listen to rumors."

"Okay," Sully said agreeably. "But I have no idea where Rub is." Actually Sully expected him any minute now. Fridays were half days out at Hilldale, and he generally hitched a ride into town and came looking for Sully, hoping to get him to spring for a cheeseburger, then listen to him talk well into the evening, tough duty, given his worsening stammer.

"Forget Rub," Carl insisted. "I didn't even mention him. I asked you a simple question."

"Ruth," Sully said, pointing at the clock above the counter, "it's 11:07. Let's see how long it is before he wants to know where Rub is."

"A simple question you haven't answered."

The bell over the door jingled then as Roy Purdy, Sully's least-favorite person in all of Bath, came in. Unlike Carl, Roy Purdy looked exactly like what he was. Newly released from a downstate medium-security prison, Roy was a poster-boy ex-con: skinny, cheaply tattooed, sallow skinned, stubbled, fidgety, stupid. To hear him tell it, good behavior was the reason given for not making him serve his full sentence, which made Sully wonder what that standard must be in the joint if Roy, who'd proven incapable of good behavior his entire life, could qualify. "What question was that?" he asked Carl.

Carl sighed mightily. "I know it's hard, but try to pay attention. I'm asking how often you think about sex. Once a day? Once a month?"

"Not as often as I think about murder," Sully admitted, regarding Carl meaningfully before allowing Roy, who'd settled onto a stool at the far end of the counter, to come into focus. Though he hadn't looked in his direction, Sully felt certain that Roy was keenly aware of his presence. Ruth, who had even less use for Roy than Sully, nevertheless grabbed the coffeepot and a clean mug, then headed back toward him.

"How's our girl?" Roy asked as she poured the coffee they both knew he wouldn't pay for.

"You mean my daughter?"

"I mean my wife."

"Your ex-wife. She didn't marry you again, did she?"

"Not yet," Roy said.

"No, I imagine not," Ruth went on. "Especially if it's true what we heard."

"What you heard?"

"That you're shacked up with a woman named Cora over at the Morrison Arms?"

"I'm sleeping on her couch is all. Till I got the scratch for my own place. She ain't nothing to me, Cora ain't."

"You tell *her* that, Roy? Is that how she understands it?"

"I can't help what other people think," he said, eyeing the pastries on the back counter. Ruth wouldn't offer him free food, but before long he'd figure out how to ask her for some. She'd give him a hard time at first, though in the end she'd cave. Where her ex-son-in-law was concerned, Ruth seemed committed to a doomed policy of appeasement, which was why, since Roy reappeared in Bath two weeks earlier, Sully'd been mulling over an alternative course of action modeled more on George Patton than Neville Chamberlain.

When she returned to their end of the counter, Ruth noted where Sully's dark gaze had settled and snapped her fingers in front of his face, causing him to lean back on his stool again. "I hope you don't think what's going on down there is any business of yours," she noted.

"I'm glad it's not," Sully told her. "If it was, I'd know how to deal with it, though."

"I ask," Carl was saying, still single-minded, "because I think about it every ten seconds or so. It's worse now than before." By this he meant before the recent prostate surgery that had left him, for the time being at least, both impotent and incontinent without—he maintained— diminishing in the slightest either his sex addiction or his ability to pleasure women. The existence of said addiction was something Sully had yet to concede, though he and Carl had been debating it since the night almost a decade earlier when Carl had come into the Horse with a rolled-up magazine and swatted Sully on the back of the head with it by way of hello. Climbing onto an adjacent barstool, he'd opened the magazine to the article he wanted him to read, smoothing it out for him on the bar. "You know what I am?" he said, his usual smug expression amplified.

"Yes, I do," Sully said, without looking at the magazine. "In fact, I've told you what you are on several occasions. You must not've been listening."

"According to this," Carl said, stabbing the magazine with his fore-finger, "I'm a sex addict. It's a medical condition."

"What you are," Sully assured him, "is an anatomical description."

Sully's friend Wirf, who happened just then to occupy the stool on

Sully's other side, was apparently intrigued, though, because he took the magazine and began reading.

"And I'll tell you something else," Carl continued. "According to medical experts, what I deserve is sympathy."

"Wirf," Sully said, rotating on his barstool to better observe his friend, who continued to read carefully. "What do you think Carl deserves?"

That rare lawyer who was less interested in law than justice, Wirf took even joking references to the latter seriously and could always be counted on for both perspective and sound judgment. "A dose of the clap," he said after a moment's reflection. "Also, perhaps, the grudging admiration of men like me and you."

Carl and Wirf then clinked beer bottles across Sully, leading Sully to regret, as he often did, drawing his unpredictable companion into barroom arguments.

"Sully's just jealous," Carl observed when Wirf went back to reading the sex-addiction article, "because stupidity isn't classified as a medical condition."

"Actually, I believe it is," said Wirf, not looking up.

"But not one worthy of sympathy."

"No."

"Or respect."

"Certainly not."

Poor Wirf. To Sully's mind, the world had been less just and true since he left it. Also less fun. "When I'm gone," he'd told Sully more than once, "you're going to discover how hard it is to find another one-legged lawyer who's always in a good mood," and this had proven true.

"Of course you think about sex every ten seconds," Sully told Carl now. "You stay up all night watching porn." Since losing his house, Carl had been living in Sully's old apartment over Miss Beryl's. When Sully, who now lived in the trailer out back, got up to pee in the middle of the night, he could see lewd images reflected in Carl's upstairs window.

"I like porn," Carl said, with the resigned air of a man who'd long ago given up trying to even understand his own behavior, much less modify it.

Sully didn't doubt that he did enjoy porn, but he guessed there was more to it. Carl's urologist had warned him it could be anywhere from six months to a year before he could achieve erections again, and there was no guarantee even then. He suspected it was mostly fear that drove Carl to sit up half the night watching smut, ever on alert for a stirring in his boxers.

"The production values are getting better," Carl continued. "Ruth? Tell him I'm right."

"Hey, Ma?" Roy Purdy called from down the counter. "If it's between me and the garbage can, I'd eat that last piece of day-old."

This was in reference to the single slice of cherry left in yesterday's pie dish. Sully couldn't help smiling at Roy's tactic. Begging for something even as you establish that it's of no value means you're not only more likely to get it but also—and here was the real beauty—you wouldn't owe much of a debt of gratitude to the person who gave it to you.

"Throw it away," Sully advised, loud enough for Ruth, and maybe Roy, to hear.

The effect of this was both predictable and immediate. Ruth slid the pie onto a saucer and banged it down in front of her son-in-law, arching her eyebrow at Sully so there'd be no mistaking the consequence of his opening his big fat mouth. "I'd eat that dry ole piece of crust too," Roy told her, pointing a yellow finger at the shard of pastry burned to the dish.

"They didn't feed you downstate?" Ruth said, prying it loose with a knife.

Roy dug in, using his fork like a small shovel. "Not well," he said around a mouthful of pie, "and that's for true."

Carl leaned toward Sully and lowered his voice confidentially. "Earlier? I couldn't help noticing that when I explained how it's worse now than before, Ruth didn't say before what? Don't you find that strange?"

"I find *you* strange," said Sully, who knew where this was heading.

"Because that would've been the obvious question, unless she already knew what I was talking about."

"Hey, Dummy. Look at me. I never told anybody. *You* did."

The night before his procedure Carl had come into the Horse and told Sully about it, swearing him to secrecy. After Sully went home, though, Carl had gotten drunk and told a dozen other men, as well as Birdie, the bartender, which meant that the next day, even before the anesthesia wore off, Carl Roebuck's broke-dick plight was common knowledge, the talk of the town.

Not that Sully hadn't been tempted to tell. After all, Carl's legendary inability to keep his dick in his pants had ruined several marriages, including his own. Sully'd told him as much that night at the Horse. "Half the married men in Schuyler County are going to see this as simple justice. You *do* know that, right? You've heard of karma?"

"Like when bad things happen to good people?"

"No, like when what goes around comes around."

"Yeah?" Carl shrugged. "Well, I hope I'm there when it comes around for you."

"It already has," Sully assured him. "What you're looking at is the result."

Though in truth, he hadn't been sure then and still wasn't now, even after the VA diagnosis. Had he gotten off easy? During the war he'd somehow managed to be standing in the exact right place while more talented men and better soldiers happened to be standing in the exact wrong one. Often that was right next to Sully. For a while there on Omaha Beach there'd been a new, utterly lethal lottery every few seconds. Through diligence and judgment and skill you could improve your odds of survival, but not by much. All the way to Berlin, the calculus of pure dumb luck had ruled, Sully its undeniable beneficiary.

But that had been war. When the shooting finally stopped and the world returned to something like sanity and he again had the leisure to reflect, things felt different. There were days he couldn't help feeling fucked with. If there *was* a God, his primary source of amusement seemed to be toying with all the poor little bastards he'd without invitation created. Carl himself was a case in point. Give a man a dick, arrange things so that it rules his life, then poison the little gland that makes the dick work and watch what he does. Seen from God's point of view, maybe this was just good sport, a fleeting release from the monotony of omnipotence. Because if you *were* God, it stood to reason your real enemy would be boredom. Sully remembered as a kid studying ants on the sidewalk out front of the family house on Bowdon

Street after he'd finished eating a melting Popsicle. Hundreds of the little fuckers, maybe thousands, all programmed to perform in unison a task Sully couldn't fathom. From their well-ordered ranks, he'd select a single ant and prevent it from doing the one thing it clearly wanted to, forcing it left or right with his Popsicle stick, farther and farther away from the moving current of its fellows, marveling that its tiny brain was incapable of processing what was happening. The only sensible play would be to abandon the struggle until the giant who was thwarting its purpose became disinterested and moved on, probably to torment some other poor creature, but clearly the ant was not programmed to desist. It wanted what it wanted. So maybe God was just a kid with a stick— vaguely curious but incapable of empathy for anything so small and insignificant. From Carl Roebuck he'd stolen a tiny gland. From Wirf, he'd first demanded a leg and then, finding the man undiminished, had taken his life. That'd teach him.

Now it was Sully's turn. *Two years. But probably closer to one.* Fine, Sully thought. *Does it ever trouble you that you haven't done more with the life God gave you?* Not often. Now and then.

"Okay, fuck you, then," Carl was saying. "If you don't want to talk about sex, I better get back to work. For which—okay, I admit it—I *am* going to need your smelly dwarf. I've got a job he's perfect for."

"Ruth," Sully called down the counter, again pointing to the clock. "Ten after eleven. Three whole minutes it took him." Then, to Carl, "So tell me about it, this job." He already had a pretty good idea, but he was interested to hear Carl characterize it.

"I'll explain it to *him*."

"Tell me first."

"And you're what? His father?"

Actually, that was pretty much how Rub thought of Sully, which might be why he felt a kind of paternal responsibility for him that he'd never managed to summon for his own son, who mostly treated Sully like an inexplicable but undeniable genetic fact. "What if that shit you want him to clean up is toxic?"

"Toxic? It's a ruptured sewer. Disgusting, I'll grant you, but hardly toxic."

"If you don't know what it *is,* then you don't know what it isn't."

Carl rubbed his temples. "I liked you better before you came into money."

"No kidding? You liked it back when you had me over a barrel, Sheetrocking sixty hours a week in subzero temperatures?"

"Forty. You *invoiced* for sixty. God, those were good times," Carl sighed, with a far-off, mock-nostalgic expression. "Seeing you Chester into the Horse, caked head to toe with mud and all manner of shit, smelling like Mother Teresa's pussy? Just looking at you was all I needed to be happy."

The weird part was that Sully missed those same days himself, not that he'd ever admit any such thing to Carl.

"Anyhow," Carl said, lowering his voice significantly. "The shit's not toxic, okay?"

"And you know this how?"

"Think about it. What's uphill of the factory?"

"Nothing," Sully said, tracing the sewer line up Limerock Street in his mind. "Except the old—"

"Right," Carl said. "The rendering plant. Remember why they closed? No, of course you don't. You can't remember yesterday. But if you *had* a memory, you'd recall they got into a spat with the town over back taxes and moved the operation to Mohawk. Gus thinks they flooded that sewer line intentionally. Kind of a parting gift."

"Except that was, what? Two years ago? Three?"

"That's what threw us off. The theory is the mill needs repointing along the eaves. Every time it rains, water gets inside. Normally that wouldn't matter, except it drains into the basement floor."

Sully nodded, finally understanding. "And the drainage keeps whatever's down there nice and ripe."

"Under ideal conditions," Carl went on, "say a heat wave after a week of rain . . ."

"Double time," Sully said.

"Sorry?"

"Whatever you paid Rub for your last filthy job, he gets double for this."

"Oh, sure. *That* you remember. Extort your old buddy Carl at every opportunity. Why do I even talk to you?"

"Triple, actually," Sully said, upon further reflection.

"Fine, I'll hire somebody else. You think Rub's the only halfwit in Bath who needs work?"

He had a point there. "Okay, then double."

"Deal," Carl said, far too quickly.

Sully'd given in too soon, he realized.

"You think you can talk him into it?"

"I don't know. He hates you."

Carl rose to his feet. "Tell him *you* like me," he suggested, heading for the men's room. "He has no opinions that aren't identical to yours."

"But I *don't* like you."

"Sure you do, booby."

When the bathroom door swung shut behind him, Sully went back to studying Roy Purdy, who was now thumbing up the last microscopic crumbs of piecrust from his plate. What he'd told Carl earlier was true. These days he did think of murder more often than sex. Roy had arrived back in Bath the same day Sully was given his diagnosis, the two events dovetailing in his mind and encouraging him to weigh his various options for the scumbag's permanent removal. Running the little prick over with his pickup truck probably made the most sense, though it struck Sully as kind of impersonal. There was a strong possibility Roy wouldn't fully comprehend what had hit him, and Sully wanted him to know. Sneaking up behind him and braining him with a shovel would probably be more rewarding. The sound of tempered steel encountering Roy's skull—that melon softness underneath the fractured bone— would be satisfying. Since turning seventy, though, Sully wasn't as good at sneaking up on people as he used to be, and here, too, Roy might die without knowing who killed him. Maybe the best guarantee that he would know exactly who was putting an end to his sorry existence would be to lace his coffee with rat poison. Some midmornings, after the breakfast rush, Ruth would ask Sully to watch the counter while she ran to the bank, so he could do it then. It'd be gratifying to watch Roy's face spasm, the realization dawning, too late, that he'd been poisoned and by whom. The difficulty was in knowing how much poison to administer. Too little and he might not die, too much and he might taste it in the first sip, after which Sully might die. Sully'd never really been afraid of death and wasn't even now that it was approaching on horseback, but he was fully committed to Roy dying first.

"I guess you liked that all right, then," Ruth said, clearing Roy's plate.

"Not bad for day-old," he said, rubbing his small paunch. "We good here?"

"Aren't we always?"

Roy evidently had no opinion on this subject. "Tell Janey I'm sorry I missed her."

Sully saw his eyes settle on the door from the diner to the attached apartment where his ex-wife lived with Tina, their daughter.

"She doin' okay, then?" he asked. "Everything all right?"

"She's just fine, Roy," Ruth said flatly. "So's your daughter, if that's of any interest."

This last Roy appeared not to hear. "Tell her there wasn't no need for that restraining order. I'm a changed man."

"She'll be glad to hear that. Keep your distance just the same."

"Like I told the judge, it ain't easy in a town this size."

Ruth nodded. "That why you hang around the parking lot out at Applebee's around closing time, waiting for her to get off?"

"I do that?"

"Somebody said they saw you."

Roy swiveled on his stool to look at Sully now, acknowledging his presence for the first time, then swiveled back again. "Tell her soon as I find a job I'm gonna start making things up to her, and that's for true."

"Maybe you'd have better luck job hunting someplace else," Ruth suggested. "Albany, maybe, or New York City. Someplace with more opportunities."

"Oh, don't worry," Roy said, getting to his feet and taking half-a-dozen toothpicks from the cup by the register. "I'll find something right here in town one of these days."

Sully opened up the paper to the classifieds and put on his reading glasses. "Here's something that'd suit you to a T, Roy," he offered.

"Sully," Ruth said, with an edge in her voice that a wise man would have paid attention to.

"Wife beater needed," Sully pretended to read. "Entry level. Minimum wage to start but plenty of opportunity for advancement. Only highly motivated self-starters need apply."

"*Sully,*" Ruth repeated.

"Hey, that's a good one," Roy said. "You make that up on the spot or you been thinkin' about it all morning, waitin' for me to come in here so you could say it?"

Sully ignored both this and Ruth, who was glaring daggers at him as well. "Yeah, but here's what I don't understand," he told Roy. "Carl Roebuck was just talking about needing somebody to clean up that ruptured sewer line. How come you didn't speak up? Let him know you were looking for work?"

Roy rose from his stool. He'd removed a toothpick from its scarlet cellophane and was chewing on it thoughtfully. "How come you don't like me, Sully?" he said. "I never done nothin' to you."

"Hold on, here's another," Sully said, as the other man moved toward the door. "Wanted. Experienced petty thief. Night shift. Ex-con preferred."

"I guess you don't think people can change, then," Roy said, his hand on the doorknob, the bell above tinkling in anticipation.

"They do, sometimes," Sully conceded, refolding the paper carefully, so his landlady was faceup again. Was it his imagination, or had her expression changed? Become ever so slightly more disapproving? "Mostly they get worse, though, is the problem."

"Maybe I'll surprise you," he said. "I been meanin' to ask, though. How you like livin' in my trailer?"

Sully snorted, though he knew what Roy was getting at. "*Your* trailer?" Because it *had* once been Roy's, or rather his and Janey's, a gift from Ruth and her husband when Janey was pregnant and she and Roy were newly married and without a place to stay. They'd parked it out back of Ruth's and lived there until Roy got arrested out at the Sans Souci with a truckload of stolen TVs and furniture. Later, after Roy was sent downstate that first time, Ruth bought the trailer back so Janey would have enough money to move to Albany and begin a new, improved Roy-free life. She'd been beyond incredulous when Sully offered to take it off her hands. "What do you mean you're going to live in it?" she wanted to know. "You've got a nice big house on the prettiest street in Bath."

"Don't worry. I don't want it back," Roy assured him. "They say them things is firetraps. I been reading up. Fall asleep with a lit cigarette some night and up in smoke you'll go."

Sully met his stare and held it for a full beat before saying, "Is that for true?"

A muscle twitched on Roy's cheek, and for a moment Sully thought Roy might barrel down the counter, but he stayed where he was. "That's for true," he repeated, smiling. "You know what I got up here, Sully?" Roy continued, pointing at his right temple.

"Well," Sully replied, "thanks for teeing it up for me."

Roy ignored this, the look on his face causing Sully to wonder what it must be like to go through life never getting the joke, to smile only when nothing was funny.

"A ledger," Roy informed him seriously. "On one side's all the people I owe. Other side's the ones that owe me. This morning, right here, I added one piece of cherry pie and a cup of coffee on the side I owe. Some people forget their debts, but not me."

Sully nodded. "I'm curious. Who's on the side that owes you?"

"One day it'll be you," he said confidently. "When I make things right? On that day you'll owe me an apology, and I mean to collect it. I'll come by some night. I know right where you park my trailer. I'll bring us a six-pack. We'll drink a beer or two, you and me, and you can admit how you had me all wrong. If I was you I'd start practicing, 'cause it's gonna happen."

"Well, I've got just the one good leg, Roy, so I don't think I'll stand around on it waiting for that blessed day."

"Oh, it'll come, all right. Some night there'll be a knock on your door and it'll be me. And that's for true, too."

"Unless I fall asleep with that lit cigarette first."

"Hey, there you go!" Roy said, pointing his index finger at Sully like he'd just guessed right in a game of charades. "That sure could happen, too."

Slinky

I BELIEVE," Reverend Tunic warbled, a hint of Martin Luther King Jr. in his cadence now, "that by *our fair city* Judge Barton Flatt meant for us to understand that this place we call home is not just comely but fair as in 'just,' that our community is a model of rectitude, an exemplar of . . ."

Here he looked heavenward, as if for an elusive word or abstract concept, apparently finding it in a jet's vapor trail at thirty thousand feet.

"Of righteousness," he concluded.

Raymer, looking up as well, felt both dizzy and nauseated, his knees suddenly liquid in the heat. How nice being on that plane would be. In his mind's eye he could see himself disembarking at its unknown destination, magically dressed for some other line of work. Something he'd be good at. Some new life undreamed of by Becka and Judge Flatt, even by Miss Beryl. Or, for that matter, by himself.

"How, then, we may ask," Reverend Tunic continued, his gaze still fixed on the heavens, "do we make the great man's dream a reality? How do we ensure that *our fair city* is the celestial one of his profound conviction?"

What in the world had possessed him to become a policeman in the first place? Had the attraction been law enforcement's emphasis on rules? As a boy he'd always found rules comforting. They implied that life was governed by basic principles of fair play, guaranteeing him his turn at bat. And that was important, because he'd already witnessed among his peers too many kids who refused to play fair unless compelled to do so by adults. The rules he'd appreciated most were simple and unambiguous. *Do this. Don't do that.* People appreciate clarity, don't they? Being a policeman, then, would be about order, about implementing the will of the people, about the common good. Right. In actuality, the job had taught him that, far from being comforted by rules, most people were irritated by them. They insisted that even the most sensible, self-explanatory regulations be justified. They demanded exceptions in their own unexceptional cases. They were forever trying to convince him that the rules they'd run afoul of were either stupid or arbitrary, and Raymer had to admit that some of them truly were. Worse, all manner of citizens suspected that laws were enacted expressly to disadvantage them. Poor people concluded that the deck was stacked against them, rich ones that a reshuffle would ruin both them and civilization. Becka, when in the right mood, would argue that marriage was an institution designed to enslave an entire gender, and at times her rhetoric got so personal that you'd have thought Raymer himself had been a member of the original matrimonial planning committee. Back at the Academy the rule of law had made a kind of sense, at least in its broad strokes. Anymore, Raymer wasn't so sure. So go, he thought. Just get on a plane and leave. Because after Becka's death something had happened to him. His faith in his profession had eroded, and in light of this, what was keeping him here?

On the other side of the judge's open grave stood a girl of about twelve—one of His Honor's nieces or grandchildren?—who was staring intently, brow knit, at Raymer's midsection. She couldn't know about the garage-door opener in his pocket, of course, but she seemed to have drawn an erroneous inference about what his hand was up to in there. When he removed it, their eyes met, and a sly, knowing smile spread across her otherwise innocent features. Raymer, feeling himself flush, clasped his hands in front of his crotch and looked past her into the distance, his eye once again drawn to that vapor trail. If he went somewhere new, who would he know? Who would know him? What would he do for a living?

A hundred yards away, off to the side of the unpaved road that separated Hill from Dale, sat the bright yellow backhoe that had no doubt dug the judge's grave earlier that morning. Raymer recognized Rub Squeers, Sully's sidekick, sitting in the small patch of shade beside it. Something about his posture suggested that he was weeping. Could he be? Was he, too, remembering a loved one buried nearby? Was he, too, yearning for a new life, a new line of work? Maybe he'd like to swap jobs, Raymer thought, because digging graves, compared with law enforcement, would be both peaceful and rewarding. The dead were past being troubled by the world's injustice. Nor did they resist order. You could lay them out on a grid by the thousands without a single complaint. Try that on the living and see where it got you. People professed to love straight lines, which provided them, after all, with the shortest distance between two points, but Raymer had come to believe that, deep down, humans preferred to meander. Possibly, he considered, absentmindedly, that's all Becka had succumbed to—a perfectly natural urge to meander. Perhaps she hadn't fallen out of love with him so much as she'd become disillusioned by the rigidity of matrimony's rules: Love, honor, obey. Do this. Don't do that. Maybe to her, as a policeman, he'd come to represent the straight line she could no longer abide. Was the impulse to meander so terrible? When you did, wasn't there always the possibility that in the end you'd loop back to where you originally were? Given time, mightn't Becka have found her way back to him? Maybe it was time, not love, they'd run out of. It was pretty to think so.

He'd been the one to find her. He'd come home early, something he almost never did, at least not lately, not since things had started to sour between them, gradually at first, then suddenly. They'd argued bitterly that morning before he left for work, what about he couldn't even remember. Nothing. Everything. Lately, even his most benign observations summoned torrents of sarcasm, tears, anger and disdain. Almost overnight, it seemed, the range of his wife's negative emotions had multiplied exponentially. To Raymer, though, something about her litany of grievance felt out of whack. That she no longer loved him was beyond question, yet something still didn't ring true. It was almost as if she was doing scenes from all the plays she knew that featured marital discord.

He kept looking for continuity, for what she was angry or bitter about on Monday to reappear on Thursday. But no. It was as if she meant to stampede him with a multitude of unrelated complaints that ranged from the fairly benign and specific—his forgetting to lower the toilet seat—to the more vague and global—his disrespect for her feelings—with every offense, large and small, equally weighted.

So when he pulled in to their driveway and saw those three suitcases sitting on the porch, he recognized what they meant or were supposed to—she was leaving him—but more than anything the sight struck him as theatrical, almost comic. The front door was half open. Had she forgotten something and gone back inside for it? He remembered crossing the lawn and thinking they'd probably run right into each other there. She'd be surprised for a moment, then determined. And what would he do? Let her go? Keep her by force, at least until he could get to the bottom of whatever was troubling her?

She was just inside the open door. She'd been hurrying, that much was clear. The rug at the top of the stairs—now in a heap, halfway down—was probably the culprit. Raymer himself had slipped on it more than once. Becka had tasked him with finding a mat to put beneath it, but he kept forgetting, and this, right here, was somehow the consequence. Her forehead was planted on the bottom step, her hair having fallen forward to cover her face, her knees two stairs up, arms behind her, rump in the air. She looked like she'd been swimming the breaststroke from the top of the stairs to the bottom and died before she could get there.

How long did he stand there, paralyzed? He hadn't even checked to make sure she was dead, just stood there staring at her, unable to process what he was seeing. Even now, thirteen months later, he cringed to recall his breathtaking incompetence at the scene. What he couldn't get out of his head was how staged the whole thing looked—Becka's body impossibly balanced like that, no blood to speak of. To Raymer it resembled a museum diorama whose bizarre purpose was beyond his grasp. She was, after all, an actress, which made what he was witnessing a performance. She couldn't hold that ridiculous pose forever. If he was just patient, she'd eventually get to her feet and say, *Is* this *what you want to happen to me? Fix that fucking rug!*

But no. It was no performance. Becka was dead. He found the tented note she'd left on the dining room table while he waited for the ambulance. *I'm sorry,* it said. *I didn't mean for this to happen. Try to be happy for us.* It was signed with Becka's usual capital *B*.

She didn't mean for this to happen? It took him a moment to realize that by "this" she didn't mean falling down the stairs, or dying, because of course she couldn't have. No, what she hadn't meant to do was fall in love. Falling *out of love* with him was something he could, in time, come to terms with. In point of fact, hadn't he understood from the beginning that his luck in marrying Becka was too good to last? But falling *in love* with somebody new? *Try to be happy for us?* How could that happen when he didn't know who *us* was?

DURING THE LAST THIRTEEN MONTHS the images from that terrible afternoon—Becka dead, the EMTs and investigators trying to work around her on the stairs, her rigored body being maneuvered onto a gurney and then out the front door, the neighbors having gathered outside to watch—had mercifully begun to fade, like photographs left in the sun. Tom Bridger's words, by contrast, had lost none of their force. Over a forty-year career, Tom had developed a medical examiner's mordant humor. Arriving on the scene, he'd taken one look at Becka, her forehead seemingly stapled to the bottom step, her rear end in the air, and said, "What the hell did this woman do? Come down those stairs like a Slinky?" He hadn't intended the remark to be cruel, not realizing the dead woman's husband was in the next room to overhear it. What made it so awful was its truth. Because Becka had looked for all the world as if she'd done exactly that—Slinkied down the stairs. Which again put Raymer in mind of old Miss Beryl, who, back in eighth grade, famously maintained that the precise word, the carefully chosen phrase, the exact analogy, was worth a thousand pictures. Back then he and his classmates had been convinced she had it backward, but no more. When he remembered the horror of that afternoon's events, the phrase "like a Slinky" still played on a loop in his brain, still made his stomach roil. The words actually had a taste: stomach acid on the back of his tongue. Their meaning had gradually evolved, morphing from horror into anger, then into despair and finally into . . . what? Lately, when the phrase "like a Slinky" scrolled uninvited across his consciousness, he found himself involuntarily grinning. Why? He certainly didn't think there was anything funny about what had happened. Even if Becka had been planning to run off with another man, he wasn't glad she was dead. At least he didn't think he was. What had happened to her wasn't justice, poetic or otherwise. Where, then, did the shameful impulse to grin come from? From some dark place in himself? *Who,* he wondered, as Miss Beryl had so often done, is *this Douglas Raymer?*

"My dear friends," intoned Reverend Tunic, who unless Raymer was much mistaken hadn't a single friend, dear or otherwise, within earshot, "I submit that it is not the duty of one man, no matter how great and wise, to bring justice and rectitude to the world. No, that responsibility belongs to us all, to each and every one of us . . ."

Except me, thought Chief of Police Douglas Raymer. Blinking back perspiration or tears—he couldn't be sure which—he was beyond weary of all obligation. No, the thing to do was abdicate. Surrender the field. Admit defeat. Become a gravedigger.

As he'd become lost in the memory of Becka's tragic end, his hand, he now realized, had unconsciously migrated back into his trouser pocket, where it was again depressing the metal plate of the garage remote. What was the range on these things? he wondered. Was a door—or several doors, if Charice was right—sliding up somewhere in Bath? In Schuyler Springs? In Albany? Raymer found himself smiling at this patently absurd notion, picturing his wife's lover, the asshole, watching his garage door go up, then down, then up again, and knowing that the man who was making this happen was nearby and armed.

Was this the compromise he was searching for? Quit the job he wasn't cut out for, but first find out who the opener belonged to and let the rotten bastard know he was busted? If Raymer could solve just this one mystery, he could let go of everything else—responsibility and rectitude, obligation and the fucking Iroquois with their supple moccasins and whatever other happy horseshit Reverend Tunic was running up his spiritual flagpole. Okay, maybe it wasn't possible to reinvent yourself, but you could move on, right? People did it every day. He didn't hate Becka for her faithlessness. She was simply, like his career in law enforcement, a mistake. Everyone but he himself seemed to have recognized this from the start. When introduced to the bride-to-be at the rehearsal dinner, Jerome, who'd reluctantly agreed to be his best man when Raymer confessed he had no other close friends, immediately sussed out the situation. "Damn, Dougie," he said. "You're marrying *up,* boy." Raymer had been pleased by the other man's enthusiasm and proud that Becka was such a fine-looking woman. And of course it felt good to have his own assessment—that he was a lucky man—confirmed. But trailing in the wake of his friend's enthusiasm was his unspoken assumption that luck this good was bound to run out.

"There's a word," intoned the reverend, "for those among us who do not each day take up the burden of making the world a better, more just place."

That same twelve-year-old girl was nudging her mother now. *Look, Mama. Look at that man with his hand in his pocket. What's he doing, Mama?*

"Do you know what it is? The word is . . . 'shirker.'"

He'd stopped sweating, Raymer realized, and his soaked, heavy shirt now felt cold and clammy. His knees felt jellied.

"And those who do so shirk not just responsibility and human fellowship but God himself. Yes, friends, the shirker shirks the divine."

And the birker birks the bovine, Raymer thought. *The perker perks the povine.*

The girl's mother was regarding him with disgust, but for once he felt his own much-abused innocence and smiled back at the woman beatifically. Over and over he depressed the metal plate, indulging again the pleasant notion that somewhere a door was rising and falling on the truly guilty.

"And what of God?" Reverend Tunic wanted to know.

Good question, Raymer thought.

"Does God love the shirker?"

Yes. He loves us all.

"No!" Tunic emphatically disagreed. "God does not."

Well, fuck him, then, Raymer thought, giddy with heat and blasphemy. *Shame on God.*

"Because a shirker is a coward."

No, God is.

"A shirker always assumes that the difficult duty of daily living is someone else's, that the thunderclouds which darken the sun and obscure the light of reason are someone else's problem."

But why should clouds *be anybody's responsibility?*

"No, friends, Barton Flatt was no shirker. Shirking is not his legacy. And as he journeys to his final reward . . ."

Dirt? Decomposition? Worms?

". . . we honor him one last time by reaffirming in his presence . . ."

His absence, surely.

". . . our faith. In God. In America. And in *our fair city.* Because only then . . ."

Raymer started, suddenly alert, his reverie instantly dispelled. Had he momentarily lost his balance in the heat, or had the ground beneath his feet actually trembled? Apparently the latter, because all those gathered around the open grave had now assumed that classic surfer's stance, arms akimbo for balance. Even Reverend Tunic, who to this point had seemed untethered to any earthly reality, danced nimbly back from the hole in the ground, as if he'd just been informed that the bell he'd supposed was tolling for another was actually beckoning him.

Raymer's first guilty thought was that if the earth shuddered, he himself must be the cause. He'd been silently blaspheming, and God, eavesdropping, had shown his displeasure. Anxious not to incur further disapproval, he was about to offer a silent but heartfelt apology when he heard someone say, "Earthquake." In general, Raymer much preferred natural explanations to divine ones, but he doubted the ground had shaken long enough—a second at most—to qualify as a quake. It had felt less like a tectonic shift than a concussion, as if somewhere nearby the earth had been impacted. Had the plane he'd been watching earlier fallen from the sky? Had he somehow made this happen by playing with the garage-door opener? He took the remote out of his pocket and studied it, bewildered. Everyone, he realized, was staring at him.

And just that quickly, Douglas Raymer, chief of police, was furious, because wasn't this the very problem he'd been trying to articulate earlier, the trouble with police work in a nutshell? *Responsibility, justice, love, rectitude, legacy.* Words with about as much substance as a vapor trail. A pompous windbag in an embroidered silk tunic could make a tidy living pretending by means of florid rhetoric to know all about such things. But let the ground shake beneath your feet, and it was cops people turned to for answers. Like it was *their* job to explain the fundamental instability of the world. Like *they* knew how to shore it up.

Gus Moynihan, the mayor, had grabbed him by the elbow. "Raymer?" he said, apparently puzzled by the device in his hand, a good mile from the nearest garage. "The damn *ground* just vibrated like a cheap dildo. You gonna just *stand* there?"

That didn't seem like such a bad idea, actually. If it *was* an earthquake, he couldn't imagine a better place to be than in the middle of vast, flat Dale, where there was nothing within a hundred yards tall enough to fall on them. Still, for the time being at least, he *was* the police chief, and action of some sort was probably in order. The thing to do, he decided, was to call Charice. She usually had answers or plenty of suggestions and, when these ultimately failed, sympathy, though even this was often laced with sarcasm. Slipping his radio off the metal hook on his belt, Raymer pressed TALK, pausing only half a beat to wonder what sort of experience Gus Moynihan had with cheap dildos, or expensive ones for that matter, before saying, "Charice? You there?"

No response.

The mourners were all talking at once, and now Raymer thought he heard somebody say, "Meteor." Had a *meteor* struck the station? Killed Charice right there at the switchboard?

The mayor started tapping Raymer's radio with his index finger. "That would probably work better if you turned it on."

Which was true. He'd turned the radio off when the service began, not wanting the damn thing to bark at him during the homily. He turned it back on, and Charice immediately said, "Chief?"

"I'm here," he said, though this didn't actually feel true. His extremities were tingling, as if whatever made the ground shudder had entered through his toes and was trying to get out through his fingertips and ears. He turned away from the cacophony of voices so he could hear better.

"You better come on back to town," she was saying. "You aren't going to believe what just happened."

"Was it a meteor?" he ventured, in motion now, though his legs felt as heavy and rooted as tree trunks.

"What?" Charice said.

"Doug?" the mayor called to him, but Raymer held up his hand. Couldn't the man see he was busy?

"Was it a meteor?" he repeated.

"Doug!" Despite its urgency, the mayor's voice seemed miles away now, though Raymer had moved only a few feet.

"You okay, Chief?" Charice wanted to know.

In fact, Raymer's field of vision seemed inexplicably to be shrinking. In the foreground was the radio he was speaking into, and in the blurry distance the gleaming backhoe. Everything else was shrouded in gauze.

Then, with his next step, the ground simply wasn't there, and even before he could account for its absence it was back again with a bang, the noise, impossibly loud, somehow *inside* his head. Had he managed to discharge his weapon again, as he had that day with Sully? Where, he wondered, might *this* bullet land?

You know my thoughts on arming morons, Judge Flatt chuckled from inside his nearby casket.

Then, nothing.

Exit Strategies

WHEN THE LITTLE BELL over the door stopped tinkling and Sully saw how Ruth was glaring at him, he almost wished Roy Purdy would return. Back when he and Ruth were more than just friends that same look would've meant that he could forget about sex for a while. These days his punishment was less certain and therefore more ominous. "Well," she said finally, "you're right about one thing."

"Really? I didn't mean to be."

"People generally *do* get worse." Clearly, it wasn't Roy who'd prompted this observation. "What is *wrong* with you?"

Before he could answer, the men's room door opened and Carl emerged, a dark stain spreading down the inseam of one pant leg. In the weeks following his surgery, he'd worn the recommended diaper but confided to Sully that doing so was humiliating, so he quit as soon as he began regaining control of his urinary function. The problem was that occasional incontinence persisted, mostly at night and first thing in the morning. Feeling like he had to go, he'd stand patiently in front of the commode waiting for water that wouldn't come, at least until he pulled up his pants, which seemed to be the signal for his unruly urethra to cut loose. Which was evidently what had just happened.

"So, when you see Rub?" he said, oblivious. "Tell him I'm going to need both him and his backhoe."

"That isn't his, actually," Sully reminded him. "It belongs to the town."

"We could borrow it, is my thinking," Carl said, and as he slid back onto his stool Sully caught an acrid whiff of fresh urine.

"What happened to your own backhoe?" he said.

"Out at the yard," Carl said. "Temporarily disabled."

There was a towel draped over the oven door, so Sully rose and moved around the counter, a risky maneuver with Ruth so pissed at him. He was grudgingly permitted to come around when he had business there and she was in a good mood, but not when he didn't and she wasn't. "I'm sure your pal the mayor would rent it to you."

"Yeah, probably, but I'd prefer that no money changes hands."

"Having worked for you, I know that preference all too well."

"So," he said, while Sully wiped up an imaginary spill on the counter between them, "you really don't think about sex anymore?"

"Not often."

"Good," Carl said, to all appearances genuinely relieved. "I'd like to think that when I'm as old as you, all that will be over."

"What makes you think you'll ever get to be my age?" Then, lowering his voice, he said, "Here, you might need this." And pushed the towel toward him meaningfully.

Carl gave him a what-the-hell look, then saw. "Jesus," he said, spinning off his stool as if the soaking had occurred right that second, not two minutes earlier in another room entirely. Sully saw Ruth process the whole thing even faster than Carl, who now regarded Sully angrily, as if he suspected he'd been the one who peed on him. Sully, for his part, somehow felt as if he had.

"A towel's no good," Ruth said when Carl commenced vigorously buffing his chinos. "Come with me," she said, motioning for him to follow her, which he reluctantly did, his face flushed beet red.

When the door into the apartment closed behind them, Sully was left alone in one of his favorite places in the world, in a silence so profound that he could hear the coffeepot's metallic, clocklike ticking at the far end of the counter. Outside, the only visible movement was the oppressive heat rippling the window glass. As he waited for a car to pass, or someone to come out of the hardware store, or a dog to trot across the street, anything, he was visited by a profound disorientation, as if what he'd assumed to be real had just been revealed as a movie set where he was the only actor, the rest of the cast and even the crew having gone home. For the day? The weekend? Or had the movie wrapped and nobody bothered to tell him? When even the coffeepot stopped clicking, Sully felt his chest fill with something like panic. Had he just had the heart attack he'd been warned was coming? Was this what the cessation of life felt like, experienced from the inside? Everything stops, except consciousness continues merrily about its business, dutifully bearing witness.

"Hey," said a voice he recognized as Ruth's until he blinked and saw it was Janey, her daughter. Over the years, their voices had become so similar that anymore he had a hard time telling them apart. Her apartment door was now ajar, and from inside came the high-pitched whine of a small appliance. "Earth to Sully."

"Hey yourself," he said, embarrassed but grateful, too, because the sound of her voice had set everything back in motion. Across the street a man strode purposefully out of the hardware store, and up the block a car alarm went off. At the VA he'd been warned about the possibility of brief "narrative disruptions," even hallucinations. Thanks to the arrhythmia, the brain sometimes got too much blood, at other times too little.

"You're getting weirder every day, you know that?" Janey said, pouring herself some coffee. There were dark circles under her sleep-encrusted eyes, through which she regarded Sully with unfeigned disinterest. "And speaking of weird, how come Carl Roebuck's in my bathroom using my hair dryer on his crotch?"

"Well," Sully said, letting the word dangle because Janey was possibly the only woman in Bath who didn't know about Carl's predicament.

"Men," Janey said, making Sully complicit in whatever lunacy this might be.

"Hey," said Ruth, returning now and gazing at her daughter. "I'd prefer it if you didn't come into the restaurant in your bathrobe."

Janey, no surprise, didn't seem to care about her mother's preferences. "Yeah, and I'd prefer you didn't bring men into my bathroom before I'm even awake and loan them my hair dryer without asking."

"Try waking up before noon, then," Ruth suggested.

Janey pointed at the clock, which said 11:29. "It *is* before noon. And I closed the Bee last night, so how about cutting me a little slack?"

They faced off for a long beat until her mother relented. "Sorry about the bathroom," she said, "but Carl had an accident." She emphasized the name ever so slightly. *Remember?* she seemed to be saying. *What I told you about Carl?*

"Oh, right." Janey shrugged. "I guess that makes it okay."

"That was *my* thought," Ruth said. "I'm glad you agree."

Janey rolled her eyes to show that she most certainly did *not* agree but wasn't going to go to the mat over it, either. "Was that my idiot ex-husband's voice I heard earlier?" Ruth apparently took this to be a rhetorical question, because she didn't bother answering. "He's taking that restraining order real serious." Turning to Sully, "What'd she give him this time?"

"Nothing," Ruth told her, but immediately looked guilty. "A cup of coffee and slice of day-old pie."

"Think of him as a dog, Ma. If you feed him, he's gonna keep coming back."

"He hasn't caused any trouble so far, or even tried to," Ruth said, glancing at Sully. "Unlike some people."

"That's the thing about Roy," Janey said, putting her now-empty mug into a plastic busing tub. "He won't, until he does. But when he does, it'll be my jaw that gets broke, like always."

"He breaks your jaw because you're always mouthing off."

"No, he breaks it because he *enjoys* breaking it."

"Like *you* enjoy mouthing off," Ruth said as Janey brushed past her.

"Well, jeez," Janey mused, pausing in the doorway to her apartment. "Let's think a minute. Where the fuck do I get that from?"

Once she was gone, Ruth turned back to Sully. "I don't want to hear it," she said.

As he'd feared, she was all too willing to pick up their dispute right where they left off. "What don't you want to hear?"

"What you're thinking."

Actually, Sully was more than happy to hold his tongue. Through none of his own doing, he was pretty sure the tide had just turned in his favor. Nothing was more likely to return him to Ruth's good graces than a skirmish with her obstinate daughter, and he seriously doubted, despite being dead game, that Ruth wanted to wage battles on two separate fronts. Apparently he was right, because after he let her win the staredown, her posture relaxed. "Thank you," she said, like she meant it.

"You're welcome," he told her. "I might've had something nice to say, though. Now you'll never know."

She shot him a look that said she was content to take her chances, poured herself some coffee, then pulled up a stool across from him, brushing his cheek with the back of her fingers, more intimacy than they'd shared in months, the gesture powerful enough to dispel what remained of his earlier disorientation. Such as it was, this was his life, not a movie of it.

"What *is* wrong with you?" Ruth said. It was the same question she'd asked before, when she was angry, though her tone was totally different now. Then, she'd been referring to how he'd goaded Roy Purdy, but now he wasn't so sure.

"He's dangerous, Ruth."

"You think I don't know that?"

He wasn't sure, once he thought about it. Did she?

"I know you think you're helping, but you're not. If he snaps, he'll put you in the hospital. Or Hilldale."

"I might surprise you," he said, borrowing Roy's line, though it sounded just as lame coming from him.

"He's got forty years on you, Sully. And he won't fight fair."

"I understand that," said Sully, whose imagined strategies for offing Roy Purdy hadn't exactly been models of fair play either. "But if he assaults me, he goes back to jail and you're rid of him."

"Yeah, but if he kills you I'm rid of *you*."

Two years. But probably closer to one. Was that what his goading had really been about, some sort of subconscious exit strategy, an attempt to leave life on his own terms instead of waiting for the fatal hiccup of a deteriorating heart? You heard about people committing suicide by speeding on a dark road and locating a convenient tree or swerving into oncoming traffic. So how did Roy Purdy fit into that scenario? Suicide by moron?

The problem with this theory was that it presupposed Sully wanted to die, which he was pretty sure wasn't true. Earlier, when Carl was explaining the job he meant to offer Rub, work that nobody in his right mind would want, Sully had actually felt a twinge of jealousy that he was at a loss to explain, even to himself. If the source of the vile gunk bubbling up through the floor of the mill was from the rendering plant, mucking it out would be beyond disgusting. No one, including Sully, could possibly enjoy such labor. Nor was he so full of self-loathing as to believe, consciously or not, so far as he knew, that he deserved such an appalling job. What appealed to him, as near as he could tell, was its necessity. That was the thing about the work he and Rub used to do: nasty as it was, it all needed to be done. And once completed, it provided satisfaction, and even pleasure, in inverse proportion to the hardship endured. Sheetrocking in weather so cold you couldn't feel your fingers until you misjudged where they were and hit them with a hammer was hardly fun, but it felt good when you finally came in out of the cold. The long shower afterward, hot as you could stand it, felt better still, and sliding onto a barstool at the Horse an hour later? Perfection. The day's labors, safely sequestered in the past, somehow made the beer colder, and if the beer was cold enough you didn't mind that it was cheap or that cheap beer was your lot in life. And come Friday, hunting Carl Roebuck down and forcing him to go deep into his trouser pocket for that fat roll of twenties and fifties, watching while the son of a bitch grudgingly peeled them off one after the other until you were finally all square, until he paid you what you'd damn well *earned,* well, what could be more satisfying than that? Until fairly recently that had been Sully's life and, no, he wasn't tired of it, just of being forced by age and infirmity to the sidelines, which, face it, happened to everyone. It was simply his turn.

And yet. Once again he studied his landlady and she him. *Be honest,* she seemed to be saying. In response, Sully assumed, to the old question about regret for not having done more with the life God had given him. Which was another way of asking whether he wished it had amounted to more than throwing up drywall in the bitter cold and digging trenches under the blazing sun, more than sliding onto an endless succession of barstools and getting into beer-fueled arguments about whether or not there was such a thing as sex addiction. Was it the dubious worth of such an existence that had caused him to momentarily doubt its reality earlier? How would killing Roy Purdy, or inviting Roy to kill him, render his existence any less pointless?

"Listen," he told Ruth. "I'll lay off him, if that's what you want."

"Want? What I *want* is for something heavy to fall out of the sky on his pointed head. How come God never lowers the boom on the Roy Purdys of the world?"

Since there was no chance this could be a serious question, he offered no opinion. "Anyway," he said, "don't worry about me. I'm just in a funk."

"Funks have causes, too," she said. "When does Peter get back?"

Ah, so she had an angle. Good. This meant she'd be less likely to ferret out the truth. "Tuesday, I think. Why?"

"Maybe he'll change his mind."

"No, he's pretty set on leaving." Then, she gave him a look. "What?"

"How upset would you be if I told you I've never really warmed to him?"

"Well, Ruth, he is my son."

"Maybe I just wish he'd act like it."

"He probably wishes I'd acted more like a father when he was a kid."

"And there's no statute of limitations on that gripe?"

"I don't know. Should there be?"

"I don't know either," she admitted. "We all fuck up, though." Here she nodded in the direction of her daughter's apartment.

"That we do," he agreed. "Actually, I think Peter's mostly forgiven me. Most of the time we get along pretty well."

Which was true. Though Peter seemingly remained baffled by how two such different human beings could possibly be related by blood, their relationship had grown easier these last few years. The eighteen months or so they'd worked together before Sully finally retired had helped. Maybe Peter still didn't understand what made his father tick, but at least he understood the rhythm of Sully's days, not to mention his nights. And for his part Sully'd been pleasantly surprised to learn that Peter wasn't nearly as soft as he looked, that he had no quarrel with hard physical labor, even if it didn't seem to satisfy or speak to him all that deeply.

Certainly he hadn't been surprised when Peter went back to teaching, and it made sense that he spent most of his free time these days in Schuyler with his academic friends. Every now and then, though, he'd wander into the Horse, where he'd wink conspiratorially at Birdie before sliding onto the stool next to Sully, and there he'd remain, seemingly content, until last call, which pleased Sully. Peter's relationship with his own adolescent son was fraught at times, and while he never asked for advice about how to handle the boy—and Sully knew better than to offer any—he seemed grateful for his father's willingness to listen and commiserate. There were even times when Sully thought he might be growing on his son, that Peter was contemplating not just forgiving but forgetting—a possibility that seemed to have occurred to Peter as well, though every time it loomed as their ultimate destination, he pulled back, as if from a hot stove. In turn Sully feared that in some respects his son remained as deep a mystery to him as ever, as mysterious as he himself must have seemed to his own father, as baffling as Will, at times, appeared to Peter. Was this just how this deal worked? How things had to be?

What Sully gradually *had* come to comprehend was his son's unhappiness, rooted deeply in his sense of personal failure. That made little sense to Sully, who thought Peter had done all right for himself. After all, he taught at Schuyler's prestigious liberal arts college, and three years earlier, when the editor of the school's glossy but failing alumni magazine had retired, Peter had taken it over and breathed new life into the publication. Also his movie, book and music reviews were regular features in Albany's alternative newspaper. Though now middle aged, he was still good looking, and his easy charm a steady magnet for mostly younger women. And he'd raised a son who'd graduated in January, six months ahead of his high school classmates, and spent the spring semester taking college courses in Schuyler. In the fall he would enroll as a second-semester freshman at Penn on a full scholarship. Much to be proud of here, Sully figured.

Peter, of course, saw all this through a different lens. His once-promising career had never recovered from being denied tenure at the state university that had originally hired him. Now, as an adjunct instructor, he was a distinctly second-class academic, and thanks to the unforgiving nature of that world he would forever remain one. His salary was a fraction of what his full-time, tenured colleagues were making, and he had no job security. He was writing reviews, not books or scripts. His marriage had failed, and thanks to Charlotte, his vindictive ex-wife, he seldom saw his troubled middle son. Nor did it take long for the new women in his life to realize that, beneath his easy charm, he was bitter and discontented.

What Sully had the hardest time doping out was how Peter expected leaving Bath would improve any of this. He understood that with Will heading off to college, things were changing, and it made sense that he'd want to live close to his son. And, sure, there were more teaching opportunities in an urban setting, but if he moved to New York City, which seemed to be the plan, there'd also be more competition, wouldn't there? And his cost of living would easily triple, probably even worse. But when Sully'd raised these issues, Peter—no surprise—took it poorly. "Dad," he said, "once Will's gone, why would I stay here? To take care of you in your old age?" Which hadn't been what Sully was suggesting at all. He'd wanted Peter to understand that there was no need to rush off if he didn't want to, that Sully himself was content to remain in the trailer if Peter wanted to stay on in Miss Beryl's large downstairs flat. That way Will could come home on vacations. In fact, he was willing to sign the house over to Peter then and there. It'd be his one day anyway, maybe sooner than he imagined. "What would I do with this house, Dad?" Sell it when the time seems right, Sully had suggested, but Peter had just smiled that knowing smile of his that always annoyed Sully to the nth degree, the one that implied Sully was trying to put one over on him.

On the other hand, could he really blame Peter for being suspicious of his motives? If Carl Roebuck ever moved out of the upstairs flat, which Sully himself had occupied while his landlady was alive, it would make sense for him to move back in, and he could see how that might make Peter nervous. Maybe he had no intention of letting Peter or anybody else take care of him, but his son couldn't know that. He was probably thinking ahead to the day when he'd fall and break a hip or have a stroke and end up in a wheelchair. He couldn't blame Peter for wanting to be far away when any of that shit happened.

Still, if Peter moved to New York, Sully would miss hearing his footfalls on Miss Beryl's porch and the ticking of his car engine as it cooled in the drive, miss having him show up unexpectedly and slide onto that stool at the Horse. And of course he'd miss his grandson, too. He actually had more in common with Will, which his father no doubt sensed. The boy may have inherited Peter's intelligence, good looks and charm, but he was also tough, a talented three-sport athlete. In his junior year, he was the starting middle linebacker on the varsity football team, and Sully had secretly smiled when it became clear that Will enjoyed hitting people as much as he had himself. The boy's tackles were always clean, never intended to injure, but they loosened molars just the same. What pleased him most about the boy's physicality was that when he'd arrived in Bath a decade earlier he'd been afraid of his own shadow.

Peter seemed proud of his son's toughness, too, but not, unless Sully was mistaken, unambiguously so. And while he was happy that Will loved Sully, he seemed less anxious for his son to admire or emulate him. Any youthful enthusiasm he expressed for how his grandfather navigated the world Peter considered his duty to temper, lest the romance of the tool belt and barstool take root. Indeed, by leaving Bath before Will reached legal drinking age, Peter might be trying to ensure that the stool next to Sully's at the Horse would not be part of Will's inheritance.

All of this, Sully supposed, was what Ruth objected to, the reason she couldn't quite, as she put it, warm to his son.

"If you're in a funk, why not go away for a while? Take a vacation," she suggested. "A change of scenery might be just what you need."

"A vacation from what? I'm retired."

She shrugged. "I don't know. From Bath. From the Horse. From this place." Here she made a sweeping gesture. "Maybe from me. From Peter, for that matter. How can he miss you if you won't go away?"

How could *she* miss him if he wouldn't go away was what she also seemed to be saying. "Where would I go?" he said, curious about what she had in mind.

"Pick a place," she said. "Aruba."

He snorted. "What the fuck would I do in Aruba?"

"What are you doing *here*?"

"You mean in Bath?"

"No, I mean *here*. As in this minute. This restaurant."

Sully's need to speak in his own defense took him by surprise. "I thought I was helping out." Helping her open the place most mornings, filling in at the grill or busing dishes, as needed. "But if I'm in your way . . ."

"You're in your *own* way, Sully," she told him. "As always. You know I appreciate the help but . . ." This time when she touched his cheek, the effect wasn't nearly so pleasant, perhaps because he was pretty sure this gesture's source was pity.

"Okay, Aruba it is," he said. "You can come along, since you think it's such a great idea. Let Janey run this show for a week or two." She could, too. Janey might be a royal pain in the ass, but she had her mother's work ethic. Three or four day shifts a week at Hattie's and another four or five nights at Applebee's, the occasional stint out at the Horse when one of Birdie's regulars called in sick.

Ruth was grinning at him now. "Should we invite my husband?"

"I wouldn't, personally, but if it's important to you . . ."

She massaged her temples, as if at the approach of a migraine. "He's been acting so weird lately."

"Really? How?"

"He's being thoughtful. Almost . . . considerate," she explained. "It's messing with my head. I'll look up and there he is, staring at me, like he's just noticed I'm there." She shrugged, and her expression looked for all the world like shame, though it couldn't be, could it? In all the years they'd been lovers, Ruth had never given any indication of being ashamed of the no-good they were up to. She didn't hate her husband, and even early on, when she and Sully were hot and heavy, she never talked about leaving him. But neither, so far as Sully knew, had she ever felt like she was betraying the man. It was Sully himself who sometimes felt guilty, because Zack, though a total doofus, wasn't a bad guy. "I'm trying to be nicer to him," she admitted. "I tried the same thing thirty years ago and it didn't work, but it might now."

"So," Sully said, letting the word trail off and allowing both what she was saying and not saying to come into focus, "is it because of Roy Purdy that I shouldn't come in here anymore, or Zack?"

"I didn't say you shouldn't come in anymore."

"No, you said I should go to Aruba."

She didn't respond right away. "You know what Janey said to me last week?"

Sully put his index fingers to his temples, closed his eyes and pretended to concentrate. "Wait. Don't tell me. That I should go to Aruba?"

"She *said,* 'Why is he in here all the time if you guys aren't screwing anymore?'"

"And you replied?"

"She *also* said, 'Do you know how fucked up it is that most mornings the first voice I hear on the other side of my bedroom wall is my mother's former boyfriend?'"

"You didn't answer my question."

"I told her it was none of her damn business." But she wasn't meeting his eye. "I can kind of see her point, though."

"Me too," Sully admitted.

"And then there's Tina." Her granddaughter. "I know she seems slow, but she's not stupid. She watches. Takes everything in."

"You're right."

She rotated the newspaper so that Miss Beryl was now looking up at her, not Sully. "What do you think?" she said. "Will that no-good son of hers show up?"

Clive Jr., she meant. Who'd been the driving force behind the Ultimate Escape Fun Park. Who'd invested funds from his savings and loan and encouraged others to do likewise, then skipped town when, at the last possible second, the out-of-state developer pulled the plug, leaving local investors in the lurch.

"No," Sully said. "I suspect we've seen the last of him."

"What?" she said, apparently puzzled by his tone. "You're feeling sorry for him now? How many times did he try to get his mother to evict you?"

Over Sully's smoking, mostly. Clive Jr. had been worried that Sully would go off someplace and leave behind a lit cigarette, burn the house down and Miss Beryl in it. But their ongoing conflict went deeper than Sully's carelessness, which was real enough. Miss Beryl and her husband, Clive Sr., seeing how miserable Sully's homelife was, had welcomed him into their home and treated him like a son. Young Clive, their actual son, had to have seen that as an intrusion and might even have felt that they preferred Sully to himself. Later, as adults, they'd never had much use for each other. Sully always referred to Clive as "the Bank" and took genuine pleasure in making him look like a fool in places like Hattie's. Did the man have any idea that Sully had inherited his mother's house? Would that corroborate his fear that his mother had favored him over her own flesh and blood?

"Maybe I'm getting soft in my old age," he admitted, sliding off his stool and pocketing his keys.

"Look," she said, "don't get the wrong idea. What I said earlier really isn't about Zack or Janey or Tina. It's . . . you really don't come in here because of me anymore." When he started to object, she held up her hand. "I'm not saying you don't care about me. I know you do. But you come here because you don't know where else to go. Lately you just sit there staring into your coffee, and it breaks my heart. And you—"

She didn't get a chance to finish. From somewhere down the street came a loud *whomp!,* a concussion so forceful that the restaurant's windows rattled. Two water glasses toppled off the shelf and shattered. A moment later the ground shuddered, as if impacted, making the salt and pepper shakers all along the counter leap and skitter.

"What the—" Ruth said. She'd grabbed on to the counter to steady herself and was looking to Sully for an explanation he didn't have. They both remained frozen until Ruth made a beeline for the front door. Sully, who no longer leaped into action, followed, out of breath, by the time he got to the door, his heart pounding. Outside, people were streaming into the street from stores and businesses. A police cruiser roared by, its siren blaring. Jocko, who owned the failing Rexall next door, came over to where he and Ruth were standing, Sully bent over with his hands on his knees.

"Jesus," Jocko said, "you don't suppose it's the Japs again, do you?"

A cloud of yellow-brown dust was rising over the rooftops at the lower end of the street, maybe half a mile away. The awful stench that had plagued the town over the last several days was suddenly even more intense, causing the morning's coffee to rise dangerously in Sully's throat.

Ruth had a hand on his elbow now. "Are you okay?"

"Yeah, fine," he said, straightening up, trying to look like a man who might just—what the fuck?—*go* to Aruba, instead of one with two years left but probably one. "I just felt light-headed. The heat after air-conditioning probably." And maybe that's all it was, because he started feeling better as soon as he said it.

Then Carl Roebuck emerged onto the sidewalk, his chinos dry again and his chipper spirits restored. Apparently with the hair dryer going and the bathroom door closed, the concussion that had captured the town's attention had escaped his own. He nudged Sully and lowered his voice confidentially. "Guess what I was thinking about the whole time I was in there blow-drying my dick," he said, only then fully registering the commotion in the street. "Hell, what's going on?"

Sully was surprised to discover he had a working hypothesis. He pointed at the yellow-brown cloud that was now expanding and drifting slowly in their direction like some dust storm in an old western. "I got a question for you, Dummy," he said. "What's over there?"

But the blood had already drained from Carl's face. Sully could tell he sure wasn't thinking about sex anymore.

Suppositories

"Y OU FAINTED *into the grave?*"
Charice's voice crackled with a mixture of radio static and disbelief. Sympathy would come later, Raymer knew, probably when she saw him. Saw the damage. Which in the warped mirror on the wall opposite where he sat, bare-assed, draped in a flimsy paper johnny, was pretty damn impressive. His broken nose was swollen hideously, and both eyes were slits.

He'd been told a doctor would be in to see him shortly, but that was nearly half an hour ago, and the examination room's air-conditioning was in brutal contrast to the sweltering heat outside. His head throbbed dully, but apart from that he didn't feel too bad, and certainly not as bad as he looked. The light-headed, elsewhere feeling he'd suffered prior to losing consciousness out at Hilldale was gone, as was the dizziness. He was tempted to just get dressed and leave, but instead of hanging up his sweaty uniform, he'd made the mistake of draping it over the AC unit. Putting it back on would be like donning a frigid, wet onesie. He shivered at the thought.

"*Into* the grave," Charice repeated, apparently willing to concede the truth of what he was telling her but still unable to wrap her mind around what had happened. "Like . . . on top of *the casket?*"

"No," he explained, "His Honor was still aboveground."

"Why are you in the emergency room?"

"It was my face that broke the fall. But never mind that. Tell me again what happened out at the mill." Because Charice wasn't the only one having trouble processing recent events. "The whole building actually—"

"So you, like, slumped forward and rolled into the grave?"

"I fainted, Charice. Okay? You know that matting they edge graves with? They say I tripped over that, but I don't really remember. Ask Gus. He saw the whole thing."

And would be thrilled to recount the whole shitshow. According to the mayor, Raymer's knees hadn't buckled or anything. Rather, he'd gone down like a tree. "One minute you were standing there and the next it was—*timber!* You went into that hole like it was dug to your exact specifications. You were just gone. You know like when you try to stuff a cat in a bag? How there's always a leg sticking out?"

Raymer had just blinked at him. Why would he have ever put a cat in a bag? Was Gus confessing to having drowned kittens at some point? Why did he imagine this was an experience other people would be familiar with?

"It wasn't like that at all," Gus insisted. "You went in clean and neat. There was just the one sound you made when you hit bottom and then the plume of dust. I don't think I ever saw anything like it, and I was in Korea."

Korea, where he'd spent the last seven months of the conflict, was Gus's particular touchstone. It was one of the few times he'd been out of upstate New York for an extended period, and his experience on that misbegotten peninsula, even more than his graduate work in government, was the reason he believed himself qualified to be mayor of North Bath. Was it over there he'd done his cat stuffing?

"Charice," he told her sternly. "I want to hear about the mill, all right? Because I don't understand how that could happen. How does a whole building just . . . fall down?"

"Not the whole building," she said, "just the north wall. The one facing Limerock Street."

"The other walls are still standing? How can that be?"

"I'm just telling you what I was told."

"By who?"

"Miller's on the scene."

"Miller."

"Jerome's there, too."

"Jerome."

"You're repeating everything I say."

"Your brother Jerome." He worked for the Schuyler Springs PD and served as a liaison officer between the department and the college and the mayor's office, doing exactly what Raymer wasn't sure, except that he was required to be on television a lot, either attempting to explain the inexplicable or obfuscate the perfectly clear.

"It's his day off, so he stopped by the station. He's got this joke he wants to tell you. When the call came in about the mill, he figured we could use a hand."

Raymer sighed. "Why's he acting like this?" Because lately, Jerome had become increasingly solicitous about Raymer's welfare, always stopping by the station on some pretense, telling him jokes and calling him buddy.

"He's worried about you."

"Why?"

"*I'm* worried about you."

"Why?"

"Chief," she said, as if the answer to this question was so obvious it needn't be voiced. His head was hurting worse now. Probably because of the fall, but possibly not. His head often hurt when he talked to Charice. "I mean, imagine, okay?"

"Please," he begged. Charice was forever asking him to imagine this or that, usually something extremely unpleasant. Like trying to put a cat in a bag, or some other Korean-type activity. "Please don't."

"Imagine you're in a great big room with ten thousand other guys."

"Actually, I'm in a small room, all by myself."

"And the guy in charge says, 'Okay, show of hands. Who's passed out at a funeral—'"

"Stop, please."

She ignored him, of course. Charice believed, for some reason, that a vivid imagination was the true path to understanding. "*Passed* out," she repeated, "right into an open grave."

"Desist," he told her. "This is a direct order I'm giving here."

"Yours would be the only hand in the air," Charice noted. "That's all I'm saying."

"Charice."

"Make it a hundred thousand guys, if you want. A million. It's still just you with his hand up, Chief."

"Actually, I wouldn't have my hand up either," Raymer said, reluctantly giving in to her scenario. "Why would I admit something like that in front of ten thousand other guys?"

"Imagine if you lied, you'd be electrocuted."

"I've got a better idea. Imagine you work for me and you have to do what I say. Tell Jerome I don't want to hear another stupid joke. Also, remind him he has no jurisdiction in Bath."

"I'll tell him, but you know Jerome."

"I do. Also his sister. Two peas in a pod." The metaphor was particularly apt in their case, as they were twins. "Have Miller come pick me up at the hospital."

"He's busy at the scene. Where's your own car?"

"Out at the cemetery. Gus wouldn't let me drive."

"I'll call Jerome then. He won't mind."

"Don't," he told her. "Do *not* call Jerome. I swear to God if he comes out here I'll shoot him on sight."

"Then you'll have exactly zero friends. All you got now is him and me, and I won't be your friend no more if you shoot my brother, 'cause that would be unnatural."

"*Any*more," he said. "You won't be my friend *any*more."

"There you go again. Making fun of how I talk. I'ma add that to my list." Charice claimed to be compiling a list of all the workplace shit he gave her. It had several distinct, if, to Raymer's mind, overlapping categories of abuse: illegal, immoral, actionable, insulting, bigoted and just plain wrong. She hadn't showed him the list but claimed it was growing and pretty comprehensive.

"Do you have any idea how bad my head hurts right now, Charice?"

"That's why they took you to the hospital. To get yourself checked out. Stay there, why don't you. Jerome can handle things."

"Miller, you mean. Miller can handle things. It's Miller on our payroll, not Jerome."

"Chief, we both know Miller can't handle anything. Don't matter whose payroll he's on."

"I don't care," Raymer said. "Send *some*body out to get me. Anybody but your brother, okay? And make sure whoever it is brings that big bottle of extra-strength Tylenol I keep in my desk. And a Diet Coke. Come yourself if you have to."

"Oh, I get it. This is a test, right? Last week you chew my ass out for leaving the switchboard to pee, and now you want to see if I learned my lesson."

"Goodbye, Charice. In five minutes I'm going to be on that bench outside the hospital. Main entrance, not emergency. Somebody better be there."

Head throbbing at a good beat now, he slid off the examination table and wobbled over to his clothes on the air conditioner. His jockeys, no surprise, were not only still soaked with sweat, but also very, very cold. *Imagine*—he could almost hear Charice say—*what it'd feel like to pull those on. Like a wet bathing suit, all nasty and cold . . . up there in your private place.* He closed his eyes and pulled them on and Charice was right, that was exactly how it felt.

HE'D NO SOONER PARKED himself on the bench outside the hospital's main entrance than Jerome's cherry-red Mustang convertible pulled up and stopped on a dime, tires screeching, chassis rocking. Jerome himself was at the wheel, of course. Nobody else was allowed to drive the 'Stang, not even Charice, who didn't even want to, but hated on general principle being told she couldn't. Her brother's explanation—that this was the car made famous in *Goldfinger,* the one the blonde chick drove before Oddjob decapitated her with his magic bowler—only pissed her off even more, because it wasn't really an explanation so much as a description, the kind of thing you'd say if you wanted to make certain you were both talking about the same vehicle. Raymer wasn't sure he understood Jerome's reasoning either. Part of it was that he didn't want to risk wrecking his 'Stang, but Raymer suspected that what he really hated was the idea of somebody readjusting the seat. He was tall—six foot six—and had very long legs. Another driver would have to move the seat forward in order to reach the pedals, which meant he'd have to readjust it later, and what if he couldn't find that exact comfortable position again, the one where his knees were ever so slightly flexed, his arms perfectly straight and the perfect distance from the wheel? He was similarly fussy about a lot of things. He really didn't want people to visit his apartment, either. It wasn't the company he objected to. Indeed, he seemed to enjoy it, but people were forever picking things up and then setting them down in the wrong place. And he particularly hated for people to use his bathroom. "I can't help it," he explained. "I don't like other people defecating where I do." "Obsessive-compulsive" was the term Charice used to describe his fastidiousness, claiming he'd been like that even as a child.

When it came to the 'Stang, though, he was beyond any diagnosis. Raymer could tell he didn't even like having anybody in the passenger seat, but he was willing to make exceptions for good-looking women. And since Raymer hardly fell into that category, he had to wonder if Charice hadn't had to twist her brother's arm to get him to fetch him at the hospital. He hoped so, because if Jerome had volunteered his services it would confirm what he'd lately been sensing—that he was behaving more and more strangely.

Rolling down the window, he said, as he always did, absolutely dead-pan, "The name is Bond. Jerome Bond." Part of the joke was that his and Charice's last name *was* actually Bond. "Are you bleeding?" he wanted to know. "Because these are genuine-leather seats."

Raymer made no move to rise from the bench.

"You gonna get in?"

"I'm still thinking."

"There's your problem right there," Jerome said. Like his sister, he spent far too much time diagnosing Raymer's problems. "Best nip that habit right in the bud, bud. Man starts thinking this late in life, no previous experience or proper guidance, there's no telling where it could lead."

"I told Charice I'd shoot you on sight if you showed up here, so what do you do?"

"Yeah, but see? I already got the drop on you." Jerome's left hand, on which he wore a special fingerless driving glove, gripped the wheel. When he raised his right, it held his revolver. Raymer sighed. It was a joke, sure, but to Raymer's way of thinking Jerome unholstered his weapon *way* too often. He never pointed it at anyone, of course, preferring to strike the classic James Bond pose, with the barrel pointed straight up, but he seemed to enjoy reminding people he was armed and that as a cop, black or not, he was allowed to be. "Come on and get in, before any blood gets shed."

Raymer rose, went around the car and opened the door, pleased to see that Jerome's revolver had disappeared back into its holster, or at least so he assumed. Still, he hesitated before getting in, because there was nothing Jerome liked more than peeling out the split second Raymer's ass hit the seat, the passenger door still open. "See that sign? QUIET? HOSPITAL ZONE? MAXIMUM SPEED FIFTEEN MILES PER HOUR?"

"You worry entirely too much."

"Yeah?" Raymer said, cautiously climbing in. "Well, I have my—" *Reasons* was how he meant to finish his sentence, but Jerome hit the gas, tires squealing, violently thrusting him back into the bucket seat, conking his skull on the headrest with the explosion of a million bright shards.

"You should only worry about things you have control over," Jerome was saying as the 'Stang fishtailed out of the parking lot. "The other shit you have to just let go. Otherwise it's like . . . a sickness . . . a cancer that'll eat away at your guts until one day—"

"Goddamn, Jerome," Raymer said. "Please, please shut the fuck up."

Then his radio barked. "Chief? Your ride show up?" Unless he was mistaken he heard a chortle.

"You and I are going to have to have a long talk, Charice," Raymer told her.

"Oh, goodie." And the radio went dead again.

He regarded Jerome for a moment, then closed his eyes. "Tell me you brought the Tylenol."

"Glove compartment."

Inside, like a chalice in a tabernacle, sat his big plastic bottle of five hundred Tylenol capsules. The only other thing in the glove box was, incredibly, the owner's manual. Badly as he needed the painkillers, Raymer couldn't help himself. Dumbfounded, he took out the manual, which was encased in plastic like a library book. "Who has the *owner's* manual to a 'sixty-four Mustang?"

Jerome looked away, embarrassed, as a normal man might when his secret stash of *Penthouses* was discovered. "Those things are collectors' items, man. Hundreds of dollars. I had to special order it."

Raymer regarded him. "You special ordered a Mustang owner's manual."

Jerome shrugged.

"And *I* have problems?" He tossed the manual back into the glove box for the pleasure of seeing Jerome wince. Later, once he got rid of Raymer, he'd probably pop the compartment open and lovingly recenter the booklet.

"Okay," he said when they came to the T-intersection at the end of the long hospital road. The traffic light was red, so he put his left-turn blinker on, toward town, then turned to watch Raymer struggle with the childproof plastic cap on the Tylenol bottle. "So this guy goes to the doctor and says, 'I'm all stopped up. Haven't defecated in a week.'"

"Defecated," Raymer repeated, marveling as he often did at how completely Jerome had excised North Carolina from his diction. Charice had as well, though unlike her brother, she enjoyed the vernacular and slid into and out of both dialects with ease. This Raymer found profoundly disorienting, like dealing with a split personality.

"Shit," Jerome clarified.

"I know what it means. In a joke the guy'd say *shit* or maybe *take a crap*."

"Maybe he's refined," Jerome suggested. "Not everybody's like you. Anyhow, it's been a week since he defecated, so the doctor writes him a prescription for suppositories."

Suddenly, Charice was on the radio again. "Oh, and another thing? When the wall fell down?"

"Yeah?" Raymer said, both thumbs clawing under the lip of the cap, his face purple with fruitless exertion, the plastic having somehow fused at the molecular level with the bottle itself.

"You gotta line up the little arrows," Jerome offered helpfully.

The problem was Raymer couldn't really see the damn things, not without his glasses, and he wasn't about to put them on now. The arrows sort of *felt* more or less aligned, but maybe not. He tried adjusting them a smidge, but no fucking luck.

Jerome held out his hand. "You want me to—"

"No."

"You still there, Chief?" Charice wanted to know.

"I'm here all right."

"It fell on a car," she informed him.

"A parked car?"

"Uh-uh. Moving. Apparently that wall came down just as it was passing by. What are the odds, right?"

Next she'd want him to calculate them.

"The good news is the vehicle in question was a beater."

"Is this a joke, Charice?" Because her twin brother and tag-team partner was sitting right next to him, also telling him a joke, and to Raymer, his head throbbing, it seemed possible the two jokes might be related by something other than the tellers' desire to torment him. "Are you going to tell me the bad news is that the driver was killed?"

Exasperated, Jerome grabbed the pill bottle, deftly lined up the arrows, popped the cap, shook out two capsules and handed them to Raymer, who swallowed them without benefit of liquid.

"Where's the cotton ball?" Jerome now demanded.

Raymer just looked at him.

"You know, the little cotton ball they always put in the mouth of the bottle?"

"Like any sensible person, I threw that away two seconds after I opened it."

"They put that there for a purpose, Doug."

"Right," he agreed. "To make it harder to get the pills out."

"No, to keep them fresh."

"Explain to me how that would work, Jerome."

He would've put the cap back on if Raymer hadn't held the bottle tight, shook free a third pill and gulped it down.

"From a liability standpoint it's lucky the car was a beater, is what I'm saying," Charice explained. "It could've been a new Lexus or a BMW. The driver might've come straight from the showroom. Whereas—"

"*Charice.* Was anyone injured?"

"The driver got a broken arm. Possibly other injuries, according to Miller."

"Miller," Raymer repeated. "So basically we have no idea. The guy could be dead."

"No, he's at the hospital. You didn't see him there?"

"Do me a favor, Charice? Call the city engineer and see if the traffic light at the hospital intersection's working properly. We've been sitting here for like ten minutes."

No response. She could go mute when asked to perform tasks that fell outside her normal purview.

"So a couple days later the guy runs into the doctor on the street," Jerome continued, apparently having concluded from his sister's silence that she was off doing as instructed. "He's limping along . . . can barely move. That's how long it's been since he defecated. The doctor can't believe it. He says, 'What's the matter? Those pills didn't work?'"

"You want to hear the strange part?" Charice interrupted.

Raymer closed his eyes and rested his head against the seat back, trying to gauge how much longer the painkillers would take to kick in. "Stranger than the part where the factory wall falls on a passing motorist for no reason?"

"Oh, I'm sure there's a reason, Chief," Charice assured him. "Things don't just happen for no reason. We just don't know what it is yet." No question, she and Jerome were twins. They both believed in a world where cotton balls had a purpose.

"There's a competing theory, Charice. There are people—smart people—who believe that *everything* happens for no reason."

"Yeah, okay, but guess who was driving that car?"

"Charice."

"It's going to make you very happy."

"Well, it can't be Jerome, because he's sitting right next to me."

"Get serious. Take a guess."

"Okay, Donald Sullivan."

"That's not very nice," Charice said, clearly taken aback.

Raymer had to admit she was probably right. It wasn't nice. But Barton Flatt was already dead, and he honestly couldn't think of anybody else he wanted to be the victim of a freak accident.

"Roy Purdy," she blurted, apparently unable to keep the good news to herself any longer.

"Why would I be happy about that?"

"Because he's an asshole."

Okay, maybe he was a little happy. He'd run into Roy at the Morrison Arms the day after his release. The creep had moved in with a sad, overweight woman named Cora, who'd apparently fallen for him, and he couldn't have been more smarmy and obsequious. In jail Roy had found religion, or so he claimed. Before, he'd apparently used his time behind bars to hone his criminal skills, but in this stint his Bible-study and psychology classes had allowed him to emerge as a wholly new and improved man. The old Roy, he'd assured Raymer, was dead and gone. All he could hope was that people wouldn't hold that Roy against him. He was anxious that Raymer in particular didn't harbor any ill will about when they were kids and Roy used to bully him relentlessly. None of that had been personal, he explained. He'd just been looking for somebody to take out his anger on. This last spell, with the help of an older con, he'd learned to let go of all that anger. It was rage that had stolen his whole damn life, and with the help of his newly acquired anger-management skills he meant to steal it right back. Perhaps not the best metaphor for a career thief, Raymer remembered thinking. Still, he supposed it was possible the man had truly been reformed. What undermined this likelihood was the note of pride in his voice when he recalled those middle-school days when he'd been the endless scourge of timid boys like Raymer.

"You'd rather have a wall fall on a harmless old coot like Sully," Charice said, "than on a true lowlife like Roy Purdy. That's just sick."

Truth be told, Raymer had no idea why Sullivan had occurred to him first. He'd resented the man for so long it'd become a habit, he supposed. "Well," he said in his own defense, "it's Sully that stole our three wheel boots, remember."

"We don't know that," Charice countered.

"Sure we do," he said. "What we don't know is how. *Or* where he hid them. What'd you find out about the traffic light?"

"Nothing yet. How long would you say it was before it finally turned green?"

"We're still sitting in front of it."

"Really? All this time?" She sounded impressed.

"Goodbye, Charice."

Jerome was grinning at him. "And the guy says, 'Are you kidding me, Doc? I might as well have shoved them up my ass for all the good they did me.'"

Raymer waited a beat, then said, "Green."

"Huh?"

He pointed, but by the time Jerome looked, the light had turned yellow, and before he'd let his foot off the clutch it was red again.

Raymer still hadn't put the cap back on the pills, so he tapped a fourth into his palm.

"Is that a good idea?" Jerome said. "*Four* extra-strength Tylenols, all at once?"

Maybe not. In the ER they'd refused him painkillers until they were sure he hadn't suffered a concussion. Two extra-strength Tylenols might put him in a coma; four could kill him. Good, Raymer thought. At least death would cure his headache. He could feel angry blood pulsing through the constricted vessels to his brain and the beat of his broken heart.

Because why not admit it? He wasn't over her. Becka. Okay, so she'd made a fool of him. At the time she went down those stairs *like a Slinky* she'd been carrying on with somebody, maybe even somebody he knew. What was it the note said? *Try to be happy for us.* Like maybe he knew the guy. Probably not, though. Men just fell in love with her at first sight. On the spot. Just as he had. Anyway, face it. Charice was right.

He was still fucked up. Here was Jerome just trying to help out, maybe take his mind off things, and Raymer, in turn, was wishing that wall had fallen on him instead of Roy Purdy.

"You have to admit it's pretty funny," Jerome said, apparently in reference to the suppositories joke.

"Laugh? I thought I'd die," Raymer said, which was literally true. He was squirming now, shoving the bottle out of sight into his pocket. A couple dozen capsules were rattling around in there like tacks, and he was afraid if he didn't put it away he might just swallow them all at once and be done with everything forever. The problem was that the bottle was too big; even if he succeeded in forcing it into his trousers, it would produce a comic bulge. This reminded him of the girl out at Hilldale who stared at him as he absentmindedly fingered the—

"Turn right," he said, too loud, startling Jerome.

"What—"

"Go through the light! Hurry."

But of course they were too late. By the time they arrived back at the cemetery, Judge Flatt's grave had not only been filled in, the whole plot had been manicured. Both the yellow backhoe and Rub Squeers were gone. Raymer dropped to his knees in the moist earth, beneath which, under the old asshole's casket, lay the garage-door opener. He'd been holding it in his hand when he fainted. Which meant his last chance to solve the riddle of his wife's infidelity was gone, along with it his final opportunity to prove himself a real policeman and not just a joke. Something like a howl escaped his throat then, and the resulting pain in his skull was beyond belief. He gripped his head between his elbows to keep it from exploding.

Jerome put a gentle hand on his shoulder. "I guess those Tylenol aren't working, huh?"

No, they weren't. Not even a little. In fact, he might as well have shoved them up his ass.

THE STILL, STAGNANT AIR in the vicinity of the Old Mill Lofts was the sort of yellow that normally presages a tornado, and the smell was staggering—yesterday's stench on steroids. Raymer swallowed hard, trying to keep his roiling stomach in check. As they were driving over here, Charice had radioed again to say there was yet another problem. As if things weren't bad enough, Carl Roebuck's crew of merry idiots, jackhammering the concrete floor, had hit an underground power line, knocking out a nearby transformer and leaving most of Bath without electricity. At the station and out at the hospital, they'd converted to the backup generator.

"Go on back to Schuyler," Raymer said when Jerome pulled over to the curb a couple blocks from the now-three-sided mill. Apparently the power outage stopped at the Schuyler Springs city line, right where misfortune historically ground to a halt. After all, if Raymer, whose job it was, wanted no part of these proceedings, what possible interest could they hold for a man whose job it wasn't? "I can snag a ride back out to Hilldale later." On the drive into town he realized that his car was still out at the cemetery. At the sight of the judge's grave, all filled in, he'd been too distraught to think clearly.

"Nah, I'll stick around a bit," Jerome said, getting out and locking the 'Stang. "You don't look so good." Raymer, light-headed and jelly kneed, had all he could do to pull himself out of the car's deep bucket seats.

What remained of the mill resembled a child's dollhouse, its long front face thoughtfully removed so its insides could be examined. Officer Miller, flexing authoritatively at the knees, had cleverly stationed himself at the epicenter of activity, where he could serve, so far as Raymer could tell, no useful purpose. A Tip Top Construction truck was parked next to the mound of bricks from the collapsed wall, and those of Carl's crew who weren't busy depriving the town of electricity were tossing them into the back. Nearby, the impressively flattened car—how had Roy Purdy escaped with his life?—was being hoisted onto one of old Harold Proxmire's flatbeds.

Miller stood observing all this as if it were his responsibility to make sure these jobs were being done properly. "Chief," he said, clearly surprised to see Raymer approaching. "I thought you were out at the hospital." Eyeing Jerome suspiciously, he gave his boss a quizzical what's-he-doing-here look. Low man on the department totem pole,

Miller worried constantly about being replaced, and Jerome, already in law enforcement, was a possible candidate. Also, he was black and Charice's brother. Was there some sort of affirmative action/nepotism afoot here?

"Mind if I ask what you're *doing?*" Raymer said.

Miller seemed pleased to know the answer to this question. "Providing a police presence, sir," he said, as if reciting from a manual. "I heard you were at the hospital, so I—"

"How about moving those people back," Raymer suggested, pointing at the gawkers that had gathered at the foot of one of the remaining walls. "Could you do that?"

"Because Charice said you'd sustained an injury out at Hilldale and I was in charge." Giving orders, he meant. Not taking them.

"Yet here I am."

Miller nodded. Clearly, he would've liked to dispute this fact, but how?

"Miller," Raymer said, "please move those people back. Now."

"You think another wall might fall?"

"This one did."

When he trotted off, Raymer and Jerome joined the mayor, who'd come directly from Hilldale, still dressed in funeral attire, and Carl Roebuck, who was studying some sort of schematic diagram and scratching his head. "What the hell's a power line doing there?"

"Providing power?" Gus suggested.

"Not anymore," a worker said, resting his gut on a jackhammer.

"Uh-oh," said Gus, eyeing the Niagara Mohawk truck that was just then pulling up. "We should've waited. NiMo's gonna ream our asses."

"My ass," Carl corrected.

"Jesus, look at this," Gus said, finally noticing Raymer. "They didn't admit you?"

"I kind of checked myself out."

"Why?"

"Because I thought you might need me?"

"Why?"

"I don't know," Raymer said, annoyed to be talked to the way he'd just talked to Miller. "That's what I came to find out."

"It's true I might want to borrow your sidearm," Gus said. "I'm thinking about shooting Carl here. How you doin', Jerome?"

"Mayor," he said, and they shook hands. Surprised, Raymer wondered how they knew each other. Had he and Gus ever shaken hands?

"How come shit like this never happens in Schuyler?" was what Gus wanted Jerome to explain.

"There's an ordinance against it," Jerome said.

Carl rotated the schematic, considering it from a different angle, and offered it to the mayor. "Show me on this where there's a power line."

"Why would I show you on that when I can take you to the actual cable your guys just jacked the shit out of."

"What I don't get," Jerome said, when Carl headed over to the NiMo crew, "is how a building can stand for a century and then one day tumble into the street."

"Well," Gus sighed, "several things have to happen. First, some imbecile has to sever the collar ties that secure the walls to the roof."

"Why would anybody do that?"

"They were working on the penthouse units, is my understanding. They meant to retie them later."

"Still," Jerome said, "the floor joists—"

"Those were compromised a couple weeks ago in order to construct the interior stairwells."

Jerome nodded seriously, apparently following all this.

How did normal people know shit like this? Raymer wondered. Or, to rephrase the question: How had he himself managed to live so long and learn so little? "Aren't you curious?" Becka always said whenever he asked why she was reading this or that. "About the world and how it works? About people and what makes them tick?" He supposed she had a point. Curiosity was probably a good thing, not always a cat killer. Still, what made people tick was no great mystery, was it? Greed. Lust. Anger. Jealousy. You could almost let your voice fall right there. Love? Some people claimed it made the world go round, but he wasn't so sure about that. Love mostly turned out to be one of those other emotions, or a mixture of them, in disguise. Even if it did exist, Raymer doubted its relevance to much of anything.

"Carl still might've got away with it," Gus was saying, "if somebody down in the basement hadn't lit a cigarette and tossed the match into a floor drain."

"Gas pocket?" Jerome said, as far ahead of the game as Raymer was behind.

"Boom," said Gus, puffing out his cheeks. "Maybe that's the lesson. You can skate on the first idiocy, and maybe even the second, but the third brings down the wrath of God." He regarded Raymer then as if he might be the physical embodiment of the principle he'd just articulated.

Suddenly the smell was just too much. "Excuse me a minute," Raymer said, turning away. There was a convenient pile of rubble nearby and into this he vomited violently, hands on his knees, reluctant to straighten up until he was sure the worst of the nausea had passed. Everyone, even the NiMo guys, who'd been happily cutting Carl Roebuck a new asshole, stopped to watch him retch. Was he throwing up because of the heat and stench, Raymer wondered, or because he was concussed? It would've been good to know, but too much trouble to find out. Curiosity trumped yet again.

When he finally straightened up, Miller, having moved the spectators across the street, had returned to his previous post and was again pointlessly supervising the brick tossing.

Raymer went over and said, "Miller?"

"I did what you said, Chief," he told him, gesturing at the people he'd moved out of harm's way.

"Yes, you did," Raymer agreed. "But look." The spectators Miller had moved were mostly still there, but half-a-dozen newcomers were now standing right where they'd been.

"You want me to move them, too?"

Raymer nodded. "And this time?"

"Yeah?"

"Stay there. That's where the job is. This here"—he indicated the men tossing bricks—"has got nothing to do with us."

"He's not what you'd call gifted, is he?" Jerome remarked when Raymer walked up.

"No," he admitted, though for some unknown reason he felt an

urge to come to the idiot's defense. Probably because Miller seemed to
have such a hard time grasping the same things that had eluded him
as a young patrolman. No doubt he himself had exasperated his boss,
Ollie North, as thoroughly as Miller was doing now. Police work, perhaps more than any other profession, attracted people for the wrong
reasons—in Raymer's case, the desire to be useful. You'd be given orders
and you'd execute these to the best of your ability. It never occurred to
him that part of the job was figuring out, without being told, exactly
what the job was. Right from the start Ollie had encouraged him to act
on his own initiative, to analyze the scene and figure out what needed
to be done. Sure, there was plenty of mind-numbing repetition, but
most days, especially in the beginning, you'd encounter something new,
and there wasn't always time for instructions. In their absence, though,
young Officer Raymer had found himself assailed by not just the usual
raft of self-doubts but also the old ambient feeling of futility that had
been his more or less constant companion since he was a boy in a disor-
derly house that he'd wanted to put right, without having a clue where
to begin. He knew nothing about Miller's background but could recognize in him the same eagerness to please that so often went hand in
hand with a reluctance to take chances. At every juncture, Miller had
to be told what to do and then what to do next. Having been ordered
to move people to safety, he'd done so. Since Raymer didn't tell him to
stay there and see the job through, he'd returned to his earlier post to
await further orders. "I keep hoping he'll grow into the job," Raymer
said weakly.

Jerome shrugged. "You put Charice out here, she'd have this whole
deal organized in about two seconds flat."

He was right, too. The station had been a nightmare of inefficiency
until Charice arrived, everything in the wrong place. By the time you
found what you were looking for, you'd forgotten why you needed it in
the first place. Charice had made sense of it all, transforming the department into a well-oiled machine. For which she was universally resented.
Not because her coworkers preferred chaos to order—they were cops,
after all—but because she'd invaded their turf and changed things
without asking for permission or even advice. She could be abrupt to

the point of rudeness and clearly didn't suffer fools gladly, perhaps not a particularly admirable quality when one is surrounded by a dozen of them. Out on the street, Raymer feared, she'd piss folks off even worse. People in Bath weren't used to being ordered around by sharp-tongued black women. If she got sent out on a call to the Morrison Arms or Gert's Tavern, she'd be lucky not to get beaten to death with her own baton, and if something like that ever happened, Raymer would have only himself to blame. "I need somebody with good judgment at the station," he told Jerome, who just shrugged, as if to concede that the chief of police had every right to remain stupid.

Rejoining them, Gus put a hand on Raymer's shoulder. "Go home before you pass out again," he said. "This'll all get worked out. You can die in the line of duty some other day."

"All right," Raymer agreed, too exhausted and dispirited to protest. Jerome wouldn't mind dropping him off at the Arms before heading back to Schuyler. There he'd fall into bed and see what happened. Maybe all he needed was a nap. Or possibly he'd just sleep right on through to tomorrow. Or better yet die in his sleep. Maybe his fainting into the judge's grave had been an omen—that his own end was near. If so, fine.

"Hey, Jerome," Gus said as they turned to leave, "you given any more thought to what we discussed?"

"I'm still thinking," Jerome told him.

"Don't take too long."

"Okay, I won't."

What the hell were they discussing that could only be alluded to obliquely in Raymer's presence? Something he wasn't supposed to know about, obviously.

God, did his head hurt.

Dump

PULLING INTO their steep gravel drive and surveying the weedy lot, littered as always with rusting hubcaps, bent rims and other orphaned auto parts, all of them liberated from the landfill and people's front yards, Ruth wondered what in the world she'd been thinking when she told Sully she meant to start treating her husband better, a resolution she felt right then not the slightest inclination to act upon. At the top of the driveway there was room, theoretically, for two vehicles, but once again Zack had failed to pull his truck over far enough, so halfway up the grade she paused, her foot on the brake, to reflect darkly on the obvious—*there was no room for her*—and its inescapable metaphorical significance, which begged a fairly basic response: back right out and drive away? Earlier that afternoon, hadn't she advised Sully to go somewhere, anywhere, so long as it was far off? Didn't the same apply to her as well? *Go,* she told herself now, *this very minute.* It didn't matter where. Would anyone even notice?

Well, that was the thing. They would. They'd get hungry. Down at Hattie's and here at home, people wanted to be fed and expected her to feed them. Though it was only midafternoon, Zack was probably already hungry, wondering what she meant to make for dinner. Was there ever a time when he *wasn't* hungry? Where did such constant appetite come from? Nor was it only her husband. At the restaurant, people just ate and ate. It didn't seem to matter much, if at all, what the food tasted like, provided there was plenty of it, whether mountains of french fries or troughs of slaw. Just as they went about the day's other necessary tasks, they ate with concentration, determination, conviction. When they were done and you asked them how it was, they looked puzzled. The food was gone, wasn't it? If something was wrong with it, they would've complained. Others responded with a particularly reveal- ing non sequitur. "Full," as if emptiness were the prevailing condition of their lives, from which eating provided a temporary respite.

Ironic that Ruth herself had little or no appetite most of the time. Especially these last few days, thanks to the brutal heat and the Great Bath Stench. Who could think of food under such circumstances? If she went away somewhere, would her normal appetites—for food, sex, joy—return, or were those gone for good? Didn't she owe it to herself to find out?

Apparently not, because instead of putting the car in reverse she laid on the horn until her husband appeared at the back door in his undershorts and barefoot, rubbing his eyes sleepily. Good, she thought. Midafternoon was his time to fall asleep in front of the television, though he always denied doing this, even when she caught him doing it. He had legitimate reasons for napping, she supposed. A successful scavenger—if that wasn't an oxymoron—had to be up early, so each morning Zack rose even before she did to open the restaurant. By five he was out the door and picking through the crap people set out on the curb on trash day. Tuesdays and Thursdays in Schuyler, where the best stuff was, other days in surrounding communities that still had trash pickup. By afternoon he was ready for a nap. Ruth, who was never not exhausted, didn't get to nap, though, so she couldn't help resenting the stolen hour. That he wouldn't admit to this theft made her more resent- ful still.

"I hear you, I hear you," he was saying now, trying to smooth down his unruly hair. What sort of man, at damn near sixty, still had a cow- lick in the exact spot where so many other men had given in to tonsured baldness? Was it possible that once upon a time she'd found that disobe- dient thatch endearing? "You can lay off."

"Just move the truck," she told him.

"I am," he said, limping down the porch steps and onto the rough gravel. Where in this enormous hulk of a man was the skinny boy she married? One hundred and twenty pounds he'd been, soaking wet. At eighteen his mother was still buying his trousers—Ruth should've given more careful consideration to what *this* might mean—in the boys' department. Now he was three fifty if an ounce. "Filling out his frame," his mother, herself a very large woman, had called it when he finally turned that genetic corner and started putting on weight. These days he also filled whole doorframes, most of which he had to turn sideways to get through. "What do you think I'm doing?"

"I think you're walking around outdoors in your undershorts."

"So what? There's nobody here but us."

"Unless Tina was to come walking up the drive?"

"She's seen me before."

Ruth massaged her temples. "Just move the truck."

"I *am*," he repeated. "Okay?"

She watched him climb in behind the wheel and then, a moment later, get out again, making a jingling motion with his right hand, which she interpreted as *keys*, or in this case the lack thereof. Since they lived out of town, where there was almost nobody to steal the truck, he usually just left them dangling in the ignition, but apparently not today. Since his search might take a while, she reluctantly turned her own engine off, got out and followed him inside.

The house where they'd lived their entire married lives had belonged to his parents or, rather, his mother, his father having died when Zack was still a boy. That old bag's name was also Ruth—Mother Ruth, they called her, to avoid confusion, though she'd quickly dubbed her "Mother Ruthless." Right from the start the woman made it clear that she held her daughter-in-law-to-be in low regard. The day they were introduced—Zack had brought her to this very house to meet her—Ruth, suffering from a combination of morning sickness and terror, had immediately asked if she might use the bathroom. Even with the door closed, she heard the cruel question: "Did you have to pick the homeliest girl in the whole school to knock up?"

Zack later dismissed the incident as unimportant. "Don't pay no attention to her," he scoffed. "She don't mean nothin'."

"You might've stood up for me."

He put his arm around her shoulder and drew her close. "Didn't I say you had a great body? Anyway, she'll like you better after the baby's born." Which showed how little he understood his mother. Give her credit, though, Mother Ruth had at least loved the baby, even though Janey was Ruth's spitting image. And of course she would have hated whoever Zack had knocked up. Her husband dead, and helpless to navigate the world outside her home, she was determined to keep a tight grip on what she had left, and that was her only son. Through him, and through his devotion to her, she meant to rule what remained of her world, and to this end she did everything in her power to undermine her new daughter-in-law. Among other things, that meant never letting her forget whose house she was living in or that she'd arrived there pregnant and without any domestic skills. Ruth hadn't learned to cook at home, and Mother Ruthless obviously didn't like having anyone else in her kitchen. "How's she supposed to learn if you won't teach her nothin'," Zack asked when Ruth begged him to intervene. Eventually, she had grudgingly copied out on notecards the recipes for a few of Zack's favorite meals. They never turned out right, though. The recipes either left out key ingredients or were unclear about technique or got the proportions wrong, which made Ruth look like a very slow learner indeed. "He likes his mother's cooking better, don't you, sweetie," Mother Ruth cooed after each new failure, and Zack had to admit he did. Only after Ruth finally tumbled to the fact that her culinary efforts were being sabotaged, and compared the notecard recipes with others in cookbooks she'd checked out of the library, did she begin to improve. Before long she was a better cook than Mother Ruth, who was lazy and gravitated to canned and frozen ingredients, even when fresh ones were available. Still, Ruth had known better than to openly challenge her, so the woman remained boss of her kitchen until she finally suffered the stroke that put her in the county nursing home. Not a moment too soon, in Ruth's view, because the kitchen hadn't been the only battleground. "You know she's stepping out on you," the old woman told her son when some busybody informed her about Ruth and Sully. By then, of course, she and Zack had been married going on twenty years.

"Mind your own business, Ma," Zack replied, having heard the rumors already.

"I told you she was a tramp from the start," the old woman continued, as if Ruth had been cheating since day one. On this day, though, she was simply standing in the next room, listening.

"You don't know nothin' about it, Ma. You're just repeating gossip."

"You know it's true as well as I do," his mother said. "You just don't want to admit it."

"What I want," he told her, "is to not hear no more about it from you."

That was about as close as he ever came to taking Ruth's side where his mother was concerned. After the stroke he visited her faithfully at the nursing home, usually late Sunday afternoons after his garage sale. With one memorable exception, Ruth refused to accompany him. A Sunday off was rare for her, and she had no intention of spending any part of it with a hateful old woman whose animosity had only deepened every single year. After her stroke, Zack was the only person who could understand her garbled speech, and the one time Ruth went along to visit, Mother Ruth had grabbed him by the wrist to pull his face down next to hers. What she whispered was gibberish to Ruth, though Zack evidently understood, because he removed her hand and said, "How many times I gotta tell you, Ma? I don't wanna hear it."

Ruth had imagined that with the old woman finally out of the house, things would be different, but they weren't. For one thing she wasn't really gone, at least not as Zack saw it. He missed her and confessed that some mornings when he came downstairs, still half asleep, he could smell the cinnamon rolls she used to bake. Once or twice he even imagined seeing his mother there, bent over the stove. To him, these were apparently pleasant experiences. Ruth supposed it was fine for a man to love his mother, but his ongoing devotion to such a mean old bat seemed both morbid and unhealthy. Furthermore, she was sick of having to share a home with a woman who (1) hated her and (2) wasn't even there. To banish Mother Ruth completely, Ruth suggested they remodel the kitchen, which was antiquated and ugly, but Zack, mortified by the suggestion, reminded her that his mother still owned the house. Besides, he said, it would be expensive and they didn't have the money. The real reason, she suspected, was his fear that in a remodeled kitchen he'd never again smell those cinnamon buns, never see Mother Ruth bending over her stove like she'd done when he was a boy. She couldn't bear to tell him, of course, that he wasn't the only one who pictured Mother Ruth in that kitchen. Ruth saw her there, too, every fucking day, which was why she wanted to gut it.

Today, entering that still-unremodeled kitchen, she was not greeted by the specter of her mother-in-law but rather the ghost of her husband's lunch, last night's leftover chicken-with-rice casserole, now converted to ripe midafternoon methane. How, she asked herself, and not for the first time, had she come to marry a man whose single genetic imperative was to break, in every conceivable way, his own containment? She slung the crusty lunch plate and dirty silverware he always left there on the dinette into the sink, the clatter causing him to pause in the doorway with an expression of fear, mixed with guilt and disapproval. *Oh, please,* she thought, *do say something,* but instead he just shook his head and continued on into the front room.

Returning to the dinette with a wet rag, she banged her hip on the corner of the counter hard enough to bring tears to her eyes. How, she wondered, could the room feel even smaller and more cramped now than it had when Mother Ruth was still standing foursquare in its center, impossible to get around, little Janey crawling back and forth between her trunk-sized legs. Why, especially of late, was she always banging into all the sharp corners and edges? Each morning in the shower she saw new ugly bruises on her shins and hipbones. She never banged into things at the restaurant, which was every bit as cramped, and there was more to bang into.

The front room, where Zack was now pulling on his pants, was dark except for the nervous flickering of the TV (an old Popeye cartoon, one of her husband's many favorites). On hot days he always kept the place closed up, believing it stayed cooler, so the aroma of flatulence was even more pronounced in here. Feeling her gag reflex kick in, Ruth went from window to window, throwing back the curtains and wrenching the windows up as far as they'd go in their dry, warped frames. She could feel her husband watching her, no doubt puzzling over exactly which bee had invaded her bonnet, but still he said nothing, evidently as determined to avoid a fight as she was to pick one. Only when the last of the windows shrieked up did he finally say, "What'd I do now?"

She opened her mouth, prepared to let him have it with both barrels, then abruptly changed course. "Is Tina here?" Their daughter tended bar most nights and didn't get home until late, so their granddaughter more often than not ate dinner with them and slept over. If she was upstairs in the spare bedroom, the kind of fight Ruth had in mind would have to wait.

"Uhmm?" said Zack, clearly trying to scroll back. Had Tina come in? "I don't think so . . ."

When he started out to move the car, she said "Zipper," since his shirt was visible in the gap in his fly.

He yanked it up. "Anything else?"

"Actually, yeah. Explain something to me," she said. "Why do you have to take your pants off to watch television." Because she really did want to know. Her own father had had the same habit, her brothers, too. Marriage, unless she was mistaken, was some kind of trigger, as if the words "I do" were a signal for them to take their pants off the minute they stepped indoors. Say this for Sully. If he took his pants off he had a reason to, and when the reason no longer applied he put them back on again. Why had she been so hard on him today? Until Roy came in, he'd barely said a word. Him just sitting there at the lunch counter staring into his empty coffee cup had made her every bit as pissed at him as she was at her husband now. Hadn't she once loved the man? Didn't she still? And what if, as she suspected, he was sicker than he was letting on? What in the world was wrong with her? In the restaurant, with Sully, just a few hours ago, she'd resolved to treat her husband better; now at home, with Zack, it was Sully she regretted being so hard on. Was it possible her anger had nothing to do with either one of them? Were they simply handy targets, stand-ins for what she should actually be aiming at?

Zack shrugged at her question about the pants, offering her his lopsided grin.

"No, really," Ruth insisted. "I'm dying to know why men have to take their pants off to watch TV." A fool's errand, of course, like an ape trying to explain the kind of behavior he engages in out of sheer instinct. You might as well ask him to explain particle physics.

Naturally, Zack shrugged. "More comfortable, I guess."

"How's that?"

He shrugged again. "More freedom?"

"But you don't take off your shirt. Or your socks."

"No reason to take *them* off."

Ruth massaged her temples even harder this time. "Go move the truck."

When he headed for the kitchen, she said, "Where are you going?"

He threw up his hands. "I need to—"

"I *should* let you get all the way out there," she said, pointing at the big wooden ashtray on the coffee table, itself a landfill acquisition, where his keys sat, plain as day.

Once he was gone, Ruth surveyed the living room. Spread out on the coffee table and sofa were the parts to at least one small appliance—a toaster oven, by the look of it—and, on the nearby love seat, two ancient vacuum cleaners that hadn't been there this morning, which meant he'd had, for Zack, a good day. At fifty-eight, he was as determined as he'd been at thirty to corner the market in broken, worthless crap, to bring it all home, take it apart and leave the pieces strewn over every flat surface in the house. She'd long ago given up trying to change him, but until recently she'd hoped to reign him in, much as America had once hoped to prevent the spread of communism. On purely philosophical grounds she'd considered her own battle worth waging, but had she really figured it was winnable? The living room before her did not represent mere defeat. She'd been overrun. Blitzed. Routed. How had that happened? Well, one bloody skirmish at a time. A small concession here, a tactical error there, troops deployed to the wrong sector, failures of imagination too numerous to count, leading in the end to spiritual exhaustion, despair and, finally, ignominious surrender. That would about sum it up.

No doubt her strategy had been flawed from the start. Why inform the enemy of your endgame? Why let him in on what you cared about most, what you meant to defend at all costs? Collect all the crap you want, she'd told her husband, just don't bring it in the house. Even birds know enough not to shit in their own nests. And with this declaration the long proxy conflict had begun. Its first arena had been the garage, which had two large bays, with room to spare for both their vehicles, or so she'd thought, although the flatbed truck Zack used to haul his shit in was half again as wide as the largest pickup. When the floor-to-ceiling shelving started going up along the interior walls, she'd thought, Overkill. (Failure of Imagination Number One: underestimating both the enemy's ambition and his tidal persistence.) By the end of that year every last shelf was bowed and groaning under the weight of more and more crap. Then, down the middle of the garage, in the space between their vehicles, came the lawn mowers—push and power—as well as rusty bicycles with flat tires and brake pads dangling from detached cables, assorted posthole diggers and Weedwackers. Suddenly the whole place was so booby-trapped that you had to go slow and pay attention both driving in and then stepping out, because there were land mines everywhere—skateboards, Wiffle balls, Hula-Hoops, even lumps of Play-Doh. Along the exterior walls, dented metal drums appeared. Into the empties Zack poured used oil and grease. The others—some decorated with smiling skulls and crossbones—contained the industrial solvents and toxic chemical baths he needed to remove rust from bike chains and other hardware.

Even more demoralizing than the junk itself was her husband's unshakable conviction that it was all valuable, or would be as soon as he could locate the handle, screw, lid, link, cap, clasp, rubber grip or wheel that had gone missing. That what you needed would turn up eventually was one of the central tenets of his scavenging faith. Another was that people who tossed things out because they didn't work anymore were stupid. That someone would go out and spend good money on a new power mower because the pull rope on the old one snapped off filled Zack with the kind of pure wonder that he was forever attempting to evoke in his unsympathetic wife. To her way of thinking, the fact that people threw away stuff that *maybe* could be repaired meant they were busy, not stupid, and even if they were stupid it didn't necessarily require you to get up at five in the morning to go digging through their trash in search of evidence. If they put an old sofa out on the curb, that didn't mean you had to load it onto the back of your truck and haul it home, all proud of yourself ("I can get that cat-piss smell out"). And it certainly didn't mean you spent your entire adult life in an activity that, if you succeeded, meant only that you'd relocated the public landfill to your own property.

In Ruth's considered opinion, hers was a winning argument, but for some unknown reason, instead of pressing it, she'd instead granted a concession—Major Tactical Error—by reminding herself that every man needs a hobby, especially someone like Zack who might otherwise be tempted to stay home watching TV in his skivvies and collect unemployment or unearned disability. And it wasn't like he fought her on every little thing. He was capable, at times, of reason. When she told him to open his own bank account, he did; and when she warned him never to touch the money in their joint account to finance his purchases at flea markets and yard sales, he agreed. Every now and then she checked to make sure he was abiding by that stipulation and damned if he wasn't. To hear him tell it, he never bought anything for fifty cents that he didn't eventually sell to somebody else for a dollar, which might even be true for all she knew. As long as he stayed out of her hair, what did she care? This had been her thinking. Let him fill up the fucking garage. As long as there was room for their vehicles . . .

Then one day she came home, and his truck was parked outside. In his bay, upside down, rested a long wooden canoe with a hole in the bottom. Her own bay, cramped and crowded now, was vacant, but upon pulling in she discovered she couldn't open the car door, thanks to a ropeless toboggan—it was mid-August!—that hadn't been there in the morning and now lay lengthwise against the shelving. She was about to resort to her horn when Zack appeared in the rearview mirror. "I meant to move that," he said, standing the toboggan up on one end so she could get out. "That boat'll be gone by next week," he added.

"Yup," she agreed. "There'll be three more of something else, though."

He smiled, apparently pleased she understood. "The business is growing," he said.

"I'm sorry, the what?" Because she'd gotten used to describing all this as a *hobby,* and embedded in that word was the concession she'd granted.

"I'm in business here," he told her. "Ma thinks it's a good idea to ramp things up."

"Well, there you go, then."

"I'm getting a sign made," he added, as if this was his trump card.

"You can't find one out at the dump?"

"It wouldn't be mine." That was the thing about Zack. He always answered her questions, even the ones that were snide, mocking criticisms, as if they were serious.

Later that night she warned him again. "Not so much as one rusty wing nut in my house."

"It's Ma's house," he said. "We just live here."

"Well, thanks for reminding me."

"It will be. I ain't sayin' it won't. I'm just sayin'—"

"I know what you're saying."

"You could take an interest," he said, sounding plaintive, and she felt her hardened heart soften a little. "In what I do, I mean."

"I'm exhausted, Zack. I work three jobs."

"I work, too. You're not the only one."

No, just the only one who makes money. Did he know that this was on the tip of her tongue? Maybe. Probably.

The following week a snowmobile appeared in her bay. "It'll be gone in a day or two," he assured her.

"Where am I supposed to park?"

"It's summer," he pointed out, not unreasonably.

By the time winter rolled around, though, her bay was crammed, from floor to ceiling. After a blizzard camouflaged both their vehicles under a foot and a half of snow, he told her, "I'm looking at sheds." Right, she thought. As if invading armies ever gave back conquered territory. The garage was now Poland. Occupied.

The next theater of war had been the yard itself. They had over an acre of land, but except for where the house and garage stood, and a small lawn, most of it was wooded. At first a few miscellaneous, awkwardly shaped items—a rowing machine, its oarlocks missing, a large collection of mismatched fireplace utensils—were partially hidden among the trees and bushes, but before long other crap appeared, such as the outboard motor that materialized one day like the world's ugliest lawn ornament. Had the time come to make a stand? Probably, but in truth Ruth decided she didn't really care (Alert! Conflict Fatigue!). Unlike many women, Ruth had never much concerned herself with appearances, and where they lived, a good half mile out of town, there were no neighbors to complain about them ruining the neighborhood and driving down property values. Moreover, it was about this time that she'd taken Hattie's over from its previous owner, a woman roughly her own age who'd fled to Florida after her mother, the original Hattie, died. A businesswoman now, Ruth began to separate her homelife from the restaurant. Mother Ruthless was still out at the county nursing home, but her speech had improved a little, and when they brought her home for holidays and special occasions it was clear that she still considered this her very own shithole and looked forward to the day when she'd be able to return and claim it. Her doctors had privately assured them that this would never happen, that she would always require round-the-clock nursing, but for the time being the house was still in her name, whereas Hattie's was in Ruth's. Let the old woman croak on her own schedule, she told herself. Then dig in and fight your fight. Sure, it was disheartening to see the property overrun with weeds— with so much shit everywhere, you couldn't mow it—but the perimeter of the house had not been breached, and that, she reminded herself, was the important thing (Grave Tactical Error! Never surrender your DMZ!). Evenings, after the sun went down, were the worst. Then the taller items in the yard, the ones he'd left leaning up against trees, put Ruth in mind of troops massing at the border. Could there be any doubt of their intention to invade?

Then, without warning, instead of the anticipated assault on the fortress, there was an unexpected pullback, indeed a sharp reduction in tensions across the entire theater of conflict. Roy got himself arrested for burglary and was sent downstate to serve his time, freeing Janey to move to Albany in search of a new life. That meant the trailer they'd been living in reverted to her parents. Eight hundred additional square feet of storage space. Not a lot, but enough to take some of the pressure off. Next, buoyed by the increasing popularity of his monthly yard sales, Zack decided to hold one every week. For a time it felt to Ruth like some sort of Zen balance—shit-in and shit-out, at roughly the same rate—had been achieved. The yard and nearby woods were suddenly less cluttered. Were the invaders being redeployed? Sent home? That's how it felt. Suddenly she could breathe again, having fought to a noble draw. They could begin to disarm and enjoy the peace. Turned out, though, the domino theory was just that: a theory. But honestly, she thought later, did she ever really believe the war was over? She must've. Otherwise, why would she have sold the trailer to Sully? Having just inherited his landlady's house on Upper Main Street, he needed it like he needed a hole in the head. But Zack was talking about upgrading to a shed, claiming the money they got from the trailer would pay for it, so why not? (In war, as in the courtroom, never ask a question you don't already know the answer to.)

The day Sully was to haul off the trailer and the new shed was to be delivered, Ruth put in an extra long day at Hattie's. Despite having waitressed her entire adult life, she was still learning the business end of running a restaurant. Even when she managed to close on time—afternoon coffee drinkers were hard to expel—she still had to spend another hour or two prepping for the next morning, ringing out the register, going over the receipts. Plus they'd had a problem in the ladies' room that afternoon, so she had to wait for the plumber to finish fixing the toilet before she could lock up and head home. In fact, it'd been such a perfect bitch of a day that she'd forgotten the shed completely until she made the turn into her driveway and saw the gleaming metal reflecting the evening sunlight through what remained of the trees. *Shed?* The fucking thing was almost as big as the house and had all the charm of an airplane hangar. Worse, she knew what Sully'd given them for the trailer, and that would've barely paid for the doors.

At the top of the drive Zack's truck sat in its usual place, and next to it, in her spot, was Sully's pickup. The two men, together with Rub Squeers, were on the ground, leaning back against the new shed, drinking beer and looking for all the world like Larry, Moe and Curly. Putting her car in park and turning the ignition off, she chose for the time being to remain where she was. Seeing her husband and lover sitting there so naturally, like best friends, gave her the bends. So did the mountain of tree stumps nearby. From where she sat she counted fourteen of them.

"I sold them stumps," Zack said when she finally got out and stood staring at them, shaking her head in disbelief. As if they represented her only possible objection to their radically altered landscape.

"Who'd buy a tree stump?"

He offered her his trademark crooked smile. "People buy some strange stuff," he said.

"I can see that," she said, regarding the enormous metal structure. "Funny how the subject of cutting down our trees to make room for that monstrosity never came up when we were discussing all this."

"We—"

"Or the size of the shed you were thinking about."

"I told you it was bigger than the trailer."

"So's Yankee Stadium."

When he only shrugged, she said, "Where'd you get the money?"

"Like I said—"

"Where'd you get the money?" she repeated, with enough edge in her voice to suggest he take care answering.

"Not from Schuyler Savings." That's where their joint account was.

Mother Ruthless, then. Even in the nursing home, still calling the shots.

Sully was looking increasingly uncomfortable. "Why don't you grab a beer and join us?" he suggested.

"I just might," she said, her mood veering dangerously. As tired as she was, she had little doubt she could make short work of any one of these men in a drunken brawl, but all three at once gave her pause. Also, who was to blame here, really? She'd allowed herself to be out-flanked by three idiots, one her husband, the other her lover, and the third, unless she was mistaken, a man who was more in love with her lover than she was but didn't know it and probably never would. "If one of you *gentlemen* would care to get me one."

Sully nudged Rub. "Dummy. Go get Ruth a beer."

"Why me?" Rub wanted to know. To Ruth, he had the look of someone who'd done his beer arithmetic already and knew that if Ruth drank one, it would be his she was drinking.

"Because I'm tired and I've got a bum knee," Sully told him.

"Why not him?" Rub wanted to know, indicating Zack, whose wife, after all, this was.

"He bought the beer," Sully reminded him. "Or you could just tell her to get her own beer. If you think that's a good idea."

Rub glanced at Ruth and saw that it wasn't, then he got to his feet and went inside.

"So," Ruth said, still looking at the shed. Dear God was it ugly. "Was there a larger model you could've bought?"

Zack nodded. "One," he said.

"But you restrained yourself."

"Wasn't enough room for it."

"You sure? There's still a couple trees you didn't chop down."

He looked at Sully now. "What'd I tell you?" Like it was the two of them who were in cahoots, not Sully and her. "I told you it was them trees she'd be sore about." Like he was some sort of expert on what she thought and how she felt. Like being married for thirty years meant intimacy. Taking him in, sitting there so pleased with himself for having gotten what he wanted, she was glad he *didn't* know what was in her heart, because it would've wiped that stupid grin off his face.

"It'll take him a while to fill it, anyway," Sully said later that night. After Zack went to bed, they'd met at their usual Schuyler motel. Once asleep, her husband never woke up until the alarm went off in the morning, so it was pretty safe.

"You're trying to make me feel better," she told him, "and that can't be done." Though in truth, sex had made her feel at least a little better, like it always did. Sully had known without asking that she'd need him that night. Most of the time he could be as dumb as every other man, though every now and then he was also capable of something like prescience. Give him credit for something else, too. He'd worked all day on his bum knee, and given how exhausted he clearly was, the last thing he needed was a roll in the hay. He might've begged off, but he didn't.

"So how long were you two scheming about this?" she asked him.

"Scheming?"

Because even if the crew from the manufacturer was responsible for erecting the structure itself, everything else—hauling the trailer over to Sully's, chopping down all those trees, pulling up the stumps and grading the cratered earth in time to take delivery of the shed—had to have gone off with military precision. "That was about a week's worth of work you did since five o'clock this morning."

"We went at it pretty hard," he said as he massaged his knee, which had swollen to the size of a grapefruit.

"All done behind my back," she said.

"He asked me to help."

"So what're you saying? The two of you are friends now?"

"I don't know. He doesn't have any others that I'm aware of."

"There's me."

Sully arched his eyebrow at this but offered no comment.

"And Mother Ruthless."

"I don't think she'd have been much help pulling up stumps."

And just that quickly she was close to tears. "I guess I thought you were all mine."

"You want me to beg off, next time he asks?"

"No," she said, though the ground under her feet had suddenly shifted, and part of her was screaming, *Yes!*

The next day, Zack came into the restaurant as she was closing up, something he seldom did. She'd never told him he wasn't welcome there, but somehow he knew that Hattie's was her domain, just like the garage and now the shed were his. "People are saying they saw you and him last night," he told her.

"Who's people?" Not even bothering to ask who the him was. Well, *people* had been talking for years, including, unless she was mistaken, her now-incarcerated son-in-law.

He recited the name of the motel.

"And you believe them?"

"I didn't say that."

"Good," she told him. "Don't."

"I just don't like to hear it," he said. "If I'm hearing it, Ma's hearing it."

Oh, her again. "She can't think any worse of me than she already does."

"Kids talk at school, too. You want them saying things to Janey?"

"What are we discussing here? What you just told me you didn't believe?"

"All I'm saying is I don't like to hear it."

"Yup. You already said that."

Once he left, she played back the conversation over and over until she began to grasp what he was telling her. She could have Sully. Sully could have her. They just had to be more discreet. Be happy, she told herself, and part of her was. But it also meant that her husband didn't think she was worth fighting for, and how was that supposed to make her feel? Or that Zack, for whatever reason, was forging his own relationship with Sully? Or the fact that in his life she was only the second most important person named Ruth?

Sully was right about one thing. It'd taken Zack a while to fill the shed. Years, as it happened. But then came the day when she passed the kitchen window and was surprised to find that the view was partially obscured by an aluminum ladder he'd left leaning up against the wall. A stiff wind the day before had knocked a shutter loose, so he probably was fixing it. But in the following weeks other things turned up leaning against the house—a pair of snow skis, a dresser with no drawers, a wrought-iron bench. She could almost feel the pressure each inanimate object was exerting on the skin of the house. All this shit wanted in. Then one afternoon she came home to find that first vacuum cleaner disassembled on the living room floor. It was possible that repairing whatever was wrong with it was simply taking longer than he'd planned. Maybe he meant to have the mess cleaned up by the time she got home. But there was another explanation that made even more sense. His mother had died the week before.

Ruth remembered how it'd been when Saigon fell, the last Americans climbing onto the embassy roof to await the choppers that would ferry them home.

Home? The bitch of it was, Ruth was already there.

IN THE KITCHEN that was finally hers and yet somehow wasn't, Ruth ratcheted open the window over the sink. Outside, Zack had moved his truck and was now pulling her car up beside it. A nice gesture, except that in order to get behind the wheel he'd have to push the seat back as far as it would go and would never remember to pull it up again for the simple reason that that would mean he'd done two things in a row right, and in all the years they'd been married that hadn't happened yet.

She was still at the sink, staring out into the yard, when he came back in, scratching his belly thoughtfully. In pursuit of an elusive thought, most men scratched the location where they imagined it might be hiding, but not her husband. "Sorry," he said weakly. "I was going to do those."

"It doesn't matter," she said, putting the rubber stopper over the drain and turning on the tap, all the fight having suddenly drained right out of her. When she reached under the sink for dishwasher soap, there wasn't any.

"You have a bad day?"

"Nope," she said. "It was just peachy. Like all my days." On the wall was a chalkboard he'd picked up at a yard sale, and on its tray a tiny sliver of chalk. She started to write *dishwasher soap* on the slate but saw it was already there, in her own handwriting, so instead she wrote *chalk*.

"What's the matter, then?"

Two responses immediately suggested themselves: *everything* and *nothing*. Both true, neither accurate. "I just . . ."

"Just what?"

"Just once I'd like to come home and find . . ."

"What?"

A new life. It would be nice to come home some afternoon and find a whole new life. Yet how crappy a wish was *that*? Pretty crappy, she had to admit. Was she actually wishing her husband dead? Not really, or at least she didn't think so. What she had in mind was more along the lines of a parallel universe in which he'd never existed in the first place. Because how great would it be, after a long day at the restaurant, to come home to a quiet house? To call out a lusty hello and hear no answer? Heaven. Instead of foraging in the fridge for something to cook her husband for dinner, she could just make herself an enormous bowl of popcorn and eat it while reading a book on a sofa that was neither grease spotted nor redolent of male. Later, getting sleepy, she'd put the book down, look around the room and instead of revulsion she'd feel . . . what? Satisfaction. Contentment. Herself, her nature, her daily life—everything in sync. Minus Zack and his clutter, these same rooms would be spare, even stark. She didn't crave better, more expensive possessions, just fewer of them. Less of everything, really. The world she'd create for herself would be sparse and orderly and clean.

Earlier, when she suggested to Sully that he go to Aruba, she hadn't just randomly picked that island out of the Caribbean hat. During a thaw that winter, when the crusty, dirt-speckled snowbanks were being tunneled out by torrents of diuretic brown water, she'd made the mistake of pausing in front of a Schuyler Springs travel agency, the windows of which—the heartless bastards—were full of island-vacation posters. Inside, she scanned a thick, three-ringed binder full of blue resorts. The one she liked best, in Aruba, featured suites with enormous, white-tiled bathrooms. There were billowing white sheers over French doors that opened onto a long stretch of empty sand, the surf beyond so close you could almost hear it. A shower with no door, nor curtains, just silver shower heads coming down out of the ceiling. Across from each was a gleaming white vanity, perfect for a woman traveling alone.

Because she certainly would be traveling alone. She had no desire whatsoever to go there with Sully or her husband or any other man, including Brad Pitt. To allow a male into a bathroom that pristine would be a desecration.

"Are you guys fighting?"

Neither Ruth nor her husband had heard their granddaughter approach. Only when Zack yipped in surprise and danced out of the doorway did Tina become visible. To Ruth it was unnerving how silently she moved through their home, the only member of the family who could descend those creaky back stairs without making a sound. Was she like that at school, too? Was that why her teachers never seemed to pay her any attention? The remedial classes she was always placed in were full of rowdy, hyperactive boys, so probably they were just happy to have one kid who neither demanded nor seemed to expect anything from them.

"Where'd *you* come from?" Zack asked her. Because obviously she'd been upstairs all along.

"We covered that this spring in health, actually," she told him. That was the other unnerving thing about her granddaughter. Ruth could never be sure when she was joking. A lot of what the girl said was funny, but her delivery was always deadpan, and sometimes when Ruth laughed, she looked blank or even hurt. "For two whole weeks."

"I must not've heard her come in," Zack said, clearly embarrassed to have told Ruth earlier that she wasn't in the house.

At this Tina winced. "We had a conversation, Grandpa." She had a special affection for her grandfather, Ruth knew, and she clearly hated to throw him under the bus. "You asked me why I was home early. I said because of the holiday."

"Oh," Zack said sheepishly, "right. Memorial Day. What else did we talk about?" He was scratching his stomach again, genuinely curious.

Tina wrinkled her nose. "It smells in here," she said. Her bad eye, the one that had been operated on half-a-dozen times, obedient when she'd entered the kitchen, now wandered off as if in search of what stank. When she was tired or upset, it seemed to have an agenda all its own.

"That's your grandma's fault," Zack told her, his loopy grin widening. "She shouldn't never feed me rice."

"I shouldn't feed you at all."

"You also asked how school was," Tina said. "I lied and said good. Like always."

"Can we skip this today?" Ruth suggested, drying her hands on a dishcloth. "About how much you hate school?"

"Summer school will be even worse. Do I really have to go?"

"Yes. So you can graduate. On time."

"I'd rather come work for you."

"You already do." After a fashion. She helped out in the kitchen for a few hours on Saturday mornings during the rush, scrubbing pots, loading and unloading the Hobart.

"Out front?"

"To be a waitress, you have to talk to people."

"Why?"

"That's what they come in for, most of them. You can't just drop plates down in front of customers and walk away. Especially the wrong plates." Which she'd done when Ruth had let her wait on a table or two.

Tina shrugged. "They just switch their plates."

"They shouldn't have to."

Also you'd have to look people in the eye, Ruth thought, and was immediately ashamed. Whenever she allowed herself to contemplate her granddaughter's future, it was always the physical disability she focused on, and that wasn't remotely fair. It reminded her of that story kids still had to read in school, the one where the guy kills an old man because of his "vulture eye," then chops him up and hides him beneath the floorboards. That's what people wanted to do with abnormalities: put them somewhere out of sight. Under the floor or back in the steamy kitchen, where people wouldn't have to see them. This sweet, slow girl? Hide her away so she won't get hurt. Hide her well enough and long enough and maybe she won't ask the question you don't know how to answer: *Who will ever want to love me?*

"I could bus tables."

"You want to clear people's dirty dishes for the rest of your life?"

"You do."

"Exactly. You want to end up like me?" Because wasn't she herself an object lesson in how hard it was, even if you kept your wits about you, to arrive at the right place when you started out in the wrong one?

"Besides," Zack said, "if you work for Grandma, who's going to be my helper?"

Which she'd been, on weekends during the school year, and also summers and vacations, for the last several years. Together they made the rounds of local yard sales and flea markets. Mostly they were looking for broken small appliances that could be easily repaired if you knew how, but also for items people didn't know the value of, which you could buy cheap and sell dear to the right buyer. For all the problems Tina had at school, she always remembered where her grandfather put things and would go fetch the item in question if someone expressed interest. Either that or she'd say, "You sold that last week, Grandpa. To the woman with the pink hair?" And she was always right.

"I meant a *paying* job," she told him now.

"Hey, don't I pay you?" Zack said. "What about the Tina Fund?" Each week he gave her a few bucks for spending money, but also made a contribution—he was pretty vague about how much—to what they'd originally designated as her college fund, until it became clear that college wasn't in the cards.

"How much is in it?"

"That's for me to know and for you to find out," he told her, his standard kidding reply.

"How can I find out, if you won't tell me?"

"You're richer than you'd guess, is all I'm sayin'."

Ruth cleared her throat. "Does your mom know you're staying with us tonight?"

"She doesn't care."

"Of course she does."

The girl shrugged.

"She's your mother. She loves you."

"She's always yelling at me."

"That's normal. When your mother was your age, she and I fought every day."

"You still fight every day."

"That doesn't mean we don't love each other."

"Are you sure?"

"Yeah," Ruth said. "I am."

She wasn't, though. Not really. In truth, the years of conflict with Janey had taken their toll. Now, with Roy back in the picture, it was even worse. That there was no end in sight to their bickering was beyond exhausting to contemplate. Gregory, her son, had been the smart one. He'd joined the military as soon as he was old enough and never came back. He called on Christmas from wherever he was living, but that was about it.

"Am I going to see my dad soon?"

Ruth wasn't surprised by the question. In fact she'd been expecting it, but she still didn't know how to answer. "Do you want to?"

Again, the girl shrugged.

"Because you don't have to if you don't want to."

A third shrug.

"You know what a restraining order is?"

She nodded.

"You know why your mother got one?"

She nodded, so shrugs and nods were evidently synonyms. "I'm not supposed to let him in."

Ruth and Zack exchanged a glance.

"If you want to see him, tell me. Or Grandpa. He can visit you here."

Her eye wandered off. After a minute she said, "*Are* you?"

"Am I what?"

"Fighting? You and Grandpa?"

As usual, no transition. Follow the bouncing ball. "We're trying to decide," Ruth told her, offering Zack the kind of grudging half smile he could regard as a truce, if he chose to.

Which he did. "*She's* trying," he told his granddaughter. "I'm a lover, not a fighter."

Ruth had to swallow hard at that. Had it been a decade? Pretty close. He was right, though, about not being much of a fighter. He'd made the mistake of confronting Sully once, early on, and though half his size Sully had backed him down.

"It's really hot in my room," she said. "Can I have a fan?"

"What's wrong with the one in the window?"

"It doesn't work."

"Is it plugged in?" Ruth asked. Because while Tina might be smarter than people gave her credit for, she did often overlook the obvious.

When the wayward eye wandered off in search of the answer, Zack said, "Why don't we go check it out? If it's broke, I got another in the shed."

After they were gone, Ruth let herself cry. She was drying her eyes on a dish towel when the phone rang. "Ma?"

"You're not supposed to call here, Roy," she told him.

"I didn't know where else *to* call," he said, "and that's for true."

"What do you want?"

"I'm out to the hospital."

Naturally, her first thought was Janey. He'd put her in there often enough before. What had happened this time? Had he waited out back of the restaurant? She always parked in the narrow space next to the Dumpster. Had he hidden behind it and surprised her there? Tried to sell her that line of happy horseshit about how he was a changed man, how the two of them belonged together, how their daughter, whom he'd never given a single, solitary thought to, deserved a father. Not that Janey was buying a word he said anymore, but she'd have to mouth off. And giving Roy lip was what always lit his short fuse. What had he done this time? Broken her jaw again? Or worse? Probably. So far, each act of violence was more awful than the last. Had he beaten her unconscious this time? Killed her? Was that what he was calling to tell her?

"If you've hurt her, Roy, I swear to God—"

"I'm the one that got hurt," he said. "Busted collarbone. Left elbow's all fucked up. Concussion."

Good, she thought. When news arrived that Roy was about to be released, Zack had found an old hairline-fractured Louisville Slugger at the landfill and given it to Janey to protect herself, should the need arise. Apparently she'd given it to him good. "Well, you were warned to keep away from her," she said.

There was a pause, then, "Wasn't Janey. A goddamn building fell on me, is what happened."

"That was you?" Jocko had come in for lunch and brought her up to speed on what happened out at the old mill, including the part about the passing motorist.

"My car got totaled. That's how come I need a lift."

"What about your girlfriend Cora? Call her."

"I tried. Must not be home."

Interesting, Ruth thought, that he didn't deny she was his girlfriend this time, like he had only hours ago. "Hold on," she told him. "I'll find the number for a taxi."

"Got no money for one of them."

She was about to tell him that was too bad when she remembered what she said to Sully that morning, that she wished something would fall out of the sky on his pointed head. A prayer answered? Not exactly, she decided. Roy *was* still alive. "Okay," she said, stifling as best she could a nasty chuckle. "Give me fifteen minutes."

"What's so funny?"

"Nothing," she said. "It's just that bad luck seems to follow you."

"That's for true," he agreed.

Not Happy

P ULL UP BESIDE that old man for a minute," Raymer said when Jerome made the turn into the Morrison Arms parking lot. Seated in a folding aluminum beach chair on the sidewalk out front, Mr. Hynes was waving a small American flag at passing motorists, some of whom tooted an acknowledgment. Despite the punishing heat he was dressed in his usual threadbare long-sleeved flannel shirt and a ratty wool sweater. "How you doin', Mr. Hynes?"

"Fine, fine, fine," was the reply Raymer had come to expect. To hear him tell it, he was never any other way.

"How many varieties you got today?" Raymer asked, their long-running joke.

"Fifty-seven," Mr. Hynes said proudly, "same as always."

"That's a lot of varieties."

"Don't I know it. What you go and do to yourself?"

"I fell into a grave."

"I believe it."

"You do?"

But he was looking past Raymer at Jerome, at the wheel of the 'Stang. "That a brother in there, driving this pretty red car?"

"Say hi to Jerome," Raymer told him, leaning back in his seat to afford the old man a better view.

"Whoo-wee! They ain't gon come repo that, is they?"

"Over my dead body," Jerome assured him. Raymer half expected him to unholster his pistol to demonstrate just how seriously he'd defend his rig. Fortunately, the weapon stayed out of sight.

"Whoo-weee!" Mr. Hynes hooted again.

"Power's out at the Arms, then?" Raymer said.

The old man nodded. "Black as night in there. Black as me. Blacker."

So much for the idea of a long afternoon nap, Raymer thought. His apartment, claustrophobic under the best of circumstances, would be a furnace without his small window-unit AC; even this exhausted, he doubted he'd be able to sleep in such stifling conditions. Across the street, though, the tippy martini glass in the window of Gert's Tavern was illuminated, which meant that it either had power or a backup generator. Half of the regulars—mostly deadbeat dads, disability scam artists, derelicts and assorted dickheads—fell asleep with their heads on the bar. Maybe Raymer would be allowed to do the same.

"Aren't you hot, Mr. Hynes," Raymer inquired, "sitting here in the sun? It's over ninety degrees out."

"Yeah, but I'm over ninety my own self. Me and the heat, we cancels each other out."

"Okay, but you gotta promise me you'll go find some shade if you start feeling light-headed. Heat like this is dangerous for an elderly person like yourself."

"You forget I come up from down south. Heat don't mean nothin' to me." He was clearly more interested in the Mustang and its driver than Raymer's advice. "What that set you back," he asked, "that pretty red car?"

"You don't want to know," Jerome told him, easing off the brake.

"See, that's where you wrong," Mr. Hynes insisted. "I *do* want to know. That's how come I ask."

GERT'S WAS DARK and cool and smelled like it always did, of stale beer and overmatched urinal cakes. Not, for some reason, like the Great Bath Stench. Half-a-dozen solitary midafternoon drinkers were there when Raymer and Jerome walked in, but the sight of the police chief in the company of a tall black man with a bulge under his arm scattered them like oil on water. When the front door swung shut behind the last of them, Gert, an enormous man in his midseventies with a shaved head and a hairy chest, strolled over. He'd spent most of his youth in the joint, though for the last thirty years or so, since buying the tavern, he'd managed to stay out of trouble. Raymer had heard that he dispensed advice, along with rotgut whiskey and cheap beer, to the town's petty criminals, who liked to run their nitwit schemes past him so Gert could point out their more obvious flaws.

"Well, well," he said, "look at you."

"Uh-huh."

"You're killing me here," he said, nodding almost imperceptibly in Jerome's direction. "You know that, right?"

If Jerome registered the insult, he gave no sign. "Name's Jerome," he said, extending his hand across the bar; Gert looked surprised, but took it. "Are you the proprietor of this excellent establishment?"

"I own the joint, if that's what you mean," Gert said.

"Sir, you take my meaning perfectly." He peered down the bar at the draft sticks. "Do you serve any microbrews?" Jerome's usual watering hole was an upscale bar in Schuyler, whose screwball name for some reason eluded Raymer. Becka had dragged him there a couple times.

"What-oh-brews?" Gert said.

"All righty, then," Jerome sighed, squinting at the sticks. "A Twelve Horse ale, if you would."

Raymer said he'd have the same, and when Gert went off to draw their beers, he volunteered, much to his surprise, "I'm thinking about resigning." He hadn't planned to say anything of the sort. Certainly not to Jerome, who would rat him out to Charice. And certainly not in Gert's, where such an announcement could circulate widely.

"You're just having a bad day," Jerome consoled him.

"They're all bad," he replied. "Today's especially bad, but every last one of them sucks."

"You're conflating two issues—your job and your grief."

"Conflating," Raymer said. "Isn't that like giving a blow job?"

Jerome thought for a moment. "That's *fellating*."

"Oh."

"You need to let her go," Jerome continued. "Losing that garage-door opener? Best thing that ever could've happened."

Out at Hilldale, Raymer had told Jerome about the device that now lay at the bottom of Judge Flatt's grave and how losing it meant he'd never know who Becka had been about to run off with when she came down those stairs like a Slinky.

Gert set two full glasses in front of them and then, recognizing that his participation in this conversation wasn't required, retreated the length of the bar and disappeared behind the racing form.

Raymer drained off about a third of his beer, half expecting his head to detonate from its coldness, but it didn't. In fact, he could feel the thrumming pain, which four extra-strength Tylenols hadn't yet touched, begin to recede from right behind his eyes to somewhere deeper in his damaged skull, taking with it the worst of his exhaustion. Maybe sleep wasn't what he needed after all. Maybe he just needed to get very drunk. Which could be accomplished, he knew from experience, on about three beers. "Oh, *yeah*," he gasped, staring at the bubbles, thousands of them, magically appearing at the bottom of the glass and sprinting up to the surface. "This . . . this is *wonderful*."

"This," said Jerome, who'd also taken a drink and was making a face, "is horsepiss. I bet all twelve horses peed in this beer and they all had urinary infections."

From down the bar and behind the racing form came a discernible grunt.

Raymer took off his dark glasses and studied Jerome. "God, you're a snob," he said.

Jerome winced at the sight of Raymer's face, his eyes swollen to slits. "Please put those back on. You know I've got a weak stomach."

He put the glasses back on. "Okay, but don't tell me I need to let Becka go," he said. "You've never been married. You're always dating three girls at a time. You lose one, you've got two spares. Plus they're mostly college girls. Interchangeable. Same exact girl, different major." According to Jerome, he dated only girls from the college's three small graduate programs, but Raymer had his doubts. Most of the female population was from the city, and their views regarding tall, handsome black men were on the liberal side. By his own admission Jerome had to beat them off with a stick, though there had to be times, Raymer suspected, when no stick was handy.

"Yeah, but summer is my slow season. The campus is practically deserted."

"Whereas Becka was a woman."

"I know that," Jerome said, sounding surprisingly serious.

"And please don't tell me fainting into that grave, breaking my face and losing that garage remote was the best thing that could've happened, because that's just plain insulting."

Jerome was fidgety. "You sure the 'Stang's all right out back?"

Godalmighty. Despite the blistering heat, he'd carefully put the top up, then double-checked to make sure both doors were securely locked—a car nerd if there ever was one. "Well, you took up two spaces," said Raymer, who nonetheless wasn't at all sure it would be okay. The parking lot behind Gert's was second only to the Morrison Arms in terms of generating calls to the police station. "Only assholes do that, by the way."

"Spoken like a man who drives a Jetta and drinks Genesee."

Raymer took another long drag of beer and closed his eyes, tracking the fluid down the back of his throat and into his chest. Lord, it tasted good. Becka had preferred wine, so he'd mostly just gone along. But how the hell had he forgotten beer? He needed nothing else, he decided. Not sleep, not riches, not a woman. Just beer and this cool dark room. He certainly didn't need Jerome telling him why he should be enjoying anything else. "If you're so worried about the car, go outside and stand guard. In fact, why don't you go back to Schuyler and drink microswill at Adfinitum."

"Infinity," Jerome corrected him.

"Right," Raymer said, now remembering the posh sign. No words, just the symbol, a drunken 8 lying on its side. "Go there. Because I intend to sit right here and drink horsepiss until the power comes back on across the street. Maybe a little longer."

"See, this is what I'm talking about," Jerome said. "All this shit's related. You've heard of chaos theory? A butterfly flaps its wings in South America and that causes a hurricane in the Gulf of Mexico?"

"Connect the dots and win a prize."

"You're depressed. That's the problem. You live in a rathole like the Moribund Arms because you're still grieving. Worse, you punish yourself by drinking cheap beer in a sleazy dive that smells like the locker room of a metropolitan YMCA."

From behind the racing form came another grunt.

"You think your job's the problem, but that's got nothing to do with it."

Raymer finished his beer and clunked the glass down on the bar loud enough to signal that he was in need of another, but when Gert didn't budge, he slid off his stool and said, "I gotta pee."

"Urinate," Jerome said. "Women pee. Men urinate."

"And defecate."

"Correct."

The men's room was only fifty feet away, though it was all Raymer could do to make it there, and he arrived too tired to pee standing up. There was no door on the stall, and the toilet seat was beyond disgusting, but he sat down anyway. This release was nearly as thrilling as that first long swig of beer had been. *Life's simple pleasures,* he thought, the phrase materializing, ready-made, in his brain. He needed to pay more attention to these pleasures. He wasn't even finished peeing before he fell asleep on the commode, then jolted awake again. How much time had passed? Had he already started dreaming? About Becka? He stood, hitched up his pants, washed his hands in the filthy sink and then dried them on his pants, the towel dispenser empty, naturally. There was only one word for the face that stared back at him from the cracked, cloudy mirror: gruesome.

When Raymer emerged, Jerome was right where he'd left him, which suggested he couldn't have napped for more than a minute or two. "The thing is," he told Jerome, recalling their aborted conversation, "you can't even keep your bullshit straight." His glass was still empty, so he went behind the bar. "First you say it's all related, then you tell me that my job's got nothing to do with my depression. So which is it?" Before Jerome could answer, he called down the bar. "I'm drawing myself another beer, Gert."

"Help yourself," came the reply from behind the racing form. "You already drove out all my customers. Empty the till while you're at it. Put me out of my misery."

"It's not bad enough," Raymer continued to Jerome, "I have to hear this same shit all day long from your sister—"

"You're a good cop, is what I'm saying," Jerome interrupted, serious again. "Like with that old gentleman across the street. All day long he sits out there on the sidewalk waving his little flag. Every now and then somebody honks. But you stopped to talk to him. That might be the only human contact he'll have all day."

"That's social work," Raymer countered. He knew Jerome was trying to pay him a compliment, but for some reason he wasn't in the mood to accept any. "The police solve crimes. Prevent crimes. Apprehend criminals."

"Police work is giving a shit."

"So what're you saying?" Raymer asked. "Because I don't want a lonely old man to die of heat stroke, that makes me a good cop?"

"Don't resign, is what I'm saying. If you do, you'll be sorry, is what I'm saying."

From down the bar, now, a chuckle.

"Gert," Raymer called. "What do I owe you?"

"It's on the house."

"Nope."

"Two bucks, then. Call it happy hour."

He took two dollars out of his wallet. "I'm putting it here on the register."

There came a genial snort. "A cop paying for a beer? The end-times approach."

Raymer ignored him. Heading back around the bar, he noticed one of the business cards he'd had printed up special for the last election, wedged into the corner of the mirror along the backbar. Yellowing, curled at the edges and covered with fingerprints, it had to have been there a good year. He tossed it onto the bar in front of Jerome. "Read this and tell me I'm not a joke cop."

"*Douglas Raymer, Chief of Police,*" Jerome read. "*We're not happy until you're happy.*"

Gert rose from his stool and headed for the restroom, his shoulders shaking.

"Read it again," Raymer suggested, sliding back onto his stool.

"We're not happy until . . ." Jerome's voice trailed off. "Huh," he said squinting at the card. *"We're not happy—"*

"Until you're not happy," Raymer finished.

The card had been the mayor's idea, something to hand out to voters in the run-up to the election. Raymer's first impulse had been to keep it simple, *Douglas Raymer, Chief of Police* in raised lettering, but Gus had objected, reminding him that this was a political campaign; it wasn't enough to just announce his existence. "Tell people who you are and what you stand for," he advised. "Your vision-for-the-police-department sort of deal." Raymer supposed he understood what Gus was getting at, but really? Tell people who he was? (Everyone knew him.) What he stood for? (He stood for something?) His vision for the department? (What did that even mean?) And cram all this on a business card?

"Something catchy," Gus explained, sensing his misgivings.

So. A motto, then. He'd come up with several, running each one by Charice, who wrote poetry when the switchboard was slow and had what her brother called sound literary judgment. *Here to serve* was his first effort, which Charice liked well enough, though under cross-examination she admitted it sounded a little, well, servile. *Serve and protect* also sounded good, but they both worried the phrase was already copyrighted by some larger, more important police force. *On the front lines,* they agreed, represented the worst of both worlds, sounding both fearful and belligerent. "Try for something more friendly," Charice suggested.

In the end it came down to a toss-up: *We're not happy until you're happy* and *If you're not happy we're not happy.* Charice liked both and saved him some embarrassment by reminding him that "your" wasn't the same as "you're" and adding the necessary apostrophes. "They both say the same thing," Charice said when he pressed for her favorite. "Just pick one." So he'd scribbled his choice down and dropped it off at the printer.

He'd passed out about fifty cards before somebody pointed out that the motto printed beneath his name didn't look right: *We're not happy until you're not happy,* it said. Raymer stared at it, at first unable to see anything wrong. But wait. There was an extra "not." How had that happened? He called the printer immediately, hoping there'd be cause for righteous indignation but already fearing that it was he, not they, who'd screwed up. "I got what you gave us right here," the girl told him over the phone. "It says *We're not happy until you're not happy.*" Somehow, he'd managed to merge the two slogans. But hadn't it *looked* wrong? Raymer asked. Couldn't they see it was the exact opposite of what he'd meant to say? This of course was the same argument he'd given Miss Beryl back in eighth grade, and she'd always reminded him that it wasn't her job to decipher what he *meant*. It was his job to *say* what he meant. The girl at the printer's expressed much the same opinion. No doubt she understood the rhetorical triangle as well.

Raymer had managed to repossess most of the cards, but the damage was done. The ones still in circulation either became collectors' items or were put on public view, like kited checks, in businesses like the White Horse Tavern and Hattie's Lunch. There was even a rumor the gaffe had been reprinted in *The New Yorker,* though Raymer doubted that. As far as he knew that magazine wasn't even sold in Bath, so how would anybody have seen it? Regardless, the local humiliation had been full and sufficient. For weeks people stopped him on the street to inquire if he was happy. Charice encouraged him to just laugh along with the joke. "Say, 'Not until you're not,'" she advised, but asking him to pull off a double negative under rhetorical duress was like expecting him to perform a triple lutz under Olympic klieg lights. Better to surreptitiously confiscate the cards whenever he ran across them.

The problem was that the damn things kept turning up, reposted as soon as Raymer stole them. How many of the damn things had he handed out? Fifty or sixty at the outside, but he'd recovered at least that many, probably more. Had somebody ordered a second printing? That was just the sort of thing his old nemesis Donald Sullivan would do. Unfortunately, he lacked proof, and without it Raymer couldn't bring himself to accuse the man, just as he'd never publicly accused him of stealing not one but three expensive wheel boots. No wonder, earlier in the day, when Charice told him he'd be pleased to learn who the mill's wall had fallen on, he'd thought of Sully right off.

When Raymer finished relating the whole sorry saga, Jerome's rigid expression was that of a man desperately trying to move a constipated bowel. "It's okay," Raymer said. "Go ahead."

Permission granted, Jerome exploded into laughter so violent that he had all he could do to remain atop his barstool. For Raymer, it was alarming to see a man as tightly wound as Jerome, one so committed to self-control, lose himself so utterly. *"We're not happy until you're not happy,"* he croaked, tears streaming now. "Oh, sweet Jesus."

"Great," Raymer said. "Enjoy yourself."

"Oh, come on," he said, wiping his eyes on his sleeve, "You *do* have to admit that's funny."

"Laugh, I thought I'd die," Raymer said, straight-faced. "I'm surprised Charice didn't tell you all about it back when it happened."

The mention of his sister seemed to be just what Jerome needed to regain his composure. "The thing you don't realize about Charice is that the woman is completely devoted to you, man."

The door to the men's room opened, and Gert emerged, eyes down. Climbing back onto his stool, though, he made the mistake of looking up, and the mere sight of Raymer was enough to send him scurrying back to the men's room.

"Jerome," Raymer said, "not a day goes by that your sister doesn't threaten to sue me. She's keeping a list of all the actionable things I do and say. If I resigned, she'd do the happy dance on the station steps."

"You could *not* be more incorrect," Jerome said, with startling gravity after so much hilarity. "You underestimate her. Keeping her back at the station when she should be out on the street. She can think rings around Miller."

"That's damning with faint praise," Raymer said. "Anyway, my point is she thinks I'm a fool."

"You *are* a fool," Jerome said, again surprising him. "So am I. So's just about everybody we know, dude. I mean, look around. Who's not a damn fool most of the time?"

"Yeah," Raymer said, "but there's a difference between *being* a fool and *looking* like one." From inside the men's room came more strangled laughter. "Look, I know you're a fool, Jerome. You don't have to convince me of that. You're in love with a fucking car."

At this Jerome's eyes narrowed, as if Raymer had crossed a very serious line.

"But still, people don't laugh at you."

"That's because I refuse to tolerate disrespectful behavior. I dress well. I speak well. I have excellent posture. I've got a great apartment. I drive the 'Stang. People take one look at me and decide to fuck with somebody else. And of course I'm armed. People do respect that, especially in a Negro male."

"Yeah, but this is *exactly* what I'm talking about," Raymer insisted. The second beer was kicking in, and he felt a terrible drunken urgency to make Jerome understand. "I'm armed, too. Maybe I don't take my gun out and wave it around like some people, but it's right here on my hip where everybody can see it. In all the years I've been a cop, I've unholstered my weapon only once, and the man I pointed it at cold-cocked me. I might as well have been holding a Q-tip. Don't tell me shit like that happens to a man whose true destiny is police work."

"Doug," Jerome said, "people *voted* for you. Okay, maybe they've had some fun at your expense, but they voted for you, man."

"They were probably thinking of all the crimes they could commit," he said miserably. "Things I'd never get to the bottom of. If I found any evidence against them, I'd lose it."

"Only in your imagination—which I have to say is deeply weird—was that garage-door remote evidence of anything."

Raymer took a deep breath, the way you do before saying or doing something you know better than to say or do. "Tell me something. Why do you think she married me in the first place?"

"Beats me," Jerome said, as if he'd already given the matter a lot of thought and felt no need to hesitate at all.

"Thanks."

"Dude. You're seeking a rational explanation for an irrational behavior. Why do people fall in love? Nobody knows. They just do."

Raymer had heard this opinion voiced more than once, but was it true? He knew exactly why *he'd* fallen in love. Becka was beautiful and sexy and clearly out of his league. He supposed, in hindsight, that last attribute should have been a red flag. It might've been a good idea to ask what she saw in *him* that other women had been so completely blind to.

But who, confronted with such good fortune, asks sensible questions? If a girl like Becka wanted you, you'd be an idiot not to want her back, wouldn't you?

"But . . . you were surprised, right?" Raymer said, recalling Jerome's reaction when he first introduced him to Becka. "Admit it. You thought, Wow! This woman's going to marry *Raymer?*"

Jerome shrugged. "Sure. That's correct."

"Thanks again." Dejected, he rose and went back around the bar. "Gert," he called. "I'm drawing myself another beer."

This produced a muffled grunt of acknowledgment, so he laid another two bucks on the bar.

"Okay, I was surprised," said Jerome when he returned, "but you're imagining things. I didn't think she was too good for you . . . not exactly."

"No, not *exactly.*"

"It was more like . . ."

Raymer waited for him to split the hair he was squinting at in his mind's eye.

"It's more like you two weren't interested in the same things. I mean, Becka liked to work out and listen to jazz and read and travel and drink good wine and dance and—"

"Stop."

"What?"

"You're just rephrasing my original question in a way that makes me feel even worse."

"But she married you. She must've seen something she liked. Same with your job. People voted for you. They saw something, too."

"You said the two weren't related."

Jerome sighed. "I was wrong about that. They're related, okay? Satisfied now?"

From behind the racing form, Gert grumbled, "*I* voted for you."

Gert *voted?* "Seriously?" Raymer said. "Why?"

"I don't recall," he said. "But I did."

Now Raymer sighed again, unsure how to feel. He scrolled back through the conversation, troubled by something Jerome had said. "Becka liked to dance?"

Jerome made a face. If *he* knew this, Raymer should've known, too, was the point intended. Toward the end Becka's primary grievance was his inattention, his knack for missing things that were "right in front of his face," like that extra "not," things he'd see plainly if he just opened his eyes. Including, apparently, her unhappiness. So yes, his failures as a husband did dovetail neatly with his failings as a policeman. Of *course* they were related.

"I should've danced with her," he said, the very idea sending a new wave of despair coursing through him. Because she really was a good dancer, sensual and provocative in the movement of her hips, always just a little slower than the music seemed to call for. He could practically see it now, like a video playing in front of him.

"Do you even know how to dance?" Jerome wondered.

"I could've learned."

Jerome looked doubtful. "Stop punishing yourself. Bottom line? You weren't rich, so it must've been love. It just didn't last."

"Yeah, but why not? It's not like I changed. I didn't trick her. Right to the end, I was the same guy she married."

"Maybe that's it. Maybe she *wanted* you to change. Grow. Try new things. Expand your horizons."

"She *was* my horizon. I was supposed to be *her* horizon."

"That's asking a lot."

"No, she found a new horizon instead, and now I'll never find out who he was." Three beers. Every time. Just like clockwork. Drunk, maudlin, pathetic. "If I knew who this horizon was, maybe I'd know what was wrong with me, horizon-wise. Suppose I meet somebody new? How do I keep from doing the same thing and losing her, too."

"Maybe it was something you didn't do."

"Like what?"

"I'm the wrong person to ask."

"The right one's dead."

"Ask Charice, then."

"How would she know?"

Jerome shrugged. "She's a woman?"

"Chief?" said Charice at that very instant, her voice startlingly near on the radio. For a moment it felt to Raymer as if she'd been privy to their entire conversation and had finally decided to add her two cents' worth. "Are you at the Arms? Because you need to get out of there."

"I'm across the street."

A moment of confused silence, and then: "The only thing across the street from the Morrison Arms is Gert's."

"That's where we are."

"We?"

"Jerome and me."

"My brother is at *Gert's Tavern*? With the lowlifes and scumbags and derelicts? *That* Gert's?"

"The mouth on that chippie," Gert grumbled from down the bar.

"Why would I have to get out of the Arms?"

"There's a cobra loose."

"A *cobra*? Like . . . from India?"

"Right."

"So what's a cobra doing in upstate New York?"

"Evidently one of your fellow residents sells exotic reptiles."

"Who?"

"Don't have the gentleman's name just yet, Chief."

"But selling poisonous snakes is—"

"Illegal, yes."

Actually, *insane* was what he was going to say.

"It seems that one of the cages got knocked over in the dark, and the snake escaped. It chased him down the corridor and out into the street."

"Good," Raymer said.

"I need to use the gents'," Jerome said, sliding off his stool.

Puzzled by his abrupt exit, Raymer watched him go. "Okay," he told Charice, "here's what you do. Get on the horn with animal control—"

"Already did. They're on the way."

"So am I."

"How about I put Miller on the desk and join you."

"No," Raymer told her. "I need you there."

"Chief?" she said. "I ever tell you about the tattoo on my ass?"

"No, Charice. That I would've remembered."

"Butterfly. Tiny little thing. If you don't let me out from behind this switchboard, it's gonna be a pterodactyl by the time I'm forty."

Then she was gone, the radio silent. I am not, Raymer thought, heading for the door, going to think about the butterfly on Charice's ass. I will not.

"Funny gal," said Gert, lowering his paper at last. "I just remembered why I voted for you."

"And?"

"You seemed sort of . . ." He was clearly groping for the right word. "Normal."

Raymer nodded. "Normal?"

"Yeah, sort of," Gert repeated, shrugging. "Rare in law enforcement. In my experience."

Stepping outside was like being bludgeoned, by the heat and stench and blinding sunlight. Raymer paused to let his eyes adjust. He wobbled, then righted himself. Across the street a crowd was milling around in front of the Morrison Arms, many of them residents Raymer recognized. These were his neighbors, he reflected, and while he didn't like to be unkind, they were not attractive people on the whole. He'd known several of them since grade school, and they hadn't looked too good back then either. Amazing, when you thought about it, how much of human destiny was mapped out by the third grade. A man wearing a neck brace, with his right arm crooked in a sling, caught his attention because he, too, looked familiar. When their eyes met, the man quickly turned away, and in this furtive gesture Raymer recognized Roy Purdy, who only hours ago had been pulled from his flattened car by a Jaws of Life machine. Was it possible he'd already gotten treated and been released from the hospital?

Raymer was about to cross the street when he heard the door open behind him. "I think I'm just going to head on back to Schuyler," Jerome said. Tone-wise, he seemed to be trying for nonchalance, but it didn't ring quite true. And though he'd had just the one beer, he didn't look right, either.

"Jerome?" Raymer said, visited by a sudden intuition. "Are you scared of snakes?"

"Me?" he said, then waited a beat. "Nah."

"Because you look kind of—"

"*Some* snakes, sure," he grudgingly admitted. "I mean . . ."

"What?"

"Look," he said, clearly annoyed he had to explain himself. "There are three things a snake shouldn't be able to do. It shouldn't swim. It shouldn't climb trees. And it sure as *hell* shouldn't stand up like a vertebrate." He actually looked relieved, having gotten all this off his chest.

"I think cobras can do only one of those things," Raymer noted.

"One's enough," Jerome said, refusing to look him in the face. "Go ahead and laugh," he finally said. "I don't care."

"I'm not laughing," Raymer said. "I'm just . . . I don't know . . . surprised, I guess. I always figured you were—"

"Brave? I would follow you into a hail of gunfire, brother, but I don't do serpents. Sorry."

"Chief?" his sister chirped from Raymer's hip.

"What now, Charice? I'm kind of busy here."

"Jerome still with you?"

Jerome shook his head.

"No, he's headed back to Schuyler. Why?"

"Just wanted you to know you can't count on him for backup. That boy's petrified of *garter* snakes."

Not true, he mouthed. Unconvincingly, given the speed at which he was backpedaling.

"I've got this, Charice."

Though in truth, he was no great fan of reptiles himself. He was glad he had a snootful of Twelve Horse ale, which, combined with the rush of seeing Jerome unexpectedly fearstruck, gave him the necessary courage to turn back to the Morrison Arms and step into the street, though the immediate result was a blaring horn and screeching tires as the Schuyler County Animal Control van came to a rocking halt only inches away, sending him up onto his tiptoes.

The driver appeared to be in his midtwenties, and when he poked his head out the window, he looked vaguely familiar. "That was close," he said. "I'm Justin. We met last year?"

Though the danger had passed, Raymer stepped back onto the curb, his heart pounding.

"I hear this right?" Justin said, sounding skeptical. "A *cobra*?"

"That's my understanding."

The young man nodded thoughtfully. "And me without my mongoose."

Raymer followed the van across the street as Justin parked as far away from the crowd as possible, then hopped out and pulled from the back a long pole with a wire noose at the end. For some reason its length deepened Raymer's already serious misgivings. He wished there'd been time for one more beer. "Just how lethal are these things?"

Justin seemed disinterested. "Do me a favor," he said, stepping into thick canvas pants that looked like waders. "Go ask those people where the snake was last seen."

Before Raymer could do so, though, there came a shriek he'd never heard outside a movie theater, so high pitched that he couldn't tell whether it was male or female. But what really made no sense was that it wasn't from inside the Morrison Arms, where the snake supposedly was, but rather from the direction of Gert's. He froze for a moment as the scream morphed into a terrible keening, then found himself chugging back across the street, once again setting horns blaring and tires screeching. In his peripheral vision he saw Mr. Hynes, flag in hand, struggling to his feet and tipping his beach chair over in the process. And what was that expression he fleetingly glimpsed on Roy Purdy's bruised, swollen face? A smirk? But there was no time to dwell on such irrelevancies. Because it suddenly came to Raymer who the screamer had to be.

Raymer found Jerome on his knees in the parking lot, staring straight ahead, slack jawed, unresponsive, and he squatted down next to him. "Where did it bite you?" he said.

Because as he hurried back across the street a narrative had formed. The cobra, frightened by the noisy crowd, had somehow slithered across the busy two-lane blacktop, probably in search of a hiding place. Had Jerome left one of the 'Stang's vent windows cracked, or could the serpent have crawled up under the chassis and—

"Bite me?" he said, still staring off into the middle distance before turning his focus on Raymer. "*You* bite me."

Raymer wrote this bizarre response off to the snake's venom and told him, "Don't worry. It's gone." Which was true: no snake was in evidence. Nor was there any sign of snakebite on Jerome's face or neck or hands. Dear God, had it slithered up Jerome's pant leg? No way. Jerome wouldn't be calmly kneeling there with a cobra sliding around in his trousers. Unless the venom had induced more or less instant paralysis. "Jerome," he said. "Look at me. Where did it bite you?"

"The 'Stang," he said, pointing at his car.

"The snake's in there?" Raymer said, pleased to have his original narrative confirmed. Maybe he wasn't such a bad cop after all. He just needed to trust his intuitions. Except Jerome was now regarding him like he was some Asperger's patient introducing a random subject into a normal conversation. As if snakes had no bearing upon these proceedings at all.

"There," he said, his face a rigid mask of revulsion and also, unless Raymer was mistaken, sheer rage. Sighting along Jerome's index finger, he patiently waited for the snake to make its next move and reveal itself. Why the hell couldn't he see it? The vehicle sat on a slant, just as they'd left it, athwart two spaces. Except now, he noticed, the bright red paint bore a deep silver furrow that ran the length of the car.

He stood up and went over for a closer look, approaching cautiously, since his mind was still fixed on the cobra. There was an identical gash along the other side, and the cloth roof was in tatters. When he bent over to peer inside, he was greeted with a powerful scent of urine. Swatches of foam stuffing had exploded out of the slashed leather seats.

Jerome was still on his knees, glaring at him now. "The 'Stang," he muttered. "Why?" As if Raymer owed him an explanation.

"Who knows . . . ," he started, but when he put a hand on his shoulder, Jerome slapped it away with surprising violence and snapped, "You crazy bastard." Was it possible that he was somehow blaming *him*? "I should've known," he said. "You were in there too long."

"In where?"

"The men's room."

Was the man insane? "Jerome," he said, "why would I want to damage your car?"

"Why would I want to damage your car?" he mimicked, as if there *was* a reason and they both knew perfectly well what it was.

Raymer gave up trying to figure it all out. Maybe Jerome *wasn't* snakebit, but he seemed to have surrendered his rationality completely. "Look," he said, "I can't stand here and reason with you. I've gotta go find that snake." (It was unlikely, it occurred to him, that he'd ever again have reason to utter these two statements sequentially.)

"I hope it sinks its fangs right in your buttocks," Jerome said.

"You mean bites me in the ass?"

"You take my meaning perfectly."

Heading back to the Morrison Arms, Raymer again called Charice on the radio. "Come see to your brother."

"I thought you said he'd gone back to Schuyler."

"Somebody vandalized the 'Stang," he explained. "Don't ask me why, but he's got it into his head that I did it."

"Uh-oh," she said. "I'll be right there."

For some reason this assurance occasioned in Raymer an unexpected wave of relief. Which was beyond nuts. He was drunk on duty and his headache had returned with a vengeance and he was about to confront a venomous reptile. What possible difference could it make that Charice was on her way? And why, he wondered, did he at this particular moment find himself picturing the butterfly tattooed on her backside? Hadn't he expressly forbidden himself to do this very thing? Okay, so the brain was a strange, unruly organ. His own probably stranger than most. Though not, thankfully, as strange as Jerome's. Something about Charice's reaction a moment ago suggested she wasn't entirely surprised by her brother's irrationality. He made a mental note to ask her about that.

At the curb he paused, looked in both directions, and then, because it was, at least for the time being, still his job to serve and protect, he moved forward.

Impulse

HANGING UP the pay phone in the hospital lobby, Roy Purdy went outside to wait for his mother-in-law in the bruising heat, his neck immobilized in a stiff brace, one arm in a sling. He was in better spirits than might've been predicted for someone who'd just escaped a freakish death. Some people might have been chastened by the experience, or at least unnerved enough to seriously contemplate their mortality. A religious man might even have considered the possibility that God had hand-delivered him a warning: that his act needed cleaning up right quick, before the real boom got lowered.

Roy, however, was neither religious nor easily chastened. If any deity meant to communicate with him, it would need to speak louder and more clearly. Because if a person was to attach *meaning* to that collapsing wall, might not he conclude just as sensibly that God, or luck, or the cosmos, or whatever was out there deciding shit, was disposed in his favor? Maybe even had his back? Had his best interests at heart? His mouthy mother-in-law had expressed the view that bad luck trailed him, but then she'd always held him in low esteem, so naturally she'd think so. But no, sir. The more Roy thought about it, the more inclined he was to agree with the hospital staff, which to a person had marveled at his good fortune. Not only was he alive when he could've been dead, but there was every indication he was going to come out of this smelling like the proverbial rose. According to the ER doctors, he'd be good as new in no time. Meanwhile, he'd find himself a lawyer willing to work on spec and sue everybody connected with that renovation, as well as the whole town. At the very least he'd end up with a new vehicle to replace the piece-of-shit beater the wall had pancaked. Add to this his pain and suffering. Who knew? There might be a huge pile of cash waiting for him. Better yet, the pretense of looking for work could now be safely dispensed with. He'd be on the workmen's-comp gravy train for the foreseeable future, living the life of Riley, whoever the fuck he was. Maybe he'd find out. See if he could do ole Riley boy one better.

Moreover, though painful, the present was almost as gratifying to contemplate as the future. Everything in the ER was free. The bastards had known it was going to be, too, the moment he was wheeled in. The woman who'd typed his information into her computer had given him the hairy eyeball. No insurance. No job. No prospects. Residing at the Morrison Arms. Sure as shit, somebody else would be picking up the tab on this one. That did Roy's heart good. Hell, they hadn't even charged him for the pain pills. They were good ones, too, the kind he'd be able to sell for top dollar, not that generic shit. Yessiree, a man inclined to look on the bright side—and Roy was one—had plenty to look at. Nobody *wanted* a fractured collarbone, but once you had one, why not make it to your advantage? Sure, it represented a short-term setback. For the next few weeks he'd be a sore motherfucker with a limited range of motion from the shoulders up, but maybe that was a blessing in disguise. He'd been of a mind to start crossing names off his list but, really, where was the hurry? Cooling his jets and thinking things through might not be such a bad idea.

Say what you want about the joint, incarceration did afford you time to reflect. On Roy's most recent stay, working in the prison laundry, he'd come to recognize—with the help of a grizzled old con by the name of Bullwhip—that he had a problem with impulse control. Oh, Roy was capable of sound, careful planning, but then he'd glimpse an unexpected opportunity and all his preparation would sail right out the window. Next thing he knew he was being cuffed and shoved into the backseat of a squad car. "Impulse control," Bullwhip assured him knowingly. "I know whereof I speak. You and me's cut from the same bolt of cloth." Normally Roy didn't like anybody identifying flaws in his character, but Bullwhip appeared so sorrowful and sympathetic that he decided to give the man a pass. Because even Roy had to admit there was some truth in the man's reluctant diagnosis. If Roy continued to allow himself the luxury of acting on every passing whim, the best he could hope for was to square up with one or two people on his list, whereas he was determined to get even with every single one of them. And Bullwhip was right. That was going to require patience.

From his shirt pocket he took the small spiral notebook he always kept handy and thumbed it open to the most recent entry, five names in all. At the restaurant he'd told that asshole Sully he kept two lists—people he owed and people who owed him—but in fact there was just the one. No need to keep track of the second batch. He couldn't think of a single soul who'd be on it. Sure, his mother-in-law was coming to give him a lift back into town and, yeah, she gave him a cup of coffee and a shitty pastry every now and then, but she'd taken far more from Roy than she'd ever given him. He couldn't name what she'd robbed him of exactly, but it was something essential, something a man couldn't do without. By holding him in such low regard, she'd shortchanged him, and wasn't that thievery? If you were lucky enough to have a good opinion of yourself—which Roy did—and everybody else was forever undermining it, saying things that chipped away at your confidence, how was *that* not theft? When he was a boy, his father had warned him how it would go. If you had something good, you could be sure some fuckwad would be eyeing it, trying to figure out how to take it away from you. And if they did make off with it, what choice did you have but to take it back? To get even? His old man hadn't been worth much, but he got that right. If Roy was a thief—and yeah, okay, he *was* a thief—who'd made him one? All those jerk-offs, that's who.

No, payback was the only list Roy kept. In the old days, back before he met Bullwhip, it had seemed like everybody he ever met was on it, or should be, but anymore it was short enough to keep in his head. He preferred this shit in writing, though. That was another trick he'd learned from old Bullwhip, who'd been a list-making fool. Write down every last name, he'd advised him. See if that don't make the person more real. Written-down names, he explained, were a hedge against weakness, against time itself, which would, as the saying goes, heal all fucking wounds. It also led to forgiveness, which Roy wanted no part of. In jail, where time was about all you had, Roy went through a good half-dozen notebooks of forty-five pages each, front and back, five to seven names per page, depending. People whose future suffering he was passionately committed to. Usually the same names, only their sequence subject to revision. When he got out two weeks ago—early, thanks to institutional overcrowding—the first thing he did was steal a new spiral notebook from the Rexall, and he'd spent part of every day since studying and revising his lists to ensure that his incarcerated thinking had been valid, and for the most part he was gratified to conclude that it was. The final entry, composed that very morning, read:

BITCH
MAMA BITCH
NIGGER COP
SULLY
OLD WOMAN

Okay, that last entry did give him pause. This was the old woman's first appearance, and he'd put her there on a whim. He'd seen her picture in the newspaper and read that the middle school was going to be renamed in her honor this very weekend. For Roy, she raised an interesting philosophical issue: could you settle a score with a dead person? The same problem had come up before in connection with his old man. "I thought you told me he was dead," Bullwhip objected when Roy brought the matter up. You couldn't square up with a dead person, Bullwhip maintained, for the simple reason that the dead were past fucking with. That's what dead really meant, if you thought about it. Beyond caring. At rest. Roy supposed he could see the other man's point. After all, many of his own most satisfying score-settling fantasies involved putting people in the ground, so if that's where they were already, why bother? On the other hand, dead people could prosper. Look at Elvis. Earning more money dead than he ever did alive. People loved him more now than before. Same with the old woman. She'd been buried in Hilldale for nearly a decade, but people still remembered her letters to the editor, and the paper had reprinted some of these. *Miss Beryl,* the article concluded, *is still very much with us.*

Roy's initial reaction had been that this was total bullshit, but the longer he thought about it, the more he wondered. What if some part of a person remained after they died, refusing to quit the scene? Like in that movie Janey dragged him to, the one with that sexy white bitch and the bigmouthed black one and the faggot with all the hair. What if some essence of the old woman lingered, still attached to this person or that place, still trying to improve everybody's grammar and get them to see things her own stupid way. If so, then didn't it stand to reason that she'd be disappointed when her hopes were finally dashed?

He also thought having her on the list rounded things out. He liked the symmetry of a five-person list and also liked that she was connected to three of the others. For some reason Sully had been a favorite of hers, and once, when Janey had done some fucking thing that made him crazy, and he'd gone looking for her with his deer rifle, the old witch had hidden her and the brat in that big house of hers on Upper Main Street, the same place Sully now parked Roy's own trailer behind. He finally got somebody to tell him where they were holed up, but he'd somehow gotten mixed up on the street number (his first mistake), so he'd stood out on the sidewalk yelling, "Come out of there, you dumb fucking cunt!" (his second), and when she didn't come out he'd lost it completely and proceeded to shoot out the windows of the wrong fucking house, scaring the shit out of the wrong goddamn old lady (the fucking trifecta). "Oh, you got it *bad,* son," Bullwhip had chuckled when Roy described what had happened. "You got it bad as me."

Which was true enough. When his blood was up, Roy just *did* shit. Didn't think, just *did,* figuring there'd be time to deal with anything else later. The problem—here again Bullwhip was the dude who'd put his finger on it—was that all too often *later* arrived in mere minutes, as had been the case that day. One minute flat for the damn cops to respond to reports that a crazy man armed with a rifle was shouting obscenities, not out front of the Morrison Arms where you'd expect it, but on Upper Main where you wouldn't, and then another minute for the bastards to disarm and cuff Roy and stuff him rudely in the back of their cruiser.

Once again he savored all these names. Janey was on top, of course, like always. Out of sight, out of mind was how it was with her. Every time he went to jail, she'd forget they were made for each other and do something stupid. The first time she sold their trailer and took the brat and moved to Albany so he couldn't find her when he got out. Like that would ever fucking work. The next time he went in she filed for divorce. Mama Bitch had probably put her up to it, but still. Then a few weeks before he got out, she shacked up with some guy in Schuyler, as if that was going to keep him away. Bullwhip had advised him to go slow, not to give in to his natural desire to beat the living shit out of Janey to get her thinking straight again. Because that would just send him right back inside. Take your time, he said. Enjoy your freedom. Maybe get a job. When things are on an even keel, that's the time to pay her a visit, talk to her all calm and smiling. Tell her you mean to make things right with her. Tell her you got a job and you mean to win her back. Buy her something nice, or take her out to dinner.

It had taken Roy about an hour to find out where she was living in Schuyler. He'd never been comfortable there, especially the closer you got to the college. The sorority girls all looked at him like he was a bug, and their boyfriends steered them away as if he was contagious. He brought the deer rifle with him but left it in the trunk of the car, pleased to realize that he was exercising the kind of restraint that would make Bullwhip proud, though he hadn't taken any of his other advice. The douchebag Janey'd shacked up with had an apartment just off campus on the street where all the frat houses were, and she opened the door before Roy could even knock. She looked hot. Hotter than ever. "Saw you coming, Roy," she said. "Story of your life, right?" But then he caught a glimpse of the douchebag in the kitchen, hanging up the phone. He had one of those well-trimmed beards that Roy would've liked to sandpaper off. And just that quick Janey was on the floor, blinking up at him, her jaw broken. The scumbag still had his hand on the phone. That's how fast it all happened. The dumbfuck should've stayed in the kitchen, but instead he rushed into the front room where

Roy stood over Janey, waiting for her to get up so he could punch her again. He actually looked surprised when Roy punched him, too, which made Roy laugh because how could you be surprised when the person who punched you had just punched your girlfriend like two fucking seconds before? Then the cops were there—that's who the douchebag was calling—and pulling Roy off the guy. The nigger cop, the same one he'd seen driving the red Mustang around town, was one of them, and in no time Roy was secured in the back of the cruiser. There was worse to come. Roy wasn't used to being manhandled by black people, but having one laugh at him was really the shits. When it was discovered that he'd been released from prison less than twenty-four hours earlier, the nigger cop laughed that this had to be a new redneck record. He and all the other cops at the station had a great time yukking it up. It was this merriment at his expense, together with the flashy red car, that vaulted Sambo onto Roy's list and kept him there.

Strange, the effect that laughter had on him, how it made the whole world go red. Most men, given the choice, would rather be made fun of than have the shit kicked out of them. Not Roy. He had, he knew, an amazing tolerance for physical pain. He'd gotten beat up more than once in the joint, and while it wasn't a pleasant experience the bruises healed. Even the broken bones. The guys that came at him in the joint mostly didn't even know him, and it was all business, nothing personal. They were there and you were there and shit happened, you couldn't always tell why. Being laughed at was different. Those wounds refused to scab over and never really healed. You never forgot the words themselves or who said them. Roy couldn't remember the last time BITCH wasn't on the top line, and he hated the thought of dropping Janey down, even one notch, but *damn* if Sully hadn't gotten under his skin this morning, making that shit up from the want ads to get him to do something stupid that would land him back in jail. He'd come pretty close, too. That Sully was living in his trailer was a different kind of joke at Roy's expense, and this didn't sit well either. No question. He was definitely going to have to settle up with Sully.

The question was how, and that would require serious thought. Most people were easy. You just had to figure out what they wanted. Robbing them of their heart's desire wasn't very hard. With other people it was more a question of what they feared. But again, it was usually pretty simple. If you asked, half the time the dumb fucks would tell you. Desire and fear. That's what made you vulnerable. With Sully the problem was that he didn't seem to want much, and supposedly he was some kind of fucking war hero, which meant he wouldn't be easy to frighten. Once, years before, he'd tried to take Sully down a peg by telling his retarded father-in-law about him and Ruth, how they were going at it right then in a nearby motel, even giving the idiot the room number, but all he did was tell him to mind his own business. This time he'd have to figure a whole different approach. He heard Sully had given up those shenanigans now that Ruth was dried up and worthless, like all women got eventually. Served them right, too. They only ever had just the one thing a man would want and then came the day they didn't even have that.

Janey was no different, Roy thought, staring at the word BITCH atop his list. There were times, when he was feeling softhearted, that he wondered if it was strictly necessary for him to square up with her at all. Why not just sit back and let nature run its course? But no, that was crazy thinking. She'd earned that top spot, hadn't she? By testifying against him in court, even though the law said she didn't have to? He'd thought about that performance every day when he was locked up, about how he wouldn't even be there except for her. Planning what she had coming to her when he got out was the only thing that made life in the joint bearable.

He wasn't over her, though. He hated to admit it, even to himself, but he wasn't. In the joint his hatred had been pure, but as soon as he laid eyes on her again he knew there was still something between them. Though she might be homely like her mother, he liked the way she looked in that Applebee's uniform, Janey all but busting out of hers. If she played her cards right, there was no need for her to be on his list at all. Seeing her again, he thought he could maybe forgive her. If she came up to him and said, "Hey, Roy," and traced one of her long fingernails along the line of his jaw, like she used to do, he just might. Instead she had to go and slap him with that fucking restraining order before he could even say hello. So, no going soft now.

But he might drop her down a slot. He might just sleep on it to see how it felt. Tomorrow, if he changed his mind, he could just put her right back on the top line. No harm done.

Reassured, Roy took out the pen he'd swiped from the emergency room and drew a line through each name and began a new page that offered a more up-to-date testimony to his feelings.

The top line now read: SULLY.

"SO," SAID A RASPY VOICE, close at hand, and when he looked up from the notebook his mother-in-law was leaning across the front seat of her sedan to stare at him. Had he dozed off? How long had she been there? Like most sneaky people, Roy hated being snuck up on. Especially when the person in question was acting like you had no clothes on.

"Ma," he said, getting stiffly to his feet, surprised by how much that hurt. The painkillers they'd given him at the hospital were already wearing off. He'd planned to sell the rest of them at Gert's, but now he was thinking he might set aside a few for his own use. "I didn't see you pull up."

Ruth nodded. "If I didn't know better, I'd have sworn you were in deep thought."

Roy got in slowly, gingerly, wincing as he closed the door. "There you go," he said, offering her the biggest smile he could muster under the circumstances, hoping to disguise the hostility that her presence always provoked. "Selling me short again."

"Is that what I'm doing, Roy?"

"It is," he said. "And that's for true. One day you'll finally get it."

"Work faster," she said. "I'm getting old."

"You and your boyfriend both," he said. He knew she and Sully had quit that, but he couldn't resist the jab. "He's always shortchanging me, too. I must be an easy target."

"I guess you are," she said, pulling away from the curb. At the traffic light, though, she looked over at him with something akin to concern. "You hurting bad, Roy?"

He shrugged. "They give me some pills."

It was a very long light. After they'd been sitting there in silence for what seemed like forever, he said, "You look like you got something on your mind." Because that's exactly how she looked.

"Yeah?"

"Might as well go ahead and spill it."

"Okay," she said, studying him again, that direct look of hers making him squirm. "What would it cost to make you go away?"

"Go away where?" he said. Not that he had the slightest intention of doing any such thing. He was curious about what she might propose, though.

"We don't have a lot of money," she said. "The house has been refinanced twice for your daughter's eye operations, and the restaurant . . ." She let that trail off. "But I might be able to put my hands on enough money to get you a one-way ticket out of Bath. Maybe a few bucks left over to give you a fresh start. First and last months' rent on an apartment or something."

"A fresh start where?" he said, still curious.

"You decide."

"Schuyler?"

"That's only three miles away, Roy. You've been arrested there half-a-dozen times. What kind of fresh start would that be?"

"Albany?"

"You've been arrested there, too."

"Just the once."

"Roy."

"Far away, you mean, then."

"That would be best."

"For who?"

"Everybody."

"I go far away, I don't get to see my wife and kid."

Ruth sighed. "It's just the two of us here, okay? There's no need for me to bullshit you, or for you to bullshit me. We both know you don't care about Tina."

"We do? We both know that?"

"Did you even send her a birthday card this year? You don't have to answer, because I know you didn't."

"How was I supposed to buy her a birthday card when I was incarcerated?"

"You weren't *in* jail then, Roy. See? That's my point. You don't even know when her birthday is. It was last week." When he offered no rejoinder, she continued, "And you don't have a wife. You have an ex-wife."

The light finally changed and she made the turn, heading back toward town. Roy let her think he was considering the offer for a minute, then said, "Till death do us part. We said the words, her and me both. You was there."

"She's moved on, Roy. That's what you need to do. If you stay here in Bath, this doesn't end well."

"You can see the future?"

"Enough to know she's not coming back to you, Roy. Not ever."

"She might."

"No."

"I guess we'll just have to wait and see."

"No. We don't have to wait. It's not like a roulette wheel. We don't have to wait for it to stop spinning. You keep hurting her, Roy. Started out, you gave her a fat lip, then a shiner. Next you knocked out a tooth, then you broke her jaw. Last time you slammed her head into a concrete wall. You don't need a crystal ball to see where this is headed. It ends when you kill her."

"Me? Kill Janey?"

"Oh, you won't mean to. You never mean to hurt her. But that doesn't stop you from doing it. To hear you tell it, it's more her fault than yours. She provokes you. Tells you to fuck off or calls you a name or something."

"Girl's got a mouth on, and that's for true," Roy conceded. "Maybe she's the one you should be talking to. Tell her to shut it."

"It's *you* I'm talking to, Roy," she said. "If I let you stay, I end up with a dead daughter, and you go back to prison for good. You understand what I'm saying? No winners."

"If you *let* me stay."

"Whatever you're planning?" she said. "I can't allow it. I won't."

They were in town now, and as his mother-in-law pulled into the

Morrison Arms, Roy caught a glimpse of something shiny and red in the parking lot behind Gert's. The old nigger who always sat in the lawn chair was waving his flag at them. Ruth waved back, then pulled into a parking space. Roy was curious to know what she thought his plan was. Women always claimed to know what he was thinking. Janey maintained she could watch thoughts scrolling across his forehead, which was bullshit. If she could do that, she'd know when to duck, and she never did. Ruth was different, though. She did often seem to know what was on his mind, more or less, and she never believed any of his bullshit. That was fine. Roy never expected her to. He mostly said things just to see how people would react. When it came to being taken seriously, he had low expectations. One of the paradoxes Roy had long ago stopped worrying about was that even though he didn't expect people to believe anything he said, it stoked his rage when they didn't. When he told them he was a changed man, why didn't they pause, even for a second, to wonder if that might be true? Okay, sure, it *wasn't,* but it *could've* been, right? To people like Sully and Ruth, he was just the one thing, when, for all they knew, he might've been something else, too. How could they be so damn sure?

"So, what kind of money we talkin' about here?" he asked, keen to hear what she imagined it would take to buy him off. Also, how desperately she wanted to be rid of him. Which she would never be. His mind was made up on that score. That nasty chuckle she'd let escape on the phone guaranteed he was going nowhere.

"I could probably come up with three thousand," she told him.

He put on what he hoped was a poker face. "Not much of a fresh start, is it?" he said. "That kind of money, you could start and be all done the same day."

"It's not a fortune," Ruth allowed, "but it's all I can offer you, and it's free. I thought that might appeal to a man who hates honest work as much as you do. Somebody who never seems to have the price of a cup of coffee."

"Five would be more interesting than three," he said, though it wasn't true. Five was just a bigger number, not a more interesting one. The only interesting part was how she'd react.

"I don't have five to give you."

"You could borrow it. You and Sully are still tight. He come into the old lady's money . . ."

"I'm not asking Sully."

He shook his head. "Just trying to help you get to five."

"You should think about it, Roy."

"The five or the three?"

"The three. I'll look into the five, but it's three I can offer you."

"Suppose I was to take the three," he said, enjoying himself now. "I'm not saying I will. But just suppose. I take the three and go some-place for that fresh start. Suppose I spend your three and find out I don't like it there and come back."

"The deal is you don't come back."

"Yeah, okay, but we're just supposing, right? So suppose I get to thinking how much I preferred my stale ole life to my new fresh one. What's to *keep* me from coming back?"

"We're going to shake on it. You and I."

"So it's like my . . . word of honor."

"Call it whatever you like, so long as you stay gone."

"Something in this deal of yours kinda goes against human nature," he said. "That's what I'm getting at. Say you give me the three. Free money, like you say. But if I break my word and come back, maybe you'll give me another three? Or this time maybe the five? Where's my . . . what's the word I'm looking for?"

"Incentive?"

"That's it. That's the word. My incentive to stay gone. I'm not saying I'd come back after we shook hands on it. But then again, I might."

"Put it this way, Roy. It's not really your word of honor I'd be putting my faith in. If you were ever dumb enough to come back here—"

But before she could give voice to what Roy was reasonably certain would be some sort of threat, one of the exterior doors to the Morrison Arms flew open, and a fat, balding man dressed in nothing but a pair of threadbare briefs that sagged revealingly in the crotch bolted from the building as if pursued by the devil. The gravel parking lot was littered with shards of broken beer and whiskey bottles. Nobody in his right mind would traverse it in bare feet, but clearly that didn't include this lunatic. He chugged past Roy and his mother-in-law with the kind of grim determination that suggested he'd weighed the dangers of what lay before him against those that lay behind and was unimpressed by the former. There was no sign of pursuit, so once he reached the sidewalk Roy expected him to stop or slow down, but he just kept churning until he disappeared around the corner onto Limerock.

Roy was first to recover. "People like you think they can read the future," he said, "but they can't. Not unless you want to tell me you seen that comin'."

"No," she admitted, "but if you told me I'd see a naked man run out of an apartment building in Bath, New York, I think I could've predicted which one it'd be."

Since Roy was pretty sure they weren't going to agree about predicting the future, he opened the door and with great care—because he really did ache all over—got out of the car. From inside the Arms came a shriek, then another. Cora, the woman he was living with, raced outside with surprising speed and agility for somebody her size. Then two more women, one holding an infant, came out squealing. Ruth had started to pull away but stopped and rolled down her window. "What's going on?" she asked.

"There's a damn snake in there," Cora said. "Big one."

Roy was interested in the possibility that what she was saying might be true, despite its unlikelihood. He knew there were timber rattlers out in the woods, but what would one of those be doing in town, inside the Morrison Arms? He supposed the smart move was to find something with a long handle—a broom or a rake, maybe—and go in and find out, but there was something else he needed to do first, something he'd told himself to remember and then forgot all about it.

"Think about my offer, Roy," his mother-in-law said.

"I will," he lied. Though it didn't look like she believed him, she rolled up the window anyway and pulled out into the street.

Cora came over then. "Oh, Roy, look at you!" she said. "I heard you was hurt—"

He held a finger up to stop her. "Dummy up a minute," he told her. "I'm trying to remember something."

"Sure, Roy," she said. "I was just—"

"*Got* it," he said suddenly.

"Where you goin'?" she said when he turned away from her. "To Gert's? Can I come? I got some money . . ."

But he'd stopped listening. Over at the curb he had a direct view of the parking lot, where he'd seen that flash of red when they got here. Seeing what it was, he smiled, then frowned, recognizing with some apprehension the approach of an impulse, the very kind that, up to this point in his life, he'd shown not the slightest ability to control. He thought of how old Bullwhip had identified Roy's problem and told him what to do different. Well, he was one to talk. He'd gotten out a few months before Roy, and after six weeks he was right back in again. When Roy asked what happened, all he'd said was, "I saw me an opportunity."

More agitated people were streaming out of the Arms now, but Roy paid them no mind. His whole brain was pulsing red.

Don't, he told himself.

Then he did.

Boogie

THE BAREFOOT, HALF-NAKED MAN who'd bolted from the Morrison Arms that afternoon was Rolfe "Boogie" Waggengneckt (Boogie Woogie, his last name being unpronounceable). He fled straight up the center of Limerock Street, right past the now-three-sided mill. By then, midafternoon, the crowd had largely dissipated, but Carl Roebuck's crew and the NiMo guys were still there, as was Officer Miller, who was providing a police presence. These men all paused to watch, slack jawed, as Boogie motored past. Though middle aged and woefully out of shape, he had run track in high school, and in his ramrod posture, churning arms and fluid stride you could glimpse the runner he'd once been. Propelled by stark terror, he made it farther and faster than anyone, including himself, would've predicted, though compared with youth and rigorous physical conditioning fear is a poor fuel, thin and easily burned through, even when there's a lot of it. So when Boogie's tank was finally empty, he stopped like a windup toy and sat down in the middle of the street, utterly spent and aware at last of the spectacular pain in his shredded feet.

Officer Miller was reluctant to leave his comfy post but reasonably certain that a barefoot man, clad only in undershorts, running up the middle of the street was the sort of thing Chief Raymer would want him to investigate. He approached the man cautiously, in accordance with best practices as detailed in the police manual, a document he'd committed to memory as a hedge against the necessity of having to think on the spot. In his mind's eye he could actually see the relevant text, which warned officers to be cognizant of the possibility that a fleeing suspect might be carrying a concealed weapon, though in this case that seemed unlikely. Nor did the man appear to be a further flight risk. Boogie's feet, oozing impressively, looked like someone had gone at them with a cheese grater, and his chest was heaving violently. Clearly he wasn't going anywhere unless somebody carried him, and so Miller, his confidence growing, turned his attention to the matter of questioning the suspect. Where to begin? He might justifiably raise the issue of public nudity, he supposed, since Boogie's dark genitals were clearly visible in the gap between his upper thigh and sagging undershorts, but opted instead to address what he considered a more urgent concern. "You can't just sit down in the middle of the road," he said.

Boogie, blinded by tears of anguish, slowly took in the fact that he'd been joined by a uniformed police officer, which meant his situation, already deeply embarrassing, was now officially humiliating. Having little breath with which to speak, he chose his words carefully. "They're not my snakes," he said.

Officer Miller wasn't sure what sort of response he'd been expecting, but this wrong-footed him completely. Who'd said anything about snakes? Was the man on drugs, imagining himself to be pursued by reptiles? His pupils weren't dilated. Though he reeked of stale beer, he didn't appear drunk, just adamant. "I'm not going back in there," he insisted. "You can't make me."

He was, however, willing to go to the hospital, so Miller radioed for an ambulance, which Charice told him to follow so he could take a statement. This did, surprisingly enough, involve snakes. According to Boogie, when the occupant of apartment 107 relocated for three months to the county jail, he'd sublet the place to a man who gave his name as William Smith. While he'd never actually met him, Smith had hired him over the phone at Gert's Tavern, Boogie's home away from home. How the man came to know about him was anybody's guess, but he apparently had gleaned that Boogie was somebody who could be hired for minimum wage, provided the job required no actual work. Smith described himself to Boogie as a traveling salesman and an entrepreneur currently testing several business opportunities in upstate New York. He would likely require Boogie's services for three weeks, though it was possible, if said opportunities panned out, that the employment could last well into June. Smith further explained that he himself would rarely be in residence. He meant to use apartment 107 primarily to store his inventory.

Boogie's duties, as described to him over the phone, could not have been more perfectly suited to his temperament and lack of ambition. He was to sign for packages that would arrive periodically during working hours, Monday through Friday, via UPS. There were rules, however. He was not allowed to have friends over—no problem there, because Boogie didn't have any—nor was he permitted to entertain women, even less of a problem. His wife had left him over a decade ago, and he hadn't had a date or any other encounter with a woman since. In fact, he was not to even answer the door unless the person on the other side of it identified himself as a UPS driver. The packages he signed for were to be placed immediately in the large kitchen refrigerator, the shelves of which, Smith explained, had mostly been removed to make more room. There would be, Smith admitted, one minor inconvenience that couldn't be remedied. Like all the other apartments at the Morrison Arms, 107 had just one bathroom, accessible only through the bedroom, the door to which would be locked at all times. When Boogie needed relief, he would have to go upstairs to his own apartment or, if he didn't feel like climbing the stairs, use the weedy lot out back. These matters would have to be attended to briskly, lest he miss a UPS delivery. Otherwise, he was welcome to watch TV and drink free beer from the well-stocked minifridge that Smith had thoughtfully provided.

Boogie's only other duty was to make sure the large air-conditioning unit in the bedroom window was kept running at all times. (Though the front room had a ceiling fan, it was otherwise uncooled.) Smith explained that the bedroom contained, among other things, temperature-sensitive pharmaceuticals. At least twice a day—once in the morning and again in the afternoon—Boogie was to go outside and make sure the bedroom unit was functioning properly. If for any reason it stopped—a fan belt broke, say, or the building lost power—he was to immediately call the number written on a slip of paper attached to the fridge with a frog magnet. In all probability no one would answer, but he should leave a detailed message. If Smith needed to communicate with Boogie, he'd call him on apartment 107's telephone. When Boogie inquired if they'd meet at some point, William Smith said it was possible but unlikely. If the terms and conditions they'd just discussed were acceptable, he could begin work the following morning.

Boogie hung up half expecting to learn that the whole thing had been a hoax perpetrated by some asshole at Gert's, maybe even Gert himself. Because drinking beer and watching TV were things he'd always paid to do at the tavern, this deal really seemed too good to be true. That very night, though, returning to the Arms, he found an envelope containing a key to apartment 107 in his mailbox, as per his conversation with William Smith, and the following morning there was another that contained half of his first week's pay in advance and in cash.

By nature Boogie was neither curious nor thoughtful nor complex. Politically, he considered himself a libertarian. He disapproved of most laws and all government intrusion. On general principle he didn't like being told what to do or what was good for him. He prided himself on never having to be told to mind his own business. Certainly anyone willing to pay him to drink beer and watch television was entitled to his privacy. It occurred to him, of course, that William Smith might not be his employer's real name and the man probably hadn't been completely forthcoming about his "business." Also that his "inventory" might not be one hundred percent lawful, but what concern was that of his? He wasn't a policeman. Once, toward the end of his first week, Boogie did suffer something akin to misgiving. That afternoon, when the television cut away from an old sitcom he was watching and the commercial didn't come on right away, in the momentary silence that ensued he thought he heard a baby's rattle shaking behind the bedroom door. While he disliked children of all ages, Boogie wasn't sure he approved of leaving an infant alone all day in a locked room. But then he'd thought the whole thing through and came to the reasonable and reassuring conclusion that he must've been mistaken. A baby would cry and make a fuss every time it wanted its nasty diaper changed; it would cry for its bottle. No, that rattle was a figment of his imagination. Or maybe it had come from outside in the corridor.

Though generally laid-back, Boogie was, however, prey to the occasional resentment. That he wasn't allowed to use the toilet rankled him. During the second week of his employment, the weather turned unseasonably hot and the front room was like an oven, even with the ceiling fan on high. Why should the bedroom's AC be off-limits? Besides, locking him out of the bedroom was downright offensive, implying he wasn't trustworthy. Also, though he'd been warned that he might never actually meet William Smith, it was borderline rude that the man hadn't stopped by to introduce himself. Because he clearly was, however briefly, visiting the apartment. The packages Boogie put in the fridge never remained there more than two or three days before being relocated, Boogie assumed, to the bedroom. Every time it looked like Boogie might run out of beer, another case or two would magically appear.

Most days there was at least one delivery. The packages, which varied in size, were mostly flat, rectangular and marked PERISHABLE. One day Boogie signed for a box that was twice the size of the others, and its contents shifted like a half-full water bottle when he took it from the UPS man. Putting the box in the fridge as instructed, Boogie stood before the open door, wondering why, if these goods were indeed perishable, the temperature inside the fridge was set at fifty-five degrees.

The next afternoon, after depositing another package in the fridge, he noticed a long handle—maybe a broom?—in the gap between the fridge and the wall that hadn't caught his attention before. Reaching into the narrow space, he pulled out an odd-looking contraption whose purpose he couldn't immediately divine. At the lower end of the shaft was a bright orange V-grip; at the upper end a set of padded tongs. Sure enough, when you squeezed the handle, the open tongs closed, and relaxing the grip caused them to open again. Obviously, the implement was designed to grab hold of something, but what? An object stored out of reach on a high shelf, perhaps? There wouldn't be much use for such a tool at the Morrison Arms. At five feet seven inches, Boogie could practically touch the ceiling when he stood on his tiptoes. Huh, he thought, that single syllable pretty much exhausting his curiosity. He stuck whatever the fucking thing was back behind the fridge. What difference did it make what it was used for? For that matter, if you yourself weren't storing anything in it, what difference did it make that the fridge was running at a lukewarm temperature? Life was full of such meaningless riddles, and one of Boogie's great skills had always been his ability to ignore anything that might've seemed troubling had he been foolish enough to think about it.

That night, however, upstairs in his own bed, he sat straight up, his disobedient unconscious mind having solved in his sleep the riddle of this bizarre tool. The tongs weren't designed to fetch inanimate objects but to seize something all too animate that was best kept at a safe distance, something that might die if the temperature got too cold and would wake angry if it was too warm. It wasn't a baby rattle he'd heard; it was a snake's. "William Smith" was collecting reptiles, to what purpose Boogie couldn't fathom.

Knowledge was not a state to which he'd ever particularly aspired, much preferring the bliss of ignorance. The realization that the only thing between him and a roomful of snakes was a plywood door seriously undermined his hard-won alcoholic equanimity. Whereas before he'd righteously resented the locked bedroom door, he now checked first thing in the morning to make sure it *was* locked. While he'd seen little purpose in going outside twice *every day* to see if the damn AC was still humming along, he now inspected it hourly. Try as he might, he could no longer get comfortable anywhere in the apartment. Television shows that had always held his attention were suddenly boring. One minute he'd be staring at the screen, and the next he'd be across the room pressing his ear against the bedroom door, straining to hear any stirring or rattling. If he drifted off, he'd awake in a panic, convinced something had just slithered over his feet, and whenever the UPS guy knocked he'd just about leap out of his skin. While in the beginning he liked to polish off at least a case of beer daily, it was now all he could do to drink a mere six-pack, which meant that by the end of the afternoon he was approaching sobriety, a condition he found both unnatural and tiresome. When he tried to eat, solid food instantly liquefied in his stomach and required him to gallop upstairs to his own apartment, and when he rose from the toilet, his sphincter on fire, he'd glimpse his sunken face in the bathroom mirror. He was becoming a wreck. Well, maybe he already was one, but still. As much as he hated the idea of missing all this money and free beer, he'd just have to tell William Smith to find someone else.

The following day, Wednesday, after a sleepless night, Boogie called the number under the frog magnet. No one answered, but the same voice he'd heard earlier came on the answering machine. "I'm not here. Leave a message."

"Mr. Smith," he said, "this is Rolfe Waggengneckt . . . uh, Boogie. I'm sorry, but I can't work for you anymore. After today, you'll have to find a replacement."

After he hung up, the phone rang before he could make it back to the sofa. "Two weeks' notice is customary," said the voice by way of hello.

"You only hired me for three, and I already worked two," Boogie blurted, not unreasonably.

"That still leaves one."

Not knowing what else to do, Boogie decided to come clean. "I know what's in the bedroom."

"The snakes, you mean?" His employer didn't seem alarmed in the least by Boogie's discovery. "Or the guns?"

Guns?

"Or the drugs?"

Drugs?

"The snakes," Boogie clarified. "I'm afraid of them."

"They're in cages."

"They're in my dreams. I can't think about nothing else."

"I'm sorry, but you quitting now is inconvenient."

"I'm sorry."

"I need you through Friday, at least."

"I'm sorry," Boogie repeated.

"How would you like it," the man whispered, "if I dropped by your apartment some night with a guest?"

"A guest?"

"Have you ever noticed how your apartment door doesn't fit flush with the floor?"

Boogie had in fact noticed this, and he broke into a flop sweat.

"As I said, I need you through the end of the week."

"Okay," Boogie said, not wanting William Smith to be visiting his apartment with any guest.

The next morning, Thursday, the phone rang shortly after he arrived in 107. "Is everything good?" the voice wanted to know.

"It's hot," Boogie told him. The thermostat in the front room had already registered ninety, and it wasn't even nine o'clock.

"Turn the ceiling fan on high."

"It is," Boogie said, but the line had already gone dead. Clearly, the only reason William Smith had called was to make sure he'd reported for duty.

The next day, Friday, was even worse, the front room a sauna when he stepped inside. After two nights in a row without sleep, his exhaustion complete, his mind was blank except for ambient dread. He immediately stripped down to his skivvies and took a beer from the minifridge, not to drink but to roll over his forehead and the back of his neck. When he looked around the apartment, something felt different. Had William Smith been there during the night? He checked the fridge. Nope, the UPS box delivered yesterday was still there. And yet, though Boogie had never met the man, his presence was palpable. Could he possibly be in the bedroom with the snakes, spying on him? Ridiculous. Boogie was becoming unhinged.

Clearly, even this early in the morning, the only thing to do was to get drunk. If the alcohol failed to dispel his terror, it would still make these final eight hours pass more quickly. He reminded himself that he was just doing, one final time, what he'd done for the past two weeks without mishap. The reptiles were all safely in cages, a danger to no one. Soon the nightmare would be over. He guzzled a beer, vomited into the sink, drank another. When this one stayed down, he popped a third and turned on the television to a game show with the volume on mute.

By midmorning unwelcome thoughts uncoiled and slithered around in his head. What guarantee did he have that Smith wouldn't telephone that afternoon and demand that he stay on for another week? Given how much Boogie knew about his varied "inventory," could Smith afford to just let him quit and hope he wouldn't rat him out to the cops? What if he was upstairs right now, slipping some serpent under his apartment door? Wouldn't it make more sense to do unto William Smith before William Smith did unto him? If he called the cops, they could be here in a matter of minutes, and his employer would be a wanted man. So Boogie went over to the wall phone and picked up the receiver. At the dial tone, though, he hung up. Paralyzed by indecision, he got himself another beer. When it was empty, he went back to the phone. This time, at the tone he dialed 911, just to make sure it *did* connect to the police station. When the lady there answered, he hung up again and drank another beer, felt a sudden gastrointestinal emergency and bolted upstairs to his apartment, barely making it to the toilet before his bowels exploded. Back downstairs, he went to the phone once more, this time determined to complete the call.

It was then that Murphy's law, which even a libertarian like Boogie was subject to, kicked into gear. Whatever could go wrong did. When he dialed 9, all the lights went out, the TV went silent, the ceiling fan ceased to squeak, the fridge quit humming. The clock on the wall stopped ticking—and along with it, very nearly, his own heart. With the curtains drawn, the room was almost completely dark. In Boogie's addled mind, hitting that 9 and the lights going out were linked by cause and effect. Was his boss so clairvoyant that he knew not only that his employee was about to betray him but also the exact moment the betrayal would occur? Or had he installed a camera somewhere in the front room so he could keep tabs on him? Boogie quickly slammed the phone down and held up his hands in the classic posture of surrender, as if Smith were in the room with him and holding a loaded gun. He held that pose for several minutes, until he began to feel silly. When he heard a siren outside he went over to the front window and peered out from behind the curtain. The world outside looked bizarrely normal. The old black dude was seated in his folding chair like always, waving his little flag at passing cars. *Get a grip,* he said out loud, the sound of his own voice suddenly reassuring. The thing to do was call William Smith and press his claim as a loyal, competent employee, not somebody who'd fink on an employer who had, except for one vague little death threat, treated him very considerately.

Again, the answering machine picked up and the voice said: "I'm not here. Leave a message."

"Mr. Smith? It's Boogie. We just lost power."

From behind the bedroom door, unless this was his own dementia, came a rattle. Could the room possibly be getting warm already?

"What am I supposed to do?" he whimpered. "If you're there, could you please pick up?"

Setting the phone down on the counter, he went over to the bedroom door and put his ear to it. Nothing but silence. Don't knock, he told himself, then knocked. In immediate response, not one rattle but several.

He grabbed the phone. "They're waking up, Mr. Smith. I can hear them in there."

Not just rattles now but, unless he was imagining it, hissing.

"So I called, just like you said," he told the man who wasn't there. "I done everything you asked." Where *was* the guy? The last time, he'd returned Boogie's call right away. Why couldn't he just pick up now and say, *Don't worry, Boogie. I know you did. It's my problem now. You go on over to Gert's and have one from the tap.*

Only when the answering machine's tape cut off did he hang up and return to the bedroom door. The hissing had stopped, and he now heard the soft sounds of creatures waking up restless, of unlidded eyes opening, of triangular heads lifting up, of uncoiling. Of other smaller, terrified things scurrying in their cages and hiding under scraps of newspaper. Also of metal and wire mesh being strained, expanded, tentatively at first, then with greater purpose.

It occurred to Boogie, standing there in his skivvies, that should flight become necessary, he was ill prepared. He'd do well to at least put his trousers on. His shoes. Though, really, this was crazy thinking. As long as there was a locked door between him and these pissed-off reptiles, he was in no danger. That door fit snug to the carpet, and nothing could slither beneath it. Unfortunately, no sooner had he reassured himself of this than he perversely pictured a tiny triangular head pushing through the crease, going rigid when it spotted him, then burrowing forward with renewed purpose.

Grabbing his pants off the back of the kitchen chair, he was frantically trying to pull them on, one leg at a time, when he heard the cage topple over in the bedroom. The sound froze him in position, balanced on one leg, his full attention on the door itself, which he half expected to open despite being locked. But then a terrifying thought occurred to him: *Was* it locked? He'd been in such a state that morning that he hadn't even checked! How could he have been so stupid? This question seemed to answer itself. Because he was an idiot. He'd been one all his life. His wife had told him this many times before cutting her losses and running. There was nothing left to do but prove it again, so instead of pulling up his trousers he hopped over to the bedroom door, one leg in, one leg out. He turned the doorknob to the right, as he'd done so many times in the past, to make sure it was locked. It wasn't, of course, and why *would* it be, Boogie thought with stunning clarity as his weight swung the door inward. Now that he knew what was in there, William Smith had no further reason to lock it up. Boogie's sheer terror would keep him out.

Tangled in his pants and heavy with beer, Boogie tumbled to his knees. The bedroom was dark, illuminated only by the light spilling in from the front room. But he was able to see more than he wanted to. He could make out the outlines of the stacked cages, the slow uncoiling of the dark ropes they contained. And of course the cage that had fallen, its door sprung.

He didn't see the cobra, though, until it stood up.

The Two Rubs

RUB SQUEERS AND HIS WIFE, Bootsie, lived in a ramshackle farm-house on a lonely stretch of two-lane county blacktop west of town where the rents were cheap. When the wind was right, as it was this evening, you could smell the nearby landfill. It was nearly dark by the time Sully pulled into their drive and parked behind their dented, two-tone Subaru. "Stay," he told Rub's namesake, who stood panting beside him in the front seat. The dog sighed mightily but obediently flopped down onto the seat, his chin on his front paws. Having spent much of the day in Miss Beryl's cellar he was anxious to be let loose, Sully could tell, but there was a patch of woods out back of the Squeerses' house where, this close to the dump, he was liable to encounter a skunk. Half an hour from now, with any luck, Sully hoped to be settling onto his favorite barstool at the Horse, not home giving the stupid little shit a tomato-juice bath.

The winter before, Rub had found the poor half-starved creature limping along the icy roadside and brought him home, thinking to keep him. Unfortunately, Bootsie, who easily topped three hundred pounds, was offended by anything skinny, so no dice. A clairvoyant, at least where her husband was concerned, she saw all too clearly that the wretched animal's care and feeding would devolve to her, so she informed Rub that in her house there was a one-mangy-cur limit, leav-ing him to ponder that philosophy's arbitrariness, grapple with its metaphorical implications and finally do the arithmetic. So that's how Sully, whose strong suit wasn't caring for things, had reluctantly taken the extra cur in. The name on his tag was REGGIE, but Sully removed the tag, renamed him and settled in to enjoy the resulting confusion. When both Rubs were around, he liked to issue commands to see if either would obey. When the dog barked, Sully would say, "Quiet, Dummy," causing both dog and man to regard him expectantly, neither sure who was being spoken to, neither wanting to guess wrong, the look on their faces identical. When the human Rub made the mistake of answering, Sully would say, "I wasn't talking to you."

The canine Rub was relatively young in years but old in experience, most of it, Sully suspected, awful. Consequently, this Rub's youth, energy and congenital optimism were in constant conflict with his memories, which dictated extreme caution and, if that wasn't sufficient, flight. After six months of Sully's benign neglect, he still started violently at sudden loud noises, and if his new master forgot and raised his voice, he'd empty his bladder on the spot. The dog seemed to love him, though, and when Rub wasn't peeing on things, Sully was able to return his dumb affection. Until recently he'd let Rub tag along wherever he was going, including Hattie's, but the animal had recently picked up a genital parasite somewhere and had taken to chewing on his dick. Unsurprisingly, the sight of his bloody, masticated little pud put people off their feed. When he was on the premises, you couldn't give away link sausages.

Even with the sun down, it was too hot to leave Rub in the truck with the windows up, so he leaned across and rolled down the one on the passenger side. "Stay," he repeated. "You hear me?" Because Rub was eyeing this potential escape route with almost human longing. "If I come outside and you're not in this truck, I'll leave you here for the coyotes." Which also frequented the dump.

Rub sighed again, even more mightily this time. Sully could read the thought bubble over his head: *If you don't want me to jump out, why open the window?*

"Don't pee in here, either."

Climbing out of the truck, Sully thought he heard a low mewling nearby, but when he paused to listen, he couldn't hear anything. Had an animal been struck by a car and crawled off into the trees or under the house to die? He stood there, waiting for it to start up again, though the only sound borne in on the hot breeze was that of interstate traffic. Halfway up the porch steps he heard scrabbling and turned to see his dog standing on the seat now, front paws on the open window frame, in launch position. "Rub!" Sully called. "I swear to God, if you're not in that truck when I come back out, I'm gonna grab that shovel out of the back and beat you with it." Apparently Rub took this threat seriously, because he whimpered and disappeared back inside the cab. Probably pissing all over the seat, Sully thought ruefully. He hadn't meant to shout.

From somewhere—closer now?—the same mewling resumed. Had the wind shifted? Or was the sound coming from under the porch? Sully considered going back down the steps and peering underneath, but the thought of shining eyes peering back at him out of the darkness wasn't terribly appealing, so when the sound stopped again, he figured to hell with it.

He'd been hoping, as he always did when he dropped by the Squeerses' house, that he'd find Rub there alone, but the Subaru in the drive, its engine still ticking, meant Bootsie, whose car it was, had arrived home from work shortly before, and indeed it was she, clutching a fistful of junk mail, who answered his knock. She was still in her uniform, her thinning brown hair still clutched in the hairnet she wore to serve food in the hospital cafeteria.

"You," she said, seeing who it was.

"Yup," Sully agreed. "Sorry to disappoint."

But she'd already turned away, leaving him to come inside and close the screen door behind him. "I keep hoping it'll be Harrison Ford, but it never is."

"Next time I'll bring my whip. Where's Dummy?"

"I thought he was with you. Didn't I just hear you threaten to beat him with a shovel?"

"Nah, that was the dog," he said, which seemed to satisfy her. "I haven't seen your husband. I waited for him at Hattie's, but he never turned up."

"I thought you two were taking down that branch today," she

said, tossing the junk mail into a wicker basket the size of a bassinette that must have contained about a month's worth. Everything in the Squeerses' house overflowed, the sink with dirty dishes, the garbage can with smelly trash, the living room sofa with the romance novels Bootsie borrowed by the gross from the library. According to Rub, she read at least one a night.

"You're right, we were," Sully confessed. Last night, just before leaving the Horse, they'd agreed to meet here at noon. Sully was to bring his ladder. He'd even thrown it in the back of the truck when he got home, but by morning he'd forgotten his promise. Even noticing it there that morning had failed to jog his memory. Much as he hated to admit it, such lapses were becoming routine. Had Rub spent the whole afternoon waiting for him? Where was he now?

Bootsie, head cocked, was regarding him dubiously over the rim of her reading glasses. He'd paused in the dining room to lean on a chair. "What's with that?" she wanted to know.

"With what?"

"You're breathing like you just ran a marathon."

Not quite, but close. Four little porch steps. Heart thumping in his chest like a sledgehammer. "I'll be all right in a minute."

"Are you like this all the time now?"

"Nah, it comes and goes. Tomorrow I'll wake up fine." He hoped.

"You still smoking?"

"I can't remember the last time I bought a pack of cigarettes," he told her.

"Okay, but that's not what I asked. You think you're talking to somebody who's never bummed a smoke?"

No surprise that she hadn't gone for his head fake. He *had* pretty much given up cigarettes during the day, but at night, out at the Horse, he'd cadge a few from Jocko or Carl Roebuck. "No," he told her, "but I might be talking to somebody who should mind her own business."

"Yeah?" she said, fixing him with her trademark stare.

"I didn't say I *was*," he clarified. "Just that I might be."

She held his gaze a moment longer, then let him off the hook. "Men," she said, causing Sully to wonder—and not for the first time—why so many women deemed him the personification of the whole infuriating male gender, an attitude he found it particularly hard to swallow coming from Bootsie and Ruth, given the men they were married to.

"I gotta get out of this uniform," she said, heading up the stairs. "It's rubbed me raw everywhere."

He didn't care to contemplate this chafing. With Bootsie, everywhere covered a lot of territory. In the kitchen, he sat down heavily in the only chair at the dinette that wasn't piled high with crap, and after a moment his breathing returned to normal. One day, possibly quite soon, it wouldn't. He knew that. What he couldn't decide was how to feel about it. He still had three or four good days to every bad one, but his VA cardiologist said that ratio wouldn't hold. Four would become three, then two, then one. Eventually they'd all be like today. That was assuming things happened slowly, which they might not.

From upstairs came a groan of pure pleasure, and before Sully could prevent it he was visited by an unwanted image of Bootsie stepping out of her uniform and examining the day's abrasions. How often did he think about sex? Too fucking often.

"What's this I heard about the old mill falling down?" she hollered, her voice penetrating the ceiling.

"Just the wall nearest the street," Sully called upward.

"Yeah, but how does something like that happen?" she asked.

So, speaking through the ceiling, he told her what he'd learned over the course of the afternoon, how Carl, meaning to shore everything up again later, had severed the building's collar ties and floor joists, leaving the long wall that bordered the sidewalk free to topple into the road on top of Roy Purdy, who conveniently happened to be driving by. Sully, who'd spent the morning daydreaming pleasantly about how he might murder Roy, couldn't decide whether or not to feel guilty. If he hadn't goaded Roy with his fake want ads, delaying his departure by a minute or two, the man likely would've passed through the area before the wall collapsed. Had Sully's idle woolgathering somehow been mistaken for a prayer and answered? God's answering prayers now? Since when?

Bootsie came back into the kitchen, clad now in one of the brightly colored muumuus she favored, beneath the fabric of which, to Sully's eye, far too much violent pendulous motion was going on. "What do you want to bet they'll be saying Carl did it on purpose, for the insurance?"

"They're already saying it."

"You think he did?"

"I wouldn't put it past him," he admitted, "but no, I doubt it." Mostly because whenever Carl had dumb ideas, he ran them by Sully first.

"You want a beer?" Bootsie said, opening the fridge.

"No, thanks."

"Good. We're out." Of that and just about everything else, judging by the empty shelves. Just how badly were they struggling financially, Sully wondered. Rub had steady work at the cemetery now, and Bootsie had her food service job at the hospital, but neither was overpaid. He had no idea what they spent their money on, but Rub always seemed to be broke.

When Bootsie pulled out the drawer under the phone book, Sully quickly turned away, because that, he happened to know, was where she kept her diabetes kit. The last time he made the mistake of watching her sink the needle into her belly, right through the fabric of her muu-muu, he'd nearly passed out. In fact, just knowing what was going on behind his back caused sweat to bead on his forehead. "Tell me when you're done."

She chortled, clearly enjoying his discomfort. "For such a tough guy, you sure are squeamish."

"If the Second World War had been fought with hypodermic needles, I'd have deserted in basic training."

"Well, you can turn around. I'm all done," she said. He waited, though, not trusting her, until he heard the drawer close again. When he finally ventured to glance, she was surveying the kitchen with the air of someone who was repulsed by the sight without being motivated in the least to do anything about it. "I don't suppose you know how to fix a dishwasher."

"You ask me that every time I'm here," he told her. "The answer's still no."

"Maybe I could get Carl to come over and detonate the whole kitchen," she said. "Just blow it to smithereens and start over." When

Sully didn't offer an opinion, she regarded him through narrowed eyes. "Don't say it," she advised.

"I wasn't going to say anything."

"Yeah, you were. You were going to say that a month from now I'd be right back in the same place."

"Not true," he said. A *week* from now was more like it.

"I'm not stupid."

"Did I say you were?"

"No, I guess you didn't," she answered. "Must've been something I heard in my head." Going over to the window, she peered out into the darkness. "You ever hear things in your head, Sully?"

All the time, Dolly, he was about to say, but suddenly she said, "Son of a bitch," with her voice so full of genuine wonder that he joined her at the window. There, lying on the ground, its outline unmistakable even in the dark, was the tree limb he and Rub were supposed to have lopped off that afternoon. Had the fucking thing fallen of its own accord? No, lying there at the base of the tree was the chain saw Rub had rented the day before. Had he gotten tired of waiting for Sully and borrowed a ladder somewhere else? Their nearest neighbor lived a good half mile away, too far to walk carrying a ladder, even an aluminum one. Had he called a tree-pruning service? Highly unlikely. Not after renting the saw. Besides, Bootsie would whack his peenie if he paid somebody else to do a job he'd promised to take care of himself. It was possible he'd called his cousins, who owned Squeers Refuse Removal, or maybe they'd driven by en route to the dump and offered to lend a hand, but he doubted it. Rub wasn't on good-enough terms with his cousins to ask a favor, and they weren't the sort to offer unasked. Sully himself was, so far as he knew, Rub's only friend.

"That's my dimwit husband for you," Bootsie said, shaking her head in disbelief. "It takes him a month to finally do what I ask him and cut the freakin' branch down, then he just walks away like the job's done. What do you want to bet it's still sitting right there a month from now?"

It was on the tip of Sully's tongue to say *Like all these dirty dishes? Like that tower of pizza boxes?* but he was wise enough to hold it. "Nah, we'll cart it off tomorrow, I promise," he assured her.

Her purse was on the counter, and she pulled out a ten-dollar bill, then stuffed it into a glass on the sink that was crusty with orange juice. "My last ten bucks," she said, holding up the glass as Exhibit A, "says this time tomorrow that tree limb's still right there."

Which pissed him off. "If you think I won't take your money—"

"You won't *win* it, is what I think," she told him, the picture of confidence, and her sly, put-your-money-where-your-mouth-is grin annoyed him sufficiently that he peeled two fives from his money clip. "Easy pickin's," she said, slipping the bills into the juice glass and setting it on the windowsill behind the teetering pyramid of dishes in the sink. "I know who I'm betting with. I just wish there was something else for us to bet on."

"In that case I'll get out of your hair before you think of it," he told her, heading for the door. "If Dummy shows up, tell him I'm sorry I stood him up. I'll be down at the Horse for a bit."

He hadn't made it as far as the living room when she said, "I got a question for you." When he turned to face her, he saw that her eyes, dry a second ago, were now full—indeed spilling over.

Jesus, he thought. Not this. Yet again he'd allowed himself to be bushwhacked by a woman's unhappiness. For this to happen, over and over, he *had* to be some kind of stupid. It had been going on his whole life, starting with his mother, the poor woman. Being married to Big Jim Sullivan, she came by her despair honestly, God knew. Though Sully wasn't its cause, he'd nevertheless taken her grief to heart, thereby learning at an early age that responsibility for feminine heartbreak would somehow attach itself to the male closest to hand. That said, he would end up far from blameless in this respect. It wasn't long after his mother was in the ground that Sully started disappointing women in his own right. One after another, actually, no stopping that runaway train once it got pointed downhill. Sometimes he was the sole source of disenchantment (as with Vera, his ex-wife), other times just a contributing factor (as with Ruth). The thing to do, once you saw it coming, was make tracks, but too often you didn't. They had a way of sneaking up on you, these disappointed women, dry eyed one minute, leaking prodigiously the next. And frozen in place, like Sully was now, you waited patiently for them to explain your part in their sorrow.

"What?" he said, because he had to say something and was, like always, curious as to what he'd done wrong this time.

"How come you never invite me out?"

He cocked his head at her. "You're a married woman, Dolly."

"The two of you, I mean. You and him. You're down there most nights, drinking beer. How come you never invite me to come along?"

"I had no idea you wanted to," he said. A lame response, but he was still stuck on *you and him*. When, exactly, had his best friend's wife become their shared responsibility?

"I don't," she said, wiping her eyes on the sleeve of her muumuu. "That place is depressing."

"Well?"

"A girl likes to be asked occasionally, is what I'm saying."

Huh, Sully thought. *A girl*, unsure why he should be so surprised that this was how Bootsie thought of herself. Because she wasn't one anymore? Because she was too overweight and unattractive? What bearing did mere facts have when it came to how you saw yourself? If Sully never thought of himself as seventy, even on days like today when he felt eighty, why shouldn't a lonely married woman who read romance novels every night think of herself as a girl?

"Okay," he said. "Maybe next time, if you feel like—"

"I just said I didn't want to, all right?"

They faced each other for a long moment until Rub began barking outside. *Good dog!*

Sully coughed. "I'm sorry—"

"Go," Bootsie told him, making one hand into a whisk broom and brushing him toward the door. "Forget I said anything, okay? It must be the heat . . ."

"It *is* brutal," Sully allowed.

At the front door she turned on the porch light and followed him out onto the steps. To Sully's amazement, Rub was still in the truck, but Sully's reappearance drove him into a frenzy of improbable laps inside the cab, as if he were sharing the small space with a vicious ferret. One moment he appeared on the dash, the next he was gone completely, the whole truck quivering from his idiotic exertions.

"Jesus," Bootsie said, shaking her head. "Look at that crazy little fucker."

"Rub!" Sully called to him. "Knock it off!" The dog whined once and went still.

Sully strongly suspected that something further was expected of him where Bootsie was concerned, some act of kindness or understanding of which he was incapable, but before he could think of some other lame thing she said, "Pizza. I just decided that's what I'm hungry for."

"They deliver out here in the boonies?"

"You have to order at least a large."

"All right, then," Sully said, everything settled now. A minute ago they'd been faced with a thorny existential dilemma, possibly spiritual in nature, only to have it unexpectedly redefined as an urge that only a delivery pizza could satisfy.

As Sully made his way over to the truck, though, the screen door slammed, and a moment later there was a loud crash. His first thought was that Bootsie had tripped and fallen, but then he realized that the pyramids of dishes in the kitchen must've collapsed. He heard Bootsie say, "Fine. *Terrific.* You think I fucking care?" It took him a moment to realize it was the mess she was talking to. At some point she'd have to separate what was broken from what was merely gross, toss the shards of glass and ceramic into the trash and return whatever could be used another time into the sink. But not tonight. *That* was what she was announcing to the cosmos. Sully thought about going back inside and offering to help clean up, then reconsidered. Granted permission to flee, you'd be a fool not to.

When he opened the truck's door and the dome light came on, the scene that presented itself shouldn't have surprised him but still did. Rub, having backed up against the passenger-side door as far as he could, now stood quaking with fear, his canine knees knocking together like a cartoon dog's. A small drop of urine glistened at the tip of his bright red penis, presumably the very last drop in the entire dog. The seat was soaked, as were the dash and steering wheel and even the windshield.

Sully turned on the wipers to confirm that the moisture was on the inside, and it was. "Rub," he said quietly, in case he was wrong about the dog being empty. "What the hell is *wrong* with you?"

Then there it was again, nearby, that same goddamn mewling. He thought about going back to the house to alert Bootsie that something sick or injured, probably a raccoon, had crawled under the house. Maybe Rub had seen or sensed it there and that's what had driven him batshit in the truck. But then the porch light went out and the mewling stopped, so Sully decided to let it go. The other Rub was probably at the Horse already, waiting for him to show up, and he'd mention it to him then. Tomorrow, after they'd taken care of the tree branch, they could shine a flashlight under the porch and see what had taken up residence there. From where he sat, his keys dangling in the ignition, Sully could just make out the shape of the branch where it lay on the ground. Odd that Rub hadn't sectioned the fallen limb, a five-minute job, tops. Had the chain saw fritzed? Was that why he left it sitting out in the open for someone to steal? Rub wasn't normally careless with tools.

On the other hand, life was full of mysteries, none more perplexing than human nature itself. His conversation with Bootsie, on top of the earlier one with Ruth, had left him feeling both exhausted and useless. Maybe Ruth was right and he should find a beach somewhere. He'd always wanted to, at least back when he couldn't afford it. Why not go someplace now, when he could? Tonight, he wasn't even sure he wanted to drive out to the Horse, though he knew he would. Turning the key, he put the truck in reverse and backed out. When the headlights swept over the felled branch, Sully imagined, for some reason, that Rub was lying dead beneath it, which would account not only for his absence but also the fact that he hadn't finished the job. This morbid scenario dovetailed nicely with Sully's growing conviction that ever since his luck turned, it was his friends who were paying the price. All that bad karma had to go somewhere. Except, no. Of course Rub wasn't lying beneath the branch. He would've been holding the chain saw when the limb fell, not standing beneath it. Sully turned on his high beams though, just to be sure, before backing on out. When the headlights caught the base of the tree, the length of rope attached to the handle of the chain saw registered in Sully's brain, but he was out in the road and shifting the vehicle into drive before the fragmentary visual and auditory evidence cohered. Even so, he had to sit there, engine idling, for a good minute until he could make himself believe it.

After jerking the truck back into the driveway, he switched off the ignition again and reached across Rub for the flashlight he kept in the glove box. Fearing the batteries might be dead, he tested it on the dog, who looked away, as if embarrassed by where all this was leading. "You already figured this out, didn't you," Sully said, and Rub didn't deny it. "All right, then. Let's go get him down."

Eager as the dog had been to get out of the truck before, he seemed reluctant to now, but he obeyed his second command and scooted down off the seat and trotted over to the base of the tree, Sully following, his flashlight playing at the trunk, to which, he now saw, several scraps of wood had been nailed, a makeshift ladder. "Hey, Rub," he said when the beam found his friend, sitting with his back to the trunk on what remained of the limb he'd sawed off, who knew how many hours ago. Even in the dark, Sully could see his friend's eyes were swollen from crying. "What're you doing up there?"

"Guh-guh-guh," Rub began, but quickly gave up.

"Go away?" Sully guessed.

"Yeah, go away," he said. For some reason Rub was always able to say whatever had just been stuck in the back of his throat once Sully himself said the words, as if he knew how to say it in German or French, just not English. If Sully guessed wrong, though, Rub's struggle would continue.

"Okay," Sully said, "but how long do you plan on staying up there?"

"Fuh-fuh-fuh—"

"Forever?"

"Yeah, forever."

"That's not a very good plan, Rub."

The other Rub barked, evidently agreeing.

"In fact, it's even dumber than climbing up there by yourself in the first place."

Difficult though it was to credit, Sully could now see the whole skein of events. Rub, fed up with waiting, finally nailing those wood scraps to the trunk; then climbing up. No doubt he'd attached one end of the rope to his belt after tying the chain saw to the other end so he could hoist it up. Probably he'd hoped he could sit or stand on the branch below the one he meant to saw off, which from the ground might've looked possible. Once up in the tree, though, he would've realized it wasn't. If he sat on the lower limb, he couldn't quite reach the one above; and to *stand* on it he'd need three hands—the first to steady himself against the trunk and the other two to operate the chain saw. Up there, he'd have seen that his sole option was to sit on the branch he was going to saw off, with his back pressed against the trunk. (Even Rub wasn't dumb enough to sit on the severed part that was about to fall off.) Only then, after the limb had dropped—okay, sure, Sully was hypothesizing here—and he lowered the chain saw down to the ground by means of the rope, did it occur to Rub that he was now stuck. With nothing to grab on to, he couldn't rise from his sitting position. Without the branch now lying on the ground, he couldn't lean forward and rotate around to face the trunk. Nor, with his back to it, could he lower himself down to the next branch and from there to the nearest rung of the makeshift ladder.

"Yeah?" Rub was saying. "Well, go fuh-fuh-fuh—"

"Fuck myself?"

"Yeah, fuck yourself."

"Hey," Sully said. "Don't blame me. You did this to yourself."

"You wuh-wuh-wuh—"

"I know. I was supposed to come help you, but I forgot. I'm sorry."

The consequence of this apology, of course, Sully might've predicted. Rub began crying again, that same mewling sound he hadn't recognized before as human sorrow. Not wanting to witness it, Sully turned off the flashlight. "Stay, Rub," he told the dog, before heading back to the truck for the ladder.

Human Rub's voice followed him from the tree. "Where the fuh-fuh-fuh-fuck am I gonna go?"

"I wasn't talking to you," Sully told him.

Sock Drawer

"WHAT DO YOU *mean* no snake?" she wanted to know.

Raymer, groggy, was sitting in the middle of his office sofa, his hands tented over his boxers. He'd worn briefs his whole life until he disrobed in front of Becka that first time and she'd reacted to them with startled revulsion. "Well," she said, "*that's* going to have to change." Apparently, it was an iron-clad policy: she dated only men who wore boxers. His sleeveless undershirts had to go as well. He hadn't really minded switching to boxers, though they took some getting used to, given how they bunched up and gapped at the fly, which was why he'd tented his hands over them now. What did it mean that he hadn't gone back to briefs now that Becka was gone? The sad truth was that during their short tenure together he'd learned to defer to Becka in most matters. She'd switched him from Colgate to Crest, from Listerine to Scope, from Arrid to Right Guard. Free now to return to his own preferences, he discovered that they'd come to match. Maybe that was what marriage meant, except that in theirs it had been a one-way street. He couldn't think of a single behavior of Becka's that he had altered in the slightest. But perhaps that was because there was so little he'd *wanted* to change, whereas she'd evidently viewed him as a fixer-upper from the start, structurally sound, the sort of property you wouldn't mind owning *after* you'd completed all the necessary renovations. First, though, you'd have to gut it, which was pretty much how Raymer felt by the end. As if the overhaul of his person was coming in over budget, and the person footing the bills was having serious second thoughts.

To judge by her expression, the woman standing over him in her off-duty attire—tight jeans and a halter top, in all rather provocative—agreed. It was as if by studying him she could envision all the improvements Becka had tried to make and was calculating how much work remained to be done, what it would cost to finish a job so poorly begun or whether it would make better sense to start over and just gut him again. How was it possible that two women with so little in common had come to share such an unflattering assessment?

"I *mean,*" he told Charice, his embarrassment giving way to annoyance, "no . . . fucking . . . snake."

He and Justin had gone through every apartment in the Morrison Arms, including Raymer's, plus the common areas. No snake, no trace. Tomorrow, when electricity was restored, it would have to be done again, this time, blessedly, without Raymer's assistance. Justin had called in additional animal-control personnel from Albany, but even so he wasn't very hopeful. It was possible the cobra had slithered into a vent or behind a wall, though it wasn't likely. Thanks to the heat wave, all the windows that didn't have air conditioners in them had been flung open in hopes of capturing a stray breeze, and the two rear doors on opposite ends of the central corridor had been propped open as well. The snake was long gone, probably into the weedy lot out back. Once it was daylight it, too, would have to be searched. Until then there wasn't much to be done. The Squeers brothers and the town's two or three other private trash collectors had already been warned to be careful when upending garbage cans into their trucks. Meanwhile, until the authorities were certain there was no danger, the Arms was off-limits to residents, all of whom had been given vouchers for a night's stay at one of the inexpensive motels out by the interstate, a significant upgrade as far as they were concerned.

Raymer himself had a voucher but for the time being had opted for his office sofa. Not wanting anyone to know he was there, he'd snuck into the station through the back door. Dead on his feet, he'd had just enough energy left to shed his sweat-soaked uniform before collapsing onto the couch, too exhausted to go over and make sure the door was locked. So Charice had found him there, enjoying a sleep so profound and dreamless that it bordered on oblivion, the kind of slumber only a very cruel person would interrupt. In fact, the kind of person who, if she was to be believed, had a butterfly tattooed on her rear end.

"What are you even *doing* here?" he asked.

"I work here, same as you. What're you saying, exactly? It got away, or there was no snake to begin with?"

The former, he assured her, though the question was understandable. Mass hysteria had been Raymer's own first thought. Somebody yells *Snake!* and everybody sees scores of them all over. But that was before he and Justin entered apartment 107. It hadn't taken Justin long to suss out what was going on in there. No pots, pans, plates, bowls or silverware in the kitchen. Just a ratty couch facing the small television in the living room. A minifridge stocked with cheap beer under the window. The larger kitchen fridge, with most of its shelving removed, had been completely repurposed. Justin had noted the temperature setting and removed the one flat box, holding it out to Raymer and saying, "Snake?" When the shape of the box altered subtly before Raymer's eyes and he took a quick, involuntary step backward, Justin grinned and returned it to the fridge. "No doubt about it, this guy's in business."

The guy being "William Smith," according to Boogie Waggengneckt, who'd never met him and claimed to have learned only the day before what was in the UPS packages he'd been signing for. Nobody else at the Arms seemed to have met the guy, either.

The bedroom in 107 was heavily curtained, so dark inside that Raymer instinctively flipped the switch, which of course did nothing at all. There was just enough light from the front room for them to make out the cages stacked on the bed and along one wall. When Justin turned on his flashlight, there was a chorus of rattles and hisses, but it was the dark, relentless, ropy movement that caused Raymer to back into the front room, his stomach roiling with rancid Twelve Horse ale. When Justin emerged a few minutes later, carefully shutting the door behind him, he was carrying a blue plastic pail of the sort you'd take to the beach for a small child. This one was full of handguns. "Not just the snake business, either," Justin said, handing them to Raymer, who examined several of them. The serial numbers, no surprise, had all been filed off. "You'll find drugs as well, I can almost guarantee it."

It had taken them and two additional officers, together with the apartment house's manager, three nerve-racking hours to complete the search for the missing snake, after which Raymer had ordered the Arms locked down and the entire complex to be surrounded with crime-scene tape.

"Did I hear you right?" Justin asked him when they were back outside in the parking lot. Justin was still in his waders, leaning against his van and smoking a cigarette. "You *live* here?"

Raymer, deeply embarrassed, winced. "I had no idea." What one of his neighbors was up to, he meant, though it was possible Justin had merely been commenting on the fact that the place was a sty and not the sort of place a police chief would call home.

"Well, you wouldn't, necessarily. These guys don't linger. They set up shop, do their business and get the fuck out of Dodge. Three, four weeks, max."

"You've run into this before?"

"Heard about it. Mostly down south."

"Why an apartment house instead of someplace out in the sticks?"

"You'd have to ask them, but cost is a factor, I imagine. Plus rural folks tend to be nosy. Observant. Welfare types mind their own damn business. They got too many problems of their own to worry about the neighbors. If it hadn't been for the power outage, you probably never would've known this guy was even here."

"Explain the fridge, then? And the air-conditioning?"

"Below sixty degrees, snakes basically hibernate. With the AC running, they'd wake up every couple of days, drink some water, go back to sleep. You wouldn't even need to feed them."

"Whereas in ninety-five-degree heat?"

"Wide awake. Hungry. Pissed off."

None of it made any sense to Raymer. "Okay, but why?"

"There's a growing market for exotic reptiles. Boas don't make bad pets, actually. Gotta remember to feed 'em, though. One lady down in

Florida drove to the market for milk. Gone, like, ten minutes. Came home to this very fat snake in the baby's crib."

Raymer considered sharing this story with Charice now. Maybe she'd go away and leave him alone.

"So what you're saying is, it got away?" she wanted to know, still obsessed by the cobra. "Got away where? What if it bites some little kid?"

"The kid dies."

"That's cold."

"We searched until it was pitch dark, okay? What do you want from me?" He intended this to be a rhetorical question, but he could tell she didn't get it. "Please? Pretty please? Could we continue this conversation after I get dressed?" He pointed at his office chair, over which he'd draped his pants. "If you won't go away, could you at least hand me those?"

She did, reluctantly, making forceps of her thumb and index finger. Could you blame her? The waistband was still soggy with perspiration. He'd have to drop the whole uniform off at the dry cleaners.

"We should be doing something, is all I'm saying," Charice told him, backing off a little. "Serve and protect, right?"

"I wish we'd settled on that instead of *We're not happy until you're not happy*."

"There you go putting in that extra 'not' again."   .

Rising, he turned his back to her, pulled on his trousers and immediately felt better, as only a man who'd never felt comfortable in his God-given body will. "Volunteers are going door-to-door in the neighborhood," he assured her, "warning people not to let their children play outside until it's found."

"What if they don't find it?"

"According to Justin, it'll probably just slither off into the woods and die of starvation. Or cross the road and get run over by a car."

"Probably, huh?"

"Or freeze to death when the weather gets cold."

"It's the beginning of summer. We're in a heat wave."

Bending over to tie his shoes, Raymer suddenly felt dizzy, and when he straightened up the room started spinning. He had to grab the corner of the desk to keep from keeling over.

"Chief?" Charice said, her voice sounding very far off.

"I'm okay," he said, blinking her back into focus, his equilibrium slowly returning. "Just a little woozy."

"When was the last time you ate?"

Good question. He'd skipped breakfast and had had no appetite after what'd happened at Hilldale. "Yesterday?"

"No wonder," she said. "Okay, then. You're coming home with me."

"Umm . . ."

Her eyes narrowed. "What's that mean, 'umm'?"

"I mean, there's a department rule against fraternizing."

"Don't worry, slick. I got my own rules about that. What we're talkin' about is food, not funny business. My damn fool brother was supposed to come over, but he's too upset over his baby got scratched. So I got a whole fridge full of food and nobody to help me eat it."

"Really?" Though still faint, he *was* hungry.

"Fried chicken. Collard greens. Black-eyed peas. Grits. Watermelon for dessert."

"We'll have to stop by the Arms so I can change."

"Hold on a minute," she said. "You believed me just now?"

"Umm." He felt himself flush darkly. By not picking up on her joke, he'd managed to insult her. "I'm sorry, Charice. I've lived right here in Bath my whole life. When it comes to black people, I know you and Jerome. And Mr. Hynes," he added, remembering the old man.

"And you think Jerome would eat a single collard green?"

"I don't know. I just wish . . ."

She waited.

He swallowed hard, aware that whatever he said next would probably be a mistake, yet another opportunity for his favorite cocktail: two parts humiliation, one part bitter regret, blend until smooth. Drink up. After all, it had been that kind of day. About as bad as any he could remember since the one when Becka came downstairs like a Slinky. He felt his eyes fill with tears. "I wish," he stumbled, thinking as much about his dead wife as the woman he was now speaking to, "that where women are concerned I didn't feel like a complete fool every minute of my life."

He half expected Charice to tell him, as Becka surely would have, that the solution to that problem was simple: stop behaving like one. Instead, she just held his gaze for a long moment and said, "Lamb chops. Jerome's favorite. And salad. You like lamb chops?"

"I do."

"You know how to light a fire?"

"If you mean charcoal, sure."

"Chief?" she said. "Could I say something?"

"Have I ever prevented you from speaking your mind?"

"This is kind of personal."

"It's all been kind of personal, Charice."

"You gotta stop worrying so much about being wrong."

This was true, of course. He'd known that much for a very long time. Back when he was a boy, he'd imagined the remedy was to stop *being* wrong. Being right would lead to the kind of self-confidence that other people seemed to achieve so effortlessly. The better solution, according to his mother, was to quit caring so much. But how? Neither she nor anybody else had been able to help him with that part.

"I mean, being wrong isn't such a big deal," Charice was saying. "We're all wrong about a hundred times a day."

"I'm wrong a hundred times before breakfast."

"For instance, I've been wrong about you from the start." Then, when he didn't respond, she said, "Aren't you going to ask how?"

"I'm sorry?"

"Are you even listening to me?"

No, he hadn't been. Not really. He'd been listening to himself. Trapped, as usual, in the maze of Douglas Raymer's thoughts, with no exit. He scrolled back.

"How were you wrong about me, Charice?"

"Now I don't know if I should even tell you."

"But you're going to. We both know that. You've never not told me something you wanted me to know."

"That's true, but I could tell you tomorrow instead of now." Her hand was on the door and she was smiling again, even more broadly this time.

"Tell me, Charice. I'm sure it's something I need to know."

She lowered her gaze to belt level. "Those shorts. Something very wrong there. I never would've pegged you for a boxers man."

HER AGED CIVIC wasn't spacious, but at least the passenger seat had been pushed back as far as it would go. Until now, Raymer hadn't given much thought to Charice's private life, though it was suggestive, surely, that the seat's default mode had apparently been determined by her long-legged brother and not some boyfriend. And Friday nights, when another young woman might have been going out on a date or drinking happy-hour margaritas with girlfriends, she'd been planning on cooking dinner for Jerome. It stood to reason, he supposed. It couldn't be easy for a young black woman here. Who would she go out with in conservative, lily-white Bath? Her brother—tall, handsome, well dressed and well spoken—wouldn't lack for social opportunity in Schuyler Springs. A college town, its demographic downstate, liberal, hip, urban. Charice might've had an easier time of it over there, though Raymer doubted it. White men, at least in his experience, might be attracted to a good-looking black woman but were much less likely to date her than a black man was to date a white woman. Would Raymer himself have asked Charice out if he hadn't been married when they met, and if he hadn't been her boss, and if she wasn't always busting his balls and threatening to sue him for job-related offenses? Okay, that was too many "ifs" to work through with any confidence. He *had* been married and he *was* her boss and she *did* bust his balls morning, noon and night, and most of the time she seemed at least half serious about suing him.

And anyway, maybe this was all a crock. What did he really know about her? She lived in Bath, but maybe she partied in Schuyler. Maybe she had a date every night. Maybe half the eligible men in town had seen her butterfly tattoo. What did it say about him that he assumed she had no social life? That supper at home with her brother on Friday nights was something she looked forward to, the high point of her week? Did the fact that she'd invited her middle-aged, depressed honky boss over to eat Jerome's lamb chops suggest that despondency had set in? Possibly. But wasn't it also possible that, while he was busy pitying her, she was already pitying him? If he wasn't careful, he'd find out.

"There's a flashlight in the glove compartment," she said when they pulled into the empty parking lot at the Morrison Arms. Except for a single streetlight farther up the block and Gert's, which must've had a backup generator, the street was pitch black. On a normal Friday night, that dive would've been packed, its raucous crowd spilling out onto the sidewalk, but not tonight. Further testimony, apparently, to just how much power an escaped cobra could bring to bear on the collective human imagination.

Opening the Honda's glove box, Raymer couldn't help smiling at the contrast between Charice's reassuring clutter and her brother's obsessive neatness. "Did you know Jerome actually special ordered an owner's manual to his thirty-five-year-old car?"

Charice sighed and said, "Poor Jerome," her voice rich with what sounded like genuine pity, though Raymer couldn't quite gauge its extent. Did she pity her brother generally, because he was Jerome, or just today, undone as he was by the attack on his pride and joy.

"What's wrong with him, anyway?"

"Wrong?" Suspicious now. Protective, too. He reminded himself that they were twins.

"Why would he think I'd key his car? Can you explain that to me?"

"I could try," she said, "but the only real explanation for Jerome is Jerome. Don't be long," she added when he got out.

He didn't blame her for being nervous. In broad daylight this parking lot was no place for a woman alone. Tonight, the lot empty, the two-story building encircled by police tape, a lethal serpent slithering somewhere in the vicinity, was enough to give anybody the willies. Aware that Charice was watching him, he did his best to imitate nonchalance as he ducked under the yellow tape and entered the building. In the black stairwell that led up to his second-floor apartment, he shivered despite the still-oppressive heat. Though every apartment here had been carefully searched only hours ago, the fact that they hadn't found it didn't mean the snake wasn't in here somewhere. Or so it seemed just then. Sweeping the flashlight's beam over the stairs, he nevertheless paused every few steps to listen for hissing. In the dark his other senses were magnified, including, unfortunately, his sense of smell. Who, he asked himself, would urinate in an unventilated stairwell in the middle of a heat wave?

Unlocking his apartment, he pushed the door open slowly, directing the flashlight beam along the perimeter of the floor, looking for movement, half surprised when there wasn't any. The Arms had a serious roach problem, and despite Raymer's repeated, aggressive spraying of his apartment's every recess, the silverfish, centipedes and assorted creepy-crawlies that lived in them all continued to thrive and multiply. When he got up to pee in the middle of the night, the bathroom light sent them scurrying into drains and behind cracked tiles. Normally enough to make your skin crawl, this actually would've been welcome now, a signal that the status quo, while disgusting, was still in force. Did exotic reptiles *eat* cockroaches, he wondered. Had the cobra managed to accomplish in a matter of hours what his dogged spraying had not? This put him in mind of Justin's story—almost certainly apocryphal—of the woman who came home to find a suspiciously fat boa constrictor in her baby's crib. Would Raymer find the cobra curled up in the middle of his bed, too cockroach engorged to rear up and hood? From the bedroom doorway, he shined the flashlight first on the bed, then the floor. Both snakeless.

Entering cautiously, he paused before his dresser, the top drawer of which contained his underwear. Amazing, he thought, just how easily a man's reason could be stampeded. Because, really, the snake had to be long gone, right? Assuming some motorist hadn't run over it, the thing could have made it all the way to Schuyler Springs by now, though bad news seldom seemed to head in that direction. One of the few places it simply *couldn't* be was in a closed sock drawer. For a snake to scale the dresser, pull open the drawer in question without benefit of an opposable thumb (or hand, for that matter), climb in and then—this was the best part—pull the drawer closed again from the inside without the aid of a handle was beyond impossible in the world Raymer knew and navigated on a daily basis. So why did it seem to him at this particular moment that it in fact had managed this feat? And why, before opening the drawer to find out, did he feel the need to rap it smartly with the flashlight and listen for stirring inside? Because he knew from personal experience that the world was rational until it wasn't, after which all bets were off. When, without warning, the world pivoted, it became in that instant unrecognizable. There you are, cruising along, confident in your knowledge of how things work, until one afternoon you come home early and there's your beloved wife on the stairs, her forehead seemingly stapled to the bottom step, the whole of her defying gravity. Suddenly you understand how wrong you've been about every last fucking thing, and that you have little choice but to adjust to this terrible new reality. What *can't* be undeniably *is* and *will be* forevermore. Except here, too, you're wrong. Because gradually, after the shock wears off, the world returns to its familiar old habits, seemingly satisfied to have thrown you for a giant loop and content to await the return of your complacence so it can slip a venomous snake into your damn sock drawer, thereby demonstrating yet again that it, not you, is in charge and always will be, you dumb fuck.

Which was why Raymer, normally calm and rational, slowly inched open the drawer that couldn't possibly contain a snake and yet might anyway. When nothing stirred or struck, he opened it a little more and then a little more still, leaning back in order to make the cobra's strike more geometrically challenging, until he could be certain of its contents: undershorts, socks and handkerchiefs. Not even a garter.

Disrobing quickly and kicking his sweaty uniform into the corner (wary of disturbing whatever might be in the hamper), he thought about showering in the dark, then immediately thought better of it. He pulled on a fresh pair of boxers—smiling to think that Charice had correctly intuited his preference for briefs, pleased that a woman her age had given this even a passing thought—and then clean socks, jeans and a short-sleeved, button-down shirt. To avoid having to return later tonight or tomorrow morning, he decided to pack a small bag. That involved getting down on his hands and knees and shining the flashlight under the bed where he kept his gym bag. This he pulled out and shook—

for consistency's sake, because, well, a snake that could access his sock drawer would have no problem unzipping a bag, crawling inside and rezipping it. Into the empty bag he tossed two sets of underclothes and three extra shirts, since he was already sweating through the one he'd just put on.

Passing by the window, he glanced down into the parking lot, empty except for Charice's Civic, just as its dome light came on and she got out. She was either too hot sitting there or growing impatient with how long he was taking. Something about her posture, how anxiously she surveyed the dark building, suggested a third, albeit remote, possibility: that she was concerned for his well-being. Was it conceivable that what her batshit brother had said that afternoon was true—that Charice was devoted to him? He doubted it. Just as he didn't believe that Becka had ever once worried about him. At the Academy, all the cadets had been warned about the emotional toll police work can take on marriages. Awakening to sirens at three in the morning, spouses would wonder if tonight was the night they'd get the call they'd been dreading. *Your husband's been shot. He's in intensive care, stable for now, but you'd better come right away.* Of course such nightmare scenarios were mostly urban, and Raymer was unlikely to get shot in Bath. On the other hand, until today the odds of his being bitten by a cobra had seemed considerably long as well. The world *was* a dangerous place, and Becka must've known that on any given day her husband might pull over the wrong car or stop at a convenience store just as some wacked-out dickhead emerged with the contents of the register in his jacket pocket, a Slurpee in one hand and a .45 in the other. Raymer had been prepared to reassure Becka that nothing like that would ever happen to him, but somewhat disappointingly the subject had never come up.

From where he stood now it was too dark and Charice was too far away for him to see the expression on her face, but it was flattering to imagine that it might reveal something other than her usual profound irritation. When she appeared to look in his general direction, he waved, but as he did she looked away again, and he doubted he'd have been visible in an unlit window anyway.

In the bathroom he added his shaving kit to the gym bag, then returned to the front room and paused for a moment, trying to think if there was anything else he'd need at the motel that evening. Strange that it should come home to him so powerfully—with the apartment's squalor far less obvious in the dark—that Charice was right about the Morrison Arms. That he resided by choice in such a shithole spoke volumes about his state of mind, if not his character. Things hadn't been right, or even close to right, since Becka. Most days he was borderline deranged with something he didn't identify as either grief or jealousy but that might be a strange hybrid of the two. But did it really matter what was wrong with him? The important thing was that the time had come to pull himself together. Probably losing that garage-door remote this morning *was* the best thing that could've happened to him. He could see that now. Just let it go. The suspicion, the jealousy, the self-doubt. All of it.

He was thinking he'd do exactly that when he opened his apartment door and ran smack into the backlit man on the other side of it, his fist raised, mid-knock. The sound that emerged from Raymer's larynx resembled a bleat as he staggered backward, his heart in his throat, his chest leaping violently. Only when his flashlight hit the floor and skittered away, coming to rest between the dark figure's feet, did he realize he'd dropped it.

"Mr. Hynes," he said when that gentleman bent down, his ancient bones creaking, retrieved the flashlight and handed it back to him. "What're you doing here?"

"*Thought* I heard somebody," he said. "You still looking for that reptile?"

"No," Raymer said, his hand over his heart, which was still thumping wildly. "It's probably halfway back to India by now."

"Thought you was a burglar," the old man said. "Sneaking around here in the dark like that . . ."

"Yeah, but Mr. Hynes?"

"Uh-huh?"

"If I *was* a burglar, what was your plan?"

"Get a good look at you," he said. "'Dentify you in the *police* lineup. Send yo' ass to jail."

"But . . . ," Raymer started, then decided against trying to talk him out of good citizenship. "Mr. Hynes? You're not supposed to *be* here. That's what the yellow tape around the building means. Until we remove that, the building isn't safe. Especially for a man of your years, all alone in the dark. What if you fell and there was nobody around to hear you call for help?"

"Me and the dark is old friends," he said. "Go way back. Before you was born, even."

"Didn't they give you a coupon, Mr. Hynes? So you could stay out at the Holiday Inn tonight? Have dinner at Applebee's? Paid for by the town of Bath?"

"How my gonna get my ass out yonder?"

"I can get somebody to give you a lift," Raymer assured him. "Hell, I'll take you out there right now." Charice wouldn't mind a short detour.

The old man shook his head. "Too late. Already had my dinner. Old people got poor digestion. Eat early. Pass my bedtime, too."

Raymer sighed. "Mr. Hynes?"

"Uh-huh?"

"You like doing things your own way, don't you?"

"Eighty-some-odd years I been at it."

"If I let you stay here, are you gonna tell on me? If that snake crawls into your bed and bites you, are you gonna throw me under the bus? Tell people I said you could stay?"

"Snake's halfway back to India by now," said Mr. Hynes. "You said so your own self."

"That's true, I did, but I'm wrong about a lot. When I say the snake's gone, I mean probably. I mean it's gone unless it isn't. If I'm wrong, it's you that gets bit, not me. So why don't you let me give you a ride out to the Holiday Inn? It'd make me feel a whole lot better."

"Thank you. I 'preciate it, but I'll take my chances. You can come check up on me in the mornin'. See if I'm dead or alive. If I'm dead, you can say I toad you so."

To Raymer that sounded like the last word, so he pulled the apartment door shut behind him, and together they started down the stairs, Mr. Hynes clutching the railing with one hand and Raymer's elbow with the other, his fingers like talons, his grip fierce. "Somebody been peeing in here," he observed, sniffing the air. "White man."

"You can tell?"

"Yup. A whitey for sure."

"How?"

"'Cause the only black person livin' here is me, and I use my own facility."

Odd, Raymer thought as they descended, how the human touch could serve to banish fear. In the company of this frail old man, there was suddenly no reason to fear some cobra. Outside, a horn tooted. At the bottom of the stairs, Raymer said, "You sure you're going to be okay here?"

"Be fine. Goin' to bed. That a black gal I see you with out there?"

So he'd watched them pull in, then. Saw Charice under the Honda's dome light when he got out of the car. He hadn't climbed the stairs because he thought Raymer was a burglar. No, he was curious, just as he'd been about Jerome that afternoon. "You don't miss much, Mr. Hynes."

"Wish I was younger," he said. "Give you a run for your money."

"You've got the wrong idea. She works for me," he explained. "Plus I'm ten years older than she is. More."

"So what?"

"Also, she could do a lot better," he added, thinking again of Becka, who'd evidently come to that same conclusion.

"So what?" the old man repeated. "Every woman I been lucky with coulda done better than me. When it comes to men, gals ain't always thinkin' straight. A man do well to remain alert to the possibility."

"She doesn't even like me, Mr. Hynes. She's keeping a list of all the things I do wrong so she can sue me later."

"Could be love."

"I don't think so."

The man shrugged. "Pass my bedtime," he repeated.

"I'll have somebody come by and check on you in the morning," Raymer promised.

"Have her do it. Maybe she got a thing for old men. You never know," he cackled, waving goodbye. "Get me a good night's sleep, just in case."

Raymer watched as Mr. Hynes shuffled down the dark corridor, one hand along the wall to steady himself. He tried to imagine his days, sitting outside in a lawn chair, hour upon hour, waving a little American flag at passersby. He recalled what Jerome had said earlier at Gert's— that taking the time to talk to a lonely old man really was what police work was all about. He would've liked to believe Jerome was right, though a better policeman wouldn't have allowed Mr. Hynes to remain at the Morrison Arms tonight. He'd have ignored his preference and made the man safe.

"I was about to go in there after you," Charice said when he emerged from the building. "What took you so long?"

"I packed a bag," he said, holding it up.

When they got into the car, she left her door open so the dome light stayed on and arched an eyebrow at him. "You think you're stayin' over? You think lamb chops is just the first course?"

"God no, Charice," he said, feeling himself flush.

Her eyebrow elevated even farther now. "What do you mean, '*God no*'? Like you wouldn't think of staying, even if you got invited? Is that what 'God no' means?"

"No, Charice," he said. "All I meant was . . ."

She was grinning at him now, which meant she'd been toying with him again, as with the fake menu of fried chicken and collard greens.

"I just wish you wouldn't be so mean to me," he said.

"I know," she said. "I wish I wouldn't, too. I just can't help myself, I guess."

"Please try."

"I know one thing," she said, turning the key in the ignition and closing the door. "Next time I'm coming in with you. No more sitting out in the parking lot, wondering if you're lying snakebit on the floor in there."

He looked over at her, but with the light out it was impossible to read her expression. It would have been nice to believe that maybe this was the beginning of a friendship, but how could you be friends with a woman if you never knew when she was making fun of you? *At least with Becka,* he told himself, then stopped. Had he completed the thought, it would've been: *he'd known where he stood.* But that wasn't true. He *hadn't* known where he stood with Becka. He'd just imagined he did.

"There might not be a next time," he told Charice, something like an intention forming in the part of his skull where his headache had been earlier. Until that moment he hadn't even been aware that it was gone. "I'm thinking about moving."

On, he thought. He was thinking about moving on.

Spinmatics

FOR A WEEKDAY NIGHT, the White Horse was busy, its booths all occupied by out-of-towners, half of whom were talking on cellular telephones. Where most were headed—Lakes George, Placid, Schroon and Champlain—they'd have no service. Those headed up the interstate to Montreal wouldn't have reception for a good three hours. So many downstaters heading north this early in the season should've been good news for Birdie, whose sweat equity made her co-owner of the establishment, but in fact she looked like someone who was about to burn her half to the ground. Weird how every single woman Sully knew—Ruth, Janey, Bootsie and now Birdie—was on the warpath, as if they'd all received the same gender-coded message on the wind. "Perfect," Birdie said, glancing up and watching Sully and the two Rubs come inside. "Now my night is complete."

Sully slid onto the only vacant stool, right next to Jocko, who was still wearing his Rexall pharmacy smock, and slapped a couple twenties on the bar to ensure his welcome. "Is it me," Sully said, "or is she happier to see us in the winter, after all the rich tourists have split?"

"Actually," Jocko said, "I've never felt particularly welcome here in any season."

"Sit, Rub," Sully said, and the dog curled up beneath his stool.

"Where?" said Rub, realizing as he did that he had fallen for the joke yet again.

"What can I get you, Rub?" Birdie asked.

He sighed. In the two decades he'd been drinking at the Horse, his order had never varied even once. Why couldn't she just bring him what she knew he wanted?

"A buh-buh-buh—"

"Beer," Sully translated.

"What kind?"

"Buh-buh—"

"Budweiser," Sully said.

"Anything else?"

Rub looked at Sully, who'd sometimes spring for a burger, sometimes not. "Go ahead," he told him. "You've had a hard day." Which meant it wouldn't be long before he launched into the story he'd promised driving over not to tell.

"A buh-buh-buh—"

"Burger," Sully said.

"Anything on it?"

"Buh—"

"Bacon."

Jocko's shoulders were shaking now. "Jesus, you people are cruel," he said.

"And cheese," Rub added, since he liked cheese and the word was easy to say.

Birdie turned to Sully. "You?"

"Just a draft."

"You should eat something. You look terrible."

"No appetite," he confessed, which was strange, because he'd been hungry earlier. Probably Bootsie and her syringe. Otherwise, he was actually feeling better, his chest less heavy, his breathing easier than it had been all day. "What's got your knickers all in a twist?"

Birdie shot him a don't-get-me-started look and then got started. "Buddy called in drunk again, an hour before his shift, so I had to scramble to find a cook."

A waitress emerged from the kitchen just then, a silver tray balanced on her shoulder, and before the door swung shut behind her Sully caught a glimpse of Janey working the grill.

"Then I broke a glass in the ice and did this cleaning it up." She held up her left hand, swaddled with half-a-dozen overlapping Band-Aids between thumb and forefinger.

"I wondered why my pinot grigio was pink," Jocko said, holding his glass up to the light.

"Yeah, sure," Sully said, "but what kind of man drinks that to begin with?"

"A confident man? A man with no need to demonstrate his masculinity?"

Sully rolled his eyes. "Yeah, that must be it."

"Then Bridget lets a table of eight skip out on steak dinners and five bottles of wine."

The guilty waitress just then happened by on her way to the kitchen. "I don't want to hear it," she said. "I've got twice the number of tables I should, and you know it."

Birdie ignored her. "It's still two full weeks before my summer staff shows up, half of which probably found other jobs and never bothered to tell me."

Rub, who disliked standing when everybody else had a seat, was eyeing a four-top booth that two couples were getting ready to vacate. He'd been hoping to find the Horse deserted, so he could have Sully all to himself. If he could convince him to move to the booth, he could tell him about Raymer fainting in the heat and falling headfirst into the judge's grave. The story would appeal to Sully, who'd probably commandeer it as his own immediately. By this time tomorrow night he'd have told half the town. But he was an inspired storyteller, so Rub wouldn't mind the theft. In fact, he enjoyed watching one of his stories evolve in Sully's hands until he himself, its source, had disappeared completely. These days his own storytelling was undermined by his stammer, as well as by his conviction that a story had to be true. Sully was hampered by neither Rub's condition nor his strictness. He shamelessly embellished, invented, reshaped and tailored every narrative, emphasizing with each new version the elements that provoked the most laughs or stunned disbelief in previous tellings, eliminating other elements that unexpectedly fell flat. At first he might credit Rub as his source, but as he grew more confident, he'd relate the story as if he himself had been the sole eyewitness. With Sully's best efforts, Rub sometimes wished he'd been there to enjoy the events his friend was describing, until he remembered he actually *had* been.

Tonight, of course, he had a vested interest in Sully taking up the story of the police chief keeling over into that grave, because if Sully wasn't regaling everybody in the Horse with the police chief's idiocy, he'd be reporting Rub's humiliating afternoon in the tree. His only hope was to replace the story he didn't want told with a better one. "There's a buh-buh-booth over there," he said, pointing to it.

"Hang on," Sully told him, his voice lowered. "I think a barstool's gonna open up here in a minute."

Because on the other side of Jocko sat none other than Spinmatics Joe, who'd been Sully's least favorite person in all of Bath until Roy Purdy made his triumphant return. Joe usually drank at Gert's, where a beer and a bump was a buck cheaper and only stumbling distance from the Morrison Arms. What's more, a man could freely express the most dim-witted opinions there without fear of ridicule. The Horse, not exactly highbrow itself, was generally tolerant of stupidity, but on any given night it was possible to cross an invisible line and find yourself an object of scorn and derision when you'd been counting on, if not approval, a little forbearance.

"Oh, Jesus Lord, Birdie," Jocko said, having overheard what Sully whispered to Rub. "Here we go again."

She shrugged. "I can't run him, Sully, not until he actually does something."

"You could eighty-six him on general principle."

Jocko snorted at this. "If that rubric were indiscriminately applied, who would remain?"

"Only people who use words like 'rubric,'" Sully conceded, "and drink pinot grigio."

"If he misbehaves," Birdie assured him, "it'll be my pleasure."

"He's about to," Sully assured her.

"Ah, fuck," said Jocko under his breath.

"That you, Joe?" Sully said, leaning forward for a direct line of sight. Jocko leaned back obligingly.

"You know it is, Sully," replied the man in question, nodding at him in the mirror that ran along the backbar. "You don't gotta ask."

"I *thought* it was you," Sully went on, nodding genially. "I left my glasses at home and haven't seen you for a while. I thought you might be your brother."

"I don't have no goddamn brother."

"Well, your parents probably thought you were enough. So, how are things down at the Arms these days?"

"It's a fuckin' shithole," Joe said. "Course I didn't have no crazy old woman kick off and leave me millions so I could live someplace nice."

Sully ignored him. "Well, at least none of those people you don't like are living there, right?"

"Ah, shit," Jocko grunted, knowing full well where this seemingly innocuous conversation was bound. He hadn't been present the night Joe got his nickname, but everyone in town knew the story. Angered by something he'd seen on the TV hung above the bar, he'd launched into a diatribe about how the fuckin' Spinmatics were taking over the whole fuckin' country. *How,* he wanted to know, could a white man get ahead when all the jobs went to the fuckin' Spinmatics. "They already took over Amsterdam," he said, when somebody asked what manner of redneck bullshit he was spouting now. "Y'all better wake the fuck up. They'll be over here next." At some point somebody had guessed what he was going on about: *Hispanics.* The man was talking about Hispanics. So far as Sully knew, Joe had not returned to the Horse once since getting his nickname.

"I always forget," Sully was saying. "Who are those folks you don't like?"

"Niggers?"

"Joe," Birdie warned.

"No, not them," Sully said. "The other ones."

"Fuck you, Sully," Joe said.

From underneath Sully's stool came a growl.

"Joe," Birdie warned again.

"You know the ones I'm talking about," Sully said, as if he weren't really listening. To judge by his tone, anyone would've sworn the two men were on the friendliest of terms and that Sully was merely trying to jog his pal's memory. "Help me out here. It's on the tip of my tongue."

There was considerable tittering up and down the bar now, and Joe stiffened at the sound. "You really are a cunt," he said to Sully's reflection in the mirror, sending most heads swiveling to look at Birdie. Now *here* was a word you never heard at the Horse, certainly not when she was tending bar. Rub got to his feet, walked in a tight circle and growled a little louder, his ears stiff.

"Rub," Sully snapped.

"What," said his friend, still standing patiently behind him.

As his pet lay down again, Sully said, "Oh, I remember," as if he just that second had. "The Spinmatics."

"And a cocksucker, too," Joe added, draining off half his beer.

"Drink up," Birdie told him. "You're out of here."

"It's a shame you don't like them better," Sully said. "Otherwise, you could get together with three or four and cut some records. Joey and the Spinmatics."

Joe apparently suffered from a limited range of invective, because instead of trying out any other names, he took a different tack, raising his glass high in the air, and slowly poured the beer onto the bar. Just as he'd feared, Jocko got the worst of the splatter.

"You still gotta pay for that," Birdie said, once this performance was over.

"Nah, I got it," Sully said, pushing one of the twenties at her.

"The whole tab?" She clearly disapproved of this largesse.

"Why not?" he told her. "Joe and I go way back, don't we, Spin? No need for hard feelings."

Joe, having slid off his stool, stood stock-still, deeply and visibly conflicted. *Did* they go way back, he and Sully? Was this asshole actually apologizing?

"Though the truth is," Sully continued, "I do prefer his brother."

At this Joe's face became a thundercloud, and he balled his right hand into a fist. Rub was on his feet again, and from somewhere deep within his rib cage came a low, guttural rumble that made Joe take note of him for the first time. Though Rub wasn't a large animal, he appeared fully committed. Joe was anything but, so he relaxed his fist.

"Rub," Sully said.

"Wh-wh-which?" said his impatient friend.

"Sit!" Sully told him.

The dog did as instructed.

"That's what I've been wanting to do," said his namesake.

When the door closed behind Joe, Sully turned to face Rub and indicated the now-vacant stool. "Well? What're you waiting for?"

Rub wasn't sure. He *had* wanted a stool, except this one was next to Jocko, who wasn't his friend, instead of Sully, who was. He'd go from standing alone to sitting alone. As with most of what he felt deeply, he couldn't begin to express it, so he just pointed at the puddle on the bar. "It's all wet."

"True," Sully said, "but Birdie'll wipe it up."

"How about if I move over one?" Jocko suggested, sliding down simultaneously.

This, of course, was exactly what Rub had been hoping for. Yet as he stood regarding it, all he could do was reflect bitterly, as he had occasion to do each and every day, on the terrible disappointment of getting what you thought you wanted, only to discover it wasn't, that you'd been cheated out of something you couldn't even name.

"Everything all right now?" Sully said when he climbed aboard.

Rub shrugged. Everything was *not* all right, though he would've been hard-pressed to explain exactly what was wrong. Part of it was his terrible, almost visceral need for Sully. It was this, together with the knowledge that yet again his friend had forgotten him, that had driven him up into the tree that afternoon, half hoping he'd have an accident with the chain saw. If instead of the tree's limb he managed to prune one of his own, Sully would blame himself, wouldn't he? If he was the one to find Rub's severed leg at the base of the tree? Surely then he'd realize it was all his fault. Eager to atone, he'd toss Carl Roebuck out of the old lady's house and move Rub in, so he could be sure his friend had everything he needed. They'd eat meals and watch TV together. Over time Bootsie would come to regret how mean she'd been to him, and she, too, would want to move in, but Sully would draw the line at that. It would be just the two of them. Their days would be full of long hours, plenty of time for Rub to tell Sully whatever he wanted, and Sully, chastened, would be devoted to getting him back on his feet. Well . . . foot. Okay, Rub wasn't crazy about the idea of losing a leg, but if that was the price of friendship, what choice did he have but to pay it? Sully's pal Wirf had gotten along fine on one leg, and if he could be happy on just the one, then Rub supposed he could, too.

But unfortunately there'd been no accident. The tree surgery had gone off without a hitch, unless you counted Rub's being stranded in the tree for hours, thirty feet off the ground with no hope of getting down, as a hitch. At some point, though, certain facts, as hard and uncomfortable as the severed nub of tree limb he was sitting on, began to intrude on his pleasant dismemberment fantasy. For instance, if Rub *had* managed to sever his own limb, he'd likely have bled out long before Sully showed up and discovered his leg at the base of the tree. In fact, the leg probably would've disappeared. That close to the dump there were plenty of feral animals around, and one of them would likely have dragged this prized discovery off into the woods. In all probability what Sully would find at the base of the tree was Rub himself, because when he passed out, from pain or loss of blood, he'd almost certainly tumble from his perch onto the hard ground below, and if he wasn't dead already, the fall would kill him. In the wake of such real-world considerations came equally cruel psychological realities. When, for instance, had he ever known Sully to blame himself for anything? If Rub had maimed himself, Sully would place the blame squarely on him for being an idiot. Nor would he kick Carl Roebuck out of the old lady's house. It wouldn't be Sully who nursed Rub back to health but a resentful Bootsie, who'd probably grow tired of her duties after a few days and smother him with a pillow so she could go back to reading her romance novels. And even if he somehow avoided this fate and recovered, he'd be chasing Sully all over Bath on one leg instead of two.

"Well?" Sully was saying. "You good now, or do you need some other fucking thing to make you happy?"

Rub sighed. "I just wisht they'd hurry up with my burger."

Sully nudged him, like he always did when attempting to improve Rub's mood.

"What?" said Rub, who didn't necessarily want his mood improved until he improved it himself.

"You said 'burger.'"

"So?"

"Usually, you say 'buh-buh-burger.'"

Rub didn't want to, but he could feel himself giving in, and when Sully nudged him a second time he smiled sheepishly. Because it *was* good to have a barstool, and not just any stool but the one he'd been coveting. And he *had* said "burger," without stumbling. There was no word that gave him more trouble, probably because he loved burgers and would've been content to eat nothing else for the remainder of his days. For some reason he recalled his father's question all those years ago: *Why don't you just give up?* That, he realized, was what he'd been feeling up in the tree that afternoon. That maybe he should just give up.

"Here comes your burger now," Sully said as the door to the kitchen swung open and Janey emerged. She set Rub's plate of food in front of him, along with a fork and knife wrapped in a paper napkin.

"You again," she said, regarding Sully.

"Me again," Sully agreed.

"Spreading cheer wherever you go."

Which meant she'd been privy to the whole business with Spinmatics Joe. By the time he arrived at Hattie's in the morning, Ruth would know all about it. On the other hand, there was no law that he had to go there. Hadn't Ruth given him full permission to stay away just a few hours ago? "I try," he told Janey weakly, but she was already bustling back into the kitchen.

"Try harder," she suggested, the kitchen door swinging shut behind her.

She had a point. Today, he'd goaded two profoundly ignorant men to within an inch of violence. Both dickheads but the point remained: for what? Had he succeeded in getting them to lose their tempers, they'd have made short work of him. He was too old for bar fights, but even if he weren't, what had he been trying to accomplish? Each time the urge had been pressing enough to suggest a purpose, but now, once his dander settled, he couldn't imagine what it might've been.

Next to him, Rub sighed. His burger sat before him untouched.

"What's the matter now?" Sully said.

"There's no buh-buh-buh—"

"Bacon?"

"Bacon," Rub repeated flawlessly.

Next to Rub, Jocko was chuckling. "Weird," he said. "He's really got a thing about that word."

"'Bacon'?" Sully said, assuming he must be talking about Rub.

"No, Joe," he explained. "'Hispanics.' Poor bastard just can't say it."

"Hispanics," Rub repeated clearly, even though he'd decided, as he always did in the end, to make the best of things and taken a big bite of burger. "That's not so fuh-fuh-fuh—"

"So fuckin' hard to say?" Sully suggested.

"Fuckin' hard to say," Rub agreed.

Sully couldn't help smiling. For some reason, when Rub's mood improved, Sully's often did, too, as if their emotions were wired in parallel.

"Because he could just say 'spics,'" Jocko continued. "That would solve the problem."

"Or one of them," Sully offered.

Rub apparently agreed, too, because he thumped his tail on the floor.

Embers

RAYMER AWOKE TO a sensation he remembered both vividly and fondly, Becka running her fingers lightly through his thinning hair, barely touching his scalp, mere proximity causing the hair to lift in yearning toward her touch. He smiled, enjoying the feeling, unwilling to open his eyes. *There's something I need to tell you,* she murmured.

I know, he told her. *I'm going bald.*

Because this had been her favorite thing to inform him about in moments of intimacy back when they were still in love, as if the shower drain hadn't already eloquently confirmed that diagnosis. *How am I going to do this when you don't have hair?*

There'll be plenty on the sides, he always assured her. *I'll comb it over.*

You will not.

I'll get implants.

Negative.

Then you'll just have to—

Find another man—this one with hair. Yes, that's what I'll have to do.

This was how he expected the conversation to go now, so he was surprised when her tone grew serious. *No, something else.*

What? he said, and when she didn't immediately respond, he added, *You can tell me.*

Then listen.

Of course neither Becka nor anyone else was actually speaking to him. Becka had come down the stairs like a Slinky and was dead. His hair was just stirring in the lovely breeze. When at last he opened his eyes, he saw the truth of this. There was no Becka. He was alone in the dark. Unable to accept this truth, he closed his eyes again, willing her return, because in addition to running her fingers through his hair, she'd whispered something to him, something he hadn't quite caught but that seemed important.

Whatever she'd wanted him to know, it was gone and so was she. Opening his eyes again, he saw he was being observed by a single red eye, something that, before he could bring it into focus, then closed. Did cobras have red eyes, he wondered. Was it coiled there at the foot of his bed? He realized he should care, but somehow couldn't rouse any sense of urgency. Had it already bitten him? Was that why he was having so much trouble waking up, its lethal venom already coursing through his veins? Was his death approaching? Was that what Becka had needed him to know? Was that why she'd visited him? If so, fine. All he wanted, really, was to lie here awhile in this delicious breeze. When his hair stirred again, he saw that the snake had reopened its red eye. In fact, a second eye winked open to stare at him until the breeze died and both eyes closed. Then they were open again, glowing a deeper red this time, though when a third eye opened, Raymer came fully awake. He didn't know much about cobras, but he was pretty sure they didn't have three eyes.

Then all at once reality returned in a rush of sensory data and memory. In the dream he'd been home in bed, but in reality he was out on Charice's back porch—it'd been too hot to eat indoors—where he'd fallen asleep when she went inside to fetch dessert. Full of delicious grilled lamb and red wine, he'd meant to just rest his eyes for a minute. God, those lamb chops! How many had he devoured? Seven? Could he really have eaten so many? Why hadn't he stopped at . . . Jesus, even four was probably too many. Because they were so delicious. That's why. There'd been a lovely bottle of red wine as well—no, wait—two bottles. He'd been tipsy even before they'd started to eat.

Dear God, what a day! That afternoon at Gert's he'd rediscovered beer and now, tonight, red wine. Delicious. As thick and bloody and textured as the lamb. Becka preferred white wine, so they'd drunk that, but red . . . wow! Why had he stopped drinking red wine? But on this particular evening the better question was, why hadn't he stopped? Had he swilled an expensive bottle of red wine that was meant to be sipped? How much had the meal cost her? Loin lamb chops, over ten bucks a pound, easy. Why hadn't he asked Charice to stop at the liquor store on the way so he could contribute something to their feast?

And just that quickly, misgiving morphed into full-blown panic. What had he done? At what point had the whole evening gone south? Idiocy, after the fact, resisted precision. That he'd somehow managed to ruin a perfectly wonderful evening was obvious. Why hadn't he seen that wreck coming? The overwhelming sense of well-being that had come over him sitting there on a hot summer night in the company of an attractive young woman really should have been a dead giveaway. When in his entire life had such profound contentment ever presaged anything but catastrophe? The very fact that at some point in the evening he'd stopped being scared shitless of Charice should have been a further tip-off. Because Charice *was* a scary woman. If you weren't scared of her, you weren't paying attention.

And speaking of . . . where was she? What had happened to her? She'd gathered up their greasy plates, his piled high with those little Gothic T-bones—had he actually picked them up with his fingers and gnawed on them? *really* done that?—and brought them into the kitchen. Had he offered to help, or even stood up to open the screen door? He couldn't remember, so probably not. No, he'd just sat there like a lump, sated, drunk, beached, his chin glistening. The kitchen phone had rung, he remembered that, and Charice had answered it, taking the receiver on its long cord into the next room. It was her receding voice (*No, it's okay . . . listen to me . . . it's just like I said . . . as usual, you're getting all worked up over nothing*) that had led him to think that it wouldn't hurt to close his eyes for just a minute. When she returned to the kitchen and hung up the phone, he'd hear her, surely. He'd fallen asleep to the sound of fat bugs pinging against the screen door, the kitchen lights blazing.

Now that same kitchen was ominously dark.

Off to the south, the sky lit up, briefly illuminating the low clouds, then darkened. Low rumbling followed, a thunderstorm tracking up the Northway. Still a ways off, but Raymer could already feel the electricity in the air. When the breeze came up again, stronger this time, the coals at the bottom of the Weber kettle—what was left of them—glowed red, snake eyes again. Wondering what time it was, he consulted his wrist, which was bare. He could picture the watch he'd hoped to find there on his desk at the station. Why hadn't he put it back on when they left? Why had he taken it off in the first place? Could he guess at the time by the coals in the Weber? When he'd fallen asleep the briquettes were still pulsing angrily. All that remained now were a few marble-sized embers about to expire. How long did it take for coals to completely burn down? A couple hours? More? The street was pitch dark. Was that because it was three in the morning, or had the downtown power outage spread? For some reason it seemed vital to ascertain how much time had elapsed, as if that would clarify how much trouble he was in.

Why hadn't Charice come out, jostled him awake and sent him the fuck home? Had she tried and been unable to rouse him? What if he hadn't just been dozing? What if he'd passed out? Given the day he'd had and the fact that he'd gone nearly twenty-four hours without food, it was possible. He had, he knew, no head for alcohol. Back when he was married and had too much to drink, Becka had complained bitterly that it was impossible to wake him once he'd fallen asleep. Which meant that Charice had to be beyond pissed off, and who could blame her? He'd devoured her lamb chops and guzzled her expensive red wine and passed out before she could bring out dessert. Served him right to wake up alone and befuddled in the dark. Tomorrow, down at the station, Charice would no doubt add tonight's boorish, unforgivable behavior to her long grievance list.

Rising, he tried the screen door, which didn't budge. Seriously? He was locked out? The breeze came up again, chilling him this time. He knocked softly. No answer. Louder. "Charice?"

Silence.

Wow. Was she really angry enough to lock the door on him? Why would she do that? Immediately, he had the answer. A man who would behave as he had tonight might just be capable of even worse behavior.

When he awoke from his drunken stupor, he might come into her bedroom in the middle of the night, determined to take advantage of her. Which was ridiculous. He'd never do such a thing, but how was she to know that?

"Charice?" he called again, surprised by the desperation that had crept into his voice. "Please?"

More silence. To this point he'd been proceeding under the assumption that she'd gone to bed, but another, even more ghastly possibility now occurred to him. Maybe she was sitting in the dark of the front room, enjoying his suffering. If so, calling her name would do no good. And even if she was asleep, did he really want to wake her? No, but guess what? He didn't want to be outside during an electrical storm, either. The porch was covered, but the sloping roof had to be twelve feet above him. Wind would drive the rain horizontally, and he'd be drenched to the skin in short order. Lightning would probably locate the metal dome of the Weber grill and then look for other grounding opportunities, which Raymer himself, soaking wet, would provide.

"Charice?" he called, louder now, cupping his hands, trying to direct the sound inside so as not to wake the neighbors. "I'm really sorry, okay? I don't blame you for being upset. But could you let me in? All I want is to go home."

Was this an insulting thing to say? Probably. He half expected to see a yellow ribbon of light come on under her bedroom door, followed immediately by an angry woman pulling on a bathrobe. *What's that supposed to mean? All you want is to go home. Now you're full of lamb chops and Cabernet, you got no further use for me? Is* that *what you're sayin'? 'Cause, I'ma add* that *to my list.*

Strange that in his imagination Charice should again be speaking in her teasing "black" voice, the one she used with him on the radio. During the course of the evening the syntax and vocal inflections that seemed to place her in a geographical and racial context had melted away. She'd sounded more like her brother, minus Jerome's inflated diction. Or was he just making that up? At one point he'd almost asked, but the subject had then turned to Jerome and how he'd come so completely unglued over the attack on the 'Stang. Though loyal to her brother, she'd admitted to being concerned about his state of mind. He'd always been high strung, she said, and obsessive, as Raymer had observed. Apparently, he'd been employing a come-hither-leave-me-alone strategy with people since he was a boy. He'd always wanted friends, and later lovers, but also was repelled by intimacy and, at times, even proximity. Careful to cultivate an air of strident self-sufficiency, he was, according to Charice, extremely vulnerable. Raymer had taken all of this in, but was unsure how much to believe. Jerome had, on various occasions, given him to understand that Charice had moved to upstate New York so he'd be close by if she needed him, but tonight she'd hinted that the opposite was true—Jerome being comforted to have *her* close by. He'd been in therapy, she confided, for more than a decade. He took anti-anxiety medications that sometimes worked as intended but at other times made him even more anxious.

"Yeah, sure, okay," Raymer said, more than willing to grant her general diagnosis, as well as the symbiotic nature of their relationship as twins, but he was still puzzled by the particulars of what he'd witnessed that afternoon. "Why would he think I'd ever do something like keying his car? And not just key it. Shred its canvas top and leather seats. Pee in it."

"It doesn't have anything to do with you," she assured him. "If I'd been there, it would've been me he suspected. And believe me. I *have* been there."

Raymer must've looked dubious, because she'd continued. "You know your problem?" she said, pointing a glistening steak knife at him. It was a question she asked him at least once a day, which annoyed him less than the fact that every day she provided a different answer. "You think you're the only one who's messed up."

"Yeah?" he'd replied, unsure why having her point out yet another human failing of his should be so pleasurable. Maybe it was because tonight her tone was not only nonjudgmental but almost, well, affectionate. For a moment he nearly expected her to put down her steak knife, reach across the table and take his hand.

"Whereas," she told him, "everybody's messed up."

"Even you?"

"Okay, not everybody," she conceded. She'd smiled then, and he must have smiled as well, because she said, "I know it's been a rough year since . . . but you're going to be okay, you know. If you just let yourself."

It had been, now that he thought about it, the very nicest moment in a thoroughly wonderful evening. How was it even possible for things to devolve so quickly? How would he ever make it up to her?

"Charice?" he said. "I want to pay you for the lamb chops. Is that okay? And the wine? That was expensive, wasn't it? I know your salary. I mean, I know everybody's salary, not just yours. But I had a really nice time. I want to make sure you know that. I don't blame you for being mad. I shouldn't have fallen asleep. Or passed out. Whatever I did. But I'm really sorry, so would you please, *please,* let me in so I can go home?"

In the silence that followed, Raymer could feel himself slipping into one of his maudlin fugue states.

"I'm thinking about resigning, Charice," he heard himself say. "Did you know that? I know you're keeping a list of all the things I do wrong, so I guess I don't have to explain why. I wish I was better at my job. I do. I wish I was better at everything. Anyway, I just want you to know . . ."

He stopped. What *did* he want her to know?

"Okay," he sighed. "I'll see you tomorrow at the station, then."

Her apartment was on the top floor of an old two-family house, the residences configured, as near as Raymer could tell, identically. Directly below her second-story porch was another just like it. Peering over the railing into the darkness below, he tried as best he could to gauge the distance to the ground, impossible to do except when the sky lit up again, providing him with the briefest of snapshots. The problem was that the land the house sat on sloped downward from the street—sharply at the rear of the house—toward a dry creek bed. The shortest distance to the ground was at the front of the porch, but there he'd be dropping onto either a sidewalk that ran alongside the house or the neighbor's paved driveway. A kid could probably do it, might even enjoy the thrill, while Raymer would probably break a femur. The ground would be softer off the rear of the porch, but the drop was an additional three or four feet there, and given the slope he might land awkwardly and tumble into the ravine below. Better to climb down, surely, than to leap.

The porch was supported, front and back, by two sturdy-looking columns. Would it be possible for a man his size to shinny down one of these? Maybe, if he absolutely had to. Which he did. He decided against the front column because, if he lost his grip, it would be unforgiving concrete he'd land on, though from the rear he'd most likely drop into a large hedge, where he might well become entrapped or even impaled. No doubt about it: a smart man would stay right where he was, curl up into a ball and ride out the storm on the porch. Deal with Charice's wrath in the morning. The sky lit up again, the storm closer now. He swung one leg over the railing.

Rotten wood, even when painted over, has the soft, porous feel of a badly told lie, and as Raymer began his cautious descent, his brain registered this alarming development even before the column, when he wrapped his legs around it, began to pull away from the porch floor it supported. In that instant a number of things ran through his mind, among them the realization that the last twenty-four hours were providing him with a graduate seminar in floors and ceilings and roofs and load-bearing support, an education that might very well be the death of him. Knowing that the column he was clinging to was no longer tethered securely to anything, he immediately felt the wisdom of clambering back up top. He still had one hand on the porch floor, but to haul his carcass over its lip he would need both hands, and even then he wasn't sure he was strong enough. Still, what other choice did he have? He couldn't very well just let go. When he reached up with his free hand and grabbed hold of a plank, however, it had the same punky feel as the column, and a split second later the handful of rotten floorboard came away in his hand, and the moment after *that* he lost his grip with his other hand, which meant he was now connected to the house by his legs alone. So, he thought, this is how it ends.

Except somehow it didn't. The column, instead of wrenching completely free of the upstairs porch, as he might've expected, pulled away from the house a groaning inch at a time, allowing Raymer to wrap his arms around it and hang on for dear life. Then, amazingly, given that the post was no longer attached to the porch it was supposedly supporting, it stopped moving altogether. For the moment, though fifteen feet off the ground, he was stable. Unfortunately, the upstairs porch, at least to judge by the grinding sounds above, was not. Looking up, he saw the structure begin to sag. After which he saw nothing at all, because there was suddenly a blinding flash of light, incredibly close, that Raymer's brain decoded as lightning, so he shut his eyes tight, bracing for the inevitable sizzle and thunderclap. This never came, but what did, again from above, was a rapid-fire crackling sound, the spindles of the upstairs railing snapping like twigs while the entire structure slumped even more dramatically. Having no desire to see all that come crashing down on him, Raymer kept his eyes sealed tightly shut and waited for the impact, but this didn't come, either. It was as if the world's effects had been abruptly hewn from their causes. When he finally did open his eyes, he discovered that his circumstance was far less perilous than he'd imagined. Yes, the column had completely detached from the upstairs porch, but it remained affixed, somehow, to the downstairs one, forming a radical V. By loosening his grip, he was able to slide right down it, then gently drop those last few harmless feet to the ground.

His mistake was remaining on the spot to marvel at the geometry of the column and the fact that the upstairs porch, despite its now-treacherous slope, somehow remained aloft. He heard the rattle of plastic wheels but didn't put two and two together until the Weber kettle hit the splintered section of railing and capsized. As often happens in such situations, luck was on Raymer's side until it wasn't. The kettle's dome, which might've killed him, landed with a dull thud behind him, then rolled down into the ravine. Even the rain of ashes and the last of the burning embers wouldn't have been terribly problematic if he hadn't been looking up.

But of course he was.

RAYMER HAD GONE only a couple blocks when he heard the familiar burp of a police siren. Turning, he made out one of North Bath's three squad cars inching along behind him, close to the curb. Then the spotlight came on, finishing the job of blinding him that the falling ash had begun. He figured it had to be Miller at the wheel. Who else would be dumb enough to treat the boss like a common perp?

"That you, Chief?"

Sure enough, it was Miller's voice. "Turn that fucking thing off," Raymer told him, hands up to shield his burning eyes.

When blessed darkness returned, he went over to the vehicle, and the passenger window rolled down. "Why are you still on duty?" he asked Miller.

"Pulling a double," he explained. The look on his face was astonishment bordering on, for some reason, fear. "What's that you got all over you?"

Raymer ignored this. "Why are you here?"

"Like I said—"

"No, I mean *here*. On this street . . . this *block*. As opposed to anywhere else."

"Responding to a call. Guy reported seeing a heavyset Caucasian man attempting to—"

"That was me."

Miller nodded but was clearly troubled. "Actually, Chief? Right now you look more like . . ."

"Like what?"

"Like, well, a Negro-type individual."

"You mean a black man?"

Miller sighed deeply. "Chief?" he said. "I'm not really understanding any of this. Am I supposed to?"

"Go on back to the station, okay? Forget this ever happened."

When the window rolled back up, Raymer returned to the sidewalk and resumed walking, his eyes still smarting from the ash. At the end of the block he realized the cruiser was still creeping along the curb behind him. Again the window rolled down.

"Chief?"

"What, Miller?"

"Is this some kind of test? If the call that came into the station was about you, shouldn't I be, like, questioning you?"

A fat drop of rain hit Raymer in the forehead, then another. There was an odd odor in the air. Strong. Nauseating. More thunder rumbled, very close now. "Instead of the station, how about driving me out to

Hilldale," he suggested. "I left my car there this morning. You can inter-
rogate me on the way."

"Sure, Chief," Miller said, clearly excited by this opportunity.

Raymer had no sooner gotten in than the heavens opened with astonishing fury. "Wow," Miller said, impressed by how the wind-driven torrents of rain rattled on the roof of the squad car and streamed down the
windshield in wavy sheets. From outside the car there came a hissing
sound, followed instantly by a clap of thunder so loud that Miller hit his
head on the roof of the car when he levitated. "That was close," he said.
They both tried to peer out the back window, but with the rain you
couldn't see much. Raymer agreed, though. The lightning strike had to
have been very close.

Miller took his hands off the metal steering wheel and made no move
to put the vehicle in gear. When the rain finally let up enough to be
heard, he said, like a man pretending that a thought had just occurred
to him when in reality it'd been troubling him for a while, "Hey, doesn't
Charice, you know, Officer Bond, live around here somewhere?"

"If you say so," said Raymer, who was about as good as Miller was at
pretending not to know something.

Miller nodded, then went back to staring at the water streaming
down the windshield.

"Look," Raymer said, relenting a little. "Officer Bond invited me
over for dinner, okay?"

Unless Raymer was mistaken, it certainly wasn't okay with Miller.
"Isn't that—"

"Against the rules? Probably. That's all, though. We just had dinner
out on her back porch."

Miller was sniffing. "What's that smell?"

Raymer was wondering the same thing. The nauseating odor was
stronger in the car than it had been in the street. Different from the
Great Bath Stench, but right up there on the unpleasantness meter.

"Chief?"

"What?"

"Are you on fire?"

"Why would I be—"

"Look that way a sec."

When Raymer turned his head, Miller yelped, grabbed a rolled-up magazine from the dash and commenced swatting the back of his head and neck with it, hard. Finally recognizing the smell as his own burning hair, Raymer let the other man have at him, though the blows rained down with such surprising ferocity that he had to wonder if his officer wasn't driven by more than one motive.

"Am I out?" Raymer inquired, when the hitting finally stopped.

"I think so," Miller told him. He cracked the door open enough for the dome light to come on, then used the end of the magazine to investigate Raymer's hair where it was longish and thick and curled up in the back. "Something might've gone down the back of your shirt, though."

Raymer leaned back against the seat and immediately felt a burning sensation between his shoulder blades, as if somebody'd just stubbed out a cigarette there.

The odor of burning hair was still thick in the car. "Didn't you feel it?" Miller wanted to know.

"No, I didn't. A man who knows he's on fire will take steps."

Miller nodded thoughtfully. "So what'd you have?"

"I'm sorry?"

"For dinner. You and Officer Bond."

"Lamb chops."

"Wow. What else?"

"Asparagus."

"Mmmmm. Just the two of you?"

"Just us two."

"So, are you—"

"No."

"You're just good—"

"Not even."

"Because you sounded like you were having a good time. You were both laughing and all."

Raymer was glad to have Miller confirm that things had been going well until they went badly, but the comment begged a couple fairly obvious questions. "Miller?"

"Yeah, Chief?"

"Do you have a crush on Officer Bond?"

Miller looked away, guilty. Even with only the dome on, Raymer could see that he was glowing red with embarrassment. "Me?"

"If you heard us laughing out on the porch, then you were there, which means you already knew where she lived when you asked me just now. Also, it was only a minute or two between when I climbed down from that porch and you showed up. Which means you were already in the neighborhood when the call came in."

Miller stared at the still-streaming windshield. "God, I hate myself," he said miserably. "Sometimes I drive by. Just to make sure she's okay, you know?"

"Does she know about this?"

He shook his head. "Please don't tell her?"

"Why don't you just ask her out sometime?"

"Scared, I guess."

"Well, she is pretty terrifying," Raymer agreed.

"Plus I don't think she likes me."

"Don't you want to find out?"

"Only if she does," he said. "And there's the . . . other thing."

"What other thing?"

"It's not that I'm prejudiced. It's just that . . ."

"She's a Negro-type individual?"

Miller closed the car door, probably so the dome light would go out and Raymer wouldn't see the tears spill over, which he did anyway. "Seeing the two of you together, laughing and having such a great time, it made me realize I didn't care. That could've been me up there eating lamb chops if I wasn't such a . . ."

He was so clearly in distress that Raymer couldn't help feeling sorry for him. "Miller," he began.

"So it doesn't bother you? Her not being . . . like us?"

"Do you mean her being a woman or being black?"

"Yeah," he said. Both. "But aren't you afraid people will make jokes?"

"People make jokes about me already. I'm used to it."

Miller nodded soberly.

"Anyway, it's not like that between Officer Bond and me, so there's nothing to make jokes about. Okay? Everything clear now?"

"Except the part about why you climbed down off her porch," he said. "Was that some kind of . . . wager?"

"Yes," Raymer told him, "it was."

Miller looked uneasy about this explanation, though he himself had advanced it. "And why do you look like a Negro? Was that a wager, too?"

"No, this was an accident involving a Weber grill." He started to explain further but decided against it. "And now I think you've investigated the incident fully. Good work."

"Really?"

"Absolutely." The rain was finally letting up. "Can we go to the cemetery now?"

Miller put the car in gear, made a three-point turn and headed back up the street. In the distance, there were fire sirens. When they passed Charice's, Raymer said, "Hold on a second."

Miller stopped.

"Point your spotlight up there."

Miller did as he was told, and Raymer couldn't believe his eyes. In addition to the impressive damage he himself had caused, the porch was now scorched black and smoldering.

"Must be where that lightning hit," Miller said. When his boss didn't respond, he regarded him strangely. "Chief? You don't look so good."

In truth, he didn't feel so good, either. His sense that Becka had visited him on that porch was still strong. He could still feel her fingers on his scalp, her whispering there was something she needed to tell him. If he hadn't awakened when he did? And if he hadn't climbed down from up there? He might be a toast-type individual.

BY THE TIME they arrived at Hilldale the rain had stopped, but there was more heat lightning to the south, and once again the rumble of distant thunder, another storm tracking in their direction. In the summer they sometimes bore down like this, relentless, one after the other, all night long.

The cemetery's lot was a muddy lake, in the middle of which sat Raymer's Jetta. When Miller pulled up next to it, he thanked him for the lift and instructed him to use the rest of his shift to stake out the Morrison Arms on the off chance that William Smith might return, though Raymer would've bet his life they'd seen the last of him.

"Chief?" Miller said, when he started to get out of the cruiser. "You gonna be all right?"

Raymer was touched by his concern. "I'll be fine after I get some sleep."

"Okay, it's just . . ."

"Just what?"

"You look kind of . . ."

While he searched for the right word, Raymer considered the possibilities: *Dispirited? Rode hard and put up wet? Chewed up and spit out?* Or did Miller just mean to reiterate that, covered in ash as he was, he still resembled a Negro-type individual?

"Sad," Miller finally said.

"Sad as in pathetic, or sad as in sorrowful?"

"Sad as in unhappy."

"Oh."

"Are you? Sad?"

Raymer wasn't sure how to respond. There was a dim-witted earnestness about Miller that he found both endearing and infuriating, kind of like coming across an old photo of yourself, smiling ear to ear, happy as a pig in shit. The possibility that such happiness won't and can't last, that its source is genetic foolishness, hasn't occurred to you yet, but it will.

"Because you shouldn't be," Miller said, an out-of-character confidence creeping into his voice.

"Why not?"

"Because you're the chief."

For the moment that was true, though Raymer felt certain the question that had been dogging him of late—whether to resign—would soon be moot. When it became widely known that someone trafficking in lethal reptiles, handguns and drugs (yes, Justin had been right; weed, methamphetamine and prescription painkillers had indeed been found in 107's bathroom) had been living for months in the Morrison Arms, where the chief of police also lived, that would be that.

"Look, Miller, I appreciate—"

"You're the *chief*," Miller repeated, downright adamant now. "Everybody's got to do what you say." Clearly, giving orders was the end Miller desperately hoped to achieve without first understanding the means. Had Raymer himself ever wanted that? To tell people what to do?

"Nobody does what I say, actually," Raymer assured him. Charice routinely ignored his orders if she considered them unwise. Likewise, her brother. Even old Mr. Hynes felt free to ignore his advice. When an armed white man in a position of authority couldn't even get black people to take him seriously, well, it said something, didn't it?

"*I* do," Miller said. Which was true. Until he learned to think, Miller had little choice but to remain a model of literal-minded obedience.

"And I appreciate it," Raymer said, anxious to draw this conversation to a close. "Well, good night, then."

"Chief?" said Miller, evidently just as anxious to prolong it.

"What, Miller?"

"Am I going to get fired?"

Raymer paused, unsure what he was asking: if the day would ever come when Raymer would have to terminate him, or if plans to do so were already afoot? "Why do you ask?"

"I knew it," Miller said, dropping his head miserably. "It's Officer Bond's brother, isn't it?"

"Jerome?"

"He's coming to work for us?"

"No."

Miller looked dubious. "Then why's he always hanging around?"

"I've asked myself the same question," Raymer admitted, recalling that afternoon's conversation between Gus and Jerome at the mill. Was Jerome considering some sort of offer? The mayor pressing him for an answer? At the time Raymer, his head throbbing mercilessly, hadn't given the matter much thought. Gus always had something going on. But maybe Miller was onto something. Was Raymer to be replaced—by Jerome? Had Jerome surmised that Raymer had found out about the plot against him and keyed the 'Stang in retaliation? If so, what part had Charice played in all this? Had she invited him to dinner in the hopes of figuring out what, if anything, he knew? That phone call she'd received just as he was drifting off on the back porch? Her casual tone had suggested she was talking to a girlfriend with boy trouble. (What had she said? *As usual, you're getting all worked up over nothing.*) But what if it was Jerome who'd called, wanting to know what she'd learned? That made a kind of sense, except that Charice hadn't seemed particularly curious during dinner. She'd spent more time trying to explain her brother's bizarre behavior than questioning Raymer about his own.

"I wonder where she went?" Miller said, what seemed to Raymer a completely out-of-left-field question.

"Who?"

"Charice. Officer Bond."

"She went somewhere?"

"Her car wasn't in the drive just now."

This was true, Raymer realized. Her Civic *hadn't* been there. He'd been so focused on her destroyed porch he hadn't really taken in the car's absence and what that might mean. A wave of relief washed over him then, because among other things it meant that when he'd been pleading with Charice to let him back in the house, she hadn't even been there. Nor had she heard his truly lame offer to reimburse her for the lamb chops or his pitiful admission that he was a terrible cop and a worse chief of police. She must've left shortly after receiving that phone call. Maybe she'd come to the screen door to explain that she'd be back shortly, seen him blissfully asleep and switched off the kitchen light so as not to disturb him. Maybe she'd locked the screen door to indicate he wasn't supposed to leave until she returned. Okay, that last part made no sense, but maybe there was still some small piece of the puzzle he was missing. The important thing was that maybe, just maybe, she wasn't pissed at him after all—although it was also true that in this same scenario she didn't know he'd managed to ruin her landlord's porch totally.

Maybe, he thought happily, they'd conclude it had been destroyed by that lightning strike.

"Miller," Raymer said, impressed that the man had actually noticed the missing car. "You may make a cop yet."

"Really?"

"You should stop stalking Officer Bond, though."

"I know," he said. "You probably think I'm a creep."

"No, but she would."

He nodded sadly. "Chief?" he said. "You think she'd go out with somebody like me?"

Not really wanting to answer this question, Raymer sought clarification. "You or somebody *like* you?" Because Raymer himself, he had to admit, was "like" Miller: perpetually bewildered and self-conscious and full of self-loathing. So yeah, it would've been nice to be able to say that Charice could conceivably fall for somebody *like* Miller, if not Miller himself.

The breeze came up just then, lifting Raymer's hair as it had done on Charice's porch, and yet again he felt, or imagined he did, Becka's proximity, her need to communicate something to him. He even had a glimmer of what it might be.

Miller was looking glum. "Would I get fired? If I asked her out and she said yes?"

"It's against the rules for *me* to date her, not you. I'm her boss. Whereas you . . ." Raymer struggled to locate the exact language needed to describe a relationship between Charice and Miller that didn't exist and hopefully never would.

"I'm nothing," he said, finally putting the cruiser in gear. "I know."

Rub's Penis

DURING THE LONG SECOND ACT of Sully's life, he'd made it a
point not only to be present for last call most nights but also to
go on record as objecting to the concept as arbitrary and puritanical.
These days, however, his third act well under way, though his core belief
hadn't changed, his behavior had. At seventy, in what at least his doctors
believed to be terminally failing health, Sully had reluctantly come to
suspect that misbehavior was a younger man's sport. He'd played it longer than most, though, and tonight, thanks to Ruth's heartfelt permission to stay away from Hattie's for a while and the fact that his breathing
had inexplicably improved as the day progressed, he fell gratefully and
effortlessly back into the routine that had suited him so well for so long.
As the thunderstorms rolled through, dimming lights and flinging rain
at the walls outside, Sully reflected, and not for the first time, that there
was no better place to be during violent weather than on a barstool. In
any weather, for that matter.

The Horse remained lively until close to midnight, when the last of
the storms headed north and word started to circulate that the power
was back on in town. People began to drift out into the (finally!) cool
night, leaving behind Birdie and Sully and Jocko and the Rubs. When
Janey finished her shift Sully offered to buy her a drink, but she just
looked at him like he was insane. What the fuck was this? Like maybe
he was hoping to take up with *her,* now that her mother wasn't inter-

ested anymore? Nothing could have been further from Sully's mind, but her instinct was probably right. How would it have looked if she accepted his offer of a drink and settled onto the stool next to him? Besides, Rub wasn't done with his litany of wishes yet. Having spent his afternoon in a tree, he seemed even needier than usual, if that was possible, so Sully let him get it all out of his system.

Half an hour before last call Carl Roebuck strolled in with a very drunk young woman roughly Janey's age on his arm. She was exactly the sort Carl always seemed to attract: dim-witted or pretending to be, large breasted, oversexed. "Let's play poker," he suggested, taking out his wallet and counting the bills therein. "Ninety-eight dollars," he said, slapping them on the bar. "And not just any ninety-eight dollars. My last ninety-eight dollars in the world."

"Show of hands," Sully said. "Who here feels sorry for Carl?"

"Let this be a lesson to you," Carl told his companion, when she alone raised her hand. "This is the wrong fucking place to come if you're looking for sympathy."

"On the other hand," Birdie said, handing him his usual Maker's, "if you're looking for alcohol . . ."

Apparently in response to the poker game idea, the young woman stood on tiptoe to whisper into his ear, all too audibly, "I thought you said you were going to take me home and fuck me."

Birdie snorted at this. "You must be from out of town," she said.

"Later," Carl whispered back. Then, to Birdie, "Say hello to Jennifer, who'd like a Cuba libre, that is, if you can stop making fun of other people's tribulations long enough to make her one. As you deduced, Jennifer here hails from Lake George and is not fully cognizant of certain *extremely personal matters.*"

Jennifer scrunched her shoulders. "I love the way he talks," she said.

"Yeah, me too," Birdie said, pouring rum over ice.

Rub, as he always did with Carl's girlfriends, commenced staring at Jennifer's chest, his expression identical to the one he always wore when contemplating big ole bacon cheeseburgers. Seeing she had his undivided attention, Jennifer extended her hand in greeting. "Hi!" she said. "What's your name?"

Rub normally didn't have much trouble with his *R*'s, but he did now. Embarrassed by his stammer, Jennifer quickly turned her attention to the other Rub. "Oh, look!" she squealed. "A puppy! Isn't he cute?"

"Would you like to have him?" Sully said.

Jennifer seemed to regard this as a joke. "What's his name?"

"Rub," Sully said, causing her to blink at the man she'd just met. Had there been some misunderstanding? He and the dog had the same name? If she asked the name of the tall man in the pharmacist's smock, would it, too, be Rub? What kind of place was this?

When Rub, excited to hear his name, stood up and wagged his whole hind end, Jennifer took a quick step back, visibly alarmed by his bloody erection. "What's wrong with Rub's penis?" she wanted to know, causing the other Rub to blush deeply.

"He chews on it," Sully explained.

"Doesn't that hurt?"

"You're asking me?"

"Nights like this," said Jocko as they filed into the back room, "I feel the need of a one-legged lawyer." Sully had been thinking the same thing, and together they raised their glasses in the direction of Wirf's prosthesis, which since his death had occupied the place of honor on the mantel. They took their seats around the poker table, Rub careful as always to sit next to Sully. Jocko located the chips and assumed the role of banker, Carl being too dishonest, Sully too careless. The dog circled around several times, sighed, curled up at the base of his master's chair and returned to gnawing.

"How would you like to own half a construction company?" Carl asked Sully.

"That would depend on who owns the other half."

"Assume it's your best friend in the world."

Sully elbowed Rub, who'd gone back to staring at Jennifer's boobs. "Hey, Dummy. Do you own a construction company?"

Carl ignored this while Rub beamed. "Assume this best friend isn't going to be able to make payroll next week. Assume that wall collapsing this afternoon was the last fucking nail in his coffin. Assume he's about to be sued by everyone from the mill's investors to the town of Bath to the asshole ex-con who happened to be driving by at the exact wrong moment."

Carl of course was always claiming imminent financial ruin, but could it possibly be true this time, Sully wondered. "Let's assume instead," he suggested, "that everybody but you saw this day coming for a long time. Assume the friend you now want to be your partner has been warning you about it for the last fucking decade."

"Assume," Carl replied, "that this friend's an asshole for picking this particular moment to say I told you so."

"Assume this same friend's a fucking prince for not bringing up the fact that you're six months behind on your rent."

Jennifer was taking all this in with growing alarm. "Are you two having a fight?"

"Not really," Sully told her. "I *am* going to take his last hundred bucks, though."

"He would, too, if I'd let him," Carl agreed.

"High card deals," said Jocko, setting the deck down in the middle of the table.

"That would be me," Sully said, leaning forward to turn over the ace of spades.

Carl sighed. "Fuck me," he said.

And Sully, feeling as you sometimes do when the world aligns in your favor, proceeded to do just that.

A Sundering

R AYMER STARTED UP the Jetta and, just in case Miller was watching in his rearview, put the car in reverse so his taillights would pulse. When the cruiser pulled out onto the two-lane blacktop and headed back toward town, he put his car back in park and turned the engine off. Rummaging around in the glove box, he located the flashlight he kept there, but naturally the batteries were dead. A sign, if ever there was one, to cease and desist, to put a merciful end to this bloody, god-awful day. Tomorrow would arrive soon enough and with it numerous opportunities for further lunacy. Hadn't he already crammed a good hundred pounds' worth of shit into today's fifty-pound sack? *Go home,* he told himself.

Except what did that even mean? Home, at least until he could make other arrangements, was still the Morrison Arms and officially off-limits. If he ignored his own yellow tape and climbed into his own bed, his sleep would likely be haunted by phantoms of the escaped cobra. His other alternatives were nearly as unattractive. He could return to the couch in his office, but he'd be discovered there bright and early by Charice, and given the evening's events he couldn't really face that. Like the other residents of the Arms, he had a voucher for a motel room, but so late, with this a holiday weekend, he'd surely be greeted by a NO VACANCY sign.

As Raymer made his way into Dale on foot, there was renewed rumbling to the south, the low clouds reflecting distant lightning strikes. The air was again full of electricity, the hair on his forearms standing up, just as it had on Charice's porch (before he destroyed it). With nothing but sporadic lightning to navigate by, he stuck to the path as best he could but managed to stray anyway. The Dale grave markers, set flat to the ground, jutted up just enough to trip him, and twice he went down, the second time hard. Rising slick with mud, he was grateful for the dark. Between the charcoal ash from the Weber and the fresh coat of mud, he could easily imagine what he must look like. It put him in mind of that book Miss Beryl had assigned in eighth grade, the one where a boy comes upon an escaped convict on the marsh. The old woman had made a special point of telling him he would identify with the boy in the story, but after reading that first chapter he'd put the book away and refused to pick it up again. When he failed the test, Miss Beryl, puzzled, had asked him if he'd found the book too difficult. He lied and said yes, because the truth was even more embarrassing. He'd quit because the scene on the marsh had terrified him, and even though the chapter ended with the convict being led away in chains, Raymer had been afraid he would return. It was a long book, one that would take weeks to read, and he knew he'd spend the whole time worried sick. For some reason he related this story as a lighthearted anecdote to Becka on their honeymoon, though she'd appeared genuinely stricken. "Don't you see?" she explained. "You cheated yourself." And maybe she was right, but really, was that such a terrible thing? Didn't people cheat themselves all the time, over more important things than eighth-grade reading assignments? "Was I right?" he asked her, because clearly she knew the book in question. "Did the convict come back?"

"Of *course* he did," she admitted. She seemed about to say more but thought better of it, which was a shame because in describing the poor kid's predicament—whether or not to rat the man out—Raymer discovered that he actually did want to know how the story turned out. (Miss Beryl was right—he *had* identified with that lonely, friendless boy.) Becka's refusal to satisfy his belated curiosity suggested that even now, so many years later, he didn't *deserve* to know. More troubling still was the possibility that this had been her first inkling that their marriage was doomed, that a cowardly boy had grown up to be a cowardly man.

These were his thoughts as he trudged through marshlike Dale, his shoes ruined, his socks squishy. He wasn't even certain he was headed in the right direction until the sky lit up obligingly and he saw the old judge's grave, its fresh mound shrunk considerably by the earlier deluge. Was it really just this morning that he'd stood here listening to that idiot preacher? It felt like last week. Pitch dark descended again, but he had his bearings now, and he had a pretty good sense of where the yellow backhoe had sat and also, a few rows off to the right, where someone had placed that bouquet of red roses.

When he located Becka's grave, he would . . . what? Try to fall asleep again in hopes that she'd return to him in a dream, as she had earlier, and tell him whatever it was she wanted him to know? If she could visit him on Charice's porch, over a mile away, surely she'd be able to contact him here, mere feet from all that remained of her physical existence. Whatever she wanted to convey had seemed urgent, though after this long, what could it be? The identity of her lover? Okay, but why now? That she'd come to understand in death what had eluded her in life— that it was he, Raymer, and not this other man, who she truly loved? Or that the time had come for him to stop obsessing about her lover's identity and move on with his life? Maybe the reason she visited him there on the porch, after the lovely evening he and Charice had spent together, was to give him her blessing. It was possible. But so, alas, was its opposite. What if she'd come to warn him about Charice, that he was about to make a terrible mistake?

Given the swift approach of this new storm, however, would sleep even be possible? Exhausted though he was, he was feeling pretty wide awake. And even if he did manage to drift off, wouldn't the first clap of thunder thwart him all over again? On the other hand, maybe sleep wasn't the only means of summoning her. If she was a ghost and near to hand, maybe she'd just appear to him? If she did, what would he say? He supposed he might begin by apologizing for not having visited before now, that a better man would've grieved her loss instead of allowing himself to be consumed by the betrayal she'd been contemplating when she came *down those stairs like a Slinky*. Because for her to have fallen in love with someone else, she'd first have had to fall *out* of love with him, and he must've had some role to play in that. And while he was apologizing, now might also be a good time to admit he never should have married her in the first place, knowing as he always had that he didn't deserve a woman as beautiful and smart and self-confident and talented and full of life as she was. Of course Becka would stray. How could she not?

The trouble with such abject groveling as an opening conversational gambit with a dead woman was that Becka would immediately identify its source as self-loathing, the very thing she'd always liked least about him. If after death some part of the old Becka remained, and he—face it, the aggrieved party—begged *her* forgiveness, he could all too easily imagine her dismayed response: *Christ on a crutch, don't tell me you're still at it?* But how was he to entreat her if not with kindness and under-standing and forgiveness?

The only thing he could be certain of was that if Becka was a real ghost, then the conversation—whatever its content and form—had to take place tonight. Tomorrow morning her visitation at Charice's would feel like a dream, and he'd interpret that dream accordingly, in the con-text of his own emotional need—his subconscious inventing her so that she could inform him it was okay to have feelings for another woman and to act on them. And tomorrow, in the cold light of day, sure, why not? Tonight, though, in the intimate dark, he wanted Becka to be real, to have come to him out of her own need, not his. Here in Hilldale he wanted more than cheap parlor tricks of his own devising.

Though of course all of this was assuming he survived the next half hour. Crazy, but he'd been treating the approaching storm as if it were a friendly presence, lighting his path to Becka's grave, yet now that it was upon him—directly overhead, in fact—there was nothing friendly about it. A bolt of lightning sizzled audibly overhead a split second before illuminating his surroundings, and in that heartbeat, before everything went black again, he saw the ground was pocked with splotches of dull red. It took a moment for him to understand what he'd seen, that the earth beneath his feet was strewn with petals, all that was left of the beautiful bouquet of roses he'd noticed that morning. Which meant he was close. Becka's grave was nearby. With any luck the next lightning flash would tell him which one was hers.

What came instead was the rain, all at once and furious, just like the earlier downpour in town, except now there was no dry police cruiser to duck into, no dim-witted Officer Miller to distract him from the deluge. What on earth had possessed him to come out here? he wondered, awed for the second time in an hour by nature's fury. Why hadn't he waited for the storm to pass in the comfort of the Jetta? In a matter of seconds he was drenched to the skin, the last of the charcoal ash leaching out of his hair, running in rivulets under his collar, down his back and into the waistband of his boxers. It occurred to him then that if this *was* a ghost story he was in the middle of, *here* was how it would end: in the morning he would be found, cold and dead, at the foot of Becka's grave. Because in a ghost story Becka wouldn't have summoned him to Hilldale in an electrical storm to tell him that all was forgiven. No, her ghost would be vengeful. She would've brought him here—Raymer swallowed hard—to kill him.

Still, if the knowing, sentient universe was waiting for that fatal symmetry, couldn't he deny it by remaining right where he was? He had no idea who lay interred beneath these rose petals, but he doubted whoever it was had anything against him, certainly no reason to call terrible vengeance down upon him. The ruined bouquet of roses suggested this was the grave of a woman—someone's beloved wife or sister or daughter. It didn't really matter who she was, so long as she wasn't . . .

REBECCA WHITT RAYMER.

The very name on the stone at his feet that he himself had grudgingly paid for. This was what that lightning flash had revealed, and when the world went dark again her name remained as sharp before him as a photographic negative. Rebecca Whitt Raymer. The thunderclap that followed the lightning strike shook the ground so violently that the wire cone used to hold the flowers in place tipped forward at a forty-five-degree angle in the loosened soil, as if offering him the thorny, denuded stems. The green cellophane that had served as a sheath was now flapping wildly in the wind, the small florist's card somehow still affixed.

This, then, Raymer thought, dropping to his knees in the mud, was how Becka meant to communicate with him. An obscene giggle erupted at the thought. There would be no dream, no conversation. The florist's card would contain a name. Raymer would read that name and finally would know. After which the lightning would find him. The knowledge he'd sought arriving in tandem with death. Perfect. Biblical in its justice, when you thought about it. The end of his selfish, foolhardy quest would be the end of *him*. Fair enough. Because he'd been, as always, an idiot. It wasn't even knowledge he'd sought. There would have been some dignity in that. No, he'd been willing to settle for information, a lesser thing entirely. He'd wanted, and still did want, her boyfriend's name. His *identity*. Beyond that he had given the man himself little real thought. Until just now, when he realized that these once-lovely red roses had been for Becka, it hadn't occurred to him that maybe he wasn't the only one haunted by her, still in love with her, unwilling or unable to move on. How had that obvious truth eluded him so completely? How many other failures of imagination had he been guilty of?

The one that troubled him most was Becka herself. In the short time they'd been married had he ever asked about what she was feeling or thinking, whether she was happy? There had been moments, especially toward the end, when he suspected something must be wrong, but she always denied it when he inquired, claiming that she just had a case of the blues, that she'd wake up feeling more cheerful in the morning. And he'd been all too happy to be reassured. Why dig deeper?

As was invariably the case with Raymer, such specific self-doubts and accusations led to other, more global ones. Was it possible to be a good cop, a good husband or a good man when you were disinclined to imagine the inner lives, in particular the suffering, of others? Wasn't this just basic empathy? Was it empathy she'd gone looking for and found in the man whose name was on the florist's card? Had he taken the trouble to understand her more deeply than Raymer ever had? Or was empathy just the tip of the iceberg? Raymer supposed he could stand it if the man was taller or trimmer or better looking, but was it possible the fucker also possessed intelligence, wit, elegance and grace? Was he *everything* he himself was not?

That, then, was what it all came down to: vanity. He simply *had* to know, even if it cost him his life. That was why it seemed he had no choice but to reach out and grab the florist's card, which he did just as the wind tugged the green cellophane free of the wire mesh. The information he was after was now literally within his grasp, but in that very instant the sky was cleaved by yet another shaft of lightning, and he felt a searing heat in his right palm, as if the little card had somehow burst into flame. He felt a desperate howl building deep in his chest and knew he would have to cut loose either the howl in his throat or the card in his fist. The howl, then, he decided, and it merged with the thunderclap as if the two had the same source.

He couldn't tell how long he'd been howling, but when it was over, he felt a profound change to his being, his psyche. An odd sensation, not unlike vertigo, like something essential had been hewn in two. He'd entered the cemetery as Douglas Raymer, a man who for a very long time, maybe his whole life, had been going doggedly through the motions. Now he felt a second presence, as if the skin and bones that had until then belonged to him, and him alone, now played host to another. Douglas Raymer, wholly familiar, was still here, the same boy Miss Beryl had thrust books at, that had been bullied by boys like Roy Purdy and later mocked by scofflaws like Sully and ridiculed from the bench by Judge Flatt. Who had run for public office on the promise that he wouldn't be happy until those he served were *un*happy. A fool, face up to it. A fool and a milquetoast who was forever banging on about becoming a better cop, a better husband, a better man.

Strange that he should feel so familiar with the second presence even before being introduced, as if he'd known this "other" all his life. Call him . . . what? *Dougie,* Raymer decided, because the presence he felt seemed younger, like a kid brother. A mean one. The thing about this Dougie? He absolutely did not give a shit. Not about Becka, not about duty, not about what people thought of him, especially Douglas

Raymer, who, in Dougie's considered opinion, ate far too much shit on a daily basis. Dougie's inclination, long held in check, was to kick ass and take names. Get the fucking job done.

It was Dougie who would know what came next. After they looked at the card. After they knew who the son of a bitch was.

Reincarnation

ONLY CARL APPEARED disappointed when the game broke up an hour and a half after it started, with all the chips in front of Sully. Jennifer, quickly bored, had fallen asleep on the sofa, and Carl now stood over her with a look of profound sadness. "Have you ever made a rash promise?" he asked Sully.

"Oh, once or twice," Sully admitted. "I was married, if you recall."

"I'm sorry, baby," Jennifer purred, when Carl put a hand on her shoulder. "I'm not in the mood anymore." She rolled away from him, under the apparent impression that she was home and in bed.

"Let her sleep," said Birdie, who had an apartment above the tavern.

"Really?" Carl said, looking for all the world like a man who'd just been granted a stay of execution.

Birdie shrugged. "The register's locked."

Outside, in the parking lot, they waved to Jocko, who tooted good-bye. Carl, nudging Sully, said, "A word in private?"

Hearing this, Rub's face darkened. He was about to be dismissed, and he hated that. Worse, he'd be leaving Sully alone with Carl, who seemed to believe they were best friends and sometimes, like tonight, even said so. When Sully handed him the keys to the truck, Rub accepted them reluctantly.

"It was true, what I said earlier," Carl told him when they were alone.

"You're really broke?"

"And then some."

"I don't know what you think I can do, but I'll help if I can."

"Nah, I think we're well beyond that."

"What, then?"

"I *am* sorry about the rent."

"Don't worry about it."

"I'll clear out if you want."

"What'd I just say?"

Carl shrugged. "Okay." Then, "Do you believe in reincarnation?"

"You mean like we die and then have to do this fucking thing all over again?"

"Yeah, like that."

"Jesus, I hope not."

"I don't know," Carl said. "Second time around we might be smarter."

"We might be dumber, too."

"*I* might be," Carl admitted. "I really don't see how you could be."

"Would you *want* to live again?"

"Fuck, yeah," Carl said, rocking back on his heels. "I mean, what a night. Look at that sky."

Sully did, and in fact it was beautiful, the air crisp and clean, the sky full of stars and a bright three-quarter moon. He recalled that afternoon at the diner when everything had appeared to stop, and his life had suddenly seemed like the set of a low-budget movie. At the time he'd wondered if maybe that meant he'd had enough, but now he wasn't so sure. "I hope you're not going to tell me it's the stars you're going to miss when you're dead."

"I don't know why I even talk to you," Carl said.

"I don't either. Are we done, or is there more to say?"

Apparently there was. "Why would I do something like that?" he said, genuinely perplexed.

"Like what?"

"Promise that girl."

"How the fuck should I know? I don't even understand why I do half the shit *I* do. I'm supposed to understand you?"

Carl thought about it. "You *really* never think about sex anymore?" he said. "Because I just find that so fucking hard to believe."

DRIVING BACK TO Rub's place, Sully handed him the money he'd lost playing cards so Bootsie wouldn't get pissed off. "How come you didn't drop when I gave you the knee?" he asked.

"I had three fuh-fuh—"

"Fucking queens, I know. But I had a full boat."

"Didn't look like it," Rub recalled miserably.

"That was the beauty of it."

"Sometimes you give me the nuh-nuh-knee and I drop and then it turns out you got nuh-nuh—"

"Nothing?"

"—and it would've been my pot."

"Yeah?" Sully said, watching Rub stuff the bills into his chest pocket. "Well, cheer up. The money usually finds its way back to you."

When they pulled into the drive and the headlights swept over the tree limb, Sully said, "When you get off work tomorrow, come find me, and we'll cart all that off. Don't forget, either, because I got a bet with Bootsie, and I can't afford to support you both." Then when Rub started to get out, he said, "Hey."

"What?"

"What's the matter with you anyway? You been acting weird all night."

Rub began to cry.

Sully sighed, having known better than to ask. "You upset because I told about you getting stuck up in the tree?"

Rub stifled a sob. "Everybody laughed."

"Well, it was funny. You laughed, too."

"I know."

"Well then?"

"I'm nuh-nuh—"

"Never gonna hear the end of it? That's probably true."

Rub wiped his nose on his sleeve. "I just wisht—"

"What?"

Rub sighed. Where to begin?

"That I'd be nicer to you?"

He shrugged again, but this was the gist of it, Sully could tell.

"I wish I would, too," he said, and for some reason this seemed to cheer Rub up. He always liked it when they agreed, and it didn't seem to trouble him that with a little effort Sully could probably make both their wishes come true. "And I'm not the only one who could be nicer, you know."

Rub looked at him blankly.

"When I was here earlier, your wife was crying."

"Buh-buh-Bootsie?" He looked genuinely terrified now.

"How many wives you got?"

"Why?"

"How the hell should I know? She's your wife." Because of course this was an invitation to think about Vera, his own wife, or ex-wife, out at the county home, muttering obscenities under her breath whenever she thought of him. Until recently he'd pretty much banished her from memory, but this was the third time he'd thought about her today. What the hell was *that* about?

"Wuh-wuh-what should I do?"

Sully shrugged. "Who knows? Take her out to dinner or something."

He took out the money Sully'd just given him and counted it dubiously.

"Jesus," said Sully, handing him another twenty. "Rub!"

"What?"

"I wasn't talking to you."

Rub, who'd been riding in the back, leaped out of the truck bed and up into the seat his namesake had just vacated.

"I wisht he had some other name," Rub said.

"And so does he about you," Sully told him, putting the vehicle in reverse.

Hill Comes to Dale

WHEN RAYMER FINALLY RETURNED to his senses, he was still on his knees at the foot of Becka's grave, the storm having passed. He had the distinct impression that he'd actually vacated his body for a time, left it to fend for itself, but for how long? A few minutes? Half an hour? The rumbling thunder was now miles to the north, and the rain had stopped, so probably closer to the latter. Taking inventory, he discovered his right hand was cramped painfully into a claw. He shook the damned thing vigorously, trying to restore circulation, but it remained frozen, numb. Had he suffered a stroke? Struggling to his feet, he became aware of an odd, tingling sensation in his extremities— toes, ears and, for some reason, the tip of his tongue. Had he been struck by lightning? Wouldn't a direct hit have killed him? Reduced him to cinders, in fact? What about an indirect hit? What if lightning struck a tree over in nearby Hill, say, then traveled along the ground in search of somebody dumb enough to be kneeling in the soaking wet in Dale and delivered enough of a jolt to short out a circuit or two but not enough to fry them all?

"Hello?" he said, trying out his tingly tongue, the word echoing in his skull like it would in an empty drum. Why did he half expect an answer?

Then he remembered: reaching out for the florist's card as the sky lit up like broad daylight, the pile-driving peal of thunder as he closed his fist around it, the howl escaping his throat subsumed simultaneously by the thunderclap. And finally the nauseating sense of having been split in two, of a malignant new presence filling up every cell of his body. Dougie, he remembered naming it. "Hello?" he said again, louder this time, akin to a man shaking a shoe and listening for the pebble trapped in its toe. "Dougie?"

Silence.

Thank God. Because one Douglas Raymer, he thought, was all the Douglas Raymer anyone would ever need, including himself. Evidently the second entity, whose rogue electrical impulse he'd detected, hadn't survived the drier, fresher, cooler air that trailed in the wake of the storm. Good riddance.

And yet it had been, he had to admit, a very close call. He'd come dangerously close to losing his mind. Hard to believe, but as the storm raged overhead, he'd actually believed that his dead wife, somehow in control of nature itself, was trying to kill him, hurling lightning bolts at him like a vengeful Fury, as if he'd been the one cheating on her instead of vice versa. Insane. He'd nearly killed himself for the sake of a card from a *florist,* for God's sake.

Soaking wet and shivering uncontrollably, Raymer made his zombielike return through the slop, arriving back at the parking lot just as the three-quarter moon scudded out from behind the clouds, so blinding it was a miracle it didn't dampen all the stars in the sky. The last of the fast-moving storms seemed to have finally broken the back of the heat wave, the temperature plummeting a good twenty degrees. That morning, standing beneath a broiling sun, Raymer had prayed for just such blessed relief, and now that prayer's answer was delivered, like those of so many prayers, like retribution itself. Unlocking the Jetta, he slid behind the wheel and studied his right claw under the dome light, marveling at its rigor-mortis determination to remain clenched. Using the thumb and forefinger of his good hand, he was able to straighten his frozen pinkie, but every time he let go of it to work on its neighbor, it snapped back into the claw again, and he finally gave up, grateful that no one was around to witness his futile struggles against himself.

It was going on one, so the sensible thing would be to find someplace to crash, but where? Charice's? No, not a chance in hell. Even under normal circumstances he would've been reluctant to show up on the doorstep of fastidious Jerome, whose upscale Schuyler condo was the 'Stang's glove compartment writ large. About the only person he could think of who might welcome him at this hour was old Mr. Hynes, but since Raymer had his own apartment at the Morrison Arms that made no sense at all. Besides, after all he'd been through, what he really needed was to be alone for a while, in a hotel room's bathtub where he could soak his freaky paw in warm water and wait for the tingling in his extremities to subside. By morning, if the hand still hadn't relaxed, he'd have to haul it into the ER. Follow the biblical injunction and have the fucking thing amputated if it continued to offend him.

Unable to grip the ignition key, he awkwardly inserted it with his left hand, finally managing to turn it in the ignition. When the engine turned over, the windshield wipers leaped unexpectedly to life, startling the hell out of him, and once he switched them off the radio blared on, loud. He cut the volume and checked the dial, which was tuned, inexplicably, to a country station. Raymer seldom listened to the radio at all, much less to this hillbilly shit. Had someone been playing around in his car? When he snapped the radio off, he noticed an ambient buzzing in his ears that hadn't been there before. He shook his head vigorously, even more convinced that he'd somehow absorbed some sort of electrical shock back at Becka's grave. "Hello?" he said again, his voice causing the buzzing to get even louder.

Then, a moment later, it stopped altogether, and a gravelly voice said, *Hello, fuckwad.*

AT THE CEMETERY'S MAIN GATE, instead of turning right onto the highway, Raymer turned left onto the gravel road that separated Hill from Dale, at the other end of which was the rarely used Spring Street entrance. That would lead directly out to the interstate, where he just might, against all odds, find a vacancy at one of the chain motels.

He'd waited back in the parking lot for over half an hour, praying for the voice in his head to say something else, but instead the buzzing in his ears had returned, only louder. Sleep. Dear God, *sleep* was what he needed. If he couldn't find a room out there, he'd conk out in the vast Lowe's parking lot. And tomorrow he'd hand in his resignation. In the unlikely event anyone objected or wanted to know why, he'd tell them he was hearing voices and going batshit crazy. Maybe he'd drive to Utica, to the state mental hospital, in hopes they could sort him. They hadn't done shit for the mayor's wife, but who knew?

So profound was his exhaustion that when Raymer came to the ten-foot mound of earth sitting in the middle of the blacktop and blocking both lanes—as if lowered from the sky—he pulled up and stared at it, unsure if what he was looking at was even real. Could it be, like the voice in his head, a figment of his insanity? At the top of the hill stood a gnarled tree, mostly dead from the look of it, tipped over at an absurd angle, exposing its root system to the open air. In the moonlight, the whole thing put him in mind of an absurdist painting, its details dreamlike, their deliberate inclusion meant to induce wonder. The most bizarre of these was the oblong box protruding from the soil at pavement level where something ornate and silvery, a handle of some sort, reflected Raymer's headlights. It took a minute for the composition to add up to a casket whose lid, he now saw, was askew. Above, a good fifty yards up the hillside, a great gash in the slope suggested that there, until recently, the hill itself and the tree and the casket had all resided.

In other words, what he was looking at had a rational explanation. His eyes weren't playing tricks. All the trees in the Hill section were old, and many were dying, literally falling over. The torrential rains had loosened the hummocky ground, causing this section to pull loose and slalom right down to the road. The external world was what it was and operating as it always had. Tomorrow, when citizens asked the chief of police *What the hell?* he'd have a comforting explanation ready. Though reassured that he hadn't come completely untethered from reality, Raymer nevertheless found himself overwhelmed with sorrow. He was, he realized, actually weeping, gently at first and then more violently, his shoulders quaking with sobs. It was as if mundane and mechanistic things were suddenly revealed to have been specifically designed with an eye toward maximum cruelty and guaranteed suffering. Bad enough that our relationships with the living should always be undermined by fear and venality and narcissism and a hundred other things, but it seemed especially awful that we couldn't be faithful even to the dead. We put them in the ground with expressions of love and admiration and eternal devotion, promising never to forget, though then we did, or tried to. The old judge they'd buried just this morning was already receding from the collective memory. Nobody except Raymer remembered his poor mother anymore, and when he was gone it would be as if she never existed. No wonder the dead protested. No wonder their caskets came lurching up out of the ground, their lids awry, as if to say, *Remember me? Remember all your promises?* Poor Becka. If she was angry at him, could he blame her? He hadn't even made any of the usual promises. He'd put her in the ground because he was her husband and that was his duty, but he'd been unwilling to forgive or forget her perfidy. Tonight, he now realized, he'd managed to get things exactly backward. It was his anger at Becka that was metastasizing into something lethal, not hers at him. She wasn't vengeful beneath the ground; he was vengeful above it, his rage fueled by the corrosive knowledge that someone else had loved her better and more truly than he ever did. Another man *had* made solemn promises and, as the bouquet of roses testified, even kept them.

The buzzing in his ears stopped abruptly.

Oh, listen to yourself. Do you have any idea how pathetic you are?

Sorry, what's that?

Well, how would you describe yourself?

Unable to decide whether he was the accused or the accuser, Raymer was speechless in his own defense.

Be honest, for once, then.

Honest?

I know, a brand-new concept.

Go fuck yourself.

Okay, but think twice about that.

I know who I am.

At this, much hilarity. *You don't have a fuckin' clue. The old lady was right.* His voice changed here. *Who is this Douglas Raymer? Who is this Douglas Raymer?* A perfect impersonation of Miss Beryl back in eighth grade. *God, you kill me, you really do.*

Raymer waited for the laughter to stop, which it finally did.

Okay, so, this black chick, the voice continued. *You say you know your-self? Then explain to me why you're messing around with her?*

Raymer could feel his shoulders shrug. He thought about Charice, what a nice evening it had been when it seemed as if she liked him. He couldn't remember the last time he enjoyed himself nearly so much. *I don't know,* he admitted.

Sure you do.

It's complicated.

It isn't. Try being honest.

Well, he thought. *Right now I could really use a friend . . .*

See? That's exactly *the kind of bullshit I'm talking about. What you* want *is to see the butterfly on her ass.*

You know what? You're not a good person.

Finally. Now we're getting somewhere.

Raymer opened the car door and vomited lamb chops and aspara-gus and red wine onto the ground, hoping he'd expelled whatever had taken up residence in his head along with the contents of his stomach. No such luck.

Feel better? the voice wanted to know when he shut the door again.

I do, yes.

After a pause, *I'm not your enemy.*

You're hardly my friend.

That remains to be seen.

Leave me alone. Go back where you came from.

I'm where you *came from.*

No, you rode in on a bolt of lightning. When this tingling stops, you'll be gone.

No.

Raymer swallowed hard and tasted the rancid truth of this.

So, I gotta ask: aren't you even a little curious?

About what?

About what's on the card, you dope.

My hand won't open, Raymer said, holding up his claw to where any-one could see it, as if he weren't completely alone.

Try again.

This time, sure enough, the fingers slowly began to flex, his skin suddenly alive with a thousand pinpricks. Inside his fist was the crumpled florist's card, which he smoothed out, as best he could, on his pant leg, then held it up to the light. GILCHRIST'S FINE BLOOMS, it said in raised letters. Below this was the ubiquitous wing-footed Mercury, bouquet in hand.

Turn it over.

Raymer opened the door and vomited again, mostly dry heaves this time.

Quit stalling.

Can I tell you something? Raymer asked.

Anything.

I'm so tired of being everybody's fool.

He expected to be laughed at, but he wasn't. *I'm here to help.*

Raymer regarded the card, thinking about the choice he was being given. *When I know, will things be different?*

Let's find out.

What if they're even worse?

Turn the fucking card over.

Raymer did. There was just one word, scripted in what Raymer guessed must've been an elegant hand before the ink ran. There looked to be five or six letters. The first was clearly an *A,* the second, most likely, an *l.* Alfred? Alton? No, the other legible letter—second from the last—seemed to be a *y.* Allen, but spelled with a *y*? Finally it came to him. It wasn't a man's name at all, just the word *Always.*

Well, said Dougie. *I don't know about you, but I find that very disappointing.*

And then the buzzing was back.

Grave Doings

WHEN SULLY ARRIVED HOME, a car he didn't recognize was parked at the curb. There were no lights on in Miss Beryl's house, at least none that was visible from the street. Standing on the front seat, his paws on the dash, Rub had also noted the unfamiliar vehicle, barked at it, then turned to regard Sully. "I see it," Sully told him. "Shut up before I whack you one." The dog cocked his head, puzzled. Sully'd never laid a hand on him, but his threats, always delivered with conviction, were hard to ignore completely. The strain of not barking caused him to let loose a short burst of urine on the glove box.

"Let's go," Sully said, getting out, but Rub had already scrabbled past him.

Strange that after so many years Sully still thought of the house as Miss Beryl's. He'd lived in the apartment upstairs so long that he still forgot sometimes and went up the back stairs only to find the door locked. If Carl, who lived there now, was home and heard his approach, he'd holler, *You don't fucking live up here, you idiot.* And though Peter and Will had been living in the downstairs flat for the last seven years, at times Sully was still surprised to see one of them emerge instead of his former landlady. Lately, the house filled him with unease, and that was even stranger. It was a fine property, one of the best on the street, which in turn was one of the best streets in Bath. Had he any wish to sell it, the place was worth a small fortune. This was in part due to his grandson, who kept the lawn mowed and edged, the hedges neatly trimmed. Since moving in, he and his father had painted the place twice and undertaken repairs and improvements in return for reduced rent. Sully hadn't wanted to charge them anything at all, but Peter wouldn't hear of it. As a result, the house looked better now than when Miss Beryl was alive and depending on Sully to keep it spruced up.

If he'd had any inkling of her intention to leave him the house, he'd have done his best to talk her out of it. He'd never before owned anything more valuable than a motor vehicle, and that suited him to a T. The old woman must've known he had little desire to become a property owner so late in the overall scheme of things, that it might well prove a burden. Had she hoped it would force him to accept a long-overdue and entirely unwelcome new role as a responsible adult? Possibly. More likely, though, she'd just meant to thank him for the moral support he'd offered when her son, Clive Jr., skipped town in the wake of the Ultimate Escape Fun Park fiasco. His unseemly departure, together with the small strokes she was suffering, had left her fragile, ashamed and disengaged, as well as increasingly housebound. Hearing Sully's footfalls upstairs had comforted her. She also knew Sully's son and grandson had unexpectedly returned to his life and that down the road the house might provide them with a place to live. Which meant that in due course the house would become Peter's. It probably pleased her to think that Sully, who would have had nothing to leave his son, now had something tangible to pass on. She could never have predicted Peter's disinterest in any such inheritance or that eventually Sully would see her gift as a regrettable psychic turning point.

Though to be fair, Sully's luck had already begun to turn before this inheritance. It was Peter who bet that first winning triple. Until his son's arrival, things had been going more or less according to form. Badly, in other words. In fact, Sully had been in the middle of one of those exhilarating stupid streaks that had characterized so much of his adult life. This one had culminated with a straight right hand, delivered right on the button, to then officer Raymer's nose, dropping him like a sack of potatoes in the middle of Main Street and resulting in a warrant for Sully's arrest. He'd spent most of that holiday season in jail. While he was incarcerated, the 1-2-3 trifecta he'd been playing every day for decades—what Carl Roebuck called his bonehead triple—had finally run. Missing out on it would have been about par for Sully's course, but Peter, on Sully's drunken instructions, had continued to make the wager at the OTB, so the winnings were waiting for him when he got out. Not exactly a fortune, but enough to return him to the economic knife edge he'd been teetering on for as long as he could remember, the most he could reasonably hope for. But then a month later the same trifecta hit again, its payoff even bigger, and at age sixty-one Sully had done something so completely out of character that he'd wondered, even at the time, if cosmic repercussions might follow: he'd opened a savings account. After all, he had a grandson now (three, actually, though the other two lived with their mother, Peter's ex-wife, in West Virginia), and one day Will would need money for college. Sully hadn't contributed a penny to Peter's own education, so this was the least he could do.

Even after that second windfall, he'd continued to cling stubbornly to his conviction that his newfound luck couldn't last. After all, his stupid streaks had always run with the regularity of European trains. Another was bound to heave into view momentarily, after which he'd be back in the soup, broke and busted up and without prospects, his natural condition. But no. Later that year, his landlady died and left him the house.

Nor was even this the end. The final stroke of good fortune—or at least Sully had hoped it would be—was more unnerving than all the others combined, because its ultimate source was Big Jim Sullivan, Sully's drunk, abusive, long-dead father. As a final fuck you to the old man, Sully had intentionally let the family house on Bowdon Street, the scene of so many painful memories, fall into ruin until the town finally had no choice but to condemn and raze it; that, Sully had imagined, would finish things off. He'd given exactly no thought to the weedy, unattractive half acre the house sat on, assuming the land itself, awkwardly situated, would be next to worthless. But one of Gus Moynihan's campaign promises had been to build a bike path through the town of Bath and out through sprawling Sans Souci Park, on the other side of which it would hook up with the Schuyler Springs path, the idea being to link their unlucky community to Schuyler's historically more fortunate one. The proposed route, the only one that made any sense, ran straight through Sully's half acre, which the town planned to spruce up with park benches and a marble water fountain. Sensing Sully's reluctance to sell, but not its source, the mayor had sweetened the deal by promising Rub Squeers a custodial job out at Hilldale. And when even that didn't produce the desired effect, he offered to void all of Sully's parking violations, which he'd been collecting for years and which were now the equivalent of a small line item in the town's annual budget.

"Raymer'll have a cow," the mayor confided smugly, confident that Sully wouldn't be able to resist putting it to his old nemesis, whose first investment as chief of police had been a wheel boot that he'd used on Sully's car the same day it was delivered. Later, after Sully and Carl Roebuck figured out how to unlock and steal the boot, he'd purchased two more, only to have these stolen as well. So despite his misgivings, Sully had sold the town his father's land and put the money into his savings account, the balance of which had now swollen to the point where, despite heroic resolve, he couldn't possibly hope to drink it up at the Horse during what remained of his life.

What all this amounted to, in Sully's estimation, was a cosmic joke. As a poor man he'd always suspected that life's deck was stacked in favor of those with means. Was it possible that, without intending to, he'd actually become one of them? Was he now and forevermore insulated against adversity? How, exactly, should he feel about that? Other people rose to the challenge and learned to live with good fortune. Why not him?

The problem was that from the moment that first bonehead triple ran, bad things started happening to people in his immediate circle. First, Miss Beryl had been felled by that final stroke she'd known was coming, and then a year later Wirf had succumbed to renal failure, no surprise there, either. It wasn't like Sully felt responsible for these sad events, but he'd have gladly returned the money for the pleasure of their continued company, and so a false equivalency was established in his mind between their loss and his gain. Since then, his ex-wife had come loose from her moorings and been institutionalized, and Carl Roebuck, so long a symbol of undeserved good fortune, had lost his wife, his house and, most recently, his prostate gland. If Carl was to be believed, Tip Top Construction had about one swirl around the drain left, after which he'd be officially wiped out. The more bad things that happened to people in Sully's inner orbit, the more karmically responsible he felt. There was never a causal linkage, of course, but that didn't alter his sense of complicity. He couldn't help thinking that he wasn't meant to have money, that when his luck changed some invisible mechanism of destiny had been knocked out of alignment.

At least until he'd gone to the VA and gotten his *two years, but probably one* diagnosis, which had restored order with a vengeance.

As he and Rub started down the dark driveway, the dog began to emit a low growl that probably meant the neighborhood raccoon was back. Sully'd been meaning to put some skirting around the base of the trailer, knowing how much the creature liked it under there, but when it rained Rub was partial to the space as well, so he'd let it go. "You better come inside tonight," he said, and Rub, somehow understanding this, trotted up the steps in front of him, still grumbling.

Inside, Sully turned on the kitchen light and tossed his keys onto the dinette next to the stopwatch Will had returned to him before leaving. It had belonged to Miss Beryl's husband, the high school's longtime football and track coach. Sully had given it to the boy when he and his father first arrived in Bath over a decade ago. Poor kid. For months he'd been listening to his parents' bitter quarrels. Peter's affair with an academic colleague back home had recently come to light and turned everything in the marriage toxic. Will had understood just enough about what was going on to be terrified about what came next. Having no idea what that might be, he'd become frightened of everything, including his own little brother. With the watch, Sully told him, he could time himself being brave. A minute today, a minute and a half tomorrow and so on. This would make him braver all the time, with the proof right there in the palm of his hand. For some reason it worked. For years the boy took the watch with him everywhere and slept with it on his nightstand. Sully had forgotten all about it. "So what's this, then?" he asked his grandson, amazed, as he often was in the boy's presence, at how big he'd grown while somehow remaining the boy he'd been.

Will had shrugged, embarrassed. "I don't really need it anymore, I guess."

"Nothing scares you these days?"

"Girls," he'd admitted.

"Yeah, but that's because you're smart."

Another shrug, this time accompanied by a grin. "I thought maybe you could use it."

Sully was moved by the gift, but also curious. "What do I have to be scared about?" After his visit to the VA, had his behavior betrayed something? Did his grandson have an inkling of his illness?

"I guess I just thought it was time to give it back," Will said, with shrug number three.

When Sully depressed the watch's stem, the second hand lurched into motion, still anxious to perform after so many years. "You think it'd work for somebody my age?"

"Depends."

"On what?"

"On whether you believe it will, I guess."

No doubt about it. He was going to miss the boy. No longer a boy, but . . .

Rub was growling again, low and deep in his chest, a sound that usually preceded by a matter of seconds a knock on the trailer's door, but none came. Nor was the dog standing with his nose to the door, like he usually did when they had a visitor. Instead he was facing the far end of the trailer, his ears flat against his skull. "Hey, Dummy," Sully said. "What's wrong with you?"

Rub glanced up at him guiltily, as if to concede that something might be, but then went back to growling, the hair up on the back of his neck now. A lamp was burning in the living room, one Sully didn't remember leaving on. The narrow corridor leading to the single bedroom was dark, but looking more closely he noticed a thin crease of light under the bathroom door. Sully, who had nothing any self-respecting thief would want to steal, never locked the trailer, so anyone could've walked in. Carl? Possibly, but Sully'd just left him twenty minutes earlier. Ruth? It'd been a hell of a while since she'd paid him an unannounced visit.

Peter, returning unexpectedly from the city? No, his car would've been in the driveway. The owner of the strange car parked at the curb? It was possible, of course, that nobody was in there, that Sully himself had left the light on that morning. Rub seemed to think otherwise, though, and Sully doubted the little dickweed would be growling if the bathroom was empty or the occupant someone he knew.

Which gave Sully a chill. What was it Roy Purdy had said at Hattie's? That he'd stop by some night for the apology he seemed to think he had coming? But that didn't make much sense, either. Roy's car had been crushed when the mill collapsed into the street, and Roy himself had been injured.

There was a heavy flashlight on the countertop. Not the best weapon, but it would have to do. Crossing the living room on tiptoe, Sully put his ear to the bathroom door. From inside came a voice he didn't recognize. "Fuck her," it said.

Sully straightened. Who would be muttering obscenities in his bathroom in the middle of the night? The voice sounded strange. Not exactly human. Had someone stopped by with a gift of a foul-mouthed parrot?

He turned the knob and pushed the door open.

At first Sully didn't recognize the large man slumped forward on the toilet seat, chin on his chest, pants down around his ankles, fast asleep. "Fuck her," he repeated, then sighed deeply, as if in profound regret.

"Fuck who?" Sully said, louder than he meant to, causing his visitor to jolt awake and blink up at him.

"Sully," said Raymer, his voice sounding completely different now.

"You're lucky I didn't brain you with this," Sully said, showing him the flashlight.

"Wow," Raymer said, blinking up at him. "I was really out. This is kind of embarrassing."

Earlier in the evening, Rub had told Sully about Raymer fainting into the judge's grave, but sitting there on Sully's commode, covered with dried mud, his eyes blackened and swollen, his hair matted, he looked like something far worse had befallen him. Such as being beaten senseless with a cudgel or dragged behind a car by his feet. "*Kind* of?" Sully said.

"Okay, very."

"Did you find what you were looking for?" Because the only reason he could think of for Raymer to be in his trailer was that he was searching for the stolen wheel boots.

But Raymer just cocked his head at this. "Sorry?"

"What are you doing in my bathroom at three in the morning?" he said, pointing the flashlight at him for emphasis. "And don't say taking a shit."

Raymer shifted his weight on the commode, causing the trailer to groan. "I stopped by to ask a favor," he said.

"Of me?" Sully replied.

Raymer seemed to understand that this explanation might be hard for Sully to credit, given their personal history. "I guess I didn't know who else to ask," he said, adding, "Would it be all right I finished up in here?"

This seemed a reasonable request. "Sometimes you have to flush twice," Sully warned before closing the door on him.

He emerged thirty seconds later with wet hands. Sully, who'd retreated to the kitchen, tossed him a hand towel. He'd been meaning to put one in the bathroom but kept forgetting—the sort of oversight that made Ruth homicidal back when she was still paying him nocturnal visits.

"The front door wasn't locked," Raymer said, drying his hands, then handing the towel back.

"It never is."

"We knocked."

"We?"

"I meant 'I.'"

"I'll take your word for it."

"And I really, really needed to pee."

"Most men can do that standing up."

Raymer shook his head sadly, the picture of dejection. He'd begun absentmindedly scratching the palm of his right hand, Sully noticed. "Have you ever been so exhausted you just . . ." He let the thought trail off.

Sully pushed a dinette chair toward him with his foot. "Have a seat."

Raymer did, the trailer again groaning and shifting under his weight. "This is like being on a boat," Raymer observed.

The two men regarded each other, the air between them heavy with the strangeness of a middle-of-the-night moment that neither could ever have predicted.

"You know you talk in your sleep?" Sully said.

Raymer winced. "Really? Just now? What did I say?"

Lying seemed easiest, so Sully did. "I couldn't make it out. You sounded like a parrot."

Sully expected the other man to be surprised by this detail, but for some reason he wasn't. Instead he just hung his head, utterly despondent. "Earlier tonight?" he said. "I may have been struck by lightning."

"May have been?"

"I only mention it because there's a real possibility that I'm fucked up." Adding, when Sully raised an eyebrow, "More fucked up. Okay, insane."

"I'm not sure that would occur to someone who really is," Sully said, and Raymer looked grateful for his opinion but dubious as to its accuracy.

"Now I've got this voice in my head."

Good God, Sully thought. The man really was off the rails. "What's it say?"

"Mostly stuff I don't want to hear. It suggested I come see you. It said you'd help."

"Help what?"

The other man took a deep breath. "Do you know how to operate a backhoe?"

"It's not difficult."

Raymer nodded. "Where do you stand on unauthorized exhumations conducted under the cover of darkness?"

"It's never come up," Sully admitted. "Let me take a wild guess. Are we talking about Judge Flatt's grave? The one you fell into this morning?"

Raymer sighed, clearly dismayed by how far and fast the news of all that had traveled. "I lost something down there."

Sully frowned. "Your wallet?" Because, really.

To judge by the other man's expression, this was the very question he had been hoping Sully wouldn't ask. "Uh . . . something else, actually." When Sully didn't respond, he reluctantly continued. "Okay, a garage-door opener."

"Those can be replaced, you know. You don't have to dig up dead people."

"My wife . . . ," Raymer began, then stalled.

Sully vaguely remembered the story. How the woman had fallen down the stairs and broken her neck. That Raymer had found her.

"Before she died . . . she was seeing somebody." His eyes had filled. "She was about to run off with him."

"Who?"

"I never found out," he admitted. "I figured he left town, but apparently not. This weekend he put a dozen red roses on her grave." He handed Sully the crumpled florist's card.

Sully squinted at it. "*Always*, huh?"

Raymer nodded.

"Okay, but how do you know he didn't call in the order and get the flowers delivered? He could be in California for all you know."

"No," Raymer said, far too confidently, it seemed to Sully, because how could he be so sure? "He's here. I can feel him."

All this time he'd been digging at the palm of his right hand with the thumbnail of his left. "What's wrong with your hand?"

The question seemed to take him by surprise. He looked at the hand he'd been scratching as if it belonged to somebody else. "It's nothing," he said quickly, shoving it into his pocket.

"Okay, say you find out who the guy is. What then?"

He shrugged. "Probably nothing. I just want to know."

"That's what you say now. What if you change your mind?"

"I won't," he promised. "Look, I understand if you don't want to help. No hard feelings. I know what I'm asking sounds kind of crazy."

Kind of? Well, yeah. And teaming up with a lifelong adversary, who'd just confessed he was hearing voices? What kind of sense did that make? Still, the idea wasn't without appeal. Just ten minutes earlier he'd been lamenting how long it had been since his last stupid streak.

Was it possible that what Raymer was proposing might just jump-start a new one? Maybe he only needed to forget about *two years, but probably closer to one* and start acting like the man he'd been for his entire adult life, until good fortune—like Raymer's lightning strike?—fucked up his circuitry. His grandson had already left, and by the end of the summer his son would be gone as well. What further use had he for model citizenship? "You're thinking of doing this now? Tonight?"

"It's not going to seem like a very good idea in the morning," Raymer admitted.

Sully couldn't remember ever seeing another human being look more utterly abject. And given his friendship with Rub Squeers, that was saying something.

Sully consulted his watch. Three forty-seven. He repocketed his keys and tested the flashlight to make sure the batteries weren't dead. Taking a deep breath of his own, he was surprised to discover that it went right down to his stomach. The heaviness in his chest had miraculously vanished. Maybe the *two years but probably closer to one* was bullshit. These were VA doctors, after all. Not the sharpest knives in the drawer. He'd told Ruth he was just in a funk. A lie, he'd thought in the moment. But what if it was true?

"Well," he said, getting to his feet, "we don't have much time."

Raymer looked stunned. "You'll do it?"

Sully shrugged. "Hey, if anything goes wrong, I'm with the chief of police."

"I'm resigning tomorrow."

"How come?"

"I guess because I'm kind of . . . unfit?"

Sully had long thought so, so he was surprised to hear himself demur. "Do you take bribes?" he asked.

"No," Raymer said, clearly offended by the suggestion.

"Do you look the other way when the right people ask you to?"

"Of course not."

"Then you've got my vote."

Raymer looked surprised. "You vote?"

"That was more a figure of speech," Sully conceded, though he did vote in general elections. "Hey, Dummy," he said to Rub, who'd been lying quietly under the table, gnawing away. "You want to stay here chewing your dick or go dig up a judge?"

The dog hopped up and went over to the door, his tail wagging enthusiastically. So maybe the idea wasn't so dumb after all.

OUTSIDE, Sully noticed the blue light of Carl's television reflecting in the windows of his apartment, first a close-up of a woman's crotch, then a midrange shot of a skinny man with an impressive hard-on. Sully picked up a small handful of pebbles and rattled them off the glass.

"What are you doing?" Raymer said.

"This is a three-man job," Sully said. "I'll dig the hole, but I'm not climbing down into it on my bum knee." Also, though his breathing was okay now, that might change. Better safe than sorry.

Carl appeared at the window, squinting out into the darkness. He must've recognized Sully's silhouette below, because he said, "What do you want now? You already took my last bent farthing."

"Get dressed," Sully told him.

"You decided to evict me after all?"

"Not tonight."

"Because that would be just like you."

"What are you, hard of hearing? Get dressed. Old clothes."

"Who's that with you? Because it looks like Raymer."

"It is," said Raymer, who'd gone back to absentmindedly digging at his palm.

"Okay," Carl said, "but only because I'm curious. The sight of you two together beggars the imagination. Give me five minutes."

"Two," Sully said.

He and Raymer went out to the curb to wait, Rub panting along with them. Sully lowered the truck's tailgate. "Jump in," Sully said, and Rub, a talented leaper, did as instructed.

"He understands you?" Raymer said, clearly impressed.

"Seems to," Sully said, raising and latching the tailgate. "You can sometimes lose him with abstract concepts."

"When I was a kid we had a dog who chewed himself like that," he said sadly.

"What happened to him?"

"He got hit by a car."

"Hey, Dummy," Sully said, and the dog perked up. "You hear that?"

CARL, noticing the dried streaks on the windshield, ran his index finger through one, verifying his suspicion that, yes, it was on the inside of the glass.

"I wouldn't," Sully warned him.

"Wouldn't what?"

"Lick that finger."

Carl sniffed it instead, then shot Sully a look of unadulterated disgust before rolling down the passenger window. "Who was the last human being to ride in this vehicle besides you?"

"Rub, I think," Sully told him. The outside air smelled clean and fresh but still thick with ozone from the storms.

"Rub's a dog."

"The other Rub."

"In this vehicle," Carl continued, "we witness the sad demise of fundamental Western values. Pride. Order. Personal responsibility. Rudimentary hygiene."

"This from a man who pisses himself."

"See, that's the difference between us. *I* was embarrassed this morning. *You,* by contrast, think this truck's normal."

That wasn't entirely true. Every now and then Sully considered giving the cab a good scouring but always decided against it. For one thing, a clean vehicle would only encourage his Upper Main Street ladies to take further advantage of him. Elderly widows, they already relied on him for small handyman jobs, as well as snowblowing their sidewalks and driveways in winter. When their middle-aged children, who mostly lived in Schuyler or the Albany suburbs, weren't available to take them to the doctor or the supermarket or the hairdresser or out to the new Applebee's for lunch, it was Sully they turned to. After all, cabs cost money, whereas he could be paid in banana bread. They always began by saying how grateful they were, and what would they ever do without him, but once this pro forma gratitude was entered into the record, they commenced complaining about the condition of his truck, the springs poking up through the truck's passenger seat and goosing their withered flanks, the floor strewn with sloshing Styrofoam coffee cups, the crowbar on the dash—how did *that* get there?—that would vibrate and inch toward them menacingly whenever he accelerated.

Mostly Sully didn't mind being at their beck and call, as his long afternoons were hard to fill. But the old women chattered at him incessantly, and when he dropped them back home they always wanted to know if he'd be free the following Tuesday, as if that were the sort of thing a man like him would know offhand. They might be old—ancient, many of them—but they wanted what all women had demanded of Sully his entire life: commitment. His determination to remain uncommitted was strengthened with each new request. Besides, why clean the cab if Rub was just going to pee in it again?

"Okay," he said. "I got one for you. What kind of man owns a construction company and no work clothes?" Despite Sully's explicit instructions, Carl was wearing his usual outfit: polo shirt, chinos and what looked to be expensive Italian loafers.

Carl ignored him, distracted by the sound of Rub's toenails scrabbling in the truck bed. "You shouldn't let him ride back there."

"He enjoys it," Sully said weakly, because of course Carl was right. "He's a dog."

"Yeah, but what happens if you have to jam on the brakes? How are you going to feel when he goes flying and gets dead?"

"You're right," Sully said. "On the drive home you can ride back there."

When they came to a stop sign, Carl adjusted his side-view mirror so he could study Raymer's Jetta as it pulled up behind them. "Who the hell is he talking to?"

Sure enough, when Sully glanced at his rearview, Raymer did appear to be in an animated conversation with somebody. "He must have a police-band radio in there," Sully ventured. But then he remembered the parrotlike voice on the other side of the bathroom door. So maybe not.

"Does he seem right to you?" Carl said. "Because to me he looks unhinged. And this business about the garage-door thingy? How does that make any sense?"

"He seems adamant."

"Or just batshit."

"He's had a rough day."

Carl snorted at this. "No, *I've* had a rough day."

"He fainted into a grave this morning," Sully said. "Tonight he got struck by lightning."

Carl considered this, then shrugged. "Okay, I stand corrected."

In good weather the cemetery's backhoe was kept under the sloping metal awning attached to the maintenance shed. The shed itself was locked, but Sully knew where Rub hid the key. As he inserted it into the lock, he remembered something. "Wait here," he told his companions, then went quickly inside, shutting the door behind him. It took only a minute to locate the backhoe's ignition key dangling by a cord from its peg. What he'd remembered just in time was that Raymer's three missing wheel boots were stashed in here under a tarp. Sully had originally hidden them out at Harold Proxmire's auto yard in the trunk of a rusted-out Crown Victoria, but such contraband made Harold nervous, so when Rub got the job at Hilldale, Sully'd moved them here, then promptly forgot all about them. He raised one corner of the tarp, and sure enough, there they were, good as new. Tomorrow, he told himself, after he and Rub hauled that tree branch away, he'd transfer them out to Zack's shed, where it was unlikely anyone would come across them by accident.

The eastern horizon was graying, which meant they didn't have much time. Tossing Carl the keys to the pickup, he climbed aboard the backhoe, and Rub leaped up beside him. "Don't get too far ahead," he told the other two. "I don't know where we're going, and top speed on this thing's about two miles an hour."

As they crept slowly through the cemetery, Sully found himself wishing that Peter was here. His son's default mode was disapproval, at least where Sully was concerned, but there were also occasions when he let his guard down and surrendered to the madcap spirit of the moment. Once, years earlier, Sully had conscripted him to help steal the Roebuck snowblower. Every time it snowed, Sully would swipe it, only to have Carl steal it back. With each theft they increased their security measures to prevent further larceny. Finally Carl had brought it out to the yard and chained it to a pole. The property was surrounded by a high chain-link fence and patrolled at night by a Doberman named Rasputin. Sully'd knocked the dog out with a handful of sleeping pills inserted in a package of hamburger, but he still needed Peter to climb the fence and liberate the snowblower with the bolt cutters he'd also swiped from Carl. All had gone smoothly, the Doberman off sleeping somewhere (they assumed), until, just as Peter severed the chain, they heard a low growl, and there stood Rasputin within a yard of him, his feet wide apart, his teeth bared hideously. For a long minute he and Peter just stared at each other until the dog began to palsy and froth at the mouth. A moment later, the pills trumped his malice, and he just keeled over in the snow.

Later, at the Horse, his entire face lit up by an uncharacteristic joyful grin, Peter couldn't get over it. *"That,"* he told Sully, "was more intense than sex." Seeing his son so happy, Sully had wondered if it might represent some kind of turning point. Maybe Peter had finally given himself permission to enjoy life from a less ironic distance. But the next morning he was his old buttoned-up self, clearly ashamed about having allowed himself to be drawn into his father's foolishness. Too bad, Sully couldn't help thinking. Though he had no desire for a son made in his own image, he hated to see Peter refuse to acknowledge such a basic truth about himself: that he liked to have fun.

Arriving at the judge's grave site, Sully handed the dog down to Carl, who held him at arm's length, penis facing outward. "Let's lock him in the truck," Sully suggested. Rub had a vivid imagination and didn't always draw clear distinctions between what was alive and what wasn't. When he saw the backhoe in action, its jaw gulping big mouthfuls of fresh earth, he might get into attack mode.

"Right," Carl said, bearing the struggling animal away. "There might still be a surface in there that he hasn't peed on."

Sully was studying Raymer, whose whole demeanor had changed since they'd arrived at Hilldale. Having set these proceedings in motion, he now looked like a man who finally understood their gravity. He was staring at the grave they were about to desecrate, but his gaze, unless Sully was mistaken, was inward. "Hey?" Sully said, swinging the backhoe's claw into position.

"What?" Raymer said, snapping out of it.

Testing the levers that lifted and lowered the inverted scoop, Sully said, "You sure about this? Because what we're about to do here is—"

"Criminal?" Carl suggested, returning from the truck. "Deviant? Perverse? Imbecilic?"

Sully ignored this. "If we get caught," he told Raymer, "it's your reputation on the line."

"What about mine?" Carl said.

"That's hilarious," Sully told him.

Raymer glanced around nervously. "Who's going to catch us?"

"We won't know until they show up."

Raymer worked his jaw as if he was literally chewing on the problem, then finally stiffened into resolve. "All right. What the hell," he said, his voice catching and producing that same parrotlike sound Sully'd heard on the other side of the bathroom door. Raymer himself must've heard its strangeness, because he immediately cleared his throat, like something foreign and perhaps nasty had gotten lodged in there and he needed to expel it. "We've come this far."

At this Carl snorted.

"What?" Sully said.

"Nothing," Carl said. "I was just thinking about Napoleon invading Russia."

Both Sully and Raymer blinked at this.

"Also the Crusades and the Spanish Inquisition and the Vietnam War," Carl continued. "Not one of those clusterfucks could truly commence until somebody said, *What the hell. We've come this far.*"

And on that note Sully pushed forward the lever that lowered the backhoe's claw into the soft earth above the casket of Judge Barton Flatt, who likely would've received—had His Honor died in time to qualify for it—the inaugural Unsung Hero award that Sully's landlady would be getting two days hence. Next year, unless Sully was mistaken, he'd be a shoo-in.

A FEW MINUTES LATER the backhoe's steel teeth located Judge Barton Flatt's casket with a fingernails-on-the-blackboard screech. All three men winced. "Relax, Your Honor," Sully called down into the hole. "It's just me, not God."

After that, though, he worked more carefully. A backhoe wasn't exactly a precision instrument, however, and it was still too dark to see very well, so a minute later when he managed to jostle the casket again he wasn't surprised.

"Jesus," Carl said. "Don't rupture the fucking thing."

Sully, who feared precisely this, paused the backhoe. "Let's find the edges," he suggested. He always kept a broom in the back of the truck, so Raymer went to fetch it. "Grab the rake while you're at it," Sully called after him. "And a couple shovels."

Raymer answered in his parrot voice, saying something Sully couldn't make out. Carl cocked his head at the sound and raised an eyebrow at Sully, who just shrugged.

Once the outline of the casket was exposed, Sully was able to work around it, deepening the hole and providing enough space for one man to stand at the foot and another along one side. When he switched the ignition off and the machine shuddered into silence, it was quiet except for Rub's excited yipping in the pickup. "Okay, girls, in you go," Sully said, climbing down and taking the flashlight from Carl.

"You're not coming?" Carl said wryly, lowering himself into the hole.

"Yeah, that'd be great," Sully said. "All three of us down there and nobody to pull us up."

"I hope you're not claustrophobic," Carl said to Raymer when he, too, dropped into the hole.

To which Raymer replied, "I am, actually."

Carl paused to regard him. "What the hell's wrong with your voice?"

Raymer cleared his throat. "It's a recent thing."

"You sound like you should be testifying from behind a screen."

Directing the flashlight's beam down into the hole, Sully noted that the casket's burnished surface now bore two deep parallel scratches, and when Carl grabbed on to one of the ornate handles, it came off in his hand. "Nice work," he said, handing it up to Sully, who tossed it onto the pile of excavated dirt.

At first, even with Carl and Raymer tugging on it, the casket refused to budge, as if it contained not the body of a man wasted away to nothing by radiation and chemotherapy but a cache of gold bullion. Then all at once it came loose with a sucking sound, its contents shifting audibly inside. "You know what?" Carl said. "I just decided I want to be cremated."

"I'll try to remember," Sully told him.

"So what's the plan, boss?" Carl said. "Haul it out?"

"Nah, just stand him up," Sully said.

"Which end would you guess is his head?" Carl wondered, scratching his own.

"The narrow end should be the feet," Sully offered.

"It's a perfect rectangle, dimwit."

"Then I couldn't tell you."

When the two of them, grunting and muttering, succeeded in wrestling the casket into an upright position, Sully handed Carl the flashlight, and he directed its beam at the section of earth below on which the box had lain. "Okay," Raymer said, dropping to his knees. "It should be right here."

"Which is more than could be said for us," Carl replied. "What I don't get is what makes you so sure the fucking thing's even down here."

"It has to be," Raymer said, running the flat of his hand over the dirt. "I'm almost sure it was in my pocket when I passed out."

"Yeah, but afterward you went to the hospital, right? Maybe it fell out of your pocket there."

"There was no carpet on the floor of the examination room. I'd have heard it fall."

"Unless it happened in the ambulance."

That scenario had occurred to Sully as well, but Raymer seemed not to be listening. "Come on, come on!" he was saying, parrot voiced again, sifting handfuls of earth through his fingers now. Thanks to the rains, the dirt at the bottom of the hole was quickly turning to slop. "It's *got* to be here."

Carl shot Sully a look that indicated it not only didn't have to be, it wasn't.

"Raymer," Sully said, "you're only making matters worse. Use the rake." Which he handed down.

The distinct possibility that they were on a fool's errand with him the fool seemed finally to be dawning on Raymer, who went at the moist earth with the rake like a man possessed, but after a few minutes it was clear even to him that there was no such device in the hole. Carl took the rake from him and handed it back up to Sully. "I don't understand," Raymer said. "This makes no sense."

"Here's an idea," Carl said. "We could dig up these other people. See if it's under *their* caskets."

Raymer regarded him blankly, as if this suggestion had been made in earnest.

"Are we done here?" Carl said, reaching a hand up to Sully, who grabbed it and pulled him out.

When Raymer made no move to follow suit, Sully said, "You just gonna stay down there?"

"I might as well," he said miserably. "In fact, I might *better*. You should just cover me over. Put me out of my misery."

"Raymer," Sully said quietly. "Enough of this."

He said something that Sully didn't catch.

"Say again?"

"I *said* . . . now I'll never know."

When Sully glanced at Carl, he was surprised that his expression was closer to pity than exasperation.

"Go sit down," Sully told Raymer, after he and Carl managed to haul him up and out. "You don't look so hot."

Taking a seat on the pile of excavated dirt, he put his head in his hands.

Sully and Carl returned their attention to the upright casket.

"Just tip him back down?" Carl said. "Or walk him?"

"If we tip him back he'll be upside down for eternity."

"You think that matters if you're dead?" Carl said.

"It would to me."

"Yeah," Carl snorted. "Like you've *ever* known which end is up."

Together they corner-walked the casket to the other end of the hole, then slowly lowered it as far as they could reach, after which they had no choice but to let the elevated end drop the last few feet. The resulting thud caused all three men to cringe.

"This is a terrible thing we've done," Raymer said in his own voice now. He'd picked up the silver casket handle and was turning it over in his hands. "We violated a man's grave. And for what?"

Sully understood how he felt. To this point his spirits had been relatively high, and if the remote had been there it might've justified, sort of, the madness of the entire endeavor. By the time they'd recounted the story at the Horse a few times, its lunacy would seem inspired. Whereas now . . .

Only Carl seemed unchastened. "Raymer," he said. "His Honor didn't mind. He was dead. Do you know what 'dead' means?"

"And in the meantime," Sully said, climbing back aboard the back-hoe, which he would now return to the shed, "we're not done here. I'd rake that dirt," he suggested to Carl, indicating the mound of earth Raymer was sitting on, "just in case it got scooped up somehow."

Raymer shook his head. "It would've been under the casket."

"You'd think," Sully admitted. "Let me see that thing a minute," he said, pointing at the silver casket handle Raymer was fondling.

He looked puzzled by the request but got to his feet and handed it up to Sully, who promptly tossed it into the hole, where it rattled off the casket. "Hey," he said, pointing at the eastern sky. "New day."

Raymer looked where Sully was pointing, but his blank expression suggested he was looking for something that just wasn't there.

HE PULLED UP in front of Miss Beryl's again just as the first rays of sunlight winked through the trees in Sans Souci Park. Carl, who'd removed his ruined loafers and muddy socks, seemed in no hurry to get out, so Sully turned the engine off and the two men sat there, confusing the hell out of Rub, who was doing frantic laps around the truck bed, loosing short bursts of urine all the while. Where did it all come from? Sully marveled. Wadding his socks up into a ball, Carl wiped away at the inside of the windshield, ostensibly to remove the streaks of dried dog piss, but in reality making an opaque brown hurricane pattern on the glass. "Look," he said, clearly pleased with his effort, "a perfect shitstorm."

"Thanks," Sully said.

"Don't mention it," he replied, tossing his socks out the window, followed by his shoes. "Why don't you firebomb this thing and get yourself a decent rig?"

Two years, but probably closer to one. What would Sully want with a vehicle that was in better shape than he was?

"You know," Carl went on, "until tonight it never occurred to me that you and Raymer are actually brothers under the skin. Surely the chief of police can afford a better car than that beater of a Jetta he drives."

"Maybe he likes it," Sully said. "Could be there are a few things about you that he doesn't understand, either. Did you ever think of that?"

"I know one thing. That man is seriously off the fucking rails."

They'd parted company back at the cemetery, with Raymer promising to go home and get some sleep. Sully wasn't sure he'd do any such thing. Carl was right. There was something manic and untethered about him. He'd seen men with that same look who, after prolonged battle, continued to function, sometimes at a high level, but in a more profound respect had simply abdicated. Lost men, not at all sure they even wanted to be found.

"And there's no radio in that car," Carl added. "I looked."

"Yeah?" Sully said.

"Yeah."

Sunlight streaked through the trees just then, its sudden glare making Sully squint. Leaning forward to peer at it from around his shitstorm, Carl said, "Amazing, isn't it, when you think about it, how the world keeps on turning, no matter how fucked up things get?"

In Sully's opinion it'd be more amazing if it stopped, but he understood his friend's sentiment. Because it *was* something the way things kept grinding with no apparent reason or need, indifferent to life and death and all else, too. He thought about that stopwatch Will had now returned to him; its second hand just kept ticking away, seemingly content with its circular journey, forever in the same direction. That said, the mechanical world probably wasn't so different from its living inhabitants, most of whom, Sully included, went about their lives, most days, taking it all for granted. His own happiness, such as it was, had always seemed rooted in his willingness to let each second, minute, hour and day predict the next, today no different from yesterday except in its particulars, which didn't amount to much. Most mornings, he'd be rising about now, hauling himself out of bed, shaving and washing up, then heading downtown to help Ruth open the restaurant. Could something so fundamental, so ritualized, ever really be changed?

Maybe Ruth was right and the reason he showed up at Hattie's every morning was that he didn't know what else to do, where else to go. Naturally he would have liked to tell her that wasn't true, that of course he still felt the old affection for her. Wasn't the fact that there was no other woman in his life proof of that? He couldn't imagine there ever would be, not at this late juncture. Surely that had to mean something. But then he thought of Raymer, wild eyed, out at Hilldale, repeating "It's *got* to be here" over and over again, an expression of personal need that the world simply refused to validate.

So maybe it *was* time to try something different. Maybe his mornings at Hattie's were, under the guise of being helpful, just selfish. If Ruth's husband, for reasons known only to him, suddenly wanted her back, and if his wife was disposed to feel more tenderly about him than she had in the past, who was he to come between them? If Janey was sick of waking up every morning to the sound of Sully's voice, no doubt a constant reminder of the damage his affair with her mother had done to their family, could he blame her? And though he would have liked to deny it, he *had* done damage. Ruth's son Gregory, Janey's brother, had left town right after high school, and he'd almost surely known what was going on. So if he was going to Hattie's out of some old habit, wasn't it his responsibility to break it? After all, Hattie's wasn't the only place in town where a man could order a plate of eggs and shoot the shit.

Except, well, it was. Sure, there were the franchise joints out by the interstate exits, but their counters were full of people on their way somewhere else. Which was what Ruth seemed to be suggesting that Sully become. A person headed to Aruba. Why not? was what she wanted to know. He had the money. As he did for a better truck. So why the hell not? *Because,* he would've liked to explain, like the second hand of Will's stopwatch, his center was fixed, his motion circumscribed by gears he couldn't see, much less alter.

Rub, tired of being confined in the back of the pickup for no good reason, gave a sharp yip and leaped out onto the terrace, where he rolled like a well-drilled soldier, regained his feet and darted off toward the trailer. Both men watched him go, feeling, unless Sully was mistaken, something like envy. Was it possible to be jealous of a dog with a half-chewed-through dick? Well, again, why not? Rub was nothing if not an optimist, and optimism, the older you got, became harder to summon and, once summoned, even harder to hold on to.

"You ever see Toby?" said Carl out of the blue.

"Why would I see her?" Sully asked, though he'd had a pretty serious crush on Carl's ex-wife at one point, a decade or so ago.

"You tell me," said Carl, who'd been all too aware of the infatuation.

"Come to think of it, I did one day last fall. Around the holidays, I think."

"Yeah?"

"Yeah, she just stopped by."

Carl straightened up. "Stopped by," he repeated. "To see you."

"She thought I might want to list this place," he said, nodding at Miss Beryl's house. "She's in real estate now."

Carl relaxed again. "Yeah. I heard she was doing okay. How'd she look?"

"Terrific," Sully said, enjoying himself now. "Never better. Sex on a stick."

"Fuck you," Carl said, then sighed. "I can't believe I drove her into the arms of a hairy-legged lesbian."

"She must have something you don't."

"No, she *doesn't* have something I *do,*" Carl corrected. "Or did, until recently."

"Give it time."

"I don't know," Carl mused. "What are men even good for anymore?"

Since that was precisely the sort of question Sully had studiously avoided asking for his entire life, he thought this might not be a bad time for a change of subject. So he decided to ask about what had been in the back of his mind since Raymer's pitiful lament out at Hilldale, that without the garage-door opener he'd never know the identity of the supposed boyfriend. "Tell me it wasn't you," he said.

"*What* wasn't me?"

"With Raymer's wife." Because if the opportunity had presented itself, Carl wouldn't have hesitated. Sully didn't doubt that for a moment. Still, the dozen roses on the grave? The card inscribed *Always*? For Carl Roebuck those gestures felt out of character, to say the least. On the other hand, you never knew.

"Fuck no," he said.

"You're sure?" Sully said, though it really wasn't necessary to ask a second time. Carl might be full of more shit than a Christmas goose, but so far as he knew the man had never lied to him about anything important.

"What? You think I'm the only pussy hound in this town?"

"Good," Sully said. Because maybe he and Raymer weren't brothers under the skin, as Carl had just suggested, but his heart had gone out to the poor bastard.

Carl had spoken again, he realized. "I'm sorry, what?"

"I *said* it wasn't me, but I know who it was."

Carl was staring straight ahead, at the pee-streaked windshield, no doubt waiting for Sully to ask the obvious question. Which he had no intention of doing. Because, he told himself, it was none of his business, but that was a lie. He didn't ask because he didn't want to know the answer. Because he was afraid he already did.

Complicity

R EADERS OF the *North Bath Weekly Journal* generally didn't look to
their hometown paper for real news about Bath. The odd, occasional news item, like this week's story about the middle school being
renamed in Beryl Peoples's honor, occasionally crept in, but usually the
Journal stuck to church socials and spaghetti suppers, weddings and
funerals, Little League scores and who made the dean's list at the community college. The *Journal*'s real mission, though, was to report the
more exciting goings-on in Schuyler Springs, where the harness track
offered exotic wagering on trotters and pacers, and new restaurants were
launched almost weekly, offering striking, unusual cuisines (Eritrean!)
that used colorful, mysterious ingredients (nettles! squid ink!) and
wine was served in "flights." In Schuyler the local bookstore cospon-
sored famous-author events with the college's English department, after
which you could go next door and dance to a live, punk klezmer (?!)
band or catch a movie at the new twelve-screen Cineplex.

No, if you wanted news about Bath, you had to subscribe to the
Schuyler Springs Democrat, a daily that prided itself on hard-hitting
investigative journalism, at least where its neighbors were concerned.
For example, the Great Bath Stench, unreported in the *Journal,* had
been the *Democrat*'s front-page news all last summer, as were Hilldale's
ongoing problems ("Dead on the Move in Bath," one headline read,
as if a zombie movie were being reviewed). Considered newsworthy

this year were the long delays and cost overruns out at the Old Mill Lofts, a project that grew sketchier by the day and to which Mayor Gus Moynihan, despite recent efforts to distance himself, was inextricably tied.

And of course all of these headaches were in addition to Gus's wife, who was in yet another downward spiral. That evening Alice had gotten so agitated over dinner that he'd called the doctor, who agreed to Gus's request and prescribed a sedative. Given her exhaustion and the strength of the drug, she was unlikely to awaken before noon.

There had always been an ebb and flow to Alice's madness, whole weeks, even months, where she'd be, or at least seem, at peace. She'd read or paint or just stare out the window into the dark Sans Souci woods. Then, for no apparent reason, she'd be on the move again, manic, jittery, wandering from room to room in their big rambling house like somebody looking for a lost object. Gus had learned to read the signs: the nervous twitch at the corner of what had before been a perfectly placid smile; books she'd previously been engrossed in that suddenly no longer held her interest; the tiny, precise brushstrokes of her paintings becoming looser, more careless, less tied to the reality she'd been trying to capture, as if the link between brain and brush had been severed.

He knew Alice could feel the sea change as well, the poor woman, when her anxiety returned yet again. Small, familiar sounds, instead of soothing her, would startle the hell out of her. Whatever was in pursuit seemed always to be in her peripheral vision, vanishing the second she turned to face it. To Gus, it seemed like she was remembering, in stages, something best forgotten completely. When he asked if anything was troubling her, she usually offered him a blank look, as if he were speaking German. Once, when he inquired what she was looking for, she responded, "Me?" He couldn't help wondering if she didn't know what he was talking about or if she'd actually answered him: it was *herself* she was in search of. Eventually, when the house proved too confining, she'd fly the coop, and he'd start getting reports of her in town, seemingly everywhere at once, freaking everybody out with that damn phone.

Yesterday, she claimed to have seen someone who'd frightened her, but when he asked who it was, she again looked at him blankly, like he was supposed to know. "Kurt?" he asked. Because it was possible. The man had been gone for nearly a decade and had no reason that Gus could imagine to return. Alice shook her head. "Kurt went away," she explained, as if this departure might be something that had escaped Gus's attention. Who knew? Maybe it was Raymer she was alluding to. He was the one who'd found her in the park that morning and brought her home. Usually she recognized him as her friend Becka's husband and understood that he represented no threat or danger, but men in uniform often scared her, and Raymer had been in his dress blues, so she might not've recognized him.

Nothing troubled Gus more than this spooky phone business. These days the phone was her constant companion, her link to something as necessary as her next breath. Sometimes, when they were having a quiet meal, the phone would "ring," and she'd rise, cross the room, take it out of her bag and "answer" it. She seemed to remember their long-standing rule about no calls during dinner, so she'd lower her voice and say, "I can't talk now," and return it to her bag. Other times she would listen patiently to whoever she dreamed was speaking, her eyes welling with tears. "Oh, dear," she'd finally say, "then it's even worse than we thought." Sometimes he wondered if he himself was the subject. "He doesn't know," she'd whisper before pausing to listen for a while. "Of course he has a right to, but what if it destroys him?" Sometimes her conversations were so compelling that Gus would get caught up in them, half believing there really was someone on the line and wanting very much to know what the other person was saying. It was all so profoundly unsettling that he was considering taking the phone away from her.

At least the inevitable crisis might be drawing near, and the next few days could reveal where they were headed. Sometimes—who knew why?—Alice's inner turbulence would calm, and she'd return to her easel, her brushes, her tranquil blues and greens and yellows, but it was far more likely that they were now on that all-too-familiar down-ward trajectory that would end in Utica, at the state mental hospital. It was the waiting he hated most. It was like attending a child with a fever, watching it climb dangerously, praying for it to break, fearing it wouldn't, knowing you were helpless to affect the outcome.

All of which was why Gus had spent a sleepless night. He'd gone to bed early in hopes of putting a merciful end to the god-awful day, but his thoughts were on a loop. It still boggled his mind that one whole side of the old mill could have collapsed into the street. And on the same day a lethal reptile whose natural habitat is India escapes from the Morrison Arms? Nor was he able to dispel from his mind the image of his damn fool of a police chief pitching forward into Judge Flatt's open grave, sending up that plume of dust. No doubt all three of these stories would be prominently featured in the Schuyler paper. Dear God, they'd have a field day! Every time it seemed he might drift off, another thunderstorm rolled through, and Gus was wide awake again. *He* was the one in need of a sedative. Why hadn't he asked for one? When one pile-driving clap of thunder shook the house, he rose and went to check on Alice, but she appeared to be sleeping soundly. Nor did the ringing telephone wake her later.

The calls started shortly after the last of the storms, and they kept on throughout the night, mostly from citizens wanting to know when the fuck they were going to get their power back. The biggest mistake Gus had made in running for mayor—what on earth had *possessed* him?— was to make his home phone number public. The idea, as best he could recall, had been to come across as a genuine public servant, open and accessible to his constituents. It quickly became apparent, however, that most of the people who wanted to talk to him, especially in the middle of the night, were drunk or insane or both, so once he was safely elected he got an answering machine to screen the loonies and used his unlisted cell phone for people he actually wanted to talk to. His recorded message for everyone else stated that each call was important to him (a lie) and that he would return the call at his first opportunity (another). It stunned him how long people would vent. Several callers reported strange otherworldly sightings: cows in the fields with their twitching tails brightly aglow, or a mystical blue orb perched atop the bayonet of the Union soldier statue on the library lawn, or stone crosses ablaze at their points out at Hilldale. Was something satanic afoot? one caller wanted to know. Sophomoric, in Gus's opinion, was more like it. With less than two weeks of school left, they'd entered prime prank season. If stone crosses were burning, it was because some nitwit had doused them in lighter fluid and set a match to them. In the morning he'd have

Raymer check with the hospital to see how many teenagers had been treated for burns.

There were other less spectral goings-on as well. The mother of a man known around town as Spinmatics Joe called to say that her son had gone out to the White Horse Tavern and not come home, leading her to suspect foul play. She gave Gus to understand that some rabid liberals had it in for her boy because he dared to speak the truth about the minorities and homosexuals and them who were taking over everything to the point where you couldn't really even call this America anymore. The final lunatic had called shortly after five to report grave robbers digging up Judge Barton Flatt's grave. Though the idea was ludicrous, just in case, he'd called the station, and an officer named Miller was dispatched to investigate. He found nobody at the crime scene, but a hundred yards from the Spring Street entrance he came upon something even more bizarre and disturbing. An enormous section of earth large enough to accommodate a mature tree and its vast, shriveled root system, as well as half-a-dozen caskets, some of them very old, had somehow detached itself from its surroundings, slid down the slope made muddy by the torrential rains and now sat like an island in the middle of the goddamn road.

Which was why, when the mayor looked out his bedroom window and saw the sky lightening in the east, he gave up on sleep. Better to rise and meet the day head-on. Rather than wait for the *Democrat* to be delivered midmorning, he'd drive into Schuyler, grab a hot-off-the-press copy and take his inevitable shellacking over an expensive cappuccino at the new Starbucks everybody was talking about. Three-fifty seemed like a lot to pay for coffee, but he heard they had nice leather chairs, and he could sink into one of those to read the bad news about his town in relative peace among hipper Schuyler folks who saw nothing so terribly wrong with small extravagances. By the time he returned to Bath and his own unhip constituents, the bad news would feel comfortably old hat. He dressed quietly and was halfway out the door before it occurred to him to check on Alice one more time, and it was then he discovered she was gone.

POOR, KIND, addled woman.

Who was to blame? It would've been nice to blame Kurt, and most of the time Gus did. Other times, like now, he gauged his own complicity. He knew, of course, that Alice's difficulties predated him, and maybe even Kurt, who claimed she'd been a feral young woman in college, her mind splintered from dropping acid, but Gus doubted Alice had ever been truly wild. She might have experimented with drugs—it was the seventies, after all—but only at someone else's instigation, and he suspected Kurt of being her personal Svengali. What a piece of work that man had turned out to be. Hiring him—Gus himself had cast the deciding vote—had been a tragic mistake. To make matters worse, he'd been warned. Two of his search committee colleagues had sensed something wrong, something didn't add up, but it wasn't anything they could put their finger on, so Gus had reminded them that vague misgivings were sometimes just prejudice in disguise. He'd certainly looked good on paper. True, he hadn't published much, but he was professionally active, attending numerous conferences and giving papers, and he appeared to know the biggest names in political science personally. His letters of recommendation were among the strongest Gus had ever seen.

One night, though, shortly after Kurt's campus visit, Gus had gotten a call at home. "You do *not* want to hire Professor Wright," the caller said without preamble. Gus's first thought was that this must be one of his search committee colleagues, but it sounded like a long-distance call. When Gus said, "Who is this?" the man said that wasn't important. What mattered was that he understand that Kurt Wright was evil. Gus remembered actually chuckling at this. Who in the academy used such language? There, words like "evil" had long ago been replaced by others like "inappropriate." The caller, whoever he was, must be unhinged. "Well," Gus told him, "yours seems to be a minority view. His letters of recommendation—"

"I wrote one of those," he was told.

"You—"

"We want him out of here," the man said. "In a year or two you will, as well. In fact, you'll be writing a letter just like mine." And with that the line went dead. Gus had immediately dialed the number displayed on the caller ID, but it just rang and rang.

Gus, who had only a few more years before retirement, was living at the time in one of the college-owned duplexes on campus. He was visiting friends in San Francisco when Kurt and Alice arrived in Schuyler, and by the time he returned they'd moved into the other half of his unit. He met Alice when he pulled in. Unaware that mail typically didn't come until late in the afternoon, she was out at the curb checking the box. Gus was immediately enchanted; she was so tall and graceful and loose limbed. He'd always liked women, even older women, who wore their hair long. His own mother had done so, well into her seventies. He introduced himself as one of her husband's new colleagues in the poli-sci department and welcomed her to the neighborhood, which was mostly faculty. She seemed a tad skittish but listened intently to everything he said, and she had one of the most beautiful smiles he'd ever encountered, though its timing felt slightly off, its trigger more internal than connected to unfolding, real-time events.

The next morning her husband called to invite Gus over for a glass of wine on their back patio later that afternoon. "Thanks for picking up the phone, by the way," Kurt said after they shook hands. Though a good twenty years younger than Gus, he had a black beard so uniformly thick that it looked fake, like a cheap disguise, and made him appear middle aged. While they chatted, he poured two glasses—why only two? Gus wondered—and handed him the one that had slightly less in it.

"I'm sorry?" he said, confused. "For picking up the phone?"

"I think your advocacy helped us jump the line," Kurt said, gesturing to their half of the duplex.

Actually, Gus had been puzzled about that. The duplexes, though nothing all that special, were much in demand because of their campus location. Also, they were relatively cheap compared with housing in Schuyler's open market. How had these newcomers landed one? He was about to say he hadn't made any calls on their behalf, but then, for some reason, he didn't. Was it because of that warning? Did some cowardly part of him want to be on evil's good side, if that's what this man turned out to be? The patio door opened just then, and Alice— how lovely she looked, Gus recalled thinking—appeared with a tray containing fruit and cheese and crackers. "And you've already met my

Alice," Kurt said, which for some reason seemed to confuse her. Had she forgotten Gus so quickly? Setting the tray down, she managed to nudge the wine bottle, which teetered and was about to fall when Kurt caught it. Half the crackers went onto the deck. "I'm sorry," she said, more to her husband than to Gus, who squatted to help her pick them up. "I'm such a klutz," she confided. "Someone should shoot me."

"That seems a tad extreme," Gus said, expecting a smile at the understatement, but she was anxiously looking up at Kurt, perhaps to see if he shared Gus's view. There was no telling and she nipped back into the kitchen.

When they finished the bottle, a nice chardonnay, Kurt went inside. Alice hadn't returned, and Gus wasn't sure what to think. Right from the start, there'd only been two glasses. Was she unwell? Why didn't Kurt feel the need to explain her absence?

"So, you've been here *how* long?" Kurt asked when he returned with another bottle. There was just a hint of accusation in the question, so Gus answered cautiously as his host expertly uncorked the new bottle.

"Almost thirty years," he admitted. "I didn't intend to stay so long."

Kurt poured him a glass, his third, then another for himself. As with the first two, he gave Gus slightly less. Had someone told him that Gus couldn't handle his liquor, or were the pours purely coincidental? Gus decided they must be. After all, inviting him over in the first place was an act of generosity, and this wasn't a cheap chardonnay.

"Thirty years *here*?" Kurt said, incredulously. "In *Schuyler Springs*?"

Okay, Gus thought, maybe this wasn't Ann Arbor or Madison, but still. Had the man already weighed Schuyler's merits and found them wanting? "It's become home, I guess," he offered weakly, deciding then that when he finished this glass, there would be no fourth.

"Still, it can't have been easy, right?"

Why was the man smiling in such a peculiar way? "I'm sorry, I don't follow."

Kurt shrugged. "I wouldn't have thought there'd be much of a gay community here."

Gus's profound surprise slowed his reaction. "There isn't," he said finally. "But then I wouldn't really know because I'm not gay."

"Oh." He shrugged again, without the slightest hint of apology. "I guess I just assumed."

Why? Because he was unmarried? Because he'd just returned from San Francisco? Gus found the unwarranted assumption particularly galling, since when he'd first arrived here one or two of his new colleagues had leaped to the same conclusion, based on what, Gus couldn't imagine, then or now. Were there still people at the college who doubted his sexual orientation? He felt himself flushing.

The man's wife was still nowhere in evidence. "I hope Alice is okay," he ventured. Yes, he was eager for a change of subject, but her continued absence *was* strange, wasn't it? Had Kurt brought out only two wineglasses because he never intended for her to join them? Perhaps even instructed her not to?

"With her one never knows," her husband said, the lack of concern in his voice sending a chill up Gus's spine. "As you'll discover, neighbor."

Gus set his wine down. *To whom it may concern,* he thought. *I cannot recommend my esteemed colleague Kurt Wright highly enough. The short time he's spent at our college has been utterly transformative.*

NOT LONG AFTER the Wrights appeared in Schuyler, the social fabric of Gus's department began to fray. Longtime friends started falling out over misunderstandings that would eventually be traced back to something Kurt had said. Rumors began to circulate. The one about Gus being gay, for instance, suddenly seemed to attain new currency. Nor were such untruths the worst of it. Gus's best friend on the faculty appeared in his office one day, her eyes nearly swollen shut from crying, wanting to know why he'd betrayed her confidence. A decade earlier she'd explained to him that she and her husband had a brain-damaged child they'd finally decided to institutionalize, a decision that had nearly destroyed them and their marriage. When Gus assured her that he'd never repeated this to a soul, she refused to believe him, claiming that he was the only person *she* had ever told. By Thanksgiving, everyone in the department seemed to know something horrible about everyone else, and Gus's once-sociable colleagues had begun to teach their classes and go home, skipping committee meetings and begging off their usual Friday afternoon happy hour at a tavern near campus. "What's going on over in poli-sci," a friend in the history department asked him. "You guys used to be the life of the party."

Kurt turned out to be a man of numerous interdisciplinary interests, and he quickly got to know faculty from several other departments, where he was surprisingly popular. Apparently he was a gifted mimic who did spot-on impressions of his colleagues in political science. "You've never heard him do you?" said an old friend of Gus's from the English department. "You should get him to," she enthused. "It's truly hilarious."

When he asked her why, she grew embarrassed. "Does he make me sound gay?" he said.

"Well, yeah, but—"

"But what?"

"That's how you sound."

"I sound gay."

"Not lilting or anything, just, you know . . ."

Later that week he ran into Charlie, the guy from the dean's office who handled campus housing. "I've been wondering," he said, "how Kurt Wright managed to land the other half of the duplex I'm in. Wasn't there a waiting list?"

He looked surprised. "Well, your taking up his case like that certainly didn't hurt."

"Me?"

"And of course Alice's medical condition allowed us to do an end run around the waiting list."

"Charlie," Gus said. "I never wrote Wright any recommendation."

"Like I told you at the time, there was no need. The phone conversation was good enough for me."

"But we never spoke on the phone."

The guy's expression changed. "That's not funny, Gus. I bent all kinds of rules for you. If you and Kurt had some kind of falling-out, I'm sorry, but I'm not booting him and his wife out of their home. I'm surprised you'd want me to."

"I don't," Gus assured him. "I'm just saying. If you talked to someone claiming to be me—"

"It *was* you, Gus. Don't you think I know your voice after thirty years?"

"Charlie—"

"Besides, think about it. You can't do Kurt dirt without harming your sister."

"My sister?" Gus repeated.

"Well," Charlie conceded. "Okay, your half sister."

That weekend Gus waited at the front window for Kurt to leave, then went next door and rang the bell. He had to ring it several times before Alice came to the door, dressed in a thin robe. As always, she didn't seem to quite recognize him.

"I hate to bother you, Alice," he told her, "but would it be okay if I came in?"

"I'm sorry," she said. Why was the woman always apologizing? "Kurt's not here."

"I know," he said, and after an awkward moment she stepped back from the door.

It was dark inside, the shades drawn, only two small lamps turned on. Gus had heard she liked to paint, but how could you paint without light? He looked around for signs of artistic endeavor—sketch pads, colored pencils, an easel—but saw nothing. "I can only stay a minute," he assured her, wondering why she always seemed so skittish. This visit was, he was starting to realize, a bad idea. He'd come over thinking she might be able to help him understand her husband, what was going on, why he was causing all this trouble and telling such outrageous lies. Did she know, for instance, that he was letting on that she and Gus were related? But all you had to do was look at Alice to know she'd be of little help.

"Is everything okay over here?" he asked, surprising himself. He hadn't meant to be so direct.

She thought about it. "Kurt says I sleep too much," she admitted.

He nodded, trying to think of what to ask next. Finally, though he knew the question was out of line, given that he hardly knew her, he said, "Are you happy, Alice?"

"Happy?"

"The walls are thin," he explained.

She blinked at this, as if she'd taken the statement metaphorically.

"When Kurt raises his voice," he said, "I can hear. When you cry, well, I can hear that, too."

Her hand went to her mouth. "I make him angry sometimes. I don't mean to."

Gus nodded. "He's not a very nice man, is he?"

She thought about it. "I probably *do* sleep too much," she said. "I just . . . can't seem to stay awake."

"Alice?" he said. "If you need a friend, I'm right next door."

She turned to stare at the wall that separated her home from his, as if trying to imagine him there on the other side, his ear pressed against the wall.

"Well," he said, "I should go. I hope I haven't upset you."

"No," she said, without much conviction, and followed him to the door. When he opened it, she said, "Gus?"

He turned back to face her, surprised that she'd used his given name. "Yes, Alice?"

"Are *you*?"

What, gay? Had her husband told her that? "Am I *what,* Alice?"

"Happy?"

"Oh," he said, feeling slow witted himself now. Well, *was* he? Because for a split second, when she said his name, his heart had leaped with the startling possibility that he loved her, impossible as that seemed. So, yes, there was a brief welling up of something that might've been happiness, before the facts—that he didn't really know her, that she was another man's wife, that he was a fool about women and always had been—put that emotion to flight. "No, Alice," he confessed. "I don't think so, no."

"I'm sorry," she said quickly, as if Gus's unhappiness was yet another thing that could be traced to some personal failing of her own, one she'd turn her mind to once she'd solved the problem of sleeping so much.

AS MAYOR, Gus had a key to Sans Souci Park's main gate. Since the hotel closed, the private estate was, except on special occasions, barred to vehicular traffic. Along the bike path that wound lazily through the grounds, there were cast-iron benches, and Alice liked to sit on the one Gus had donated years earlier that bore their names. He'd hoped to find her there this morning, as the park's serenity and solitude sometimes had a calming effect on her. Why not just let her sit on their bench as the first rays of sunlight pierced the trees? Here she could talk to her heart's content on her princess phone without bothering anyone. Unfortunately, she wasn't there.

Feeling suddenly bereft, he pulled over, got out and took a seat on the bench himself, leaving the car running and the driver's-side door open so he could listen to the scanner. Before leaving home, he'd called the police station so they'd be on the lookout. He felt he needed to *do* something, but what? It was pleasant here on the bench. Closing his eyes, he listened to the breeze in the upper branches of the pines. Just that quickly he was asleep—then he jolted awake again, jittery, wondering if it was the scanner that had awakened him. Had he missed an announcement? That Alice had been located? Through a break in the trees he could make out the old hotel, grand and sad, the rising sun's rays reflecting off its upper-story windows. *The Sans Souci.* Without care. An idea sold to people with cares galore. Everybody, basically, with cares in desperate search of cures. People who wanted to believe in magical waters. Lourdes in upstate New York. Come to think of it, he could use a cure himself. Had he ever before felt so much like giving up?

One of the things Kurt had recognized in him was a buoyant, dim-witted optimism, his faith that anything broken could be fixed. Somehow he'd intuited that Gus meant to challenge the town's self-defeating, dead-end pessimism, to free it from the imaginary shackles of its unfortunate history. So what if its springs had run dry and Schuyler's hadn't? The rest of what ailed the town could be remedied, couldn't it? Yet he'd badly underestimated what that would require. Something in these people's natures, he'd reluctantly concluded, was rigid, unalterable. They needed to believe that luck ruled the world and that theirs was bad and would remain so forever and ever, amen, a credo that let them off the hook and excused them from truly engaging in the present, much less the future.

Were they wrong? Gus was no longer so sure. Maybe they were simply realists. Not a week went by that he didn't get a call from some downstate developer wanting to get the skinny on the Sans Souci. A potential gold mine, he told them, rich in history and style. People used to come from as far away as Atlanta to take the waters. "But says here it's located in this Bath place? Not Schuyler Springs?" "We're sister cities," Gus would assure them, but he could tell they'd concluded that Bath was the ugly sister, the one who never got asked out and made her own clothes, though all the other girls loved her.

Who knew? Maybe Bath *was* bad luck. Out at Hilldale the dead were resurfacing after decades in the ground, a triumph of the past over the present. How could you expect people to imagine a better future when Great-Great-Grandma Rose launched herself out of the poisoned earth, seemingly in protest. In town the ground was so full of yellow pus that when it rained, the air became not just disgusting but probably toxic. On what basis could you tell people they were wrong to concede defeat? Or convince them that every problem has a solution when those you offer in good faith turn out to be so rickety and jerry-rigged that they tumble down in the street? How do you get a community to believe in itself, in its own fundamental goodness, when in its midst there are people who secretly fill apartments with illegal poisonous reptiles? How do you keep everyone else from peering into their own flawed hearts and seeing vipers stirring there?

The other thing that Kurt had understood was that Gus wouldn't be able to resist the challenge of fixing Alice. Not only would he want to repair whatever was wrong with her, he'd confuse his compassion for a damaged soul with love. Okay, he'd tried. Give himself that much credit. Like Bath, however, there was more wrong with Alice than he'd realized, and nothing he'd tried had worked. Though he hated to admit it, he'd bitten off more than he could chew, and now he was gagging. This sin had a name: pride. Nothing now remained but what pride goeth before.

From somewhere outside the park came the squeal of brakes, and Gus winced, expecting the crashing sound of torn metal and shattered glass. When none came, he pictured Alice crumpled on the pavement.

Would it be a blessing? The question was just there, shocking, vile. How could he think such a thing? What kind of man permits such a thought, even in passing?

The police scanner crackled, then was silent.

ONE AFTERNOON, not long after he'd called on Alice, Gus returned home to find a man seated back on the patio, staring off into the woods with his feet up on the table. It took him a moment to recognize Kurt without his beard. He watched him for a moment from behind the drape, trying to decide what the chances were that his visit here was related to his own next door. Pretty good, he concluded. Also pretty good that Kurt had heard him drive up and was only pretending to be lost in thought.

Hearing the patio door slide open, he looked up and offered Gus his unpleasant smile, though he neither rose nor lowered his feet.

"Glass of wine?" Gus offered.

"I thought you'd never ask." His point being that it'd been nearly a year since he'd invited Gus over, an invitation that had never been returned.

He opened a bottle of white and brought it outside, along with three glasses. "Would Alice like to join us?"

"It would be better if she didn't."

Gus poured wine into two glasses and left the third sitting there on the table. He made sure one pour was slightly more than the other and handed that one to Kurt, who chuckled and said, "You noticed that." A manila folder with Gus's name on it sat in the center of the table. "People generally do notice things," Kurt continued, "especially when you direct their attention, but they act on very little. Then they wonder why their lives are so full of regret."

Gus took a sip of wine and winced. Was the bottle corked, or was he tasting the acid that was suddenly in the back of his throat? Probably the latter, since Kurt didn't seem to notice.

"For instance, you knew right from the start that something was wrong with Alice, but did you bother to ask? Did you own your curiosity and say, *Kurt, buddy, what's wrong with that fucking woman? Did she get dropped on her head as a kid, or what?*"

"What *is* wrong with Alice, Kurt?"

"The fuck should I know?" he said, picking up the third, unused glass and examining it closely, as if for smudges. "Something, though, wouldn't you agree?"

Gus felt a surge of anger at this, followed by a welcome jolt of courage. "Okay, then, what's wrong with *you*?"

At this Kurt tapped the empty glass against the edge of the table. It didn't shatter, but a crack now zigzagged from rim to stem. "Kurt's not a very nice man, is he," said Kurt, and it was true, he *did* do Gus's voice amazingly well.

And just that quickly Gus's courage was all used up. "Please don't do that," he said weakly, meaning the mimicking, not breaking the glass.

The other man had leaned toward him confidentially. "If you need a friend," he said, "I'm right next door."

"I said don't."

Kurt shrugged and poured more wine into his own glass.

"What do you want, Kurt?"

He appeared to think about it. "What do I want? It might be hard for you to believe, but the truth is I never know for sure. I try to live in the moment. Right now, for instance? This little bit of time we're sharing? Is *very* rewarding. Honestly, the look on your face when you heard your voice, your words, coming out of my mouth? Wonderful. You didn't know whether to shit or go blind."

"You really are evil, aren't you."

"Hey, don't say I didn't warn you." When Gus blinked at this, Kurt continued, "You do *not* want to hire Kurt Wright . . . We want him out of here . . ."

Gus felt a wave of nausea wash over him. For a moment he thought he might faint. "That was you."

"Well, I thought you deserved a heads-up."

"How did you learn to do voices?"

"Same way you get to Carnegie Hall, pal. Practice, practice, practice. I record important phone calls. All I need is a sentence or two. Man or woman, doesn't matter. Children are tougher."

"Except my conversation with Alice wasn't over the phone. I was in the room with her. You weren't."

"Yeah, pretty darned sneaky there, Gus. Waiting until I left? But I forgive you. Anyway, sometimes when I go out, I leave a tape running. Not that I distrust Alice. She'd never. But honestly? Some of the things that woman says when she's alone are fucking priceless."

"Why are you telling me all this?" Because a sane person wouldn't, would he?

"Every artist wants to be appreciated, is part of it," Kurt said, pouring again. "But also I'm easily bored. Take now. Rich though this experience has been—and I'm not just talking about you here, don't flatter yourself about that, but also the college, this whole fucking upstate New York backwater—it can't help getting old. The planning is always fun, but the execution? At some point the law of diminishing returns always kicks in, and things become rote. I've been bored with you and yours for a while now."

"I'm sorry to be such a disappointment."

"Hey, not your fault. You were *way* overmatched. Anyway," he said, pushing the manila folder toward him. "I need a couple small favors, and then I'll be out of your hair."

Inside the folder was a preaddressed, stamped envelope, as well as a one-page letter of recommendation, marked SAMPLE.

"I warned you about this, too, if you recall," Kurt said. "You can disregard that letter, if you want. I only include it for possible talking points. But by all means use your own—what's the word I'm looking for? Voice, that's it. However, as this new post I'm about to be offered is administrative, I'd take it as a personal favor if you stressed how well I play with others."

"Should I really use that phrase? 'Play with others'?"

"Knock yourself out. Nobody will hear the double meaning until it's too late. And don't trouble your conscience over all this. When I'm hired, which I will be, it won't be because of your recommendation. As you know, these things are pretty pro forma, a hedge against regret—for which, it inevitably turns out, there is no hedge."

Gus held up the envelope. "Aren't you concerned I'll call this Janet Applebaum and tell her all about you?"

Kurt waved this off. "No need. Already done. Trust me. The good woman has been forewarned, and in no uncertain terms. Unfortunately, I think she may have concluded that the person warning her was deranged, just as you did."

"You *are* deranged."

"Jeez," he said, emptying the last of the bottle into his glass. "I've drunk the lion's share of this, haven't I?"

Gus took a sip from his glass. The wine tasted better now, the fear-induced nausea having pretty much passed, leaving in its place little but sadness. "What's wrong with Alice, Kurt? What have you done to her?"

"You give me too much credit. It's true I may have undermined her confidence from time to time, but I never told her anything about herself that she didn't already know. Like most people, Alice was complicit every step of the way. But I doubt any permanent damage has been done. If she had a good man, she'd be right as rain."

"Instead she's got you."

"Poor Alice," he agreed. "I think she's fond of you. She has no idea you're gay, of course."

"I'm not, Kurt."

He shrugged, as if the point wasn't worth arguing over. "Next you'll be telling me you have no political ambitions."

To this, Gus offered no response.

"Jesus," Kurt said, rubbing his temples. "I can actually *see* your mind working. You're thinking, Good guess—right? Every English professor has a novel in his desk drawer; every poli-sci prof wants to prove that those who teach can sometimes do?"

Which was pretty much what Gus *had* been thinking. But really, how could this psychopath know about his long-range plans? He'd never spoken about them to anyone.

"The house is a good idea," Kurt said. "The one on Upper Main Street, by the Sans Souci? The one you keep going back to look at? Needs work but, as they say in the biz, it's got good bones. And Bath prices can only go up."

"You've been following me."

Kurt snorted at this. "You think I'm *behind* you, Gus? Really? Because what should be coming into focus right about now is how far *ahead* of you I've been, right from the start. But getting back to the house? Good idea. Outsiders seldom fare well in small-town politics. Gotta sink those roots into the community, have some skin in the game. So yeah, make an offer. Use locals to renovate, even if they fuck everything up."

Conclusions Gus had already come to. Why did it make him feel better to have a man he viscerally loathed confirm the wisdom of his strategy?

"Which leaves only the other thing you've been mulling over. Will people in a jerkwater town like Bath vote for a gay?"

"This again."

"Hey, it's not me you have to convince. Good-looking woman at your side just might do the trick, is all I'm saying."

Gus put the letter back in the envelope. "You said you had a *couple* favors."

"Right," he said, sitting up straight and doing a little drum solo on the table with his thumbs. "Almost forgot. If it's not too much to ask, I was hoping you might look in on Alice while I'm gone. Make sure she's okay? Moving again so soon is kind of freaking her out. I'm flying out to California the day after tomorrow. I need to find us a place to live, meet my new staff, give them their marching orders, arrange for the movers, a hundred other things. I should be back by the middle of the month, though, and like I said, after that we'll be out of your hair."

Kurt rose, his glass empty now, along with the bottle, and extended his hand. When Gus hesitated, he actually looked hurt. "Come on," he said, "nobody died. Why be a bad sport? I'd feel better if we parted as friends."

Hating himself, Gus shook the man's hand.

"I have your promise? You'll look after Alice while I'm gone?"

"Yes, that I will do."

"You know what," Kurt said. "You play your cards right, you could come out of this with what you want." He shrugged, again. "Or what you imagine you want."

———

SO, GUS THOUGHT, in the end it had been a bargain, and Alice herself a plastic chip. Had he sensed this even from the start? Over the next few weeks the exact nature of the covenant took shape. Gus had looked in on Alice, as promised. Though she was even more fretful than usual, she didn't seem to need him for much beyond a half gallon of milk or a dozen eggs if he happened to be going to the store. He didn't wonder why their station wagon was absent from the driveway, since Kurt would've driven it to Albany to catch his flight and left it in long-term parking. Alice didn't drive and had no use for it. One morning he asked her why, given that she was trying not to sleep so much, she always kept the place so dark, the drapes drawn tightly shut in the middle of the day. "He likes it like that," she told him.

"But Kurt isn't here," he pointed out. "How do *you* like it?"

She seemed to consider this, her own preference, for the first time. With the drapes pulled back, the apartment flooded with natural light, Gus began to notice things were missing. He'd only been there once before and hadn't been paying close attention, but hadn't there been a laptop set up in the kitchen nook? A Bose radio?

"Has Kurt telephoned you?" he asked the following day. She responded, as if to a trick question, "I don't think so." He noticed the phalanx of pill bottles lined up along the kitchen windowsill, all prescription drugs: Paxil, Xanax, a few others.

"I'm not well," she explained when he asked what they were for. "They help me to not be so frightened."

When Kurt had been gone a week, Gus asked if he might have a look in their bedroom. If Alice saw anything strange in this request, she gave no sign. Some of Kurt's clothes were hanging from the rod in the closet, but fewer than Gus would've expected. His dresser drawers contained underwear and some stray, unmatched socks, a few yellowing handkerchiefs—the sort of things Gus had crammed into the back of his own drawers—but where was the good stuff? Gradually it came to him that what he was looking at was a snake's shed skin, which in turn caused him to recall something in their final conversation that had barely registered at the time. Twice Kurt had used the phrase "be out of your hair." The second time he'd said *we*. The first time he'd used the pronoun *I*. The first had been a slip. Kurt wasn't coming back.

Slowly, as if the thrown-back drapes were allowing for all manner of illumination, Alice began to show signs of similar understanding, though she continued to insist that Kurt would shortly return, after which they'd begin their new lives in California. To Gus, such statements felt like trial balloons. Would he contradict her? "Why don't I cook us dinner tonight?" he suggested one morning before heading in to work. He'd prepare the food in his kitchen and bring it over. They could eat outside on the back patio with the sliding door open so Alice could hear the phone if it rang. "Should I?" she said, clearly tempted when he offered her a glass of wine, and he told her he thought one glass wouldn't hurt. He also advised her to consult a local physician about how many of the medications she was taking were really necessary. After dessert, when he rose to go back next door, he said, as if the thought had just that moment occurred to him, "How would you like it if I looked after you from now on?"

She regarded him with an expression that he took to be midway between knowledge and innocence. "You're a very nice man," she said, "but what about Kurt?"

"I can talk to him about that when he comes back."

That night he lay in bed thinking about the year he spent in Korea near the end of the conflict. He never lied to anyone about the nature of his service there, but unless asked he didn't volunteer that he'd spent his time not in combat but in the quartermaster's office. It was there he'd learned what things were worth, how to manage their flow, how to make friends and get things done for the common good. By the time he returned stateside he was prepared to take full advantage of the GI Bill, and at Albany State he'd learned the intricacies of another elaborate system and what it took to succeed in it. He'd had a rewarding academic life at the college and moved through it honestly, or at least not dishonestly. But when the phone rang he was remembering with great fondness the boy he'd worked with in the quartermaster's office.

"So," Kurt said, "how is the lovely Alice?"

"We had dinner on your patio. She still thinks you're coming back for her."

"But you know better."

"Are you two even married?"

"Lord, no. What gave you that idea?"

"Your academic vitae, for one thing? For another, she refers to you as her husband?"

"Oh, right."

"So you're telling me we'll never see you again."

"I don't intend to return to Schuyler Fucking Springs, if that's what you mean."

"Of course that's what I mean."

"Rest easy," he said, and for some reason Gus trusted him. "And speaking of easy. Do you have any idea how easy I'm letting you off?"

Actually, he did have a pretty good idea. "Goodbye, Kurt," Gus said, but he'd already hung up.

IN THE INTERVENING DECADE Gus had mostly managed to put Kurt out of his mind. The morning after he was elected mayor, though, he'd located the name of the dean, Janet Applebaum, to whom he'd sent Kurt's letter of recommendation. It turned out she was no longer in administration, having returned to full-time teaching. "I know who you are," she said, with thinly veiled hostility, when he identified himself. "Do you have any idea the misery that man caused here?" Careers ruined, apparently. Marriages wrecked. A suicide. "He's gone, then?" Gus inquired, and the woman said yes, he had been for some time. Last she heard he was in Europe working for . . . NATO? The UN? She couldn't remember.

Feeling slightly ill, he thanked her and was about to hang up when she said, "So . . . what kind of man does what you did? Knowing what you knew, how could you write that letter?" But there was something in her voice, something besides righteous indignation, that he recognized. "Didn't you write one just like it yourself?" he asked. The resulting silence was his answer.

Well, he told himself at the time, if a life had been lost, another had been saved. Once off the majority of her medications, a new Alice had emerged that Gus hadn't known existed. Not exactly extroverted but fully engaged with the world, not hiding from it in the dark. Before long, the years she'd spent with Kurt began to recede like a bad dream. Gus learned never to bring his name up in conversation, because it always rendered Alice mute, remorseful, he supposed, for the lost years. In the months leading up to their wedding, Alice's spirits were so buoyant that he allowed himself to believe that Kurt was right, and no lasting harm had been done. All she needed was a good man.

They'd had a simple civil ceremony and departed immediately for a honeymoon in Italy. That winter he'd made an offer on the old Victorian on Upper Main and spent a small fortune renovating it. When they returned stateside it was to this house, the old duplexes now rented to other faculty. Alice professed to love the house, but he could tell it was so big that it intimidated and maybe even frightened her. She wasn't sure she liked the idea of having separate bedrooms, though he'd explained there was no reason for both of them to be awakened by town business in the middle of the night. After a time, the old anxieties began to return. "I just get like this sometimes," she said when he asked what was wrong, why she was so agitated. "But he's gone," he objected. After all, Kurt *was* the root cause of her problems, wasn't he? If not him, then who?

That fall—he was in his final year of teaching—he got a call from the campus police. Alice was causing a disturbance at her old duplex where she seemed to believe she still lived. "You're not my husband, are you?" she exclaimed when he arrived there to gather her in, her tone suggesting it wasn't so much that she questioned being married to him as that he hadn't measured up to her preconceived idea of what a husband was supposed to be.

THIS MORNING, sitting on their bench in Sans Souci Park, what troubled Gus most was what he'd never know. What was it Kurt had said? That if he played his cards right he could have what he wanted, or imagined he wanted? Well, had he played his cards right, or had Kurt played them for him? The choices had seemed to be his when he made them, but now he wasn't so sure. To the other man's credit, he'd kept his word and hadn't returned to Schuyler, at least so far as Gus knew. He doubted it was him that Alice had seen today. It was possible she hadn't seen anybody. When she was spiraling out of control, what his wife saw in her head was more real to her than the world that entered through her senses. Absent evidence to the contrary, he'd continue to believe they'd seen the last of Kurt Wright. The other thing he'd never know was whether a good man was all that Alice needed. Because he himself wasn't a good man. He knew that now for a certainty. He'd meant not just to be good *to* Alice but also *for* her, but she'd been better for him and his career than he for her. Sensing her innate kindness and fragility, people were drawn to her, and they appreciated how protective he was of her. By some strange calculus, this had actually translated into votes. Kurt, of course, had foreseen that it would.

He'd played his cards right, he decided. He'd gotten what he imagined he wanted.

LONGMEADOW, a relatively new subdivision of mostly two-story town houses, was weirdly familiar to Gus. Had some young faculty member at the college won tenure years ago and, too poor to crack the Schuyler market, concluded that buying here was better than paying rent? The developer had planted trees and shrubs, but sales had been slow, and some of the plantings had shriveled and died of neglect. Though the units appeared to be fully occupied now, to Gus it looked like the kind of neighborhood that would never achieve what realtors liked to call maturity. It would segue directly from new to shabby.

He'd been afraid that Alice might be gone by the time he got there, but no, she was right where she'd been sighted on the stone bench outside the rundown community center, having one of her imaginary phone conversations. She was wearing the same long, flowing skirt she wore most days, along with one of her blousy tops, for which he was grateful. When she woke up agitated, she'd sometimes leave the house in just her robe and slippers or, worse, her nightgown. Pulling into the lot, he turned off the ignition and, since she was too wrapped up in her conversation to have noticed his arrival, just sat there, watching, trying to calculate how much of what he was witnessing was his fault. After a while, though, he got out and joined her on the bench. Seeing him, she said, "I'll have to call you back," and put the handset in her bag. "Is something wrong?" she asked him.

"No," he said. "I'm just glad I found you."

She blotted his wet cheeks with her sleeve. It was as much intimacy as they'd shared in a long time. They'd had little enough, God knew. His fault, not hers, though in the end maybe not his, either. Maybe God's, or nature's. How in the world were you supposed to know?

"Are you sad?" she said, taking his hand.

"Maybe a little," he admitted.

"Why?"

"Because I want you to be well."

"I *am* well."

"Good."

"Sometimes I get sad, too," she admitted. She was studying the nearest town house, and suddenly it dawned on Gus why the street seemed so damned familiar. Raymer and his wife had lived here, perhaps in that very place—what the hell was her name, Becky? Jesus, his brain was turning to mush. No, Becka. She'd slipped on a rug at the top of the stairs and broken her neck when she fell, the poor woman. Raymer still blamed himself, you could tell. Maybe blaming yourself was just something men did.

"She told me things," Alice said, still staring at the town house. Odd how she could sometimes read his thoughts.

"Like what?"

"What was in her heart."

Now Gus studied *her* carefully. Was she criticizing him for keeping what was in his own heart a secret?

"Was it Kurt you saw earlier today? The man who scared you?"

"Kurt's gone."

Gus was crying again. He could feel the tears. "Poor duck," he said. "You get so confused, don't you."

"Do I?"

They rose, and she followed him obediently to the car, but as he helped buckle her in, she kept looking past him at the Raymers' former home. "You're going to be okay," he promised her.

When he turned the corner and the town house was no longer in sight, she began to calm down, but just then her phone rang, if only in her mind. It took her a moment to locate the handset in her bag. "Hello," she said. "Oh, yes, hi."

And something occurred to Gus for the first time. In the fiction of these conversations, Alice never called anyone. He never heard her say, *Hi, it's me. I hope I haven't caught you at a bad time. I was just thinking how long it'd been since we last talked.* No, it was always someone calling her. She was the needed one, the one who would listen without judging or arguing. The wise, trusted friend. The person you turn to when the chips are down. "You're being too hard on yourself," he heard her say now. "I know how difficult it is," she continued, "but the important thing is to remember you're not alone. I'm right here."

Electricity

THE SHORT DRIVE to Hattie's was the best part of Ruth's day, twelve selfish, quiet minutes to herself. This was true even when she had her granddaughter with her, like today. After all, being with Tina was a lot like being alone. How such a still, silent child could have come from a long line of mouthy women was a mystery. But then life was full of such puzzles.

Including electricity. Last night Zack's shed had been struck by lightning with such force that it had ruptured a seam in the roof. The sound of the accompanying thunder had been apocalyptic, levitating all three of the house's occupants off their separate beds. A moment later Tina, blinking sleepily, had appeared at Ruth's bedroom door, looking for all the world like her mother at that age. Ruth had never seen a kid so terrified of thunderstorms.

"It's okay, Two-Shoes," Ruth said, using her pet name from when she was little. "You can come in." And so she'd crawled into bed next to her and was instantly asleep again. A moment later, it was Zack in the doorway. "Come see this," he said, and so she went into his room, whose rear window overlooked the shed. At the apex of the roof where the lightning had struck, a strip of corrugated tin now stood up like a sentinel, and at its tip was an eerie blue flame that was somehow burning steadily in the gale. When the skies opened and the rain came down in sheets, they expected the flame to be doused, but it continued to burn like a mirage, rain leaping off the metal roof all around it, until gradually the flame faded and disappeared, at which point Ruth realized that she and Zack were holding hands, something they hadn't done in years. What they did next they hadn't done in even longer.

Zack had awakened at five on the dot, dressed quietly and gone downstairs to make himself a cup of instant coffee, his usual routine. Ruth, half awake and already deeply regretting what had transpired, found this adherence reassuring, suggesting as it did that her husband wasn't placing too much importance on what had happened between them. With any luck he understood that, like the lightning strike itself, this bout of sex was an anomaly, statistically improbable, unlikely to happen again in their lifetimes. When was the last time she'd even been in this room? She wouldn't even clean it. She was willing to wash his sheets with her own and those from Tina's room whenever she stayed over, provided he strip the bed himself and bring everything down to the basement. After they were laundered, she left the sheets and pillowcases outside in the hallway, and he made the bed himself. Why had she even followed him in here last night? What had led him to believe that sex was remotely possible? The fact that she hadn't withdrawn her hand from his as they watched the blue flame? And why had he wanted her to see that in the first place? Sure, it was a strange sight, almost miraculous, but why her? Tina was normally his appreciative audience. Had he stopped in her room first, seen she wasn't there and only then come to Ruth's? Somehow, she didn't think so. He hadn't seemed interested in waking the girl. No, the flame was something he'd wanted to show Ruth. That watching it had led to sex seemed as surprising to him as it was to her. It hadn't been great, but it hadn't been nothing, either, and this morning, nothing was what she very much wanted it to be.

When she heard his truck back down the steep drive, grinding the gears when he shifted from reverse into second—seeing little to be gained by first—and head toward town, she lay awake for a few minutes, still trying to make some kind of sense of what had happened and why. Was it just that she'd been celibate for so long? Or was there some connection between the blue flame they'd seen atop the shed and the long dormant, barely guttering flame of their dimly recalled intimacy? Stirring the curtains was a lovely breeze, fresh and delicious, the essence of not-yet-arrived morning, and she might've lazed there a bit longer except she heard the alarm go off in her own room and didn't want Tina to find her in Zack's, since she might tell her mother, who in turn would want to know all about it, her curiosity further stoked because it was none of her damn business.

At some point during the night Tina must have awakened and shuffled back to her own room because the bed was now empty. Later, after Ruth had showered and was joined in the kitchen by her groggy granddaughter, the girl claimed to have no memory of the jolting thunderclap or of coming to her bed, and Ruth then wondered if the entire sequence of events—from lightning strike to blue flame to sex—had actually happened or was just a particularly vivid dream. Outside, though, the black scorch mark on the roof was visible even in the dark, and the strip of corrugated tin still stood erect, so at least that part was real.

"Can we go by Main Street?" Tina asked when they hit the outskirts of town.

"Why not," Ruth said, though they were running late and this was several blocks out of the way. Actually, she wasn't anxious to get to the restaurant. Having told Sully it might be best for him not to come by so much, she now thought she'd miss him if he took her advice to heart. Hard on the heels of that worry came another. Had Sully died in the night? Was that what the blue flame atop the shed had been about—announcing his departure from the world? Had some part of her understood it even then? Just yesterday she'd been thinking how nice it would be to live in a world without men. Had that daydream somehow set something in motion? Was what had happened between her and Zack a grim acknowledgment that he was now the only man in her life?

When they passed the Upper Main Street house Sully owned but refused to live in, Tina leaned forward to peer at it. Back in the fall the poor girl had developed a crush on Will, Sully's grandson. Ruth doubted Will was even aware of it, and he certainly hadn't encouraged it, but according to Tina he was kind to everyone, even the uncool girls, and not stuck up, like he had a right to be, popular as he was. When he came into the restaurant with his grandfather, he made a point of saying hello. Always using her name and asking how she was. Like it really mattered. So she'd fallen hard. But now he was off to New York City for a summer internship and then college, and she didn't know when or even if she'd see him again. That she still wanted to drive by the house struck Ruth as particularly heartbreaking.

Only when they'd gone another couple blocks did it occur to Ruth that Sully's truck hadn't been out front, which meant he was up and out early. Sometimes, when he couldn't sleep, he'd be waiting out back of the restaurant when she arrived to open up. If he was there this morning, she'd give him a little grief, but in truth she'd be glad to see him, if only so she could rest easy that the blue flame hadn't been about him. God, life was a complete mess.

"You know about sex, right?" Ruth was surprised to hear herself ask.

Tina turned to regard her blankly.

"I'm talking to you," Ruth said. "If you hear me, raise your left hand."

Tina raised her right.

"Very funny," Ruth told her, though not at all sure she was joking. Her granddaughter had always had trouble distinguishing left from right. Ruth had tried to help her when she was little by taking her wrists and holding both hands straight in front of her, palms out, and explaining that the thumb and index finger of her left hand would naturally form the letter *L*. Later in the day, she'd tested her on the concept, and Tina dutifully held both hands out in front of her, palms in this time, and confidently identified her right hand as her left. Had she been joking even then?

"I'm serious," Ruth said. "Boys want sex. Even the nice ones."

Tina regarded her for another long beat, her face still an expressionless mask, then went back to staring out the window, as if neither of them had spoken.

"You know you can get pregnant, right?" Ruth continued. "You know how all that works?"

Tina raised her right hand.

"What's that mean? That you heard me, or that you have a question?"

That half smile again.

"You want to know what I thought when I was your age?"

Again she raised her right hand.

"I thought you could get pregnant if a boy touched your breast." Which was true. She *had* thought that, though she'd been much younger than Tina. "Then one did."

She turned into the alley between the restaurant and the Rexall drugstore. Her daughter's car was parked behind the Dumpster. There was no sign of Sully's truck, nor had it been parked in the street. She thought again about the blue flame.

"Did you?" said her granddaughter.

"Did I what?"

"Get pregnant?" There was definitely a smile now.

"Are you having fun? Messing with Grandma?"

The girl nodded, her smile broadening. "Was Grandpa the boy?"

Ruth turned off the ignition. "I hadn't even met your grandfather yet."

"Then who was it?"

"Just a boy. Nobody you know. He died."

"When?"

"In the war."

"Which one?"

"The one he was fighting in."

"Are you mad at me?"

"No, I'm mad at the war."

"Why'd you let him?"

"Go to war?"

"No, touch you."

"I didn't let him. He just did."

"Did you let other boys?"

"Why are we talking about me?"

"I'm trying to learn."

"Yeah, right," Ruth said, putting the keys in her purse, then adding, "It felt good, I guess." The admission caused her to flush, though she couldn't decide which version of herself she was more ashamed of, the girl she'd been when she first started letting boys feel her up or the one attempting to dissuade her granddaughter from sexual activity. "It made me feel like I mattered. There was nobody else around to tell me I was special, so when boys said I was, I believed them."

The smile was gone from Tina's face now. "So I shouldn't believe what boys say?"

"Oh, hell, Two-Shoes, I don't know. They believe it themselves when they say it, or some of them do. What's important is how you feel about yourself."

"And how do *you* feel about yourself?"

"Now?"

The girl shrugged.

"Old," Ruth admitted. "Stupid. Confused."

Tina just looked at her.

"I know what you're thinking," Ruth said. "If I'm so stupid and confused, why am I giving you advice?"

"That's not what I was thinking."

Ruth leaned across the front seat and took her granddaughter in her arms, holding her tight. "I just don't want you to get hurt," she said, her tears spilling over.

"Mom says you don't love Grandpa."

"She does, huh?"

"She thinks you love Sully."

"She told you that?"

She shook her head. "She *thinks* it."

"And you're a mind reader."

The girl nodded seriously.

"Okay, what am I thinking now?"

"We're late."

"Good guess," Ruth said, because that's what she *had* been thinking. Day was upon them.

When she wiped her eyes on her shirtsleeve and took a deep breath before getting out of the car, Tina said, "You're the hurt one, Grandma, not me."

———

THEY WENT IN through the back, Ruth propping the heavy door open to help air the place out. Deliverymen would start arriving soon. In the back room, with the dishwasher and the small walk-in cooler, she noted that Cleary had been in and mopped the floors. He was a drinker and not to be depended upon, especially after Friday nights. Sometimes on Saturday mornings she'd find him stretched out on the long stainless-steel drainboard, but last night he'd mopped up and even emptied the trash. "I could use a hand unless you have homework to do," Ruth said.

"It's the weekend."

"Did you finish that book you were supposed to read? *Animal House*?"

"*Animal Farm,*" she said. "*Animal House* is a movie."

"Did you finish it, is what I asked."

The girl just looked at her. She'd answered the question already, was *her* point.

"You could start by unloading the Hobart," Ruth told her. Last thing out the door, she always ran a load. If they were busy this morning, she'd need every available mug.

Out front, she put the coffee on and filled the grill with bacon and sausage links in orderly phalanxes. It was her practice to cook them halfway, then return them to the grill as individual orders came in. If Sully were here, he'd have grabbed a hunk of yesterday's stale bread and used it to soak up the sputtering grease. Though he claimed to have no interest in cooking, Ruth had never seen a man more comfortable in a kitchen. He seemed to intuit its rhythms, to know when she'd need to sidle by him in the confined space between the grill and counter, whereas her husband, both at home and in the restaurant, always managed to be standing in front of whatever door—fridge, oven, pantry—she needed to open. His size was part of it, of course, but he was simply incapable of anticipating what came next, even when the operative sequence was entirely predictable and unfolding right before his eyes. While Sully, even when he had his back to her, was able to sense where she was and why, and he'd take a small step forward or back that allowed her to get where she wanted to go. He had similar instincts in bed, which had been nice. If only, she often thought, he was as emotionally prescient. But of course men had to be told things, repeatedly. And even then . . .

When Tina, hands wet from the dishwasher, came out with a double tray of water glasses and coffee mugs, she momentarily lost her grip and managed to bang them all against the counter, rattling everything. "Easy," Ruth snapped. She had an order in to her Albany restaurant-supply house, but until it was delivered, she was short on glasses and couldn't afford to break any.

"Sorry," the girl said, aggrieved.

"You will be if you wake your mother up." She knew Janey had taken a shift out at the Horse last night and would've laid dollars to donuts that she'd gone out drinking afterward, knowing that Tina was spending the night with her and Zack. She watched her grand-daughter stack cups and glasses on the shelf and wondered whether, a few years down the road, she'd have a child of her own, one Grandma Janey would find herself watching. This possibility was so depressing that she turned her attention back to the splattering grill, flipping the bacon and sausage links with her long spatula. In her peripheral vision she noticed Tina, returning to the back room with her empty trays, stop in her tracks. "Grandma?"

"What?"

When she didn't answer, Ruth looked up and saw that the door leading to her daughter's apartment was open. In it stood Roy Purdy, bare-foot and shirtless, his jeans slung so low that a few wisps of curly pubic hair were visible above the beltline. His pale chest sported the tattoo of a sword, the tip of which disappeared comically beneath his foam neck brace. His face was still grotesquely swollen, and his eyes were dilated. How long had he been standing there watching them?

"Not much of a welcome," he said, apparently to his daughter, though his eyes remained on Ruth. "Aren't you going to give your poor old dad a hug?"

Ruth stepped in front of her granddaughter. Still holding the long spatula, she was tempted to use this lethal instrument to extend his inso-lent smirk from ear to ear. "What're you doing here, Roy?"

"Well, Ma, I guess you could say I'm here by invitation."

And then she was in motion. "Out of my way," she said, pushing past him into the apartment, where in the murky bedroom Janey lay splayed on top of the sheets, naked. *Dead,* was Ruth's first impression, and for a moment Janey was her little girl again, toddling around on fat little legs, arms outstretched and crying *Up! Up!* He's finally killed her, she thought. But then she smelled the sex in the airless room and saw that her daughter was not only breathing but gently snoring. There was an empty bottle of Southern Comfort, Roy's revolting liquor of choice, on the nightstand. Turning on the harsh overhead light, Ruth kicked the mattress, hard.

"What?" Janey said, bolting upright and squinting at her. "Fuck."

"What's he doing here?" Ruth said, pointing the glistening spatula at Roy, who'd drawn himself a glass of water out front before following her back into the apartment.

Janey looked at him and groaned, then turned to Ruth. "Don't start, Ma," she said, sliding under the top sheet and pulling it up to her chest. "I'm warning you, okay? Just don't."

"Too late. I've already started."

Roy thumbed the cap off his prescription pill bottle expertly and shook a capsule into his palm, then washed it down with the entire glass of water, his Adam's apple bobbing dutifully.

"He needed a place to stay, all right?"

"They're not letting nobody back into the Arms till they find that damn snake," Roy said, looking around aimlessly for a place to set down the glass.

"I'm not talking to you, Roy," Ruth told him. "I'm talking to my dimwit daughter."

"Right," Janey said. "I'm stupid. *You're* smart; *I'm* stupid."

"What would you call it? You take out a restraining order against this man, then invite him into your bedroom?"

"That's right, Ma. I did," Janey said, the bit in her teeth now. "And you know what? I fucked him, too."

"She sure did," Roy corroborated. "Like old times, right, babe?"

Ruth turned on him. "Which ones, Roy? When you punched her in the face? Banged her head into the wall and gave her a concussion? Those the old times you're talking about?"

He ignored all of this, staring at Janey. "So tell her."

She was sitting there, massaging her temples, her breasts exposed again, the sheet having fallen. "Tell her what, Roy?"

"You know. How we're gonna be getting back together. Be a family again, like before, only better."

Janey regarded him with undisguised disbelief. "Don't be a complete moron, Roy. Of course we're not getting back together."

"Singin' a different tune last night, girl. You forget already?"

"It was a good fuck, Roy. That's all I said. I was horny, okay?"

"Well, there you go. More where that came from."

Janey stared at him for a long, incredulous beat, then addressed her mother. "Okay, fine. It was stupid letting him in, but you know how scared I get when there's lightning."

"Lightning," Ruth repeated. "The man beats the shit out of you—"

"All that's in the past," Roy said, scratching himself below the belt-line of his jeans, then inspecting his fingernails.

"Did you notice," Ruth said to Janey, "how he balled up his fist when you contradicted him just now? Did you? You think he's through whaling on you just because he *says* he is? Last time you were in the hospital for three days. And it's *lightning* that scares you?"

"A person can't help what they're scared of," Janey said, but clearly at least some of what Ruth had said was getting through. Either she'd seen Roy clench his fist or trusted that her mother had. "And he didn't beat me up. You can see that, right?"

"That doesn't mean he's not going to."

"All that's in the past," Roy said, his new mantra, though the hand not holding the water glass was a fist again. "And that's for true."

"It was just the once," Janey said, apparently referring to the sex, not the previous beatings. "He knows that."

"That's where you're wrong, girl. I don't know no such thing."

"Well, then you *are* a fucking moron, Roy."

"What's that you just called me?" he said.

"Get out of here, Roy," Ruth said, "before we call the cops."

"Who's gonna do that?" Roy wanted to know. "You? Or her?"

It was then that Ruth remembered her granddaughter out in the restaurant, hearing all this, no doubt, probably cowering in a neutral corner like she used to do when she was little and these same two people started screaming at each other until the hitting started. "You need to go, Roy. Before this gets worse."

"Whose fault would that be? You're the one give her that mouth."

Seeing her come toward him, Roy made no move to let her pass. "Step aside, Roy," she told him.

And just that quickly she was on the floor, blinking up at him, tasting salt. Janey screamed.

"There now," Roy said, pleased, as if he'd just won an argument.

Try as she might, Ruth was having trouble drawing the various elements of her unfolding experience into a coherent whole. Roy was standing directly over her, his right hand bloody. He'd struck her, she realized, with the empty glass. There was a large bloody shard in her lap.

"So whose fault is this right here, huh, Ma?" Roy was asking, his voice sounding far off. "Tell me that."

"Momma!" Janey was screaming from even farther away. "Don't, Roy!"

Ruth had managed to get onto her knees when Roy hit her again, this time with his fist. The back of her head hit the wall, causing very little pain but a frightening explosion of sound.

Before she could bring things into focus, Roy was on his knees himself, straddling her, and when he drew back his fist, she closed her eyes and thought, Fine. He was punching her, not Janey. If he beat her to death, well even that was okay. He'd finally be put away for good, and Janey and Tina would at last be shut of him. Perhaps because the roaring in her head sounded like surf, she thought again about that gleaming white bathroom in the Aruba brochure, how pristine and perfect it was. Maybe heaven was like that. A clean place, with pure sunshine streaming down from an unseen skylight, the cleansing surf so near you could hear individual waves breaking.

When Roy's next punch didn't arrive and she could no longer feel him astride her, she was suddenly frightened. Had he turned his attention to Janey, or maybe even to Tina? But no. When she opened her eyes, Roy was sitting across from her, his back up against the foot of the bed, looking as dazed and confused as she felt. There was a bright bloom of blood on one ear. Where he'd been standing a minute earlier Sully had magically appeared, holding a skillet. Ruth began to cry, she was so happy. Not because Roy wasn't going to be punching her anymore or that Janey had been delivered as well, but because Sully was alive. Whatever that blue flame on the roof of the shed had been about, it wasn't him. She'd been mean to him yesterday, telling him to quit coming by the restaurant so much, to find someplace else, but he'd come anyway. Nor was this the ghost who'd been haunting her lunch counter lately, a geezer staring morosely into his empty coffee cup, his shallow breath an audible rasp. A dying man, it now occurred to her. The man who stood before her here was the Sully of old, fearless, game as hell, fully committed in this necessary moment to the murder of Roy Purdy, fuck the consequences.

But then he remembered her and their eyes met and he dropped the skillet, no longer interested in Roy. She must've drifted away for a moment, because when she returned he was kneeling next to her. When she tried to say his name, he said, "Shhh," then took her face between his hands, holding her head still, so there was no place to look but at this man she'd taken up with so long ago because she was lonely, lonelier than she'd known a human being could be. She had understood how wrong it was, how doing what they were doing might open the door to some bad things down the road. Had they just now got there? She would've liked to ask Sully if he thought that the present scenario could be traced back to what they'd done those many years, because, if so, then Roy was right—it *was* all her fault. But her mouth refused to work, and whenever she tried to speak Sully kept shushing her. It was all over, he was saying, she was safe now and so were Janey and Tina, that there was nothing to worry about, she was going to be okay and at the hospital they'd fix her up as good as new. She was glad to hear all of this because in truth everything felt very wrong, the kind of wrong you couldn't ever make right. But then again, what did she know? What the hell had she ever known, really, about anything, even as a girl, when that first boy had touched her breast and she'd let him, because it felt good and *she* felt good, when most of the time she didn't. It had taken her years and years to understand that most other people didn't feel good, either, that the world's work was to make you feel like it was disappointed in you, that you'd never measure up, not really. But Sully said no, it was all going to be fine, and somewhere in the distance there was a siren that was getting closer, so Ruth closed her eyes and stopped trying to speak and allowed herself to believe every word that Sully was saying.

Secrets

M R. HYNES WAS ALREADY at the curb in his folding chair, waving his tiny American flag at passing cars, when Raymer, freshly showered, emerged from the Morrison Arms. As he ducked under his own crime-scene tape, it occurred to him that he, the white chief of police, and Mr. Hynes, an improbably patriotic old black man, were the only two residents who had scoffed at the law. Of course the other tenants, an eclectic assortment of derelicts and petty thieves and deadbeats, were taking advantage of the relatively luxurious accommodations offered by the Holiday Inn at the town's expense, but still.

Seeing Raymer approach, Mr. Hynes started to rise, but Raymer motioned for him to remain seated. "How many varieties you got today, Mr. Hynes?"

He grinned broadly, enjoying their long-running joke. "Fifty-seven. Same as always."

"Well, that's sure a lot of varieties to come up with day after day. How do you manage it?"

"Hard work. Just have to keep after it when other people quit."

Quit, Raymer thought. That was today's first order of business: write his resignation letter, give his two weeks' notice. Without the garage remote, his chances of discovering the identity of Becka's boyfriend were now officially nil. If that asshole Dougie didn't like it, too bad. After the Hilldale fiasco, he was all done listening to Dougie, who had proven unreliable. But since he probably didn't exist in the first place, this was like saying that Raymer himself was unreliable, which wasn't exactly news.

"How'd you make out with that pretty black gal I seen you with last night?" the old man wanted to know.

"She works for me, Mr. Hynes. We didn't *make out* at all."

"Send her on over here, then. You don't want her, I'll take her. She could be my fifty-eighth variety, you know what I mean."

"I'll mention you're available."

"I like the look of her. Not all skin and bones like some of 'em. I thought it was her you was talkin' to earlier."

Raymer had no idea what this was in reference to. "Talking to when?"

"Hour ago, when you come in. I hear you goin' on about this and that, so I go over to the window thinkin' it might be her you was talking to, but instead it's just you arguin' with your own self."

"I think you're exaggerating, Mr. Hynes. I might have been mumbling, is all."

"You need to get you a real person to talk to, is what I'm sayin'. How'd you get all filthy like that?"

"Grave robbing."

"Awright, don't tell me. See if I care. I got secrets, too. Everybody got secrets."

"Anyway," Raymer said, "I'm glad to see that snake didn't get you."

"Not yet," he cackled. "I'm too quick for it. Time it stands up, I'm gone. You 'member Satchel? I'm quick like him."

"Do me a favor," Raymer said, resting a hand on the man's bony shoulder, "and don't sit out in the sun too long today. It's nice now, but it's supposed to get hot again."

Mr. Hynes promised he wouldn't. As he was getting into the Jetta, his radio barked, followed by Charice's voice: "Chief?"

He glanced at his watch. Her shift didn't begin for another hour. This didn't bode well. "I'm sorry, Charice," he told her. "But I don't want to talk about last night, okay? Can you respect my wishes on this? If I offended you—"

"You seen the paper?"

"Which?"

"The *Dumbocrat*."

"No, why?"

"You made the front page."

So someone had seen them out at Hilldale. This boded even worse. "Charice," he said. "We put him back just like he was."

"What? Who're you talking about?"

"What're *you* talking about?"

"The photo of you climbing down off my porch. On the front page of the damn newspaper. The man that lives in the flat below me? He's a photographer. Works for the *Dumbocrat*. Must've run to the printer with that photo in time to make the morning edition."

"Oh," he said, remembering the bright flash of light that had momentarily blinded him as he was shinnying down the column. He'd thought it was just a distant lightning flash, reflecting off the low clouds. "Shit."

"Right. I'm about to lose my job, aren't I."

"Of course you aren't. Listen, I'm heading in now. Be there in five."

"The mayor wants to see you."

"Lovely."

"You'd better come up with a good story."

"I'll tell him I got struck by lightning."

"Too far-fetched."

"It's true. I *was* struck by lightning." Okay, not on her porch, but he might've been if he hadn't climbed down. "Now there's something wrong with me." Seared into the palm of his hand, where he'd grabbed the florist's card, was the perfect image of the staple used to attach it to the green cellophane. He'd tried his best to scrub it off in the shower but managed only to inflame the spot. Now it itched as if there were, just below the skin, a real staple. "Something *else* wrong with me," he corrected.

"Like what?"

"I feel . . . funny."

"Funny odd or funny ha-ha?"

"There's this constant buzzing in my ears. And I'm having strange thoughts."

"For instance."

Like, maybe I'm in love with you? He couldn't say that, of course. He tried to think of another example, something odd but not so deeply bizarre that she'd conclude he'd lost his marbles completely.

Before he could come up with anything, she asked, "Is someone with you? Your voice sounded weird just then. I mean, apart from what you said."

Wait, *had* he spoken out loud? Actually told Charice he was in love with her? Just a few minutes earlier Mr. Hynes accused him of talking to himself. Could it be true? "Umm . . . that's the other thing," he admitted. "These random thoughts that are just there in my head? Apparently I say some of them out loud."

"I'ma add that to my list," she said. "All this weird shit. In fact, I'm doin' it right now 'fore I forget. *Chief says . . . he's in* love *with me.*"

"You left out the word 'maybe.'"

"You write it down *your* way, I—"

"You're doing it again, Charice," he said.

"Doing what?"

"Using that black voice."

"I'ma write that down, too."

"Last night you—"

"You were different last night, too," she said, all trace of the dialect now gone.

Suddenly their evening together, which had begun so well and ended so catastrophically, was with him again. He'd promised himself to put it out of his mind, but here he was thinking about it anyway, awash in humiliation. "Can I ask?" he said. "What happened?"

"I thought you didn't want to talk about it."

"Charice."

"That phone call I got? Was from Jerome. Asking me to take him to the hospital. He thought he was having a heart attack."

"Is he okay?"

"They kept him overnight for observation. A panic attack, they think. He's had them before."

A car went by, tooting its horn at Mr. Hynes. When Raymer looked up, a man was just coming out the back door of Gert's Tavern with

a bag of trash in each hand. A car was parked next to the Dumpster
where the Mustang was vandalized yesterday. From where Raymer sat,
only one taillight and a section of fender was visible, not enough to identify the make or model. From where Mr. Hynes was sitting, though, the
whole car would be in view, and it came to Raymer again that he might
well have seen whoever keyed the 'Stang.

"Charice?" he said, returning to the matter at hand. "I thought you
were mad at me about the lamb chops."

"Say again?"

"I ate all your lamb chops. I was a pig."

"Of course you ate my lamb chops. You were invited for dinner.
Jerome would've ate 'em all. I'd've been lucky to get one."

"I guzzled your expensive wine and fell asleep."

"Shows what you know, if you think that swill was expensive."

"So you're not really mad at me?"

"Of course I'm not."

"Then why'd you lock me out on the porch?"

"Lock you out?"

"The door was locked."

"No, it just sticks when it's humid. You have to lift up at the same
time you push or pull."

Now that she mentioned it, he remembered that when she first let
them out onto the porch, she'd not only lifted the handle but kicked the
bottom of the door.

"I left you a note," she said.

"You did?"

"Put on the table right in front of you. Said I didn't know how long
I'd be, but to wait if you wanted to."

"It must've blown away," he said, recalling how still it had been when
he dozed off, how the breeze had come up by the time he awoke. "The
kitchen was all dark."

"The bugs were swarming. Like a hundred of them on the screen."

"God, I'm such an idiot. Go ahead and write that down, too, if you
want."

"Already did."

He knew she hadn't, though. Was she writing any of it down? Or was this list of hers just a running gag, like the Heinz one he shared with Mr. Hynes?

"Charice?" he said. "Do you believe in ghosts?"

"What? I'm black, so I have to be superstitious?"

"Charice."

"No."

"No to which?"

"No, I don't believe in ghosts."

"Because Becka visited me last night. Twice."

"Your dead wife visited you."

"Out on your porch, the first time. She came to me in a dream."

"How does you dreaming about Becka make her a ghost?"

"Later, in the cemetery, she tried to kill me." He'd been wondering what a statement like this would sound like out in the open air. Now he knew. Batshit.

"What do you mean, 'later, in the cemetery'? What were you doing out there?"

"I went to apologize."

"To a dead woman. In the middle of the night."

"You make it sound kind of crazy."

"Where you were struck by lightning. Even if you were, how's that Becka?"

He sighed. "I really have lost my mind, haven't I."

A quick negative response would've been welcome, but none was forthcoming. Finally she said, "You had a bad day."

"Today's going to be another. Should I go visit Jerome?"

"No," she said quickly. "Absolutely not."

"He still thinks I keyed his car?"

"Probably. When he gets like this . . ." In the silence that followed, he could hear her concern.

Nor did he blame her. He'd never seen anyone come quite so unglued as Jerome had. He remembered the relief he felt turning away from him and heading back to the Morrison Arms, even if it meant coming face-to-face with a cobra. Raymer replayed the short journey again, stepped off the curb and heard screeching brakes, the animal-control vehicle rocking mere inches from his left knee, again saw the people milling around in the parking lot. Roy Purdy had been among them, he recalled. It wasn't just the neck brace that had made him stand out, or even that he'd been working so hard to blend in. It was that, for a brief moment, everyone else in the crowd was facing the Arms. Roy was looking at Gert's, then spun away when he saw Raymer.

All at once the buzzing in his ears was gone. *Got him,* said Dougie.

"Got who?" Charice said.

Raymer ignored her. "Is there something you're not telling me, Charice?"

She hesitated before answering. "Like what?"

"Does the mayor want Jerome to run against me for chief of police, because—"

"No, it's nothing like that."

"What's it like?"

"Thing is, I'm not supposed to know. Nobody's supposed to."

"But you do."

"No secrets between me and Jerome. I wish there were."

"How about you and me, Charice? Are there secrets between us?"

"Okay, but you didn't hear this from me. The muckety-mucks in Schuyler and Bath are talking about consolidating services. Police. Fire. Garbage collection."

"Bath doesn't have garbage collection."

"It will. The idea is to get rid of redundancies. One administration. A single chain of command."

"Firing people."

"Trimming expenses."

"Firing people."

"Becoming more lean and efficient."

"Firing people. So how does Jerome fit in?"

"He'd oversee the transition. That was his master's thesis."

Raymer, who didn't usually leap to cynical conclusions, did so now. "Perfect fall guy, when it doesn't pan out. No wonder he's having panic attacks. When people find out who's behind all this efficiency, somebody's going to—"

"Shoot him," Charice finished the sentence for him. "Right. That possibility has also occurred to him. He's actually thinking about moving back to North Carolina."

"Would you go, too?" he said, suppressing the urge to beg her not to.

"Come out from behind this desk, you mean? Go someplace else where I could maybe do some real police work?"

It made Raymer's head swim, all of it. "Will Bath even *have* a chief of police?"

"Unclear."

"And Gus supports this?"

"His idea, is my impression. Remember his campaign slogan? *Let's be Schuyler Springs?*"

"Fuck him," Raymer barked, surprised at how strong his feelings were about this.

The long moment of silence this occasioned made him wonder if maybe Gus was actually standing there next to Charice's desk. Had he been listening to the whole conversation? Maybe he and Charice had made some sort of pact to keep tabs on him.

"Chief?" she said.

"Yeah?" he said, clearing his throat.

"Was that you? Who just said 'Fuck him'?"

"I don't know," he admitted.

"YOU AGAIN," the man said, when Raymer reappeared. "I thought you was gone."

"You know Roy Purdy, Mr. Hynes? Moved into the Arms a couple weeks ago?"

"What he look like?"

"Skinny. Tattoos," Raymer said. "His neck's in a brace."

"Live with that nice Cora woman?"

"I wondered, did you see him over at Gert's yesterday?"

"People here all hangin' out at Gert's. I don't pay 'em no mind."

"I meant out back. In the parking lot. You've got a good view of that from here."

"So?"

"Remember the tall black man I was with yesterday?"

"One with that shiny red car? Somebody ruint his paint job, I heard."

"Did you see who did that, Mr. Hynes?"

"My eyes don't do too good from a distance."

"How about closer up, though. You were sitting right about where you are now. You didn't by any chance see Roy Purdy come walking out of that alley, did you?"

"Would I be getting the boy in trouble if I said so?"

Raymer thought about lying but decided not to. "It's possible," he said.

"Good," said Mr. Hynes. "'Cause I 'spect he the one peein' in the stairwell."

That sounded about right to Raymer as well.

"I got it narrowed down," the old man said. "It either him or you."

A LUNATIC. That's what he looked like in the grainy newspaper photo. Taken from the kitchen window below Charice's, it caught Raymer at the moment the column detached from the porch above, his surprise at this unexpected turn of events having registered at just that instant. He'd been shinnying down, of course, but judging from the photo, he might as easily have been climbing up, a home-invading burglar. His bruised, swollen face looked like some sort of visual prediction of the damage done by a fall that hadn't yet occurred. The caption read: *What's up, Chief?*

Studying himself, a middle-aged man clinging for dear life to a load-bearing post, he again recalled the question Miss Beryl had pestered him with on his essays all those years ago: *Who is this Douglas Raymer?* Who, indeed? Three-plus decades later he still had no answer for her. Worse, he had just forty-eight hours to come up with one. At the moment all three sides of the old woman's beloved rhetorical triangle remained blank. He couldn't think of a single thing to say about his former teacher, couldn't bring his audience into sharp focus. How many of these people would even remember her? Would those few who did think of her fondly? If so, would they hold his many personal and professional failures against her? After all, if she was such a great teacher, how had she managed to turn out a man who campaigned for chief of police on the slogan *We're not happy until you're not happy?*

Tossing the newspaper into the wastebasket, he looked up and saw the cobra, hooded and erect, atop a nearby filing cabinet. He stared at it transfixed, then hit the intercom. "Charice?" he said.

She came on the speaker immediately. "Chief? I didn't see you come in."

"I snuck in the back. Could you come in here a minute?"

When the door opened two seconds later, he pointed at the cobra. "How'd that get in here?"

"Huh," she said, going over to it.

"Try harder," he suggested.

"It looks *very* real."

"That was my thought. My heart's still pounding."

She took the statue down and examined it. "Ceramic?"

"If you say so. This office was locked yesterday when I left."

"Hold on," she said, narrowing her eyes at him. "Are you saying *I* put it there?"

"I'm asking who else has a key."

"Chief. Cops work here. And know how to unlock doors without keys."

"I don't," he pointed out, for the record.

"I'm not talking about *you*," she said, leading Raymer to question was this a compliment or an insult. "Also, lots of criminals are in and out of this station. Might've been one of them."

"I was wondering about Jerome. If maybe this was his idea of a joke."

"Jerome has an alibi. He was at the hospital all night. Sedated. Besides, like I told you. Jerome's scared to death of snakes. Even ceramic ones."

"Maybe he had an accomplice."

"So I *am* a suspect?"

"I'd like to rule you out."

"I got an alibi, too. Last night? I was with the chief of police himself."

"Not all night."

"Damn straight," she agreed.

"And you got here before me this morning."

"Chief?"

"Yes, Charice."

"I don't know where the fucking snake came from."

"Would you write my Beryl Peoples tribute for me? For the middle-school rededication? Because if you'd do that, in return I'd be willing to believe you had nothing to do with this."

"Not a chance. Never even met the lady."

They regarded each other with what seemed to Raymer like a bottomless well of mutual disappointment, until she finally said, "Put *who* back where he was?"

"Sorry?"

"When I told you that you were on the front page of the *Dumbocrat*, you said you'd put *him* back where *he* was."

"I did?"

"Somebody called the station early this morning. *And* the mayor, too. Reporting that Judge Flatt was being disinterred."

"Really?"

"Means 'dug up.'"

"I know what it means, Charice."

"And you *did* admit to being out there at Hilldale getting zapped by lightning."

"Charice?"

"Yeah?"

"You'd make a good cop."

"What I been saying."

"What else was in the log?"

She went out and came back in with it. "You want everything?"

"Just the meaty parts."

"All in all, a wild night. The mayor's wife went AWOL again. We found her, though."

"Where this time?"

"Longmeadow Estates."

"Really?"

"Yeah, why?"

"That's where Becka and I used to live." He remembered coming out of the condo in the morning and seeing her loitering across the street, anxious for him to leave for work so she and Becka could have coffee. He'd told her many times that she didn't have to wait outside, to just ring the bell whenever, but the next morning she'd be there again, patiently awaiting access to her best friend. Possibly her only friend. For some reason Becka had refused to accept the conventional wisdom that Alice Moynihan was increasingly untethered from reality, preferring to believe that she was just odd, overly sensitive, like a psychic, to things other people never even noticed. Was it possible that Becka had paid *her* a visit last night as well? Why else would she return to Longmeadow Estates after so long? "What was she doing out there?"

"Talking on her phone."

"Bless her heart. Okay, what else?"

"Mrs. Gaghan called again. Said her son went out drinking at the White Horse last night and never came home."

"That would be Spinmatics Joe?"

"One and the same."

"What'd you tell her?"

"Not what I wanted to. Also, there was an A and B over at Hattie's an hour ago. Guess who?"

Dougie knew immediately, and a second later so did Raymer. "Roy Purdy."

"Except this time it wasn't the ex-wife he beat up. It was her mother."

"Ruth, right?"

"Messed her up pretty bad."

"Is he in custody?"

She shook her head. "Slipped out in the confusion when the ambulance got there. Apparently he got injured in the scuffle himself."

"With an officer?"

"No, your old friend Sully showed up in the nick of time. Brained him with a skillet."

"Good," Raymer said, surprised for perhaps the first time in his life to think of his old nemesis with straightforward affection. Something was nagging at him, though, having to do with their adventure out at Hilldale that hadn't seemed right. Not important right now, of course. "I'm pretty sure it was Purdy who keyed Jerome's car, by the way. I saw him in the vicinity. When we pick him up, have the arresting officer check his keys for red paint in the grooves."

"He can't have got far. He doesn't have a vehicle after yesterday."

"Yeah, but there's a woman at the Arms he's tight with. Cora something. Make sure she didn't loan him her car. Put out an APB on it if she did. Where are we with animal control?"

"Justin just called. He's going through the place again this morning with four or five other AC guys. They figure the snake's long gone, though."

"Have they removed the other reptiles? And the rodents?"

She nodded. "Good luck renting that unit."

"No sign of our William Smith?"

"According to Miller, a white cargo van drove by after midnight, going real slow. The driver must've seen the crime tape, because then he hauled ass."

"Miller didn't pursue?"

"He said you'd ordered him to surveil the building. His word, 'surveil.'"

"Did you know he's got a crush on you?" Raymer said, immediately feeling guilty about betraying the dope's confidence. "He's working up the courage to ask you out."

"Miller." Clearly, she was mortified.

"Go easy on him," Raymer suggested, though secretly buoyed by her reaction. "Anyway, when they're sure there's no snake, you can start letting people back in. Is the mayor in his office?"

"No, at home."

"Do we have any departmental stationery?"

She looked at him like he was crazy. "Of course."

"Bring me a sheet. And an envelope," he called after her when she went to fetch it. She returned with the envelope and two large sheets. She obviously had no idea how short this letter was going to be. "What's today's date?" he asked. When she told him, he thanked her and said that would be all for the moment. He printed the date at the top right of the page and started at the left margin with *Dear Gus*. Which was wrong, of course, so he wadded the page up and trashed it. Once more, Charice had been right. She'd probably considered bringing him three sheets. Again he wrote the date and then a new salutation, *Dear Mayor Moynihan*. Next, the body: *I quit*. And finally: *Sincerely, Douglas Raymer*. He folded the page into thirds, paused, then unfolded it and added *Chief of Police* after his name, smiling as he did so at the thought of Miss Beryl. He had produced possibly the world's smallest rhetorical triangle, but it pleased him to note that all three sides were represented: a clear subject, a specific audience, the identity of the speaker established not once but twice. Nothing to do now but deliver it.

When he stood up, though, he saw that Charice hadn't left the room but had circled around and was reading over his shoulder. Unless he was mistaken, her eyes were tearing up.

INSTEAD OF GOING directly to the Moynihans' house on Upper Main, Raymer took the department SUV and drove on impulse out to the White Horse Tavern. Except for the battered old sedan that belonged to the woman who tended bar and lived in the apartment on the second floor, the lot was empty. He parked next to the reeking Dumpster and walked the perimeter, looking for what, exactly, he couldn't say. Maybe some indication of an altercation. Spinmatics Joe was a bigot and an idiot and a loudmouth, so it was possible that when leaving the bar he'd insulted someone who'd stomped him unconscious and dragged him into the tall weeds. No sign of that, nor did he seem to be in the Dumpster, though Raymer's examination there was on the cursory side, his stomach heaving at the stench.

Oh, well, he figured, getting back in the car, it had been a thought. Dougie's? His own? Hard to say. He just sat there for a minute scratching his palm, which was still itching ferociously. It felt good to scratch the staple, but as soon as he stopped, the itch redoubled. Heading back into town, he hadn't gone more than a quarter mile before he saw the dark, violent skid marks that ran onto the gravel shoulder. Pulling over, he backtracked along the blacktop until he found a shard of thick, foggy glass on the shoulder that he held up for a better view. From a reflector, was his guess. He used the jagged edge on the staple: ecstasy, followed by even worse itching. In the weeds nearby he found several more shards, one of them crusted with something rust colored. He sniffed it, then returned to the SUV for an evidence bag that he slipped this into. There was a Bic pen on the dash, so he took its top off and used the long, plastic tooth to dig at the staple. From where he stood he could make out what he hadn't noticed before, the section of tall weeds that had been flattened and a trail leading off into the woods.

He was contemplating all this when a car with a bad muffler pulled up behind his own, then Officer Miller got out. "Chief?" he called, as if Raymer's identity were in doubt. "What're you doing?"

"I was about to ask you the same thing."

"Heading home. I just finished up my double," he added, in case his boss meant to question his right to go off duty.

"Feel like a walk in the woods?"

"Uh, Chief?" he said, pointing at Raymer's hand. "You're bleeding."

Well, this much was true, a stigmata blooming where he'd gouged the skin with the cap of that Bic. "Shit," he said, wiping his palm on his pant leg. Examining the wound more closely, he was surprised by how deep and angry it was, while Miller chuckled nastily.

"What's so funny?" he snapped, pissed off that it struck the other man as amusing.

"Sorry?" Miller said, and Raymer understood from the startled look on his moronic face that he hadn't laughed at all. The chuckle had come from somewhere else. No need to wonder where. "You okay, Chief?"

Raymer ignored him. "I think we're going to need an ambulance," he said.

"It doesn't look *that* bad," Miller said, still mesmerized by the bloody palm, or perhaps that anybody could unwittingly damage himself so badly.

"Not for this," Raymer assured him.

Miller looked around curiously. "For what, then?"

"For what we're going to find in the woods."

"You're not making sense, Chief."

"You see where those weeds are all flat?" Raymer said. "Don't walk there. In fact, after you radio for the ambulance, just stay on my footsteps."

He didn't have to go far. Joe Gaghan lay on a bed of brown pine needles, amazingly still alive, his respiration just strong enough to blow a tiny blood bubble from the nostril that wasn't completely plugged. Raymer knelt beside him and checked his pulse, which was barely there. A moment later Miller came crashing through the brush.

"Oh my God," he said, pulling up short. "That's a body."

Raymer made a mental note to take Miller with him everywhere. When it came to inspiring confidence in others, he was really without equal. "Did you call the ambulance?"

"On its way," he said.

In fact he could hear it, far off. "Good," he said. "Somehow the guy's still alive."

Miller took a cautious step closer and took in the sickening, grotesque angle of Gaghan's left leg, bent so unnaturally at the knee. "I can't believe he made it so far on that leg," he said.

"He didn't," Raymer confirmed. "He was dragged down here by whoever hit him."

"You mean—"

"Right. He was left to die here."

"Who'd do such an awful thing?" Miller said.

Really, Raymer thought, his palm throbbing now, the pain as intense as the itch had been. Take him with you everywhere.

The Tree You Can't Predict

STAGGERING UP the street like a drunk, his head still ringing from the skillet, Roy wasn't expecting to catch a break, not with *his* fucking luck, but he'd gone only a couple blocks when he heard a horn toot—with just one ear still functioning, it sounded far away—and there was fucking Cora behind the wheel of her shit-bucket of a car, waving him over. In another minute or two there'd be cops everywhere, all looking for a skinny, tattooed longhair in a neck brace, a description that would fit Roy and Roy alone.

Cora had inherited this ride—an ancient Ford Pinto—when her grandmother croaked, and this pissed off her mother, who'd been expecting to inherit the worthless piece of shit herself. Yellow on one side, purple on the other, it was impossible to know what was original and what had been cannibalized from even-worse beaters at the junkyard. Wearing her Mets cap as usual, Cora leaned across to unlock the passenger door and called, "Hey there, Roy. You partying already?" Only when he tumbled inside did she get a good look at him, his ear half severed, one whole side of his face red and swollen. "Roy," she gasped. "You're hurt!"

"Goddamn it, Cora, tell me something I don't already know," Roy said, jerking the rearview mirror around to assess the damage. That fucking Sully. Fucking, fucking, motherfucking Sully. "Son of a bitch damn near took my whole ear off, the cocksucker."

"Who? Who done this to you, Roy?"

"Fuck it," he told her, "just go." From experience both deep and broad, Roy knew how quickly things headed south in the aftermath of one of his legendary bad impulses. It was a miracle, really, that he wasn't already cuffed and secured in the backseat of some cruiser. Even with the help of this dim-witted bitch, he'd end up in one before long.

"You want me to run you out to the hospital?"

"Fuck no," he said. The cops would be all over the hospitals, both here and in Schuyler.

"You need somebody to sew that ear back on. It's just dangling there."

He swiveled the mirror back in her direction. "I noticed that, Cora." In fact, the sight had made him a little sick to his stomach. Worse, his equilibrium was clearly fucked, even sitting down. And his own voice sounded as tinny and far away as this idiot's, which made him wonder if the skillet ear was permanently fucked. How had such a gimpy old fuck managed to sneak up on him like that anyhow? Well, to ask the question was to answer it. His blood had been up. Not just up, but roaring-in-his-fucking-ears up. Every time he'd punched his mother-in-law—the same cunt who'd tried bribing him to leave town the day before—it had crashed like a wave on a beach. Of *course* he hadn't heard Sully coming up behind him. He wouldn't have heard an army of Sullys on horseback.

"Where do you *want* to go, then?" Cora said.

Good question. Part of him thought Gert's. Just slip into one of those dark booths along the back wall and start a tab. Drink one beer after another until the fucking cops thought to stop in and haul his ass off. Let Cora pick up the tab, or Gert himself. The fuck did he care? No tabs where he was headed. The problem was the cops would dope this out right quick. And there was another, too. Gert wasn't what you'd call squeamish, but seeing Roy's ear he might tell him to take a hike and not come back until he looked presentable, which at his shithole meant not bleeding freely. Or he might not let them run a tab; the prick had a sixth sense about that. Besides, holing up in some bar and waiting for the fucking cops to come collect him just didn't sit right with Roy. He ought to at least try to make a run for it, right? He was going down hard for this one, no question. He'd be away for a long time, which meant he had a moral obligation to take full advantage of his last few hours of freedom. What he needed was some kind of a plan, but Sully, the fucker, had scrambled his brain. "Take me to that CVS out by the highway," he told Cora.

"The Rexall's closer," she pointed out.

Fucking woman, Roy thought, yanking the rearview back again to see if his injuries could possibly be as bad as they'd appeared thirty seconds ago—and they were. "Will you just do like you're fuckin' told?"

"Why you bein' so mean to me, Roy? I'm just trying to help is all. I'll do anything you want. Just treat me nice, okay?"

He threw up his hands in mock surrender. "Okay, Cora, okay. See how nice I'm treatin' you? See how nice? So can we fuckin' *go* now?"

He expected her to drive around the block, but instead, being a dip-shit, she did a three-point turn in the middle of fucking Main Street and headed back where he'd just come from, right past Hattie's, the very place he was trying to escape. A small crowd had gathered outside to watch the EMTs load his mother-in-law on board. A uniformed piece of shit was trying to explain to Janey why she couldn't ride in the back with her mother, but being a total cunt she just shoved him aside and climbed in anyway. Then he spotted Sully, half a head taller than the other assholes, and the sight of him gave Roy something like an idea, though it was gone again almost before it arrived. Never mind. Roy knew that once something occurred to him it wouldn't take long to reoccur, and right now he had more pressing concerns, like the cop car speeding toward them. He slumped down in his seat as it screeched to a rocking halt at the curb.

Cora, if you could believe it, had actually slowed down and put on her left-turn signal. "The Rexall's right here," she explained. Like he'd fucking forgot where the Rexall was, or like he hadn't just fucking *told* her to go to the CVS.

"No, goddamn it—"

"Stop yellin' at me, Roy," she said, though she turned her blinker off and pulled back into the right lane. "I'm just sayin' all them stores carry the same shit and this one's right here."

"Did you happen to see that fuckin' ambulance back there, Cora? That cop car?" he said, peering to look out the back window. "Me slidin' down in my seat here? What's all that fuckin' shit tell you?"

Just that quickly the crying kicked in. "Did you do something bad, Roy? They gonna make you go back to prison?"

"Not if you shut the fuck up and drive, they won't."

"I gonna get in trouble for helpin' you?"

"Fuck no, Cora."

"'Cause they took my little boy on account of they said I'm unfit and I'm trying to get him back, so—"

"Just fuckin' listen to me, girl. You ain't gonna get in no trouble. The cops question you, just say all you did was give me a fuckin' ride. Tell 'em you're just a dumb cunt and didn't know no better. Don't worry, they'll believe you."

Cora began to cry silently, and neither spoke again until she pulled in to the CVS lot, where Roy once again scrunched down in his seat.

When she killed the engine and wiped her tears on her sleeve, he said, "Lemme see that hat a minute."

"What for?" she said, handing over her Mets cap.

"Never mind what for. Maybe I'm a big fuckin' baseball fan, okay?" Trying it on, he flinched when the sweatband came in contact with his demolished ear.

"You're gettin' blood all over it," she said, wincing.

He adjusted the plastic strap. "Jesus, Cora. What do you need with such a big head, anyway? There ain't a fuckin' thing in it."

She giggled, thinking this was a joke. "Just 'cause you got a little peanut head," she said. "Just 'cause it's full of shit."

This, Roy thought as his hand shot out, its heel connecting flush with the side of Cora's head, is the wrong fucking day to be talking trash. Her temple bounced back off the driver's-side window.

"Ow, Roy," she said, tearing up again. "That *hurt*. All I was doing was havin' a little fun. Can't you take a joke?"

He considered answering by hitting her again, then remembered he needed her help. "Look at me, Cora, and tell me I'm in the fuckin' mood to joke with you."

"You got me all mixed up, Roy. I don't know what you want me to do."

"Well, shut the fuck up a minute, and I'll tell you again. Can you do that?" When, acting on his instruction, she didn't respond, he said, "Well, can you?"

"Yes, Roy, I *can*. It's what I'm *doin'*, okay?"

"All right, then. First thing you need to get is one of them butterfly clamps for my ear. You know the ones I'm talkin' about? They'll be over with the medical supplies. Band-Aids and shit. You understand?"

She said nothing. Just looked at him.

"Do you fuckin' understand? Say you do before I fuckin' hit you again."

"You told me to shut up, Roy. That's what I'm doin'."

"You *want* me to hit you again?"

"I want you to be nice. If you can't be nice, you can just walk back into town."

Or, Roy thought, *I could wring your fuckin' neck, see if your fat ass would fit in the trunk and drive down to Albany and park this shit-bucket in the bus terminal and let people find you when you begin to stink.* Which she already did, with some kind of cheap perfume or other. The thought of the Greyhound reminded him that just yesterday his bitch-in-law had offered him three grand to disappear, an offer that hadn't impressed him at the time, which just went to show he hadn't really been thinking straight. Because what was to stop him from taking her money and going somewheres—Atlantic City, maybe—and coming back when he was broke. Fortunately, he was beginning to think straight now, at least enough to realize he needed Cora for a while longer.

"And an orange juice, okay?" he continued, wiggling the plastic tube that contained his pain meds. "Something to wash down these little beauties."

"Can I have one or two?"

Not a fuckin' chance. "Of course," he told her. "I always share, don't I?"

When she reached for the door handle, though, he grabbed her wrist. Because suddenly he didn't like the look on her face. "Don't do what you're thinkin'," he told her.

"What do you mean?"

"You're thinkin' about goin' in there and tellin' somebody to call the cops." Because in her place, that's what he'd be thinking.

"It ain't what I'm thinkin', Roy."

"Like hell. Don't lie to me. I can tell you are just by looking at you."

She began to cry again. "It was just a passing thought, I swear."

He was taking a chance, letting her out of the car, but it wasn't like he had a lot of options. "You got one minute," he said. "Don't make me come in there after you."

"I need some money."

"Use your own. I'll pay you back later."

"You never paid me back from Tuesday."

"What are you talking about?"

"At Gert's."

"You said that was your treat."

"No, I said—"

"Will you just *get* the fuckin' shit, like I told you? I'll pay you back for that and Gert's, too."

"You promise?"

"And get a couple six-packs," he added. "We'll go out to the reservoir."

"Really?"

"And some Pringles."

She sighed, beaten. "Okay."

He was asleep, or maybe passed out from the pain, before she was inside the CVS. Then she was back again. He could tell she'd been gone for more than a minute, but not much more. And she didn't look scared like she would've if she ratted him out. She had two big plastic bags full of stuff that she put on the seat between them.

"Let me see that orange juice," he said.

She handed him the large plastic bottle, its contents ice cold, just the way he liked it. He was so parched that he drank half of it straight down before remembering the painkillers. Shaking the remaining pills into his palm, he counted eight. Returning four to the vial, he swallowed the others with the remaining juice and tossed the empty container into the backseat. "What?" he said.

Cora was back in behind the wheel and staring at him. "You said I could have one."

"You can," he said. "When half *your* fuckin' ear's hangin' by a thread."

"I like how they make me feel," she explained. "And you said."

"You know how to get to the lake?"

She nodded.

"Then go, before the beer gets warm."

Still she just sat there. "It come to almost twenty dollars."

"It did fuckin' not."

She showed him the receipt. Seventeen bucks and change. "Okay, so what?"

"And the other afternoon at Gert's was almost thirty."

"That was your treat."

"Then pay me for this, at least."

"When we get to the lake."

"*Now,* Roy."

"The beer's gettin' warm, girl. You know I don't like warm beer."

She turned the key in the ignition. "What you don't like is spendin' your own damn money."

No argument there. He'd lifted a couple twenties from Janey's purse while she slept, so he could afford to give Cora one of them, but that was the thing about money: you never knew how much you were going to need. In Roy's experience, the deeper the shit you found yourself in, the more it cost to dig yourself out, and at the moment he was hip deep. One thing was for true. He'd gotten his last free cup of coffee at Hattie's. He done killed the golden goose. Well, not killed her, exactly, but good as. No more day-old pie for ole Roy. It had been worth it, though, the thrill of shutting that bigmouthed bitch the fuck up, wiping that superior look off her face. He could still feel his knuckles throbbing pleasurably. Later, he'd take his list out and draw a satisfying line through her name.

Cora was studying him sadly now. "Janey's never gonna take you back, Roy," she said. Like this was what they'd just been talking about. Like she hadn't pulled this brand-new subject right out of her ass.

"What'd I say to you about that?" Roy'd told her last week at Gert's that he didn't want to hear Janey's name coming out of her mouth. In fact, it was when she brought Janey up that he'd decided the beer was Cora's treat.

"I'm just sayin'."

"Anyway, what the fuck do you know about it?"

Cora put the car in reverse and checked the rearview. "You should start being nice to me. I'm the one that likes you, not her."

"Well, if she don't like me, how come she fucked me?"

Cora hit the brake and looked at him, her eyes like little slits. "Fucked you when?"

"Last night."

"You're lyin'."

"I'm gonna take a nap," he told her. The painkillers were kicking in, giving things that gauzy feel. "Wake me up when we get to the lake."

He closed his eyes and kept them closed while he counted to twenty. When he opened them again the vehicle was in motion, about to pull out of the CVS lot. Cora was crying, and that made him happy. He hadn't been sure she'd believe him about Janey. Roy could hardly believe it himself, but clearly she did, which meant she'd try even harder now to please him. He doubted he'd have much further use for her, but you could never tell.

Drifting off, he thought again about Janey, how nice she'd fucked him. It was like she'd been in jail, too, just like him, and starved for it like he was. They'd always been good in bed, and she'd admitted as much. Okay, she hadn't agreed to getting back together, but she hadn't said they wouldn't, neither, not till Mama Bitch started egging her on this morning. Anyway, she'd been his again, if only for a couple hours. Even if it was just because she was horny, like she said.

HE AWOKE when the wheels of Cora's shit-bucket left the pavement. Sitting up, he saw they'd just pulled in to the campground's dirt lot. It was still only nine in the morning but hot already, and even this early there were half-a-dozen other cars there. By noon the lot would be full, the beach full of brats in water wings screaming, "Mommy, Mommy, Mommy, look at me." Or worse, "Mommy, look at that man's ear!" Fuck that shit. The shoreline was dotted with camps, most of them unoccupied this early in the season, for as far as the eye could see. "Take that dirt road," he told her, pointing.

"You can't go in there," Cora objected. "See the sign? Where it says PRIVATE?"

He could see it fine, not that he gave the tiniest little shit. "Private's what we're looking for," he told her. "Someplace we can drink our beer in peace." He'd only been asleep the fifteen minutes it took to drive here, but he was feeling better now, the pulsing pain in his ear and cheekbone more muted. He'd also awakened with the beginnings of a plan, and that always made him cautiously optimistic, even if his plans seldom panned out. No matter. He enjoyed making them anyway, thinking them through, admiring how they were going to work until something came along and fucked them all up.

Cora, he saw, had stopped crying. "It's nice back in here," she admitted, inching the car slowly along the rutted one-lane path. As Roy had foreseen, only every sixth or seventh camp looked occupied, with a car angled off in the trees, a motorboat bobbing at the end of a dock, wet bathing suits pinned to a clothesline strung between trees. With the windows rolled down it was cool among the tall pines, the air rich with the scent of their needles. Only once did they encounter cars coming from the opposite direction. Cora pulled over to the right as far as she could and tooted a hello at the other driver, smiling broadly as the two vehicles squeezed by each other.

"Don't be drawin' no attention," Roy scolded her, though, really, when he thought about it, why the fuck not? They were in a half-purple, half-yellow car, after all. It wasn't like they weren't going to be noticed.

"How about right here," Cora wanted to know when they came to a stretch where the camps were all dark and deserted looking. "We could sit out on that deck."

"Keep goin'."

"Why?"

" 'Cause I said so."

They continued on, and when he looked over at her, damned if she wasn't crying again.

"You ever wonder how come some people have all the luck?" she croaked.

To Roy that was like wondering why the sky was blue. It just was.

"How come Janey gets to look like she does and I got to look like me?"

"Try not eatin' everything in sight," Roy suggested.

"I don't, Roy. And I've tried diets. They don't work. I bet Janey doesn't even have to diet."

"I'm not gonna tell you again about not sayin' her name."

"But that's what I mean, Roy. She gets to be her and be all lucky and I don't even get to say her name. And I'm the one bein' nice to you."

"She was nice to me last night, and that's for true."

"One night."

Roy shrugged.

"It's not fair, is what I'm sayin'."

"What ain't?"

Sniffling, she wiped her eyes. "All of it," she explained. "The way things are."

Roy would have liked to agree with her, having come to the same conclusion on any number of other occasions, but you couldn't go around agreeing with a bitch as dumb as this one without being dumb yourself.

"Take you," she continued. "You only just got out of prison and now they're gonna send you back. Other people do bad things. Politicians and them. *They* don't go to jail."

"Some do."

"But mostly it's us, Roy. People like you and me. We're the ones get blamed. You know it's true. Some rich lady? They don't take her kid away. They take one look at me and say I'm unfit. They look at you and off you go to jail. Don't that make you mad?"

Dumb-ass women make me mad, Roy thought. *You in particular.*

After a while she said, "Wouldn't it be nice if one of these little places was ours?" He couldn't tell if she'd shifted gears or was on the same subject. "We could live there and nobody'd bother us."

"These places ain't even insulated. You'd freeze your ass off, is what you'd do."

"I bet some are."

"They aren't, I'm telling you. Try listenin' when people tell you shit."

"Yeah, but how do you know? You been in any?"

Actually, he had. He'd robbed close to a dozen camps on this very road one winter and would've hit a bunch more if he hadn't run into bad luck. He'd parked his van on a paved driveway next to one place around nightfall, and while he was inside he came upon a bottle containing five, six fingers of top-shelf whiskey. Not enough to bring home, really, just too good to leave behind. It was mid-December, and with the power off the camp was freezing, but there was a big overstuffed chair with its own little ottoman thingy, and he had on long johns and a parka, so he put his feet up and finished the shit off, drinking it slow and right out of the bottle, feeling the heat of the amber booze spread from his chest to his extremities. He made a mental note not to fall asleep, even as he did so. He couldn't have dozed for more than half an hour, then at some point it began sleeting, and by the time he meant to leave, the pavement was a sheet of ice. He hadn't noticed the driveway's gentle slope down toward the water. The van was rear-wheel drive, and when he put it in reverse the wheels just spun and spun. He wasn't going anywhere unless he called for a tow, and he couldn't very well do that. Another night he'd have probably just gone back inside and spent the night and tried again in the morning, but since it was supposed to snow like a bitch, his only choice was to hoof it out to the main road in the freezing rain. Good thing he did, too, because that night they got close to two feet, which meant his van full of stolen shit was going to stay right where it was for the foreseeable future.

He was sick for a good week, but as soon as he felt a little better, he went over to Gert's and presented his circumstance to him as a hypothetical situation. Gert had never had much use for Roy, but he was good at problems. He listened carefully and finally said, "Report the vehicle stolen," taking Roy by surprise. "The only people out there in the winter are cross-country skiers," Gert explained, "and how do they know the camp's owner didn't leave the vehicle there. We get a midwinter thaw, you hike back in and see if the engine starts. If somebody reports it to the cops before you can get it out, you can say whoever stole the vehicle must've done the burglaries. They'll know it was you, but they probably won't be able to prove it."

Roy thanked him for the advice, which seemed both sound and rigorous. All damn winter it snowed, and no real thaw, either, but that

April he got a lift out to the reservoir and hiked back in. Sure enough, the van was right where he'd left it—except, just his luck, a mother-fucking tree had fallen on it. When he told this last part, Gert just rubbed his bald head thoughtfully and said, "That's the trouble with crime. There's always that falling tree you don't predict." Roy could see his point, but he still thought Gert was selling crime short, blaming it for something that wasn't really its fault. That tree you couldn't foresee, well, it fell on the innocent as often as it did on the guilty. He himself was a case in point. Right now his neck wasn't in a brace because he'd been doing something illegal, only because he'd been in the wrong place at the wrong time. Shit fell. Trees. Walls. Fucking meteors. Why blame all that on crime? Still, there was no denying Gert had been right about the rest of it. Seeing who the van was registered to, the cops knew it was Roy who'd stolen all that stuff, too, but they couldn't prove shit, and his having reported the van's theft wrong-footed them, too. Besides, the people who owned all those camps were mostly from somewhere else, so who gave a fuck?

"I bet some of them got woodstoves," Cora was saying, determined to believe they could survive an upstate New York winter in an un-insulated camp on a frozen lake, miles away from their nearest neigh-bor. "When it gets cold, you just put a log in it and sit around and play games and be all nice and warm."

"They'd find you in the spring," Roy assured her. "Or the half of you raccoons didn't eat after you froze to death."

Cora sighed mightily, clearly baffled by his reluctance to join her in such a pleasant fantasy. "Don't you like dreamin', Roy? About things bein' better? I know it's just make-believe, but so what? Don't you like imaginin' how nice it'd be to have things, like maybe one of these camps, or a new car to go places in?"

"Hell, girl, I'm imaginin' shit right now. Like how happy I'd be if you'd give that jaw of yours a fuckin' rest." By now they'd driven around to the far side of the reservoir. He pointed up ahead. "Pull in there."

Miracle of miracles, she did as she was told, parking alongside a camp that looked unoccupied. There were others nearby, but you could barely see them through the trees, and there wasn't a single vehicle in sight. An invisible loon called out over the water, and the breeze whispered in the upper reaches of the pines. Cora was looking around, confused. "I don't get it," she said. "Why we had to come all this way."

Jesus, was she stupid.

"WHAT THE FUCK are these?" he said, holding up the package of clamps that was at the bottom of the second CVS bag.

They were seated on the rickety dock now, their feet dangling in the water. The cove they'd chosen was narrow and secluded. The few camps visible across the reservoir were the size of the little green houses on a Monopoly board. A motorboat appeared out in the middle of the lake and just as quickly disappeared again. Roy had already chugged one beer and opened another. Cora was still sipping her first. They'd submerged the other nine beers in the cool water under the dock.

Cora winced. "Them butterfly clips you wanted?"

Well, yeah, that's what the fucking package said they were, but any damn fool could see they weren't what Roy needed for his ear. "These here are paperclips, dumb ass."

"They was out of the others," Cora explained. "I told the man what you wanted, and he showed me where they'd be, but they was all gone."

"So you bought *these* fuckin' things?"

Cora shrugged. "I thought maybe one of the smaller ones, if you had a little bit of cloth or a paper towel?"

He just looked at her. "I ought to throw you right in the fuckin' lake is what I ought to do."

"I *done* the best I could, Roy. They didn't have them others, okay? They probably would've at the Rexall, but you didn't let me go in there."

"I suppose they didn't have no Pringles neither?" he said, holding up the big bag of Cheetos she'd bought.

"I like Cheetos," she said. "Besides, it was my money, so my choice."

"Well, I ain't paying you back for none of this shit."

"Fine," she said. "Don't eat the Cheetos, then. Go hungry. You can just sit there and feel sorry for yourself." When he got to his feet, she said, "Where you goin'?"

"The fuck do you care?" he said. Her idea to wrap his ear in something soft before securing it with the clip was dumb, but he didn't have a better one.

"You gonna break in, Roy?"

"Maybe it's unlocked."

It wasn't, of course, but the wood was punky, and a couple good kicks sprung it clear of the frame.

"You're gonna get us in trouble, Roy," she called from the dock.

"I'm already in fuckin' trouble, Cora."

The only mirror in the whole fucking place was the cloudy one in the dark bathroom. Apparently the owners weren't planning to use the place until later in the summer, because the electricity still hadn't been turned on. The tiny room had just one small window, high up, and even when he pulled the curtain back he could barely see a thing.

Removing the smallest of the butterfly clips from the package, he squeezed the metal wings, opening its jaw as far as it would go, pried it open farther with his thumbs, then tested it on his good ear. Still too goddamn tight. The next-larger size looked more promising, but it was sturdier, too, and he wasn't able to bend the frame by hand. Inserting its open mouth against the edge of the sink and putting his weight on it did the trick, though, and he felt the metal give. Unfortunately, now the gap was too wide, and it fell right off his good ear. *Fucking bitch.* There was a threadbare washcloth draped over the towel rack, so he tore it in half, then in half again. If he could wrap the ear first, then secure it with the clamp . . . After several excruciating tries, he somehow managed to wrap the ear without passing out. As soon as he touched the makeshift bandage with the clip, though, it unraveled. *Fucking, fucking, fucking woman.* There was only one other solution he could think of. It took him a while to talk himself into it, though. "On the count of ten," he said out loud, taking the dangling part of his ear between his thumb and forefinger. When he got to five, though, he thought, What's so fuckin' special about ten?

And pulled.

———

CORA WAS STILL on the dock but standing now, clearly scared shitless, when he emerged from the camp, holding a swatch of paper towels, already soaked with blood, to what little remained of his ear. "I heard you screamin', Roy. You okay?"

"Do I look okay, Cora?" He held out the piece of ear he'd torn off for her inspection. When she let out a yelp and took a hasty step back, he flung the thing as far as he could out into the lake, where it plopped harmlessly, floated for a second, then sank out of sight. "Where'd that beer go?"

She was sniffling again. "I was keepin' it cool for you," she said, pointing to where she'd wedged it, upright, between two rocks.

"Get it for me," he said.

"Okay, Roy," she said, but before she could haul her fat ass over there, a small wave, probably from some motorboat, lapped up against the shoreline and knocked the can over, the beer foaming out.

"Bring it here," he told her.

"It spilled, Roy."

"Bring it here, I said."

When she did, he flung the can out into the lake, and it hit not far from where his ear had landed, bobbing there.

"Bring me another."

She did. "I'm sorry I do things wrong, Roy," she said, her lip quivering.

He popped the fresh beer, drank it half down, then sat on the end of the dock, looking out at the still-bobbing beer can. "Don't just stand there looking dumb," he told her. "Sit your ass down."

She sat next to him, warily. "You don't have to pay me back," she said.

"I know I don't."

"I'm real sorry about your ear."

"Me too."

"You aren't mad at me?"

"Hell yes, I'm mad at you," he said, though he wasn't, or not as mad as he'd been earlier. For some reason his rage had leaked away with all that blood. At least she'd quit mouthing him.

"I try," she told him. "I try real hard."

He just shrugged. He was seeing the whole ear business more clearly now. "Ain't none of this your doin'," he admitted. That's what ole Bullwhip would say if he was here. It was Roy's own damn fault for letting an old cripple like Sully sneak up on him. Cora might be dumb as a rock, but she wasn't the one who hit him with a fucking skillet, and it wasn't her fault the fucking drugstore didn't have the right clips. They probably wouldn't have worked anyway. What he'd needed to do was to get the fucking ear sewed back on, but that hadn't been an option, and that wasn't her fault, either. Okay, the Cheetos *were* her fault. She should've gotten Pringles like he fucking told her, but even there she had a point. It *was* her money.

They sat quietly for a while until Cora said, "Is it real nice in there?"

"In the camp?" he said, finishing his beer. He was going to have to pace himself, he realized, if he hoped to make it through the day. Both the beer and the painkillers he had left. What he meant to do later was gradually becoming clear to him. "Pretty nice, I guess. Go take a look, if you want. You see something you like, take it."

"I'd rather just sit here with you, real quiet," she said, putting her hand on top of his. Roy didn't like to be touched by ugly women and normally wouldn't have permitted this, but for some reason he did now. "I can imagine all the nice things they got. I always like things the way they are in my head, you know?"

Actually, he had no fucking idea what she was talking about, though it did call to mind his old man, who'd always maintained that wanting things was a waste of time. To him, though, it wasn't so much that you'd be disappointed when you didn't get what you wanted as that you would be when you did. Roy remembered the day his father made sure that message was plain as could be. They were driving home from somewhere and stopped at a diner, taking seats at the counter. The menus they were given had pictures of the food: majestic bacon-and-turkey club sandwiches, enormous meatball heroes, turkey with stuffing and mashed potatoes slathered in gravy, an open-faced steak sandwich on triangles of toast. At twelve Roy was always starved. "Can I—?" he began, but his old man had noticed where he was looking.

"No," he said. "Order off the kids' menu." Because stuff there was cheaper, Roy knew. A boiled hot dog. A thin grilled-cheese sandwich that would come burned. Kiddie spaghetti.

As a rule Roy didn't argue, because that just got him cuffed or worse. Out in public, though, he could sometimes lodge a small protest, so when the waitress came over to take their order he said, just loud enough for her to hear, "I think I'm too old for the kids' menu."

"How old are you?" she said, giving Roy a wink to let him know she was on his side, though his father noticed.

"Ten," he answered before Roy could. Because that's what it said on the menu: kids ten and under.

"He looks older," the waitress said.

Roy saw his old man stiffen and give the woman a long, dark look. Down the counter, though, were some guys dressed in button-down shirts and ties, the kind of men his father always steered clear of, as if he suspected they were judges and one day he'd have to stand before them in court, and Roy saw him register their presence now. He'd make no scene here, Roy realized. "You gonna tell this young lady what you want," his father said, "or make her guess?"

"What can I have?" Roy said.

The waitress was older than his father but apparently liked being referred to as "young" and had decided to be playful. "Yeah, Dad. What can he have?"

His father seemed to decide something on the spot. "Whatever he wants," he said, loud enough for the men down the counter to hear.

"Really?" Roy said, incredulous. Never before had he been given such freedom.

"Just don't order more than you can eat."

The open-faced steak sandwich, as pictured, was thick and red in the center and served with a mountain of thin crispy-looking fries. "Even this?" he said, pointing at it, the most expensive item on the menu.

"Why not?" his father said, though Roy noticed his smile didn't sit quite right on his face, as if it were masking another emotion entirely. "But you gotta eat it all. Every last bite."

"Looks like he's just the man for the job," said one of the guys in ties, grinning and jovial. Roy himself shared the man's confidence. Like he was indeed just the boy to tuck away a man-size steak.

When the food came, though, it was a different cut of meat from the one on the menu. Worse, it was cooked gray all the way through, tough as shoe leather, and the thick, crinkle-cut fries were doughy and cold. Roy immediately wished he'd ordered a cheeseburger, like his father, but he knew better than to say so, or that the steak wasn't at all like the one in the picture. He kept hoping his father would notice the difference and complain about it, but he didn't. When he finished his burger, he pushed the plate away, then pretended to read a section of newspaper somebody had left on the counter. Roy could tell he was watching him, though, out of the corner of his eye. "Every last bite," his old man repeated under his breath when Roy showed signs of slowing down.

"There's gristle."

"That too," he said, the forced smile gone now, the menace in his voice unmistakable. Maybe it was this that drew the waitress back down the counter. From the look on her face, she'd met men like his father before and hadn't enjoyed it.

"Hey, good job!" she said, whisking the plate away—who'd want to eat those last few pieces of gristle?—before his father could object. "How about a hot-fudge sundae?"

"Sure," his father said before Roy could say he was too full. "And make sure he gets a cherry on top." He rose, then, and sauntered back to the restrooms.

The sundae was huge. Roy managed to choke down a couple bites, including the cherry, though through all the sweetness he could still taste the sour meat, and soon realized he was finished. There was simply no more room in his stomach. When his father came back and saw the waste, there'd be trouble. Maybe not here in the restaurant, but later, in the car, or maybe at home, the belt. What was keeping him? Roy wondered. He leaned back on his stool, expecting to see him come out of the lavatory, but he didn't.

The waitress working the counter now had her head together with the one who was waiting on the booths, and Roy thought he heard the phrase "out the back." The big man in the filthy apron who ran the grill was called over, and after Roy's waitress said something, he went into the men's room, emerging a moment later and shaking his head at her. She then came over to where Roy sat staring at the sundae he couldn't eat another spoonful of and wondering if he'd be able to hold back the hot tears he felt forming.

"I shoulda known," she said, and when he made no reply, just swallowed hard, trying to keep the food down, she showed him the check, the amount circled at the bottom. "What am I supposed to do with this?" He knew what his father would've told her she could do with it, but he was only twelve, and it'd be several years before he'd be brave enough to offer any such suggestion. "They're gonna dock my pay for this," she told him. Everyone at the counter was watching them now, as well as the people in nearby booths. "Come on, Darla," one of the tie-wearing men objected, "it ain't the kid's fault," and apparently she felt the truth of this because she seemed to soften a little. "You live around here?" she asked.

He said he did.

"Can you get home on your own?" When he nodded, she said, "Well, then, git."

Out in the parking lot, in the space where they'd parked, now empty, Roy vomited up everything, the cherry recognizable in the mess, and immediately felt better. The good news was that the diner was right on Route 9, which meant he could either walk or hitchhike the four miles home. He decided to walk, because it'd take longer and maybe his father would think that was punishment enough. Pushing himself down the busy road, he toyed with the idea of being angry at his father for playing such a low trick on him but decided in the end that it wouldn't get him anywhere. Besides, it was the waitress he was really mad at, her "I shoulda known" that he wasn't able to forgive, as if the mere sight of him and his father was warning enough. That and the look she gave him when the man down the counter had taken his side. Like she could see his whole pitiful life stretched out before her, causing him to ball his hands into fists.

Still, it had been a valuable lesson. His father was right: wanting things that weren't worth wanting or wishing things were different *was* a waste of time. Women like Cora—all women, probably—could never understand that, even when the evidence was staring them right in the face. Cora had some dumb-ass idea of Roy in her mind that she preferred to Roy himself. No doubt that asshole treated her nice. Told her she was pretty when she could see for herself that she wasn't. Told her she was a good mom when she probably left the fucking kid alone in his playpen with a full diaper and crying his fucking little eyes out. Dream Roy didn't stick her with the check. He even shared his meds. Whereas the real Roy? The one sitting with her on the dock? Well, that Roy saw things for true. He knew the steak in the picture wasn't real, any more than Dream Roy was real. Just as he knew that later this afternoon, after the beer was gone, only one of them would be getting back into Cora's shit-bucket car.

Though he'd only been twelve, he congratulated himself on not blaming his old man. He hadn't gone more than half a mile when he heard a horn toot and his father pulled up alongside the curb, motioning for him to get in. "So," he said, "you learn anything back there?"

Roy nodded.

"All right, then," his father said. Pulling back into traffic, he seemed satisfied with how everything had worked out. He wasn't angry anymore, Roy could tell, which meant no belt when they got home.

"She was pretty mad," Roy said, "that waitress."

"Maybe next time she'll mind her own damn business," his father said. "Think twice before she opens that big, fat mouth of hers."

They were silent for a while until Roy said, "Everybody stared at me." In fact, he could still feel their eyes on him as he slid off his stool and moved to the front door and out into the parking lot.

"I bet they did," his father said. "But here you are. You didn't die."

Which was true. There he'd been, and here he still was.

"Pass them Cheetos," he told Cora. Actually, he kind of liked Cheetos, except they made your fingers all orange.

The bag, he noticed, when she handed it to him, was half empty. She'd gone to town on it when he was in the camp pulling his fucking ear off. He thought about saying something about that, curious to see if he could make her cry one more time, but in the end—again—he decided not to. Instead, he ate a handful of Cheetos. "These aren't too bad," he admitted.

She smiled at him, orange lipped.

Gert Gives the Matter
Some Thought

S ULLY WAS STANDING by the window when Janey came in, her eyes
swollen nearly shut from crying. This early in the morning, the waiting room of the emergency unit was empty except for Sully and Tina,
Ruth's granddaughter, who so far as he could tell wasn't really there
herself. He'd never had much luck with the girl. She didn't respond
to teasing, and with girls her age he didn't have many other rhetorical
strategies. He would try to engage her, but she always stared at him
vaguely, like you look at a television screen when your mind has wandered elsewhere. This was different, of course. Tina sat perfectly still,
staring off into some middle distance. In fact, she was so motionless that
he kept glancing over to make sure she was breathing.

Janey made brief eye contact with Sully before going over to her
daughter, squatting right in front of her. "Hey, there, Birdbrain," she
said, having apparently decided to attempt good cheer. "You okay?"
When the girl's unfocused gaze didn't even flicker, Janey grew serious.
"Tina, honey. I know you don't want to, but you have to come back,
okay? I know it was real bad, what happened back there, and I know
you think you're safer where you are, but you can't stay there because it's
not a real place. Remember how we talked about it before? And what
the doctor said about how the longer you stay away, the harder it is to
come back? There's nothing to be afraid of anymore. It's just you and
me here. And Sully. You've always liked him."

News to Sully, if true.

"None of this is your fault, sweetpea. You know that, right? I did a real dumb thing. Made your dad get all mad. But he's gone now, and nobody's gonna hurt anybody anymore. You understand? As soon as you come back we can all start making things better, you and me. Grandma, too. And Grandpa'll be here just as soon as we can find out where the hell he is. Grandpa's your special friend, right?"

Tina blinked slowly at the mention of her grandfather, and it seemed to Sully that her eyes started to focus, but then they quickly went blank again. Sully couldn't blame her. She had only to look at her mother to know that her cheer was forced, her optimism just wishful thinking. Things weren't going to be okay again for a long time, maybe never.

Janey gave in. "Okay, sweetpea. You can stay there a little while longer, but after I talk to Sully you've got to come back, okay? Then we're going to start over again, like we do. It always gets better, remember? What comes after down? Up, right? Up's the only direction left, and that's where we're headed, as soon as you come back."

When Janey rose, her knees cracked audibly, and it occurred to Sully that the woman coming toward him wasn't young anymore. Could it be that the last hour had plunged her so deeply into middle age? "Thanks," she said, joining him where he stood at the window overlooking the parking lot below. "I assume it's you who brought her here."

Sully nodded. When the cops finally arrived at the restaurant, he'd led them back to the apartment only to discover that Roy Purdy had regained consciousness while they were out front with the EMTs and skedaddled. The regulars were milling around by the entrance by the time Sully finished talking to the cops, but they seemed to get the picture when he shook his head and pointed at the CLOSED sign. It was then that he sensed he wasn't alone inside and found the girl curled up in the fetal position in the far booth. "People forget all about you, don't they?" he said, sliding in across from her. When she didn't respond, he said, "I need to do a few things here. Then we'll go to the hospital, okay?"

She nodded, but that was all.

The first thing to do was turn off the grill and toss out all the bacon and sausage, now reduced to cinders. Out back he found a cardboard box and tore it down, took a Magic Marker and some tape near the register and made another CLOSED sign for the deliverymen who would come to the back. Under the sign on the front door he taped a second: UNTIL FURTHER NOTICE. By now Tina was sitting up in the booth. "Can you think of anything else?" he said, but she gave no indication of having heard him. "Let's go out this way," he suggested, pointing. The front door was locked; the back would lock behind them.

In the truck she cocked her head at the brown cyclone Carl had made on the inside of the window. As he drove to the hospital she kept staring at it, and by the time they arrived she'd drifted into the space she now occupied. Unable to rouse her, Sully'd flagged a nurse to help get her out of the truck and into the emergency room. "What's wrong with her?" the woman wanted to know, and he told her she'd just witnessed an attack on her grandmother. That explanation didn't seem to satisfy her, and she looked Sully over suspiciously, but he didn't know what else to say. When she was little Tina had been tested for autism, and Ruth had said that in times of stress—especially when her parents were fighting—she occasionally entered these fugue states, but he'd been under the impression she'd outgrown them. Wrong again.

"Is she going to be okay?" Sully now whispered to Janey, nodding at the girl. He admired how Janey had just talked to her, a side to Ruth's daughter he'd never witnessed.

"Eventually," she said. "It's her defense mechanism. When things get too bad, she just checks out. I wish I could do the same thing."

"One of the nurses said she was sending in a doctor to examine her."

"God," she said, turning back to look at her daughter. "She saw the whole thing, didn't she?"

"She was standing in the doorway when I got there, so yeah, probably. You don't remember?"

"It's all murky," Janey admitted. "I remember screaming for him to stop. His fist hitting Ma over and over. Then you coming in. That look on your face. But it's like it's all happening underwater."

"You're lucky," said Sully, whose own recollection was all too vivid, as if playing on a color video in his brain: Ruth's battered, bloody, ruined face almost unrecognizable, her eyes meeting his for just that split second before rolling back in her head. "Are they saying anything, the doctors?"

"They're not using the word 'coma,' but she's still unconscious, so . . ."

"They don't come much tougher, though," Sully said. "She'll fight."

"I know, but, Jesus, Sully, he knocked out half her teeth. Broke her nose, fractured both cheekbones . . ."

She allowed him to draw her into his arms then, and he held her until she sobbed herself out. At one point he glanced over at the doorway, half expecting to see Zack come in. Their embrace was innocent enough, but Sully couldn't help wondering if that's how it would appear to her father. He recalled Carl's observation about the world still turning no matter how fucked up things got. *No matter how we fuck them up* was what he'd meant because, face it, things didn't fuck themselves up. Sully's chest, he realized, felt heavy, though what it was heavy with— sorrow, fear, rage—wasn't immediately clear.

"I keep remembering what I said to her yesterday," Janey said, finally stepping back. "About how it's always my jaw that gets broke. Like it was her turn, or something. And that's what happened."

"Yeah, but you didn't cause it," he said. "It wasn't you that beat her unconscious."

"No"—her eyes hardening—"but I fucked the man who did. And then I just watched. I screamed for him to stop, but I didn't *do* anything. I let her take my beating."

"She wanted to. Why do you think she came between you?"

"I'm gonna find that son of a bitch and kill him. I swear to God."

"No, you're going to take care of your daughter. Leave Roy to me."

"You have no idea where he is, even."

"I'll find him," he said, glancing at the girl again and hoping she was still checked out. "Your dad still doesn't know what's happened?"

"I left a message on the machine at home in case he's still on his rounds. He's probably out in the shed."

"I'll swing by the house."

"Would you?"

"Right now, in fact."

He was halfway out of the room when he heard her say, "When you find Roy?"

"Yeah?"

She came over to where he stood and whispered directly into his ear, "Hurt him. Promise me you'll hurt him bad."

ZACK MUST'VE HEARD Sully's truck turn in to the drive, because by the time he shifted it into park he was standing in the shed's open doorway, wiping his hands on a rag. He had on greasy jeans and a threadbare plaid shirt, his gut hanging out over his belt, his cowlick in full bloom. If the word "doofus" didn't already exist, Sully often thought, you'd have to invent it to properly describe him. When he didn't get out of the truck, Zack came over, looking worried. "You okay?"

Sully held up his hand, and the other man waited patiently for him to regain his breath. "There," he finally said, though that one word used up all the air in his lungs. The heaviness he'd felt in his chest back at the hospital was even more intense now. The pressure came in waves, making it difficult to inhale. The last one washed over him as he turned in to the drive, a real doozy, but it was almost past now. "Just let me sit a minute."

"Sit all day," Zack said, good-natured as always, this man whom Sully had wronged for so long. He'd stayed away these last couple weeks, afraid that Zack would have a two-man job he'd been putting off, some sleeper-sofa that needed to be lugged out of the shed and into the bed of the truck, work Sully simply wasn't up to in his present condition. "I got no place to be."

"You do, actually," Sully told him, and again was out of breath. "Ruth," he finally managed.

Zack cocked his head. "She all right?"

Sully held his hand up again, waiting for the last wave to draw back down the beach. "She's in the emergency room."

Hearing this, Zack looked more perplexed than anything, like maybe he suspected Sully was playing a trick on him. "You sure?"

"She's in pretty bad shape. Roy beat her up."

"Ruth," Zack repeated, scratching his chin now. "Not Janey."

"Janey's there with her. And Tina."

"They okay?" he said.

"Janey is."

"Tina go into one of her trances?"

Sully nodded.

"I can usually get her to come out of them things," he said, not bragging exactly, but clearly proud of his knack.

"Well, they can probably use your help, then," Sully said, because, really, what did it take to light a fire under this guy?

"You say Roy hurt her pretty bad?"

"Yeah," Sully admitted. "Pretty bad."

"She gonna die, Sully? Because—"

"I don't know. But prepare yourself. You're not going to recognize her. She's all . . ." He couldn't find the words for what she was or possibly imagine how Zack might prepare himself.

He was now looking over at the shed. Watching him process information in real time gave Sully a window in Ruth's frustrations with him—she, so preternaturally quick and perpetually waiting for her husband to catch up. Anybody else would have been halfway to the hospital by now, running stop signs, honking at drivers in front of him to pull over. If the world were populated by people like him, there'd be no need for stop signs, speed limits or, probably, laws of any sort.

"Her and me . . . ," he began, then paused, his eyes suddenly full. "You see that up there?"

Sully'd been so intent on the task at hand that he hadn't noticed the slender shard of metal, a good seven or eight feet in length, that was standing straight up, like a weather vane minus its horizontal arms, on the peak of the shed. At its base, where the lightning had struck, was an enormous scorch mark, which meant they'd been fortunate. Sully'd heard stories of outbuildings that weren't properly grounded exploding when directly hit by lightning. Many of those were barns filled with hay, but still.

"Last night, what her and me saw up there?" Zack was saying, his voice full of wonder even now. "You couldn't hardly believe it. This big ball of light. Fuzzy, like those frosted lightbulbs, but really bright. It sat right there at the tip, balanced, like it might fall off. Like something in a dream that don't make sense, but there it is anyhow. Something come to visit. Trying to tell us something."

Sully didn't need to follow the sight line from the roof of the shed to Zack's bedroom window. If he and Ruth both witnessed the glowing orb, they were both standing at the same window. Her bedroom was on the other side of the house. He recalled what Ruth told him yesterday about how strangely Zack had been behaving of late, as if he was really taking her in for the first time in years. Was the miracle Zack was trying so hard to describe the glowing, unnatural orb atop the shed or the fact that he and Ruth had witnessed it together in the middle of the night in a room she had led Sully to believe she never visited?

"You think maybe it was warning us about what was going to happen? That Roy was going to—"

"I think you need to go to the hospital."

Zack swallowed hard. "What if I'm too late?"

"I don't think you will be."

"Okay," he finally agreed, patting his trousers for his keys and shaking his head. When he started for the house, it occurred to Sully to ask, "Roy hasn't been by here this morning, has he?"

Zack paused, thoughtfully. "No, I haven't seen him since—"

"It doesn't matter," Sully told him, turning the key in the ignition.

"I heard he'd shacked up with some woman named Cora at the Morrison Arms."

"I heard the same thing."

Incredibly, he'd stalled again. "Could you ever do something like that? Like he done to Ruth?"

"No. Of course not."

"Me neither," he said, but he seemed to have something else on his mind, so Sully waited, his foot on the brake. "I always knew about you and her," Zack said finally.

"I figured you did," Sully said, feeling another wave of the heaviness descend upon him.

"Okay if I showed you something?"

"Yeah, but—"

From the back pocket of his jeans he took out a bankbook and handed it to Sully. His expression was one of pride, like a man sharing photos of his grandchildren. "That number there," he said, pointing to what appeared to be the balance. It was well north of three hundred thousand dollars.

"Ruth knows about this?"

He shook his head, pride morphing to shame.

"That's a lot of money, Zack. Where'd it come from?" Not that it was any of his business.

"Buy something for fifty cents, sell it for a dollar."

"I understand the principle," Sully said. "But you'd have to do it over half-a-million times."

"Then I must've."

"Why not tell her?"

He shook his head. "I kept wanting the number to be even bigger, I guess. She never thought the business was worth anything. Didn't even think it *was* a business. She never really thought I was working, at least not like she was, all those years she waitressed, then at Hattie's. I guess I wanted her to know I was working, too. The bigger the number I could show her—"

"Well . . ."

"But that wasn't it, really," he continued. "The real reason I didn't tell her is I promised Ma."

"I don't understand."

"Ruth was right. I know that now. Ma was always trying to drive that wedge between us."

"What did you promise?"

"That I wouldn't tell Ruth about all this money until she told me about her and you. And now I've waited too long. If she dies, I'll never get to tell her."

"Then go," Sully said. "Hurry."

He took a deep breath. "Okay."

But when he turned and headed toward the house, Sully called after him, "You know it's over, right?"

"Yeah?"

Sully nodded. "You don't mind that we're old friends, do you?"

"No," Zack told him. "That's all right. I'd prefer you didn't start up again, though."

"We won't," Sully promised. "It's been over for a long while. I'm sorry it ever happened."

That was one thing that hadn't changed, Sully thought when Zack disappeared inside. The worst part of his affair with Ruth had always been the lies, both told and implied. And it still was. Because Sully wasn't sorry for having loved Ruth. For loving her still. Not even a little.

YELLOW CRIME-SCENE TAPE still stretched across all three entrances to the Morrison Arms when Sully pulled into the lot and parked next to two animal-control vans. He reached under the seat for the tire iron he kept there, felt its reassuring heft, then placed it on the passenger seat so it would be handy. A couple dozen people, residents of the Arms by the look of them, had gathered in the lot, apparently awaiting permission to return to their apartments, though Roy Purdy, no surprise, was not among them. Nor was there any sign of the girlfriend's half-purple, half-yellow car. Sully had seen the beater around town, and he remembered its driver, too, a morbidly obese woman in her midthirties who usually wore a Mets cap to conceal her balding head. For some reason, he was pretty sure he'd seen both it and her this morning, but where? In the hospital parking lot? Possibly, but somehow that didn't seem right. Had he passed it going over to Ruth and Zack's? No, it had to have been earlier. Outside Hattie's, then, as Ruth was being loaded onto the ambulance? How could the vehicle have registered on him then, in the midst of all that commotion? And yet that was the possibility that felt most right.

Old Mr. Hynes was there, as usual. Seeing Sully approach, he said, "Donald E. Sullivan, Esquire," his standard greeting. Sully had no idea where he'd come up with the middle initial, but it wasn't his. "You don't look so hot."

"I don't feel so hot," Sully admitted.

"How come? Young fella like yourself."

"Call it chickens coming home to roost," Sully told him. "You look all right, though."

"'Cause I *am* all right," the old man cackled. "Don't no chickens roost on me if I can he'p it."

"They're still looking for that snake, I see."

"Still lookin'," the old man snorted. "Ain't enough for folks to worry about. Now we got *rep*tiles."

"Speaking of snakes," Sully said, "you know who Roy Purdy is?"

"*Po*lice was by earlier, looking for him. Heard he had himself some trouble earlier this morning."

"He's got more coming if I can find him before they do."

"Whack him a good one for me, if you think of it. He like to let fly with that word I don't 'preciate."

"I think I know the one you mean."

"Learned it on his daddy's knee, probably, like most crackers do."

"That's where I learned it," Sully told him.

The old man nodded up at him. "James E. Sullivan, Esquire," he said. "Big Jim, they called the man. I 'member him."

"Not fondly, I'm guessing."

"They's worse."

"Name five."

"You know what you should do, Donald E. Sullivan, Esquire?"

"Tell me."

"You should let the *po*lice find that boy. Let *them* whack him 'stead of you. You look like you the one might get whacked. Fact, you look like you been whacked already."

"I'll be extra careful," Sully promised.

"Do that," the old man said, "and you just might be okay."

"JESUS CHRIST," said Gert, looking up from his newspaper when Sully slid onto a stool at the far end of the bar. "What happened? Did the Horse burn down?"

"Not that I know of," Sully told him, blinking, his eyes still blinded by the utter darkness. "Why?"

"When was the last time you darkened *my* doorway?"

"It's been a while," Sully admitted. Near as he could tell, he and Gert were alone in the joint, though it sounded like someone was banging around in the kitchen.

"Why *is* that?" Gert said. He'd set the newspaper down but made no move to rise from his own stool.

"You think it could be the service?"

"Service," Gert said, as if this were indeed a foreign concept. "So service is what the man wants."

"I don't suppose you've got anything for heartburn."

"Hah!" the other man said, finally sliding to his feet. "Do I have anything for heartburn." Coming up the bar he grabbed a plastic tub of Maalox tablets large enough to contain a human head and banged it down in front of Sully. Next came a quart of Pepto-Bismol, then, finally, a fifteen-hundred bottle of generic ibuprofen. From the bar gun he shot a tall glass of water. "Knock yourself out. No charge."

Sully chewed a couple Maalox, made a face, then washed down three ibuprofen with the water.

"No?" Gert said, holding up the Pepto.

"My mother used to drink that shit by the juice glass."

Gert returned all three remedies whence they came.

"Where the hell is everybody?" Sully said. It was only ten in the morning, but Gert's alcoholic clientele generally showed little regard for normal drinking hours, and his morning business was usually brisk.

"That fucking snake's got everybody in a tizzy," Gert said. "It was dead last night, too."

Sully nodded. "Your whole crew was out at the Horse. Joe and the rest."

"Spinmatics Joe," Gert chuckled. "His mother's calling every hour on the hour wanting to know if I've seen him. Seems he never made it home last night."

"He left the Horse around ten," Sully told him. "Must've gone somewhere else."

"Like where?"

"Good question. There and here are the only two places I know of that'll serve him, and after last night, it's just here."

"Birdie eighty-six him?"

"That was my impression, unless she's changed her mind."

"When was the last time you knew that to happen?"

Years earlier, Birdie and Gert had been a couple, until she gave him his walking papers. Her refusal to take him back struck him as pure inflexibility, a serious character flaw.

"How about Roy Purdy?" Sully said. "He been in this morning?"

Gert met Sully's eye, then shook his head. "I'm sorry about Ruth."

"You heard?"

"It's all over the street. I wish I could say I'm surprised."

"How about that woman he lives with? Any sign of her?"

"Cora? She was in last night looking for him. Haven't seen her this morning." He was studying Sully carefully now. "You look like you need to eat something besides Maalox."

He wasn't hungry, but Gert was probably right.

"I could probably get Dewey to scramble you a couple eggs," he offered.

Sully rolled his eyes. "Dewey."

Gert gave him an up-to-you shrug that conceded the validity of Sully's misgivings. Dewey was Sully's age, and until midday usually had the shakes so bad he could barely grasp a spatula. Back before Ruth bought Hattie's, he'd been the regular breakfast cook there, but she'd had to let him go when customers at the counter complained they could smell him even when he was grilling onions. Here at Gert's he wasn't ever allowed out of the kitchen, so orders were shouted to him through a closed service window that opened only when he rested a plate of food on the ledge.

"Dewey!" Gert hollered.

"What?" came his reply.

"Scramble Sully a couple eggs! But wash your hands first! You know how particular he is!"

"Fuck him, then!"

"And bacon!" Gert added.

"No bacon!"

"Ham?"

"No ham! Linguica!"

Gert arched an eyebrow at Sully.

"Why not?"

"Well, you *did* just chew two Maalox for heartburn," Gert pointed out.

At which point the front door was flung open and a shaft of bright light pierced the interior gloom. A man Sully vaguely recognized came down the long bar with the confidence of a blind person who knew the layout by heart. Taking the stool next to Gert's, he squinted toward the other end, his eyes adjusting. "Sully?" he said incredulously. "You lost, or did the Horse burn down?"

Gert moved to the row of taps and drew a tall PBR without feeling the need to ask the man if he wanted one. "What's the good word, Freddy?"

"They're letting people back into the Arms," he said, then drained half of his beer and smacked his lips in appreciation.

"They find the snake?"

"Just now," Freddy said. "You're gonna love this. Four of those animal guys in waders up to their asscracks going apartment to apartment. Two hours they're in there. No snake. So they come outside and give the all clear, it's safe to go back inside. One of these fuckwads is holding the door open, and guess what slithers out, right between his legs."

"Yet another government agency to be proud of," Gert chuckled.

"I gotta give the guy credit, though," Freddy said grudgingly after draining the rest of his beer. "He put his boot right down on top of it. That took brass balls, waders or not."

Gert drew him another beer and then returned to Sully, who said in a low voice, "Imagine you're Roy Purdy."

"To what fucking end would I do any such thing?"

Sully ignored this. "You've just violated your wife's restraining order, not to mention the conditions of your parole, and just to make sure you're completely fucked, you beat your mother-in-law half to death. You're stupid, but not retarded. You gotta know this whole deal ends up with you back downstate, which means you're on the clock. Do you run or go to ground?"

When it came to role-playing, Gert, as everyone knew, was without equal. All his life he'd been a sucker for similar conundrums. He leaned one elbow onto the bar to get comfortable. "My car got crushed yesterday, so for me running's a problem."

Sully nodded. "Say you've got your girlfriend's."

Gert snorted. "I don't run anywhere in a half-purple, half-yellow piece of shit that's held together with duct tape. I just don't."

"Then?"

Gert's eyes glazed over and crossed slightly as he dove deeper into his role as violent moron. "I'm scared and they gave me painkillers at the hospital, so I'm not thinking straight. I fall back on what I know."

"You actually know something?"

"Home invasion. Among my few skills is an ability to put my elbow through a pane of glass without cutting myself too bad. Over time I've become something of an expert at reaching inside and unlocking doors by feel."

"It's broad daylight, though. Somebody might see you."

"Point taken. Someplace out of town, then. A house with no neighbors."

"Aren't you worried the owners might return unexpectedly?"

"*They're* the ones should be worried. Because me? At this point, I really don't have much to lose."

Freddy, apparently feeling neglected, called from down the bar. "Gert! You hear they found Joe?"

Gert swam, blinking, back to the surface. Reality, Sully could tell, wasn't nearly as compelling as the adventure he'd just been yanked from. "Where?"

"Lyin' out in the woods. Somebody ran over the poor bastard, then dragged his body out there and left him to die."

Gert shook his head. "I could've told him that straying so far from downtown Bath was a mistake."

"They don't think he'll live," Freddy said. "Who'd do something like that?"

"Some Spinmatic, probably," Sully ventured.

Freddy chuckled appreciatively. "He never could fucking say 'Hispanic.'"

"Unless . . . ," Gert said, lowering his voice and slipping back into character.

"Yeah?" Sully said.

"It's just possible that under duress I remember my very first criminal endeavor, which even now, adjusted for inflation, is one of my biggest paydays. The old Sans Souci. I think to myself, Why not? It's sitting out there in the woods, vacant, nobody to hear the glass shatter when I put my elbow through it." Gert was smiling now, nodding. "The more I think about it, the better I like it. If I'm lucky, I buy myself a couple days. Maybe a week? After things die down, who knows? Maybe I make a clean getaway. Okay, probably not, but stranger things have happened."

"You aren't worried about the caretaker? A stray groundskeeper?"

"Not really. I've heard somewhere that security's provided by a private firm out of Schuyler that swings by a couple times a day. Probably don't go inside at all, and even if they do, so what? They're going to check all two-hundred-plus rooms on the chance some dimwit like me might be hiding in one of them?"

Gert was regarding Sully seriously now, his eyes focused again. He shrugged. "Best I can do. Idiots can be hard to predict."

"Thanks," Sully said, meaning it. "If this pans out, I owe you."

The kitchen window opened, and Sully's breakfast rattled onto the sill. Gert set it down in front of him, along with cutlery wrapped in a paper napkin. "If it pans out," he said, "that's where they'll find your body."

With the food in front of him Sully found that he had something like an appetite, so he dug in. He'd eaten most of it when the phone on the backbar rang. Gert answered it, closing his eyes as if in pain. "Nah, he hasn't been in," he said. "I know . . . right . . . sure thing, Mrs. Gaghan. I'll do that."

Sully pushed his plate away, the linguica suddenly a hot poker under his breastbone. Or maybe it was the thought that if he hadn't taunted Spinmatics Joe at the Horse last night, he would've remained on his stool and avoided the speeding motorist, and his wretched mother would still have a son.

"Here," Gert said, and handed him a towel, having noticed that he'd broken into a sweat. "Spicy, that linguica."

Words to Die By

THE WEATHERED, off-white cargo van caught her attention when she arrived to open the store. Since Kreuner's Country Market—a combination gas station / convenience store / car wash—had been held up twice in the past eighteen months, she was always alert for suspicious vehicles, though more so at night, around closing time, when the register was full. She might not have noticed the van at all if it hadn't sat cockeyed beyond the car-wash bays where nobody ever parked. As always she pulled up beside the Dumpster out back, leaving the more convenient spaces in front for customers. Letting herself in through the rear entrance, she turned on just one bank of lights, enough to see by without announcing to every Tom, Dick and Harry that Kreuner's was open for business. It took fifteen minutes or so to ready the register, reboot the gas pumps and start coffee brewing for the self-serve canisters. It was still percolating when people started lining up outside, anxious to get a cup for the short drive into Schuyler or the longer commute down the interstate to Albany. Inevitably one of them would peer inside, see her going about her business, rap on the door and point at his wristwatch. When this happened, even if it was a couple minutes early, she'd flip the switch that turned on the rotating sign and the overhead fluorescents, unlock the door and begin another day.

She described the driver of the cargo van as disheveled and sleepy eyed, as if he'd spent the night in there and was having a hard time coming fully awake. He claimed to have pulled in just a few minutes before her, then to have drifted off, waiting for her to open, but Karen—the attendant—doubted this was true, though she couldn't say why anyone would lie about something so inconsequential. Nor could she explain why she felt wary about someone so determined to act friendly and harmless. Except for those sleepy eyes, she told Raymer, there was nothing special about how he looked or talked, though she thought maybe he was from somewhere down south. He wore jeans and a white T-shirt that was yellow and stretched at the collar and a baseball cap with some sort of circular logo she didn't recognize. He'd bought coffee, orange juice, a crumb cake and a pack of cigarettes, then said something like *Hey, you know what, as long as I'm here I might as well wash my van.* Again she got the distinct impression he was deliberately trying to mislead her, but to what earthly purpose? It was as if the guy was biding his time, waiting for the other customers to leave, so it'd just be the two of them in the store. She wasn't too worried, though, she said. She kept a can of Mace under the counter. Anyway, she must've been wrong about him, because they'd been alone at one point, and he hadn't tried anything. He just paid up and washed his van and left.

Raymer asked if he paid with a credit card, and she said no, that he'd given her cash, which maybe was a little strange. These days most people paid for purchases of more than ten dollars with credit or debit cards. But even more odd, now that she thought about it, was how he'd backed his rig into the wash bay. She couldn't remember a customer ever doing that before. It was almost like . . .

"Right," Raymer said. *It was almost like he didn't want anybody to see the front of the van.* "Which bay did he use?"

"The far one," she said, which Raymer might've guessed.

Caught in that bay's drain he found a sliver of thick brown glass that was a perfect match for the shards already in his evidence Baggie, and there were other, larger shards in the bottom of the trash bin.

"The mayor still wants to see you," Charice informed him when he returned to the SUV.

"Tell him later. I'm busy."

"I did. He said it's important."

"Tell him to go fuck himself," Dougie barked.

The radio crackled but otherwise was silent.

"Sorry about that," Raymer said. What troubled him most about Dougie's unwelcome interruptions was that they were beginning to feel like a natural physical impulse—a hiccup or one of those irritating dry coughs that wouldn't go away. "I'm sorry. Lack of sleep. Where is he?"

"Out at Hilldale. He said something about the dead being on the move again. Does that make any sense to you?"

Raymer actually heard only the first part. When she said "Hilldale," it reminded him of something that had been nagging him ever since he'd left the cemetery. But what? Something to do with the garage remote? He tried to concentrate and tug whatever was hiding in the back of his brain forward into the front, but the signal was too weak and managed to make the buzzing in his ears grow louder.

"Chief? You there?"

"Sorry, I was thinking."

"So you're heading out there? To Hilldale?"

"Eventually."

"Chief?"

"What, Charice?"

"You're scaring me."

There was a knock on the window, and Raymer jumped. Oh, it was just Karen, the clerk. "Sorry," she said, "but I just remembered something else. When the van pulled out? It was making this funny scraping noise."

"You could hear that inside with the door closed?"

"A customer happened to be leaving right then, so it was open. It was kind of a screech. Like—"

"Metal on a tire?"

"Yeah, like that."

HAROLD PROXMIRE, sole proprietor of Harold's Automotive World since his wife's death, was busy prying a crumpled section of panel away from a cargo van's front tire when Raymer pulled in.

"I had a feeling," he said when Raymer came over and showed him his badge. They stood regarding the vehicle Harold had bought a couple hours earlier. "Stolen?"

"I have no idea," Raymer confessed, "but there's a pretty good chance it was involved in a hit-and-run on County Road last night."

"Who got hit?"

"A man named Gaghan."

Harold shook his head. "I don't think I know him. Dead?"

"Amazingly, no. At least not yet."

"I wondered when I saw that reflector was missing," Harold said, pointing at the side panel. "The guy claimed his kid drove the thing into a ditch, but it's got Georgia plates, and that's a long ways off. There wasn't any blood that I could see."

"He visited the car wash before he came here."

"There was something wrong about him," Harold said.

"How so?"

"Just an idea that struck me as soon as he got out of the van," Harold said. "It was like he hadn't made up his mind about something. It's just me and the kid—Andy—working this morning, and he was around back smoking . . . well, smoking. So it's just me and this guy and his eyes keep wandering around the yard, like, I don't know, maybe he wants to make sure it's just him and me. Then Andy appears, and I see something change behind his eyes. Like he made up his mind right then to sell me the van."

"Instead of?"

"Who knows?" Harold shrugged, ashamed of himself, Raymer could tell. "I don't normally have such thoughts. It's probably the . . ."

"The what?"

"I'm kind of ashamed to admit it."

"I'm not here about you, Mr. Proxmire, if that helps."

"It does, a little. I've got this thing growing in my head. A cyst. Fibrous, they say, not cancer. But they can't operate. Anyway, I get these headaches."

"And smoking dope helps."

"It does. A little, anyways. I know the kid shouldn't be smoking, but

I can't very well tell him he can't when I do. Without him I wouldn't even know how to get it."

"I assume there's paperwork on this vehicle?"

"There is. I'm on the up-and-up here, mostly."

"Mostly?"

"Well, this *is* the car business."

Harold's office was the living room of a single-wide mobile home. He handed Raymer the van's title, which he hadn't even had time to file yet. Raymer wasn't sure what a title issued by the state of Georgia was supposed to look like, but something felt off about the weight of the paper this particular document was printed on. The owner was identified as Mark Ringwald.

"How much did you give him?"

"Thirteen hundred. I told him the van was shot, even before this latest accident. Over two hundred thousand miles. I'd basically be using it for parts. I figured he'd want to dicker, but he didn't. He seemed more interested in me paying in cash. That should've made me suspicious right there."

"You keep that kind of cash around?"

Harold pointed to an ancient safe in the corner. "Have to, in this business."

"So how'd he leave? In a taxi?"

"Andy gave him a lift in the tow truck."

"To Bath?"

"Schuyler. The train station. Said he needed to be in Albany by early afternoon."

"And this was when?"

"Couple hours ago?"

"Is this Andy still here?"

They went outside and Harold hollered for the boy, who appeared from in between rows of junkers. Raymer could smell the marijuana on him from thirty feet away.

"Yo," he said, eyeing Raymer nervously.

Harold regarded the kid and sighed deeply. "Andy," he said, "the person you're addressing here is Mr. Raymer. He's the chief of police in Bath."

The boy stood up straighter. "Oh," he said. "Yo, *sir.*"

"He wants to ask you about the man who sold us the van."

Now it was the kid's turn to sigh. "All I bought was a couple ounces. For my own personal use, I swear." His eyes flickered over to Harold for just a second, then returned to Raymer.

"Andy?" Raymer said, kind of liking the kid. He might be a stoner, but he'd just had the opportunity to throw his boss under the bus and he hadn't.

"Yeah?"

"For future reference? It's better not to answer questions until they're asked."

"Yeah, okay," the boy said. "I can see how that would work." But then he surprised him by taking a quick step backward and pointing at Raymer's hand. "Dude," he said. "Are you, like, a holy man?"

His palm, Raymer realized, was bleeding. Apparently he'd been scratching it again, and the fingernails of his left hand were rust colored. "Far from it," Raymer assured him. "So, Mr. Proxmire says you took the owner of the van to the train station."

The kid nodded but kept staring at Raymer's hand, even when he turned the palm away. "Bill, yeah."

"He told you his name was Bill?"

"Yeah."

Raymer put the hand behind his back, which caused the kid to blink and then finally meet his eye. "What'd you talk about?"

"I told him the bus was way cheaper, but he said he had a thing for trains."

"What else?"

He glanced at Harold again. "He offered me a job if I wanted to come with him."

"Doing?"

"Steady work, was all he said. But I told him I'm not really, like, allowed to leave the county. And he said, 'You gonna spend your whole life doing what other people say?' and I said, 'No, but like I'm *really* not allowed to leave the county,' and he said, 'Yeah, you mentioned that,' and I said, 'What's in the box?' because he'd set his backpack on the floor, but he was holding this box on his knees like it was real important and he wanted me to ask what it was, so I did, and he said if I came to work for him maybe he'd tell me, but I said, 'I'm not kidding, if I leave the county I'm in, like, mega-trouble,' and he said, 'That's three times now you've told me that,' and I said, 'Here we are, this is the train station.'"

"He said he was going to Albany?"

"Yeah, and then somewheres else, Chicago or Denver, someplace like that."

"He volunteered this, or you asked him?"

"He said to come look him up when they let me leave the county, like I could just show up in Chicago or Denver and there he'd be. You gonna arrest me?"

"Not today."

"Thanks, dude," Andy said, clearly relieved, but then alarmed again because Raymer had allowed his hand to slip back into view. "You know, you might really *be* a holy man. You got the mark, dude. It's right there, plain as day."

"You think so?"

"That's what my mother would say. She's real religious."

"Okay, then I got a message for you."

"From who? Like God or something?"

"Or something," Raymer said, holding out his stigmata. "Lay off the weed."

"Okay, I will," the kid said. "I mean it, too."

Back in the SUV, Dougie said, *Are you understanding all this, or do I need to paint you a fucking picture?*

I get it, Raymer told him.

THE TRAIN STATION IN Schuyler Springs was little more than a brick hut and a concrete platform. The small indoor waiting room was empty. A couple sat on the bench outside, the woman asleep with her head on the man's shoulder. Four trains a day ran between Albany and Montreal, two north, two south. The first of the Albany-bound trains had departed an hour ago and the next wasn't until late afternoon.

Raymer showed his badge at the ticket window. "Nice likeness of you in the paper this morning," the man said.

Sensing that Dougie was about to offer a rude rejoinder, Raymer closed his mouth and swallowed hard, which seemed to do the trick. "Thanks," he said. "I'm looking for a guy who might've bought a ticket to Albany this morning. Medium height and build. Wearing a white T-shirt, stretched and yellowing at the collar. Eyes kind of heavy lidded, like he's half asleep. Probably wearing a backpack, possibly carrying a small box or Styrofoam cooler."

"Sorry. Not ringing a bell. You can buy tickets from the machine, though," he said, pointing at one just inside the door.

"Does it take cash?"

The man shook his head. "Plastic only."

"Could I get a readout? Names on the credit cards? That sort of thing?"

"You'd have to call the manufacturer, get them to open it up."

Raymer went over the machine, and it looked like some asshole had scratched off the company's contact info and etched in its place a generic suggestion.

Think, Dougie said.

I am *thinking,* Raymer told him.

Oh. I'll wait, then.

The kid said the guy had a thing about trains.

And you believe him?

Why come here if he wasn't taking a train?

I wonder, what's nearby?

RAYMER PULLED IN TO the bus station just as the coach bound for Montreal was backing out of its bay. The man Raymer was after had told both Harold and Andy about his Albany destination, but . . .

Which direction was he heading when he ran over Gaghan?

North, said Raymer.

Right. So get moving.

Crashing through the depot's double doors, Raymer flashed his badge at a uniformed female employee who, not noticing it and seeing where he was headed and assuming he was late and trying to catch the departing bus, held up both hands and stepped right into him. He heard her grunt at the impact but kept going, having no time to apologize.

About the last thing the bus driver expected to see was someone darting right in front of him, so he was slow to brake and rocked to a halt inches from Raymer's knees.

"Put it in park," Raymer told him when the door whooshed open, then climbed the three steps, holding out his badge so the driver could see. The bus was surprisingly full, with just a few empty seats. "Don't open the doors unless I tell you to."

To his surprise, the man did exactly what he was told without a fuss, looking at Raymer as you would at somebody you knew better than to fuck with. Had anyone ever reacted to him like that before—respect tinged with fear? Not the sort of response anyone should enjoy, Raymer thought, having already enjoyed it.

You see him? Dougie wanted to know.

I sure do.

Last row, by the window. Next to him was one of the few empty seats, which made Raymer smile. Wherever this guy went, people just naturally gave him a wide berth.

You positive?

I just said so.

"Who's he talking to?" Raymer heard a woman ask the fellow she was seated next to.

The bus's air-conditioning was on full blast, and Raymer noted that the man was now wearing a long-sleeved shirt, though the dingy collar of his T-shirt was visible at the neck. The clerk at the market hadn't recognized the circular logo on his hat, and neither did Raymer at first, until he looked more closely and saw it was a stylized snake eating its tail. The eyes beneath the bill were as described—sleepy look-ing, heavy lidded, bored. He was looking out the window—feigning nonchalance?—but Raymer sensed from the cant of his head that he was completely attuned to his approach. Only when Raymer reached his row did the man turn to regard him lazily, a thin, obscene smile playing at his lips.

Don't, Dougie advised, but Raymer sat down next to him anyway. "William Smith, I presume?" he heard himself say at the precise moment he understood this to be true. Because here was not just the hit-and-run driver but also the dealer in poisonous reptiles. Miller had glimpsed him when he was staking out the Morrison Arms last night, the van speeding away once the driver saw the crime-scene tape. A better cop would've given pursuit and pulled the asshole over, and in so doing probably saved the Gaghan man from being run over a few short minutes later. But Miller would have been no match for the guy sitting next to Raymer, and it would've been his body that got dragged into the woods instead of Spinmatics Joe's. The young woman at Kreuner's store and old Harold Proxmire had dimly sensed how lucky they were to have stood so close to this man and still be alive. Even when drunk, Boogie Waggengneckt had understood through his alcoholic fog that the roomful of snakes he was babysitting were a stand-in for something far more deadly. The very thing Raymer was suddenly sitting next to.

Though certain of all this, he knew even better that he wouldn't unholster and point his weapon. If the gun discharged in the crowded bus, who knew how many innocents would fall?

William Smith was grinning at him more broadly now. He'd turned so that his back was flush against the side of the bus. The box in his lap had several small holes punched along its top and sides, and Raymer recognized their purpose.

"Hey, neighbor," the man said.

"I'm going to need you to come with me," Raymer told him. "Quietly, so we don't scare all these folks. Do you understand?"

Smith's smile faded. "Ain't me that needs to understand," he said, releasing the metal clasps on both sides of the box.

"Must be a valuable one," Raymer said, "if you didn't want to leave it behind."

"Oh, it is," he said, raising the lid. "This little fella come all the way from Africa just to make your acquaintance."

It was, Raymer thought, one of the most beautiful things he'd ever seen. Sleek black, with bright red and yellow markings, a lovely coil with no end or beginning, at least until it opened its eyes, which seemed as sleepy as those of its owner. Then it raised its head for a better look at Raymer, who would have liked to move but found he could not. It was as if the law governing cause and effect had been temporarily suspended. Though he hadn't been bitten, the venom was already coursing through his veins, paralyzing him. The good news was that Dougie wasn't similarly constrained. To Raymer's astonishment, he said, in his odd, parrotlike croak, "You're holding an empty box, dumbfuck."

Apparently this was not what William Smith expected to hear. In fact, his surprise was so great that his sleepy eyes went damn near wide open, and in them Raymer was able to read his thoughts: Had the snake somehow escaped? How was that even possible? Leaning forward, he peered over the box's lid.

Raymer had no idea a snake could unhinge its jaw so completely or open its mouth so wide. The whole of Smith's left eyebrow disappeared beneath its triangular head. For what felt like several seconds, it hung there like a brightly colored ribbon, attached to his face, before dropping into his lap. From somewhere behind them came a woman's piercing scream. Then Dougie reached out with Raymer's hand, picked up the snake, returned it to the box and secured the lid. Smith was rubbing his eyebrow, which was already ballooning impressively, and looked at Raymer with something like embarrassment. "Fuck," he said. "I knew better than that."

Words to die by, Raymer thought. Or maybe it was Dougie; he couldn't really tell. At the moment the distinction felt unimportant.

TWENTY MINUTES LATER, back in the SUV and sitting with his eyes closed, his head back against the seat rest, Raymer could feel the familiar old world gradually reassert itself. On the bus it had seemed as if his heart might leap out of his chest like a movie alien, but his breathing was finally returning to normal. Thanks to the air-conditioning, which he'd set on stun, with all the vents pointing directly at him, the sweat was beginning to dry tight on his forehead and the back of his neck. It would have been nice to close the driver's door and let the AC really kick in, but that would mean bringing the snake box inside with him. At the moment it sat on the nearby curb where he could keep an eye on it. Now that the snake no longer posed a threat, his dread of it had re-asserted itself, and every time the box jiggled, he checked to make sure the metal clasps were securely fastened, that the pissed-off demon hadn't somehow managed to spring them.

In the depot things also appeared to be settling down. Several passengers had sustained minor injuries in the panic to rush off the bus, but they were being treated by EMTs. For a time tempers had flared. People seated in front hadn't seen what happened and were annoyed by the delay. Traumatized folks toward the rear refused to reboard until the bus was thoroughly searched and no other snakes were discovered. Raymer had found the whole scene dispiriting, a tableau of human self-ishness, and when two Schuyler cops arrived, he was happy for them to take charge.

Two ambulances had been summoned. William Smith had been loaded into the first, and it had already departed. No siren, nor any need for one. Raymer had stayed with the man as he convulsed, getting off the bus only when that stopped abruptly, midspasm, and he felt his stomach rise. The second ambulance was for the woman Raymer had steamrolled on the platform. He remembered only jostling her, but witnesses reported that he'd knocked her completely off her feet with what they described as a forearm shiver. Raymer had glimpsed her swollen, dazed face as the gurney was eased into the second ambulance. No sooner had it backed out, siren blaring, than Justin's animal-control van pulled into the same space. Taking note of the box sitting on the curb, he came over to Raymer's SUV. "That my snake?" he said, squatting down next to it.

"Make it so," Raymer told him.

Justin checked the clasps, then carried the box to the van, where he put on rubber gloves and grabbed a pair of long-handled tongs before opening it. When the snake curled into a multicolored ball around the metal shafts, Raymer had to look away.

"Okay, then," Justin said when he returned. "I'll go through the coach to make sure there's not another snake."

"There isn't," Raymer told him.

"I know, but it's the protocol. And it'll make the passengers feel better. Stick around, all right?"

Raymer promised he would. At which point he must have dozed off, because he jolted awake when Charice's voice crackled over the radio. "Chief?" she said, sounding frantic. "You there?"

Don't answer, Dougie advised. He'd been silent since they were both on the bus, and Raymer had even dared hope he might be gone, but no such luck. *Let her stew.*

"Something just came over the Schuyler police scanner. A disturbance at the bus station? Is that you?"

Raymer reached for the handset. *You do and I'll bite you myself,* Dougie cautioned.

Oh, please. Raymer's hand was poised over the receiver. *With whose mouth?*

Okay, fine. I can't literally *bite you.*

"They're reporting Bath's chief of police is on the scene," Charice was saying. "There's been a fatality? Please tell me that's not you."

I really have to take this.

Wrong. The fact that she wants to talk to you doesn't necessarily mean you want to talk to her.

But I do want to talk to her.

No, let's be honest. You want to see the tattoo on her ass. For once in your life, play your cards right.

Raymer saw that Justin was returning. "Is it true?" he said, going back into his crouch. "What somebody told me inside? You picked the snake up with your bare hand and put it back in the box?"

Dougie chortled at this. *Yeah, right.* He *picked it up.*

Raymer ignored him, preferring to converse with an actual human being. "Not very smart, I admit."

"Well," Justin said, "FYI? What you grabbed was a coral snake. One of the most lethal reptiles in the world."

"How come it didn't bite me right when he opened the box? It had the chance."

Justin shrugged. "Educated guess? The box was in the guy's lap, right? Next to the AC vent? The cold air probably lowered its internal temperature. It took a couple seconds for it to become alert. Otherwise . . ."

"Right," Raymer said, feeling his stomach churn again.

"You probably don't care about my opinion, but that was a hell of a job you did on that bus."

Dougie snorted.

"What'll happen to the snake?"

"Well, corals are very valuable. Some herpetologist will want it."

"Chief?" Charice was on the radio again.

Justin straightened up. "I'll let you get back to work."

Raymer nodded and picked up the handset. No objection from Dougie this time. "Charice?"

"Thank God," she said, sounding genuinely relieved, maybe even a little bit more than relieved, and Raymer smiled. "Are you okay?"

"Define 'okay.'"

"Unharmed."

"I'm good. The mysterious William Smith, however, is no longer among the living."

"The snake dude? You found him?"

"He was our hit-and-run driver from last night."

Her voice became quiet now, almost reverential. "You had to shoot him?"

"No, he had a snake on the bus, and it bit him."

"Who says there's no justice?"

When Raymer offered no response, she said, "Chief? Are you going to turn this good thing into a bad thing?"

"A man died, Charice."

"Yeah. A very bad man."

"Also, I hurt a woman. She got in my way, and I knocked her down. They just took her away in an ambulance."

"But you didn't mean to."

"No, but I'm still a menace. I'm losing what's left of my mind. There's a voice in my head telling me what to do."

"Don't listen to it."

"Not an option," he told her, beginning to understand that, like it or not, he was stuck with Dougie. Short of being struck by lightning a second time—and the odds against this were famously long—he had no idea how this alter ego might be banished. "Besides. This voice? It's smarter than I am. It told me to go to the bus station. And I never would've found Gaghan in the woods without its help."

"Chief? This voice? If it's in your head, it's you. *You* can't be smarter than *you.*"

"It's telling me not to trust you, Charice."

This seemed to bring her up short. "Me?" she said.

"*Can* I trust you, Charice? You're not in cahoots with Gus, are you? Because—"

"It's you I work for, not the damn mayor. You."

"Tell Jerome if he wants my job, he can have it."

"He doesn't."

"Charice?"

"Yes, Chief?"

"I'm sorry if I've stood in your way. On the job. You're my best officer. It's just . . . I don't want you to get hurt."

"I know. You said already you're in love with me."

"You keep leaving out the *maybe,*" he told her. Then, looking up, he added, "Uh-oh."

"What's that mean? 'Uh-oh'?"

"The News Channel 6 van just pulled in."

"Good," she said. "Go take a bow. You nabbed a criminal. Removed a public menace. Solved two cases."

"I'd just say something stupid. I'm not happy until you're happy. That sort of thing."

"Actually?" Charice pointed out. "You said it right that time."

"See?" he said, turning the key in the ignition. "Even when I'm right, I'm wrong."

"Please tell me you'll go out to Hilldale. The mayor's calling every fifteen minutes . . ."

After the word "Hilldale" her voice gradually faded into the ambient buzzing in his ears. What he'd been trying to recall earlier, its signal too weak to pull in, was nagging at him again, the connection stronger now.

"Charice?" he said. "Send Miller out there. To the cemetery. Get the custodian to let him into the maintenance shed."

"What for?"

"Because that's where our stolen wheel boots are."

"And you know this how?"

"Call it a hunch."

The radio was silent for a beat, then, "Chief?"

"Yeah?"

"You can't resign."

"Why not?"

"You're just getting good."

HALFWAY BACK to Bath, stalled at a red light, he felt the buzzing in his ears spike and knew what that meant. And sure enough: *Happy now?*

No, Raymer told him.

You're grinning.

How would you know?

I feel it. I can feel you grinning.

Okay, maybe I'm a little happy. Would that be okay with you?

You could thank me.

What for?

Letting you flirt, uninterrupted, with Butterfly Girl, he said. Then, after a pause, *She's playing you like a fiddle.*

Again, how the fuck would you know?

You just don't get it, do you? What you *know, I* know. *That's the deal.*

I trust her, Raymer insisted.

It's your funeral.

A horn honked, and in his rearview mirror Raymer saw that another car had pulled up behind him. Distracted by his conversation with Dougie, he'd evidently sat through a green light. He waved back at the guy in apology.

Then he decided to try a different tack. *If I asked you a question, would you answer me honestly?*

Ask away.

Becka's lover? Do you know who he is?

Sure. So do you.

Sully's son, right? All those times she claimed she was out with her theater friends at that wine bar . . . Adfinitum?

Infinity.

She was actually meeting him.

Raymer had seen Peter Sullivan around town. Good looking. Well dressed, in that tweedy college fashion. Clearly educated. Did something out at the college, Raymer didn't know exactly what. Definitely the sort of man Becka would've been drawn to. They could talk about books and plays and art and music. The kind of guy she should've married to begin with, who'd help her understand what a mistake she'd made in ever taking up with Douglas Raymer.

The driver behind him was honking his horn again, though Raymer ignored him.

Anyway, here's what I'm coming to realize, Dougie. So what? Fine. I don't care.

Bullshit.

I thought I did, but if this with Charice . . .

Finish one lunacy, please, before you begin another.

Becka's dead. It's all finished. Not finding that garage-door remote was a sign. Charice is right. It's time to move on.

More honking, louder now, the guy really laying on the horn. Raymer felt like his head might explode.

Dougie gave him a Bronx cheer. *Listen to yourself.*

Yeah? Well, listening to you almost got me killed.

You think you can be shut of me that easily?

Maybe not. I don't know. Maybe I'm stuck with you. But that doesn't mean you give the orders. I'm in charge here, not you.

Now the horn was one long, steady blast. Raymer closed his eyes, but this only seemed to intensify the sound, as if the horn was right in his own car. The light was green again, but it turned red before he could step on the gas. The driver behind him was apoplectic, his fat face beet red with rage as he kept laying on the horn, urging Raymer through the intersection. Rolling down the window, the man poked his head out and shouted, "Hey, asshole! What the fuck's *wrong* with you?"

The change that registered on the man's face when Raymer got out of the SUV and came toward him was gratifying to behold, rage segueing into misgiving and then pure fright. His window hummed up again, and the door lock thunked. Slapping his badge up against the windshield with his left hand, Raymer motioned with his right for him to roll down his window. The guy looked from the badge to Raymer's face, then back to the badge and finally to the ugly stigmata on his palm, as if trying to resolve conflicting testimony. That this was obviously a policeman seemed reassuring enough for him to roll the window back down and offer Raymer a sheepish, toothy grin, which vanished under the impact of Raymer's fist. The man's head swiveled violently to the right, spittle flecking the passenger-side window, and he slumped forward in the seat, his body held upright by the seat belt. When Raymer saw that the man's eyes had rolled back in their sockets, he felt a surge of well-being. *This,* it occurred to him, was how Sully felt all those years ago when he'd punched *him* in the face. Why, he wondered, had he denied himself the pleasures of physical violence for so long? It was a shame, in fact, that there was only one belligerent asshole in the car, because it would've felt good to coldcock a few more. The static in his ears was almost as loud as the honking had been, but as he went back to his car he found himself happily humming a tune from a couple decades earlier and recalled the lyric: *I'd rather be a hammer than a nail.*

The light was green again, so he put the SUV in gear and proceeded cautiously through the intersection. The car behind him didn't budge, grew smaller in the mirror and, when Raymer turned onto the Bath road, disappeared altogether. After he'd gone about half a mile, the buzzing quieted, and he pulled over on the shoulder and adjusted the rearview so he could examine in its rectangle the face that had so frightened the asshole back there. If he'd shown that face to Becka, he wondered, would she have stayed in love with him? Was this what women wanted? Even what *he* wanted?

Returning the mirror to its proper position, he was looking straight at his palm. The ghost staple was still visible at its center, but the red, swollen, probably infected area around it had doubled in size and now resembled a bullet wound. He scratched it, hard.

Harder. What ecstasy.

Tell me again, said Dougie. *Who's in charge here?*

Home

WITH THE HOTEL SHUTTERED, the road through Sans Souci Park was blocked off, but a narrow, unpaved and rutted service road ran just inside the stone wall that bordered the property. A PRIVATE: NO TRESPASSING sign was nailed to a tree at the entrance. When Sully ignored it, Rub cocked his head and regarded him dubiously. "I see it," Sully told him. There were times when he suspected the little fucker could read.

In response the dog sneezed violently.

"I don't want to hear it. Just sit there and behave, or I'll take you back and lock you in the trailer."

Rub sneezed again, even louder, perhaps indicating that he considered this an empty threat, which it was.

The road wound through the tall pines for a good half mile before running into an empty small parking lot behind the hotel. Disappointed not to find the multicolored car he was looking for, Sully pulled in to the lot and parked anyway.

"Twenty minutes," he told Rub, figuring that if he could read maybe he could tell time as well. "If you're not back by the time I'm done, I'm leaving you here. Understand?"

Rub appeared to, because he commenced leaping with joy, his skull encountering the cab's roof with a bang, which had to hurt, though apparently not enough to prevent further leaps with the same results.

"Stop, before you kill yourself," Sully said, leaning across him to open the passenger door. "Twenty minutes!" he called as Rub disappeared around the corner of the hotel, with the whole of Sans Souci Park to race around in.

Alone now, he turned the engine off and let the past wash over him. Strange, when he thought about it. The park was no more than a hundred yards from Miss Beryl's house, but it had been years since he'd been on the grounds. As a boy, at least for a time, there'd been no place he loved more.

After an earlier incarnation of the hotel closed, his father had been hired by the estate as its principal custodian and caretaker. It was his job to make sure that the weather wasn't blowing in through some broken window, that burst pipes and other problems were promptly reported, the damage contained. The most valuable furniture and fixtures had been put in storage or sold off when the hotel closed, but there was still plenty of stuff worth stealing, and it was Big Jim's job to provide a visible presence to discourage thieves and late-night partiers out in the woods, where they left their empty whiskey bottles behind. It was also his job, or so he told Sully and Patrick, his older brother, to run off local boys who, if they were allowed to, would scale the wrought-iron fence and chew up the elegant lawns with their football games. There was no part of his job that Big Jim took more seriously than putting the fear of God into those lawless little bastards.

Sully and his brother, on the other hand, were given the run of the property. Mostly that meant exploring the woods, pretending, as boys will, to get lost, though in reality this was impossible. The park's many trails eventually wound through the trees and back to the hotel, and you couldn't walk more than half a mile in any direction without encountering the stone wall or a perimeter fence that in turn would lead you to either the Schuyler entrance at one end or the Bath entrance at the other. In foul weather, though, if their father was in an expansive mood, he allowed them indoors and gave them more or less free rein to explore the hotel, so long as they didn't break anything. In the ballroom, where the remnant furniture was gathered into one corner and draped with sheets, their favorite activity was to get a running start and slide in their socks across the burnished floor, until one day Patrick caught a nail that gashed his foot from toe to heel, earning him thirty-some stitches. The library sported a massive pool table with leather pockets, useless to them until one day they managed to pick the lock on a nearby closet containing several cue sticks, a rack, a bridge and a set of balls minus, for some reason, the eight. Because the floor had a slight slope, over time the table's surface had gone several bubbles off of plumb, which Sully and his brother learned to accommodate and even enjoy. Hit your shots with just the right speed and touch, and you could actually bend your ball around another inconveniently in its path and let gravity pull it into the corner pocket. Because he learned to play on this table, Sully imagined that the incline was part of the game's design, and years later, when he took it up again, he had to relearn the game completely. He never did love playing on a level surface nearly as much, minus the thrilling element of gravity.

So vast and wondrous a property would have been any boy's dream, but for Sully and his brother it was also a refuge from their unhappy home on Bowdon Street, where their poor mother was a virtual prisoner, too ashamed to leave the house because she often sported a black eye or a fat, busted lip. Big Jim, who gave her these, was by contrast hail-fellow-well-met in all the neighborhood taverns, where, as unofficial lord of the Sans Souci, he held court and dispensed his not-terribly-secret largesse. Given his numerous and varied responsibilities, he considered himself poorly compensated, which in his view justified his lucrative sideline. Despite not offering many amenities—the water and electricity having been turned off in all but a handful of the rooms—he was still able to rent them out by the hour at very reasonable rates, more than doubling his custodial salary. Indeed, on occasion he was said to take women there himself.

People warned him, of course, that it was just a matter of time before his high jinks were discovered and he got fired, but Big Jim refused to listen. After all, the men he reported to lived in Albany and New York City. Having lived his entire life in Bath, he had a distorted sense of distance. The former, thirty-five minutes away by car since the completion of the Northway, seemed to him well out of range, and the latter might've been on the other side of the moon. How could men living so far away know what he was up to? They had their hands full dealing with the warring factions of the family that held a majority stake in the property and couldn't agree on what to do with it. Better yet, when these same men visited the Sans Souci with a prospective buyer, they always announced their intention many days in advance so Big Jim could make sure everything was shipshape.

What eluded Sully's father was that not much ever happened here that they didn't hear about eventually. What protected him wasn't so much their cluelessness as the fact that they themselves didn't own the place. If he had a modest concession going on the side, what did they care? If he acted like a big shot around town, if he was a loudmouth and a braggart and a bore who exaggerated his own importance to the Sans Souci and sometimes treated the hotel as if he owned it, well, it was no skin off their asses. They were either lawyers or in the employ of lawyers, which meant their primary concern was liability. Yes, they wanted Big Jim to keep unauthorized people off the property, but mostly to prevent the possibility of a lawsuit if they got injured. Did they know he was a drunk? Sure. Did they mind? Not particularly. Caretakers of large estates generally ran to alcoholism.

They did, however, mind that he was a smoker, especially since he'd assured them he wasn't in his job interview. A century earlier the original Sans Souci had burned to the ground, and while the current owners could agree on little else, they were absolutely determined that their hotel should not burn down until they decided to do it themselves and collect the insurance. Discovering cigarette scorch marks on the furniture, the owners' representatives repeatedly reminded him that smoking was a firing offense, and each time Big Jim promised to quit, claiming he'd been meaning to anyway and this was the very incentive he needed. And, yeah, sometimes he'd actually try to quit for a week or two. By the time they visited again, though, he'd have relapsed. The pack of Camels would be visible through his thin shirt pocket, and a full ashtray that he'd forgotten to hide would be sitting there in the library, and there were fresh burn marks on the oak bar where he liked to entertain women before leading them off to a room with a bed. Then, yet again, they'd read him the riot act and say this was positively his last warning, that next time he'd be replaced. Plenty of men in Schuyler County were looking for work.

Why did they give him so many final chances? Well, groveling before men in suits was one of Big Jim's few real skills. And of course these men were anxious to return to Albany and New York City, so he never had to grovel for long. Though they threatened to check up on him more regularly, he knew they hated visiting the Sans Souci and wouldn't unless they were forced to. True, this abasement left a bad taste in his mouth, and Sully and his brother knew to steer clear after he'd been dressed down, but the humiliation lasted for only a week or two, after which their father's sense of well-being and self-worth always returned, along with his boastful arrogance. "Where the hell do they think they're gonna find somebody who doesn't smoke?" he would ask rhetorically. "For the kind of money they pay?"

Like so many men who resent the authority of others, Big Jim hated for his own to be questioned. Sully and Patrick certainly knew better. The same, however, could not be said of the local boys who ignored the KEEP OUT signs posted at regular intervals along the perimeter fence, signs that ironically provided an additional foothold when they climbed over. Though they were the least of his problems, their father managed to convince himself otherwise, telling anyone who'd listen that if these little assholes were allowed to run rampant, playing football and tearing up the pristine lawns, he'd lose his job. He seemed not to understand that the sport they enjoyed even more than football was goofing on Big Jim Sullivan. Quick and nimble where he was slow, lumbering and—depending on the time of day—inebriated, they taunted him relentlessly into giving chase. When he did, they scattered like roaches to every point on the compass, forcing him to decide which of the bastards to pursue, not that it mattered. There wasn't a sick wildebeest in this particular herd, nor was Big Jim the lion of his imagination. The boys particularly enjoyed letting him get close. One would pretend to fall or twist an ankle, only to leap away like a gazelle at the last second, scamper over the fence, drop down just out of arm's reach on the other side and blow Big Jim a rich wet strawberry for his efforts. For them, their pursuer was nothing short of a marvel. How effortlessly their antics brought him to a full boiling rage. What was wrong with the guy? How could he fall for the same tricks every day, seemingly incapable of learning from experience, no matter how recent or vivid? They loved, as only thirteen-year-old boys could, his inept malignancy, perhaps glimpsing in this the greater adult world they were about to enter, where rules were made and enforced by fools of every stripe. Seen in this light, wasn't mocking Big Jim Sullivan a moral imperative? With the wrought-iron fence between them and him, it must've seemed to be.

Still, how could such fine sport not end badly? How entirely predictable was it that eventually a boy would lose his grip while scaling the fence? And so, one day, it did. An iron spike atop the fence entered a boy's throat just below his chin and exited his stunned, open mouth. Two of his pals claimed it wasn't really an accident, that he never would've slipped if this large, powerful man hadn't given the fence a great shake. Big Jim denied this, claiming the wrought-iron fence was too sturdy and heavy to budge at all. Whatever the truth, the boy hung there like a hooked fish, his arms flailing frantically at first, then dangling, useless and limp, at his sides. The fire department was summoned, and the boy, deep in shock, was finally lifted free of the spike, after several horrible failed attempts. Astonishingly, he survived.

But the incident was the last straw, and it cost Big Jim his job, making his prediction of what would get him fired seem prescient. To hear him tell it, he lost his job for *doing* it, and what the hell kind of justice was that? As if in all other respects he'd been a model employee. Nor in the weeks and months that followed was he ever able to understand why the incident occasioned such an outpouring of moral outrage from the community. Given how viciously people turned on him, you'd have thought he'd done something wrong. Now that he was unable to treat them to a room at the Sans Souci, his former friends, ingrates all, behaved as if he were some sort of monster. Clearly, they'd been jealous of his status all along and loved reveling in his misfortune. It was enough to give a man grave doubts about the entire human race.

Losing his employment at the Sans Souci sparked Big Jim's final long descent into the bottle. A social drunk before, he became a deeply solitary one afterward—silent, morose, self-pitying, aggrieved. His wife bore the brunt of his moods, as she always had, though Sully absorbed his own share of verbal and physical abuse. "Don't talk back," his mother pleaded on the few occasions he stood up for her. "It just makes him worse." Sully couldn't see where this was true at all. Cowering and weakness were as likely to provoke and intensify his father's rages as confrontation. Patrick was a case in point. For reasons Sully could never fathom, he often took their father's side, despite faring no better than his brother. He was two years older, though, which meant he got to escape the house on Bowdon Street that much sooner. At the time Sully thought his brother a coward for abandoning their mother, but he did the same thing himself when his turn came.

In a sense he'd left home even earlier. As a high-school junior he tried out for football, and Clive Peoples, Miss Beryl's husband and North Bath's coach, impressed by his recklessness, took him under his wing. He and his wife, who'd been his eighth-grade English teacher, opened their home to him, and by senior year he was spending more time in their Upper Main Street home than he did on Bowdon Street. Sully tried his best to earn his keep and repay their many kindnesses, shoveling their sidewalks and driveway in the winter, mowing their lawn in the summer and, in autumn, raking the mountain of leaves that fell from the ancient elms that lined their street, duties that otherwise might have fallen to their son, Clive Jr., a soft boy four years younger than Sully who seemed happy enough for him to assume the role of older sibling. Less work for him, in effect. Sully was not only clever with tools but also unafraid of starting jobs he wasn't sure he knew how to finish, and the elder Clive was delighted by how handy he was becoming. It was Miss Beryl who understood his motivation. Any task that kept Sully away from Bowdon Street was worth undertaking. He'd enlisted right after graduation, telling neither of his parents until it was time for him to report. Though his mother might've seen it coming, she didn't have a clue.

"You're leaving?" she repeated, stunned by his announcement, as he stood there in the kitchen, his duffel bag slung over his shoulder. The look on her face was the same one she always wore in the instant before one of his father's ringing head slaps.

"You're *staying?*" he replied heartlessly.

She glanced nervously into the front room, where his father sat with the drapes drawn, as usual, the television on but the sound turned down. Sully couldn't remember the last time they'd spoken but was certain the old man, despite his typically feigned disinterest, was listening. "Why would I leave?"

What she was really asking, of course, was: *Where would I go? How would I live? Who would pay?* Having no answers to these questions, he told her what she already knew. "He treats you like a dog. Worse."

Again, she glanced fearfully into the front room. "He just has a bad temper, is all."

"No, he's mean and stupid and a coward. And that's before he starts drinking." Thinking, *Come out here, old man. Come out here and take your medicine if you don't like what I'm saying.* Ready to set down the duffel bag and go at it right there in the kitchen, if necessary.

"Deep down," she said, "he loves us."

"No, he doesn't."

She lowered her voice. Pleading. "If I leave, he won't have anybody."

"He doesn't deserve anybody."

She took his hand, then. "You don't have to be hard," she said, "just because the world is."

No? he thought. Because he'd come to the exact opposite conclusion. America would soon be at war, and he would be in it. *Hard* would be what was called for, he knew that much. Which was why he'd kissed her goodbye that morning but left without so much as glancing into the front room, already the kind of hard his mother hoped he wouldn't become.

It wasn't, unfortunately, the kind that would have allowed him to slip out of town without saying goodbye to Miss Beryl. He thought about it, though. Unlike her husband, she hadn't been enthusiastic when she learned Sully had enlisted. When he asked her why, whether she thought the coming war was wrong, she'd replied that all wars were, to one degree or another, but it wasn't that, not really. And while she feared he might be killed, this wasn't it, either. What truly frightened her, she explained, was the violence he would be doing to himself. He wasn't just placing himself at risk; he was putting his *self* at risk, the same self that

Thoreau thought was worth defending and protecting, the self whose primacy Emerson had argued for. (They'd read "Civil Disobedience" and "Self-Reliance" in her eighth-grade class.) The young, she claimed, were always being asked to risk who they really were, deep down, before they'd even had the opportunity to become acquainted. In her view it was wrong to ask them to gamble something they didn't even know they possessed, much less what it might be worth. "Also," she added, "I fear you may have enlisted for the wrong reasons."

"Why do you think I did?" he asked, curious as to how well she understood him.

"I suspect"—she sighed—"because you're young and you didn't know what else to do."

Though he *was* young, he hadn't liked being reminded of it, and he enjoyed even less that this tiny, bent woman who'd been so kind to him should also be so wise and, not just wise, but wise to him as well. Somehow she always managed to outflank him, which gave him little choice but to retreat into youthful bravado he didn't really feel. "I just think," he told her, "that somebody needs to hand Adolf his hat." In response, she'd given him that kind, knowing smile of hers, the one that said she understood him perfectly, as always.

All that had been the week before he left. Now, when he arrived at their house, Coach Peoples was sitting on the porch reading the newspaper. Setting down his duffel, Sully climbed the porch steps and they shook hands.

"So you're off, then," the coach said, prolonging the handshake.

"Yes, sir." Sully nodded.

"Off to hand Adolf his hat."

Which made Sully smile. Miss Beryl had repeated what he'd said to her, and not unkindly, he felt certain.

"She's inside, Sully," Clive Sr. told him, giving him a look that said all too clearly that he understood how difficult—okay, impossible—this goodbye was going to be, that women in general and this one in particular wanted not just everything you had but also, and especially, what you didn't have and never would. And in return they'd offer what you didn't want or had no use for or, even worse, was good for you. Which was precisely what Miss Beryl did when she looked up and saw him standing there in the kitchen doorway. "Might I entice you with a cup of tea?" she said, as if young men his age had a long, storied history of being so enticed.

"I hate tea," he told her for the umpteenth time, but then, not wanting to hurt her feelings on this special occasion, he relented. "Okay, maybe just this once."

It did seem to cheer her, that and the fact that he took a seat at the kitchen table. "Cream and sugar?"

"Will that make it taste like beer?"

"Donald," she said, setting the steaming cup down in front of him. "How I hate to see you go."

"I know. You said."

"I'm sorry. I had no business trying to talk you out of your decision. I'd forgotten how stubborn you are."

No point arguing that, so he didn't. He took a sip of tea, made a face and pushed the cup away. "Good God."

But she was serious now. "You must tell me. How did you leave things at home?"

He looked around the kitchen. "This is more my home than that place," he said.

"Oh, your poor mother," she said.

"I would never say that to her," Sully assured her.

"I know, Donald, but if you think it, she feels it. Don't you know that?"

"How can I not feel what I do feel?"

"You have a point there."

He smiled. "I do?"

"You do," she said. "You often do. That doesn't mean I have to agree with it. Dare I ask how you parted with your father?"

"With him in one room and me in another."

She gave him a puzzled look. "Do you understand forgiveness?"

"The concept, I guess."

"I mean how it works."

"Somebody's an asshole and you tell him it's okay?"

"That's a willful misrepresentation."

"As in untrue?"

"As in half true."

"Well, at least I got half. Why are you smiling like that?"

"Because I'm going to miss your company," she said.

"I'll miss yours, too," he told her. "And Coach's."

"But mine a bit more."

He turned to look over his shoulder, to make sure the man was still out on the porch and not standing behind him, awaiting his answer. "I guess," he said, surprised to realize it was true and a little ashamed for what felt like a betrayal of a man who'd treated him more like a son than his own father ever had.

"We don't forgive people because they deserve it," she said. "We forgive them because *we* deserve it."

"I guess that's something I don't understand."

She shrugged. "Guess what? I don't, either. It's true, though."

"Maybe I'll feel more forgiving when I get back."

"You *do* know that there's such a thing as being too late?"

He did, but with a young man's comprehension, confident but incomplete. "You're smiling again," he told her.

She pointed at his cup. "You drank your tea."

It was true. He didn't remember doing so, nothing beyond that first awful taste, but the cup was empty, and in his chest there was now a warm glow.

"One day you'll know yourself," she predicted. "Your *self,* I mean to say."

"You think so?"

"Yes," she said, gathering their cups. "I do."

She was releasing him, he realized with a shock, to the looming war. Was it her affection, he wondered, that made him feel afraid for the first time? That made him want to stay here in her warm kitchen? He couldn't, of course, and they both knew it. The die had been cast, and he himself had rolled it.

Word of his father's death came when he was in England during the final days of preparation before Normandy. News of his mother's didn't reach him until Paris. When he returned stateside, what seemed like a hundred years later, he'd visited their side-by-side graves. Just the once, though. Because standing there in Hilldale he'd felt nothing, which meant, he supposed, that Miss Beryl had been right; there was indeed such a thing as being too late. Normandy, the hedgerows, the Hürtgen Forest, the camps and finally Berlin . . . they all added up to this: too late. Had he found himself in war, as young men were often thought to do? Perhaps. He'd acquitted himself well in battle, proven competent in the face of fear. But had he also lost something he wasn't sure he possessed to begin with? Had his *self,* the one Miss Beryl was worried about, been harmed? He remembered the look on her face when she first saw him again, an expression comprising relief and the old affection, but also a recognition that the boy who'd gone away to war both was and wasn't the man who returned from it.

IT WAS MOST LIKELY a waste of time, and Sully, suddenly feeling unequal to the task he'd set for himself, thought about just letting it go. If Roy Purdy was here at the Sans Souci, the half-purple, half-yellow beater most likely would be in the lot. Still, it was possible he'd just had the Cora woman drop him off, so Sully took the tire iron just in case. The hotel's delivery door was locked tight, and there was no sign of forced entry, so he methodically surveyed the perimeter, checking doors at various entry points and looking for broken windows. It took him close to half an hour, and by the time he returned to the lot, exhausted, another vehicle was there, a late-model Lincoln Town Car. Its owner was a large, soft-looking man who appeared to be in his early to midsixties. He wore reflecting sunglasses and a dark, carefully trimmed beard, probably to disguise his weak chin. Bald on top, he'd let his hair grow long on the back and sides and gathered it in a ponytail. He was bending down to scratch Rub's ears, causing the dog to emit tiny, euphoric blasts of urine.

He straightened up when he saw Sully approaching with a tire iron and looked relieved when he tossed it into the truck. "Cute little mutt," he said. "Shame about his . . ."

"Dick?"

"Yeah. How'd it get like that?"

"He chews on it."

"You can't make him stop?"

"I haven't tried," Sully said, opening the driver's door. "It's his dick."

"Yeah, but—"

"Let's go, Dummy," Sully said, stepping aside so Rub could scrabble up onto the seat.

"I'm thinking about buying this place," the man said, taking off his dark glasses.

It was on the tip of Sully's tongue to say, *Bully for you,* but he held it.

"Well, not for myself," the man added, as if Sully had challenged his statement. Without the glasses he looked vaguely familiar. "I represent a developer."

"Right," Sully said, getting into the truck to signal his complete disinterest in whatever the hell this guy was doing there.

"Time-shares," he continued, apparently oblivious. "You're familiar with the concept?"

"Not really," Sully said, turning the key in the ignition. The man's disappointment made him look even more familiar. "Do I know you?"

Was that a smile? The man's beard shifted, so maybe. Or was it a grimace?

"You might've seen me in town. I've been around a couple days, talking to people. Getting the lay of the land, so to speak. You live around here?"

Sully nodded.

"You like it?"

He shifted into reverse, determined to make his getaway. "Never really thought about it," he said. "It's home, is all."

"Home," the man repeated, as if Sully had said something profound. "Right."

Sully backed up, did a three-point turn and returned to the service road, where he glimpsed the man in his rearview. Shifting into reverse, he backed into the lot. The man strolled over and said, "Hi, Sully."

He extended his hand through the open window. "Hello, Clive."

Dougie Reneges

THOUGH NOW HALF its former size, the section of Hill sitting in the middle of the road looked only slightly less bizarre under the bright afternoon sun than it had under last night's full moon. The partially exposed caskets had been dug out of the turf and loaded onto a flatbed, presumably to be interred again somewhere else. Raymer recognized Sully's odd friend Rub Squeers among the men hacking away with pickaxes and spades at what remained of the wandering hill, no doubt searching for other caskets. Overseeing this work were Mayor Gus Moynihan; the town manager, Roger Graham; and Arnie Delacroix, from Public Works, who was in charge of Hilldale's day-to-day operations.

Gus was talking on his cellular telephone but was the first to notice Raymer's approach. He quickly hung up, slipping the phone into its pretentious little holster. "Here he is," he proclaimed, "our man of the hour."

Unsure how sarcastic this was, Raymer simply said "Here" and handed Gus the envelope that contained his resignation. The other two men were staring at him, slack jawed, so he said, "What?"

"You look . . . ," Roger began, then paused, apparently stumped for the right word.

"Demented?" Arnie suggested.

"Yes, that's it," Roger confirmed.

Dougie, Raymer figured, staring out at these men. As if Raymer had given him permission to make his presence known and felt.

"Is that *blood* on your forehead?" Arnie wanted to know. "And in your *hair?*"

"Not to mention on your shirt?" Roger said, pointing at the rust-colored smudges on Raymer's sleeve.

Gus was now examining Raymer's envelope with distaste, because it, too, bore traces of blood.

"Sorry," said Raymer, reluctantly showing them the palm of his right hand.

"Whoa!" All three men stepped back.

"What *is* that?" Roger demanded. "A gunshot wound?"

Raymer couldn't blame him for thinking so. That's what it looked like. The swelling was worse than the last time he looked, the skin an angrier red. His fingers looked like overcooked sausages, and the wound itself was oozing. "It's sort of a burn," he told them. "It itches."

"It's infected, is what it is," Gus said, horrified. "Go to the emergency room and have it looked at. That's an order."

"Aren't you going to read that?" Raymer asked, proud of his perfect if tiny rhetorical triangle.

"No need," Gus said, folding the envelope and putting it in his jacket pocket. "Charice already told me. You can't quit. Okay, it's true. This morning when I saw that picture in the newspaper I was ready to carve out your gizzard with a butter knife, but since then you took out a major bad guy single-handedly. Saved a bunch of people on that bus from being snakebit."

Raymer, though pleased by the positive spin Gus was putting on those events, was all too aware that the truth was different. William Smith, or whatever his real name might be, was at best a minor bad guy who'd taken himself out. Nor had Raymer really saved anybody from being snakebit. If he hadn't tried to arrest Smith, the snake would've remained safely in the box.

"And it looks like that man you found out in the woods is going to make it. Joe Whatever. That was first-rate police work. You saved his life."

"I'm still quitting, though."

If Gus heard this he gave no sign, and before Raymer could prevent him he reached up and put a hand on his forehead. "Jesus, Doug, you're burning up. Go to the hospital and get on antibiotics for that hand. And eat some ibuprofen. Then go home and make yourself presentable. You can't go on television looking like Jeffrey Dahmer."

"Television?"

"The evening news shows."

"Not a chance. You have my resignation in your pocket."

"Never happened. You never wrote it."

"I can't go on TV. I'll look like a fool."

"I'll be right there with you."

"Then we'll both look like fools."

"It'll be a piece of cake. They'll ask you what happened and you tell them."

"Tell them what?"

"The truth."

"And when they ask me about the photo in the *Dumbocrat*?"

"They won't. I just got off the phone with one of the producers. All they care about is the bus station. They want you to be a hero."

"What if they ask me about digging up the judge?"

"They won't, I'm telling you."

"Wait," said Arnie. "Somebody dug up *Judge Flatt*?"

"Of course not," Gus told him. "Doug's just exhausted and confused. Look at him. The man's hallucinating."

"Yeah, but do we want him on television?" Roger asked, not unreasonably.

"He just needs some antibiotics to bring his fever down," Gus said. "That and a nap. He can sleep in the car. He'll be fine. In fact, show the reporters your hand. Tell 'em it's a snakebite. They'll eat it up."

Just then Raymer heard his name being called and saw Miller hurrying toward him excitedly. "Guess what?" he said.

"You found the wheel boots?"

"In the maintenance shed. Right where you said they'd be. How'd you know, Chief?"

"You can stop calling me that. I just resigned."

Miller looked genuinely terrified at this news, as if it meant he himself would now be given the position. Which probably would happen in the fullness of time. It *had* happened to Raymer, after all. "You can't resign, Chief."

"That's what I just told him," Gus said, and Miller nodded eagerly, happy to have his judgment confirmed by someone in authority.

"Just watch me," Raymer said.

Roger was now wincing like people do at a horror movie whose plot involves a chain saw.

"What?" Raymer said.

"Stop scratching it!" the other man screamed.

YOU SHOULD THINK about it, said Dougie.

What?

Going on TV.

No chance.

Just let me do the talking.

Yeah, right.

It was tempting, though. Not that he considered himself a hero. But it did buoy his spirits to think that Gus was willing to pretend he was one on live television. They wouldn't be telling any outright lies. If Joe Gaghan survived his injuries, then Raymer had, in fact, saved a life. By all accounts the life of a complete fucking asshole, but still. At least his mother would be happy. It was also true that he really had done some solid police work in locating William Smith. Okay, he hadn't, as Gus suggested, pulled it off single-handedly. It was Dougie who'd led him, practically by the nose, from evidence to inference to hypothesis to solution, by asking all the right questions. And when Raymer had been paralyzed by the sight of the serpent, it was Dougie who'd snatched it and put it back in the box. Still, he'd used Raymer's hand, so that was something.

We're a team, said Dougie, who as usual was eavesdropping. *That's how you should think of it. As a partnership.*

Except you don't exist, Raymer replied. *You're an electrical charge, and as soon as I finish here I'm heading to Gert's and drinking beer for the rest of the afternoon and evening. And every time I go to the head I'm going to piss a little bit of you onto the urinal cakes. That's how* you *should think of it.*

Where are we going? Dougie wanted to know.

You know where.

Yeah, but why?

Fuck off, Raymer barked, surprised that his voice sounded more like Dougie's than his own. *Leave us alone.*

Becka's grave looked different now. The rose petals that had blanketed the ground last night had mostly blown away, the few remaining now brown and curling in the sun, along with the denuded, thorny stems. Farther down the row, under a hedge, Raymer spotted the plastic cone that had held the roses her boyfriend had left there. *Always,* Peter Sullivan had written. Why not name him? Raymer had made the identical pledge to the same woman before God and family and friends, both he and Becka swearing *I do,* only to discover a few short years later that they didn't. With her death *Always* had transitioned to *Nevermore* for all three of them.

The sky above was a deep, reassuring cloudless blue that Raymer found gratifying. In the unlikely event that Ghost Becka actually existed, if she was still intent on frying him, she'd have a hell of a time manufacturing a charge out of such benign atmospherics. Best not to taunt her, though, so he just said, "It's me, Becka. I'm back. How about that, right? Two visits in twenty-four hours after none for . . ." He paused here, deciding on a new tack. "I've been doing some soul-searching, and I just wanted you to know . . ." But this thought trailed away as well.

What *did* he want her to know? That he forgave her? (He wasn't sure about this.) That he understood? (Did he?) And did he even know for a fact that she'd fallen for Sully's son because he was smart and good looking and educated and could talk about all the things Becka had been so hungry to discuss? Maybe it was none of that. Maybe it was just hot sex. Also, he didn't have any evidence that it *was* Peter Sullivan. Better to stick to what he did know.

"I just wanted to tell you I risked my life today. Apprehended a criminal. Also saved somebody's life, or so they tell me. Oh, and I figured out where Sully stashed those wheel clamps. I told you it was him. Anyway, for once you would've been proud of me."

Silence. He half expected a little sarcasm from Dougie, but none was forthcoming.

"I don't think I ever made you proud back when you were alive. I feel bad about that. Maybe you wouldn't have been all that proud of me even today. Because mostly, I admit, I'm still the same, well, the same guy you married. I still make a mess of things. I just wanted you to know that—for me?—this has been a pretty good day. The first really good one since you died. I guess what I'm saying is, I'm through blaming you for finding somebody . . . better. So I think it's time, you and me, we made a deal."

He gave her time to . . . what? Provide some kind of sign?

"Because I think I finally figured out what you want, and why you've been so upset with me. I think you want your privacy. Is that it, Becka? You want me to *not* know what was in your heart? You want to keep that secret."

He paused here, again giving her time to consider.

"Anyhow, that's my deal. If you're interested. You get to keep your secret and I get to figure out what comes next. Would that work for you? I think maybe I know who the man is. But I won't bother him, I promise. I won't ask him how it happened. Which one of you it was. Because, you're right, it's none of my business. So . . . what do you say?"

There was the smallest breath of breeze just then, gently lifting Raymer's hair as it had on Charice's porch. He felt himself smile.

"Chief Raymer?"

The voice was so near that he assumed it must be Dougie doing a weird impression, but he turned and saw it was Rub Squeers. He was holding something, and it took Raymer a moment to realize what it was.

"I fuh-fuh-fuh-fuh-found this yesterday—" said Rub, perspiring with the effort of speech. "At the buh-buh-buh-buh—"

"Bottom of the grave?"

"Bottom of the grave," Rub agreed, clearly relieved to be understood. Raymer took the remote from him.

When the other man was gone, Raymer stood with his back to Becka's grave, turning the device over in his hands. Once again the breeze lifted his hair.

But when he turned around again, it was Dougie who spoke in a voice that sounded just like Raymer's own, *No deal, toots.*

After all, it wasn't like he and Becka had shook on it.

Charade

H AVING SLEPT THROUGH most of the day, Carl Roebuck awoke
with a start at two-thirty in the afternoon with his hand in his
boxers. Sadly, such lunacy was becoming the new normal. Unable to
fall asleep most nights until it was nearly time to get up, he arrived
on the job a sleepwalker, blinking, addled, unable to focus. A triple
espresso wouldn't have kept him awake, not that there was anyplace
in Bath where you could get one of those. When his crew broke for
lunch Carl usually went home with the idea of taking a catnap on the
couch, but once there he'd fall into a sleep so profound that even his
brand-new cellular telephone, placed a few feet away on the coffee table,
its ringer on high, couldn't rouse him. Quitting time was five-thirty,
and he usually made it back to the job site in time to check on the
day's progress, assess new hazards and prioritize, with the help of his
job foreman, tomorrow's challenges, which, like today's, would likely
go unmet.

This morning, after the Hilldale fiasco, Carl had promised himself
that this day would be different. After showering off the mud, he put
on a fresh pair of boxers and turned on the morning news with every
intention of getting his sorry ass in gear as soon as it was over. It was
Saturday, normally not a workday, but given the week's events at the
mill—which was now officially a clusterfuck—there was much to be
done, all of it urgent. First, he needed to locate Rub Squeers and get

him started mucking out the yellow shit that was seeping up from the basement floor so that on Tuesday the masons could start rebuilding the collapsed wall, and his regular crew could get back to work on renovations. Convincing Rub to work on a holiday weekend wouldn't be easy unless Sully was somehow involved. For the privilege of spending the whole day with his best friend in the whole wide world, Rub wouldn't just stand in liquid shit, he'd eat it. Sully, on the other hand, would require a lot of convincing, and even then, there was the question of whether he was capable. Lately, Carl was beginning to wonder if something was seriously wrong with him, some medical condition he was keeping secret. Any exertion at all left him gasping for breath. This morning he'd been okay once aboard the backhoe, but he'd had a hell of a time climbing up onto it and getting back down later. And they'd only worked for an hour. Could Sully manage eight or ten, two days in a row, if that's what it took? Even three? How much of that vile, viscous shit was down there? They wouldn't know until they knew. The only thing he was certain of was that it'd be double time the whole ride, and double time had a way of turning two days' work into three. And where was he going to find the money to pay them?

It had been his intention, had he not fallen asleep and wasted the whole damn day, to join Sully at Hattie's for breakfast and give him the opportunity to repeat his offer of a loan. Though Carl was reluctant to accept help from a man who'd been saying for years that it was only a matter of time before he succeeded in completely bankrupting his old man's business, the idea of paying Sully with his own money did have a certain appeal. Could it really be considered Sully's, though? Over the last week or so Carl had lost over five hundred dollars to him playing poker at the Horse, which meant the money Sully'd be loaning him to pay them with had very recently been in his own pocket. Would this be like paying them double time *twice*? It was all very complicated, and trying to resolve the conundrum had made his head hurt. Which was why he'd closed his eyes, and now it was seven fucking hours later and his head still hurt.

There was a Cary Grant movie on TV, the one with Audrey Hepburn. Her recently deceased husband has left her an airline bag that everyone believes contains something—a key? a combination? a code?—worth a million dollars. Except the actual contents of the bag appear worthless. Carl had seen the movie several times and remembered it was the stamp on an envelope that everyone was overlooking. That's where they were in the movie right now, the bag's contents spread across the bed in a Paris hotel room, Audrey and Cary picking through the combs and toothbrushes and other useless shit. "The stamp, stupid," Carl told them, though the first time he saw the movie he hadn't tumbled to the stamp's value, either. Cary Grant, in Carl's considered opinion, was even dumber than he himself would've been had Audrey been coming on to *him* in that hotel room. At the very least he would've had the sense to sweep all that crap onto the floor and have hours of sex with her, even if she was too skinny. They could always resume the search later, and so what if they never did figure out it was the stamp? At least they'd have gotten laid, which would've been something.

But that was it in a nutshell. People just couldn't gauge their own circumstances with anything like objectivity. Okay, sure, Audrey and Cary were in a pickle. In addition to being ignorant of the stamp's significance, they had an American embassy official and three murderous if charismatic thugs breathing down their necks—and speaking of necks, Audrey's really was exquisite. Still, the way Carl saw it, they had each other for company, and if you had to be in trouble somewhere, there were worse places than Paris. Carl's own circumstances, except for the thugs, were much worse, having neither stamp nor girl nor, for that matter, a working dick should some girl magically appear. He was alone in North Bath, New York, so really there was only so much sympathy you could extend to these people.

At least he didn't *think* he had the stamp. Was it possible that, like the characters in the movie, he did possess something whose value he was overlooking? If so, what? It didn't have to be worth a million. Fifty thousand would suit his immediate purposes. Okay, in the end he'd probably need a million, though 50K would tide him over until the end of next week, when his next loan payment came due and he yet again had to make payroll. Was a measly 50K so much to ask for? He looked around the flat for something worth fifty grand, but Toby, his ex, had taken everything worth taking. If not *what,* then *who?* Gus Moynihan, after bailing him out on two occasions, had made it clear he didn't intend to ever do so again. Sully, since his luck changed, was sitting on some cash. Probably not as much as he needed, though. Who else did he know that might have that kind of dough? Somebody who might be willing to part with it. Who thought giving it to Carl Roebuck would be a good idea.

She answered on the first ring. "Schuyler Properties. This is Toby."

"Hey, babe, it's me."

"No," she told him. "Absolutely not."

"Absolutely not *what?*"

"Whatever you want. Money, I assume."

"It could be sex."

"It's working again?"

One night after the operation, he'd gotten drunk and called her, hoping for sympathy, or at least not derision. "Not yet," he admitted. "Soon, though."

"You hope?"

"Well, hope's all I've got left. You took everything else."

"I had a much-better lawyer than you did."

"Mine was free, though." Better than free, actually. Feeling bad about losing in court, Wirf had loaned Carl some money, then died before he could repay it.

"You still see Sully around?"

"Pretty much every day. We went grave robbing just last night." He thought this admission would surely stir Toby's curiosity, but they'd been married too long. She was familiar with his narrative head fakes and seldom fell for them. "He mentioned you the other day, actually."

"Remind him that I want to list his house. In fact, if you convince him to put it on the market, I might consider loaning you some money. How much were you thinking?"

"Fifty."

"Dollars?"

"Grand."

"You always were a stitch."

"Yeah? Well, what you always were rhymes with stitch. I keep hearing about what a kick-ass realtor you've become." Indeed, every time she sold another million-dollar property in Schuyler, someone felt obliged to give him the details. "Besides, if you sell Sully's house I'm out on the street. Why would I help you make me homeless?"

"I don't know, Carlos. I really don't."

He couldn't help smiling at this. "Hey," he said.

"Yeah?"

"It's been years since you called me that." It had been her pet name for him back when they were first married and she still went for his head fakes pretty much every time. Back when he could still laugh her into the sack. Back when she used to love him. Before he gave her so many reasons not to.

"Yeah, well . . ."

"Here's a crazy idea," he said.

"If it's yours, it's bound to be."

"We should go out sometime, you and I."

"That's well beyond crazy."

"Sylvia wouldn't like it?" Sylvia Plath was *his* nickname for her poet girlfriend. Not entirely apropos, of course, since Plath was a suicide, not a lesbian, at least so far as Carl knew. But he didn't have a large store of information about women poets, and Plath had to work better than Emily Dickinson, who wasn't a lesbian, either, so far as he knew.

"We split up, actually."

"No shit? How come?"

"Same reason you and I did."

"She cheated?"

"Yup."

"She's an idiot," he told her, only a little surprised to discover he meant it.

"Just her? Not you?"

"No, me too."

"You really need fifty *thousand*?"

Suddenly, unexpectedly, he was ashamed. "Nah," he said. "Really, I'm good. I was just calling to see how you're doing."

"Oh."

"Which is? I mean, after Sylvia?"

"You *mean,* am I ready to come running back to you?"

Which *was,* he realized, kind of what he meant. Or even exactly. "Would that be so terrible?"

"Yeah, it really would."

"I guess," he admitted. "So, who's next?"

"Maybe nobody."

"But if. Like, would it be a man or a woman?"

"Yup. One or the other."

On TV, one of the charismatic villains, dressed incongruously in a Stetson, is strolling past the crowded booths of the Paris stamp bazaar, himself clueless. All of a sudden he stops. There's a quick series of shots, all close-ups of stamps, accompanied by pulsing music. Then tight on the actor as he spins toward the camera. Eureka! Cary Grant's observing all this from afar, still in the dark. Dumb fuck, Carl thought. Dumb, stupid fuck. Too dumb to live, really, though Carl knew he would. He doesn't deserve Audrey. Or any woman, really. Well past his prime, he's making do on charm borrowed from his own youthful self. Maybe even he knows this, and maybe that's why he didn't take her back at the hotel when he had the chance.

"So what happens next?" Toby wanted to know, confusing him. Was she watching the movie, too?

"After what?"

"After you lose the company."

So, yeah, of course she was onto him. Didn't take that head fake. "Maybe I won't."

"For the sake of argument, let's assume you do."

"Why?"

"Because I'm curious to see if you can."

What would he do after he lost Tip Top Construction, the company his father built and loved? The company he himself always loathed but had never managed to divest himself of.

Now Cary's standing right where the guy in the Stetson was a moment earlier, and damned if he isn't visited by the same blinding revelation! He, too, spins toward the camera, his face aglow with understanding.

"What do you think I should do?" Carl asked.

"What you've always wanted to," Toby told him.

"What's that?"

"Poor Carlos," she said, as if to a child, and then she was gone, the line dead.

So much for that idea. No, the truth was simple and clear. He was all kinds of broke.

There were footsteps in the gravel below, so Carl went over to the window expecting to see Sully limping up the driveway. If so, did he have any choice but to ask? How would he broach the subject? *What we were talking about this morning, your offer? Of a loan? Well, actually, here's the thing . . .*

Except it wasn't Sully. The man's back was to him, so it took him a moment to recognize the balding blond head below as Raymer's. Taking something from his trouser pocket, he pointed it at the garage door. The remote they'd been looking for out at Hilldale? How the hell had he found *that*? When the door didn't budge, he took several steps closer and tried again. Carl thought about calling down and telling him that the door wouldn't open with that or any other device for the simple reason that no automatic opener had ever been installed. Instead, fascinated, he stood at the window and watched as Raymer discovered this for himself, pulling the door up by its handle, peering inside, running his hand along the frame where the metal tracking would've been had there been any and then, dejected, closing the door again. Sighing visibly, he put the remote between his teeth and, staring off into space, dug vigorously at his swollen, bloody right palm with the fingernails of his left hand, which, for some reason Carl couldn't begin to comprehend, seemed to give him some kind of relief. Though perhaps not, because when he took the device from between his teeth, he threw back his head and howled like an animal caught in a trap. Then with all his might he hurled the remote toward the street.

If this was an invasion of the man's emotional privacy, Carl couldn't help himself. When Raymer moved back down the driveway like a zombie, he hastened to the other end of the apartment so he could watch him from the windows fronting the street. There he saw Raymer get into the police SUV parked at the curb, and when the engine roared to life Carl expected him to pull away, but instead he got out again, crossed the street, retrieved the remote from Mrs. St. Peter's lawn and slipped it back into his trouser pocket.

When Raymer finally left, Carl continued to peer down into the street. He was pretty sure he understood what he'd just witnessed. Raymer had suspected Sully's son of being his wife's lover, and now he realized he was wrong. Carl, knowing who the guilty party was, could've put an end to the poor guy's suffering, but it was none of his business, was it? Still, it made him wonder if somebody of his own acquaintance was observing his every mistake while remaining unseen and unwilling to help. Wouldn't it be a kick in the nuts if that was how things worked? If we each knew things that other people needed desperately to know, yet were forever clueless about how to help ourselves?

Back in the living room, Audrey, trying to escape Walter Matthau, has run into a theater and managed to get herself trapped onstage in the prompter's box. Somehow Cary Grant, dumbfuck right to the end, has entered the building through a different door and is down below the stage, looking up at all the trapdoors. As Matthau, revolver in hand, crosses the stage, telling Audrey he knows right where she is, that the jig is up and that she might as well come on out, Cary tracks his footsteps by sound alone. Along the wall is a bank of levers used to spring those various doors open. But which one to pull?

This time, too, Toby answered on the first ring. "I figured out what I want," he told her.

"What's that, Carlos?"

"To be more like my father," he said. The old man had been married to his mother all those years until she died and never remarried, and never, to Carl's knowledge, even looked at another woman. He expected Toby to laugh, but instead she said, "Your wish is granted."

Matthau, always the squirrelliest of men, is standing directly in front of the prompter's box. All you can see of Audrey is her big, terrified eyes, maybe the most beautiful eyes Carl had ever seen. He was glad she isn't destined to die, that Cary's down below and, though truly a dumbfuck, he will somehow guess which lever he needs to pull. Though Carl knew all this, the suspense was still unbearable.

He glanced down at his boxers and was shocked to see they were tented.

Crazy Like a Fox

THE SERPENT THREAT REMOVED, Gert's was mobbed and every booth occupied, the bar three deep, two bartenders going flat out. Raymer's timing was good, though. The couple occupying the darkest booth along the far wall, the one he most coveted, away from all the mayhem, were insulting each other at high volume. "I'm not the one that's fucking crazy," the man shouted. "You're the one that's fucking crazy." Someone down the bar shouted, "You're both fucking crazy," leaving the angry couple no choice but to form a temporary alliance, bellowing in perfect unison, "Fuck you!" A second later, though, they were squaring off again, and whatever the man said next—Raymer didn't quite catch it—must've tripped the woman's switch, because she lunged across the booth, knocking over their pitcher of beer, and punched him in the face, the blow landing with enough force that his head rebounded off the back of the booth. "Don't," Raymer told her when she drew her fist back, about to let fly again. "I'm serious. Don't do it."

"Give me one good fucking reason," she said, her features contorted into a mask of unreason, so Raymer showed her the badge that he now realized he should've given Gus along with his resignation letter. He still had his revolver, too, as well as his radio, though he'd left the latter in the car, not wanting Charice to interrupt his drinking.

"She assaulted me," the man whined, a thin trickle of blood leaking from one nostril. "You're my witness."

"Because he's a goddamn asshole," the woman explained, as if establishing a companion's generally rum character was a time-honored defense in cases of physical assault.

"Pay your tab on the way out," Raymer told them, then stood aside so they could sheepishly vacate their booth.

"See what you went and done?" the man told his date when he saw Raymer slide in.

Gert came over and wiped off the table with a smelly rag. "Jesus," he said, noticing his ruptured fruit of a hand.

Outside in the parking lot, Raymer had discovered that the sharp-edged garage-door opener, though useless at Sully's, was the perfect tool for digging at the inflamed, itchy edges of the wound, which had taken over his entire palm. Thin red cobwebs now crept up his wrist. He slid his hand out of sight under the table. "What was that beer I was drinking when I was in here the other day?"

"You mean yesterday afternoon?"

"That was yesterday?" Raymer said. Because it felt like last week.

"Twelve Horse ale."

"Right," he agreed, Jerome's low opinion of it now coming back to him. "I'll have one of those. In fact, bring me two. I'm going to murder the first in about two seconds."

When Gert left, Raymer raised up on one haunch to regard the puddle of beer he was sitting in. At least he hoped it was beer.

"On the house," Gert said when he returned, sliding two bottles of Twelve Horse and a glass in front of him. "I heard you saved the life of one of my regulars."

"Thanks," Raymer said, sliding the glass back to him, then draining half the first beer in one go. It tasted every bit as wonderful this afternoon as it had yesterday. Since turning in his resignation, he'd been wondering what he might do next. Suddenly his path seemed clear. He would become an alcoholic. He would sit in dark, smelly bars like this one in the middle of the afternoon drinking cold, cheap beer. "I should probably tell you," he said to Gert. "That as of this afternoon I'm officially unemployed. I might not be able to pay my tab."

Gert made a sweeping gesture that took in his entire establishment. "Welcome to the fucking club."

In three more swallows he'd finished the first beer and settled into grateful ownership of a large booth all by himself, confident that not a single raucous drunk wanted any part of his company. With his uninjured left hand he rolled the cool empty bottle over his forehead, the exquisite pleasure of this proving that—yes indeedy—he *was* running a fever. That said, he'd felt worse, even quite recently. He seemed to have moved beyond exhaustion to whatever came next. The primal scream he let loose over at Sully's must've dislodged something. Dougie? That would be nice. Because that guy, he'd concluded, was an asshole. Somehow he managed to bring out both the best and worst in his host, making Raymer at once a better cop and a much-worse human being. Admittedly, he never would've tracked William Smith down without Dougie's help, and good had come of that, but it was also Dougie who'd encouraged him to dig up Judge Flatt for no sound purpose and it was also under his influence that he'd punched out an innocent (albeit obnoxious) motorist. Nor was Dougie as smart as he seemed to think he was. Without a shred of evidence, he had encouraged Raymer to believe that Becka's boyfriend was Peter Sullivan, which, granted, he'd been all too willing to accept. And maybe worst of all, after Raymer demonstrated some actual maturity by crafting an agreement that benefited both Ghost Becka and himself, the bigmouth had reneged on the deal. So if he'd somehow managed to expel Dougie with that primal scream—he'd been silent ever since, and the buzzing in Raymer's ears had stopped—so much the better.

Also apparently expelled at the same time, unfortunately, was his judgment. Because face it: instead of sitting here guzzling beer, he should be at the hospital getting his hand amputated. Would Charice think poorly of him and find him less attractive as a one-handed man? he wondered. To feel so disconnected from his own well-being was mildly alarming, but this was more than compensated for by the fact that, for the first time in his life, he didn't give one tiny little shit about anything. Was this what freedom felt like? If so, bring it on. All he was missing, he decided, was someone to tell how perfectly happy he was.

On the wall between the two restrooms was a pay phone, a suspiciously thin Schuyler County phone directory dangling from it by a chain. Half the pages had been torn out, but he was in luck, the number he needed having been left behind. "Jerome," he said when the man finally answered, his voice sounding groggy. How best to engage somebody probably still suffering the lingering effects of powerful sedatives? "I know who keyed your car," Raymer told him.

"I do, too," Jerome replied dully.

Raymer paused only briefly to puzzle over his lack of interest, then continued. "It was this asshole named Roy Purdy."

"No," Jerome said. Not contentious, just confident. "It wasn't him."

"Actually," Raymer said, "we've got a witness." Though this wasn't quite true. All Mr. Hynes had seen was Roy emerging from the alley, but still.

The silence on the other end of the line lasted so long that Raymer wondered if he'd somehow missed the telltale click of his having hung up. Finally, Jerome said, "You. You keyed the 'Stang."

Raymer let out an exhausted sigh. "Why would I do that, Jerome? I mean, we're friends, right? Why would I?"

"I have to go now," Jerome said.

"Don't hang up," Raymer said, surprised by the angst in his voice. "Hold on a minute, okay? There's something I've been meaning to tell you. Something I have to come clean about."

"You hate me. You keyed the 'Stang."

"No, Jesus, will you listen?"

"I know what you're going to say."

"No you don't. I think . . . I might have feelings for your sister."

"Now you're trying to fuck with my head."

"That's not true," Raymer said. "Why would you even think that? I mean, is that so weird? You said yourself that she was devoted to me. I should've realized how I felt about her sooner but . . . I don't know . . . it's just been really hard to let go of Becka. Hard to, well, to forgive her, I guess. Because she could've come to me, right? Explained how things were? Why she didn't love me anymore? Told me who the other guy was? She could've done all that, right?"

"I have to go now," Jerome repeated.

Raymer was visited by a sudden intuition. "Jerome? Are you drunk?"

"Maybe a little."

"Charice told me about last night . . ."

"'Bout me slipping my moorings?" he said. "It's true. Came straight unglued, ole buddy. Guess why."

"Sure, Jerome. Because I keyed your car. Except I didn't, okay? That's what I'm trying to explain, if you'd just listen. It was this asshole Roy Purdy. He's a racist dickhead, okay? He probably saw us go into Gert's and—"

"I have to go now."

"Look, how about I come over? I'll bring a six-pack of one of those microswills you like. We can talk this through."

"No," he said. "Definitely not."

"What if I promise not to use your bathroom," Raymer said, recalling what Charice had told him about that.

There came a muffled, whimpering sound. Could Jerome actually be crying?

"Or we could go out someplace," Raymer offered. "We could go to that wine bar in Schuyler. Adfinitum."

"'Finity," Jerome blubbered.

"Right. Would you like that? I can be there in twenty. Jerome?"

But the line was so utterly lifeless that Raymer wondered if he'd hallucinated the whole conversation. Because, Jesus, he really was burning up. Putting the receiver back in its cradle, he realized that in the last few minutes Gert's had taken on a phantasmagoric quality, with hulking, grotesque shapes moving through the tavern's almost liquid twilight, laughter too loud and not quite in sync with the mouths it issued from. Was he drunk? Was that even possible on one beer? Okay, two beers, he realized when he slid back into the wet booth, because the second bottle of Twelve Horse in his hand was somehow empty, too. Had he drunk the whole thing during his short conversation with Jerome? Suddenly he was frightened, though not of anything he could name. Some kind of slippage, things going too fast, then all of a sudden too slow, tectonic plates sliding along a fault line and giving him vertigo. Placing some bills—it was too dark and he was too messed up to worry about denominations—under the empty bottles, he scooted back out of the booth and stood up, so light-headed he had to grab on to the side of the booth to keep from falling.

Dougie, he thought with odd satisfaction, was a weak stick. Couldn't handle his booze worth a lick.

PULLING UP in front of Jerome's town house twenty minutes later, Raymer feared, now that he was here, that maybe coming was a mistake. Earlier, when he'd mentioned to Charice that he might swing by to cheer Jerome up, she'd told him without hesitation that it was a bad idea. What if she was right? What if he didn't want to be cheered up? What if Raymer was exactly the wrong man for the job? If Jerome was determined to believe he'd keyed the 'Stang, how could he convince him otherwise?

He'd just about decided to return to Bath—his injured hand pulsing to the rhythm of his respiration, his fever still raging—when the garage door rolled up unexpectedly. A green minivan sat in the bay, and Raymer waited for it to back into the street. When it didn't, he got out and walked up the driveway wondering who the minivan belonged to, then realizing that of course Jerome, suddenly without wheels, must've rented it. But a minivan? Jerome? Wasn't that the automotive equivalent of Twelve Horse ale?

It was dark inside the garage, and the vehicle's windows were tinted, so at first Raymer didn't realize Jerome was slumped forward onto the steering wheel. *Dead,* was Raymer's first thought. *Jerome is dead.* Had it been a heart attack just as he was about to back out? Was that possible? How could he be alive one moment and not the next, though when you thought about it, this was true of every human being who'd ever lived. At some point you are, until you aren't. "Jerome?" he said, his face close to the driver's window. "You okay?"

No response. The man's forehead still slumped on top of the steering wheel. Alive, though, yeah? Raymer couldn't be sure in such poor light, but his chest did appear to be gently rising and falling. "Jerome?" Raymer said, louder this time, and when he again didn't stir, he rapped sharply on the glass with his knuckles, and Jerome bolted upright, his eyes wide with panic, his arms straight out before him with his hands perfectly positioned at ten and two on the wheel, his body braced for impact. The shriek he let loose was high and keening and unguarded, the sound of abject terror. It took Raymer a moment to realize what must be happening, that Jerome, jolted awake in the driver's seat, had concluded the vehicle was in motion, that he'd fallen asleep at the wheel and was at that very instant about to crash into the wall right in front of him. When that didn't happen, the screaming stopped as abruptly as it had begun, but only for a moment, because then he saw Raymer peering in at him and let loose again, this second screech even more bloodcurdling than the first.

Raymer waited patiently until he stopped screaming, then opened the door. A bottle of single-malt scotch, a scant two fingers left in the bottom, fell out and shattered on the concrete floor, though his friend didn't seem to notice.

"What the hell?" Raymer said.

Jerome leaned away from him as far as he could—not very, being belted in—as if from someone with exceptionally bad breath. "What?" he muttered.

"Everything's all right. You're in your own garage. You're safe. Okay?"

Jerome sat up straighter, though he seemed reluctant to take his eyes off Raymer, like he suspected he was lying to him. Finally, though, he began to take in his surroundings. Yes, it did look like his garage. His vehicle didn't appear to be moving. He relaxed his grip on the steering wheel, then let his hands fall. "Whoa," he said, blinking. "I must've—"

Passed out, Raymer thought, though there was no reason to complete the sentence. "You scared me," he said. "I was afraid you were . . ."

He let his own thought trail off, because for some reason the garage door was descending. Turning, Raymer expected to see someone standing in the doorway that led into the kitchen and pressing the button, but nobody was there. Again his knees jellied—the same vertigo that had hit him at Gert's. Looking back at Jerome, he saw his eyes were streaming, his shoulders shaking.

"How *could* you?" was what he wanted Raymer to explain.

"I didn't," Raymer said, getting annoyed. How many times did he have to tell him it was Roy Purdy? And come on. Wasn't the 'Stang really just another fucking car? It was people's lives, not automobiles, that got fucked up beyond repair. He was about to tell Jerome to get a goddamn grip, but now that his eyes had fully adjusted to the cavelike dark, something caught his attention. The rental's rear seats were down, and the entire vehicle was crammed with cardboard boxes and suitcases and stereo equipment and mounds of clothes. "You going somewhere, Jerome?"

He stifled a sob and nodded resentfully.

"Where?"

"Away."

Again the garage door lurched into motion, this time lumbering upward.

"To where?"

"Away from you," Jerome said. His gaze was fixed on that bloody hand, as if the wound there was so disgusting, like a ruptured goiter, that he couldn't bear to be anywhere near it. Raymer, embarrassed, hid it behind his back.

"Because really," Jerome was saying, still going on about the fucking 'Stang, "it's hard to believe anybody could be so cruel . . ."

From outside came the sound of a car racing up the quiet, residential street at unsafe speed. Raymer turned away from Jerome just in time to see Charice's car rock to a halt at the curb. She'd tried to raise him on the radio several times while he drove to Jerome's, pleading with him to tell her where he was, but he'd ignored her. Now here she was, leaping out of the car and sprinting toward them as if the building was on fire. Never mind. He didn't care why she was here. He was just insanely happy to see her. In fact, his heart did a somersault, which could only mean one thing—that even without meaning to he'd moved on from Becka, the only other woman who'd ever made his heart behave like that. Was it even remotely possible that the sight of him might someday inspire in Charice, or any woman, such profound joy?

But suddenly she froze in the middle of the driveway, looking first at her brother, then Raymer, then Jerome again. "Don't," she pleaded. "Dear God, please don't."

Don't what? Raymer thought, but when he looked down he saw what must have upset her so. At some point, without realizing it, he'd apparently taken the remote out of his pocket so he could use its sharp edge to dig at the infected wound. The device was wet and sticky with fresh blood, and the pain was simply breathtaking. Apparently Jerome also wanted him to quit, because he'd taken his gun out and was pointing it at him. "No more," he said, his eyes wide with terrible determination. "I can't bear it."

"Don't, Jerome," Charice was saying. She'd come closer but was still outside the garage.

Jerome had begun to tremble, the gun in his hand shaking visibly. Raymer understood the situation was serious—pointing a loaded firearm at another human being always was—but he still had to suppress a powerful urge to giggle, recalling Jerome's favorite pose, copied from the *Goldfinger* movie poster, where 007, his long-barreled pistol pointed skyward, left hand cradling his right elbow, was the epitome of suave confidence in the face of danger.

"I told you!" Jerome was saying to his sister. "Didn't I tell you he knew? He's known all along!"

Known what? Raymer thought, but the garage door was descending again, in response, yes, to the bloody remote in his hand, just as it had been doing since he arrived. Stunned that this could be so, he watched the door motor closed and then turned guiltily back to Jerome, as if he were the one with some serious explaining to do. After a moment the light went out, leaving Raymer and Becka's lover alone in the unfathomable dark.

"We were so in love," Jerome said. "You have no idea."

Congratulations, said Dougie. *Well played.*

Something with No Name

R OY WAITED FOR full dark before returning to town and stuck to the back roads. By now every cop in Schuyler County had to be on the lookout for Cora's turd-bucket. His plan was to park on a dead-end street a couple blocks from Sully's place, but then he remembered the service road through Sans Souci Park that ended at a small maintenance lot out back of the hotel. There, Roy figured, the car might sit unnoticed for a week or more. Not that he really gave a shit. After tonight he wouldn't have any further use for it.

The old hotel loomed massively in the dark when Roy pulled in, and for a few minutes he just sat there, listening to the engine cool and staring at the fucking thing. He couldn't help it. The place just messed with his head and always had. Close to three hundred rooms, it had. Back before the springs ran dry, the hotel was always full of rich morons coming from all over to "take the waters." But really, how could that be? Sure, that was back before TV, when nobody had fuck all to do, but Roy still couldn't fathom it. If it were beer bubbling up out of the ground, maybe, but water? "Yeah, but you got to remember," Bullwhip explained when he told him about all this shit. "People crazy, and that's a fact. Want what everybody else wants, even if it don't make no sense. Take tulips . . ."

That was how it always went with Bullwhip. One minute you were talking about one thing, and before you knew it the subject was tulips.

The man knew all kinds of worthless crap. Most of the time you couldn't tell whether he was pulling your leg or talking for true. But according to him, there'd been this stretch over in Europe when everybody went crazy for tulips. Like there was anything you could *do* with a fucking tulip. Suddenly they all had to have some, and that made them expensive. People swapped gold and silver for tulips. "No fuckin' way," Roy had objected, but Bullwhip was adamant. "Read up on it," he said, as if you could go to the prison library and find a fucking book about tulips.

Still, it did make you think. If you could make all these Europeans want tulips—people who couldn't even agree on what fucking language to talk in—then maybe you *could* sell them water. Invent some crazy-ass story about how this was special water that would cure whatever the fuck ailed you. People wanted to believe shit. Take God. It was obvious to Roy that God was all bullshit. If you were God and you wanted people to believe in you, it just stood to reason you'd show your face every now and then. Instill some goddamn fear. Get people to toe the fucking line. Otherwise, everybody who wasn't completely stupid would draw the same conclusion. Roy found himself wondering if Bullwhip believed in God. If he was still there in the lockup, he could ask him before long.

Staring at the place, he felt, in addition to incredulity, something akin to nostalgia. For an all-too-brief period, the Sans Souci had been his principal source of income, a sweet deal while it lasted. This guy he knew, Garth, had been hired as a night watchman during one of the hotel's renovations. "You wouldn't believe all the shit comin' in there every fuckin' day," he told Roy one afternoon when they were both drunk. Brand-new furniture and fancy mirrors and televisions and stereo systems, arriving faster than they could be inventoried, just sitting there stacked in the original boxes. "Careless," Roy had observed. "Somebody could rip it all off, and they wouldn't even notice." Garth was basically a pussy and refused to participate in actual theft, but for a share of the profits he thought maybe he could manage to forget to lock up the service entrance. Just be smart, was all he asked. Don't take too much, and not all of the same shit. A TV or two, but not six. Couple videocassette players. A few paintings, maybe, if Roy saw any he liked. If anybody thought stuff was fucking vanishing, Garth would hear about it, and they'd lay low for a spell.

Which was how they played it there at the beginning, Roy carting away no more than would fit easily in his van. But after a month or two, with no alarms going off, he thought they needed to revise the strategy. Because who the fuck was Garth to say how they'd do it? He wasn't the one taking all the chances. Every time Roy slipped in that back door he risked somebody seeing his van parked where it shouldn't be. Why not aim for one big final score? He considered proposing this new tactic to Garth, then thought twice. Better to just make an executive decision.

"How it always goes," Bullwhip chuckled when Roy recounted the sad tale. How in fact somebody *had* noticed that shit coming in the front door was going out the back. How they were waiting for him the night he pulled up with the rented U-Haul. How they hadn't said a fucking word to Garth, since he was their number one suspect. "Human nature," Bullwhip elaborated. "People greedy. Don't know when to stop. Don't know how. It's stupid." Normally Roy didn't like being called stupid, but Bullwhip always seemed to include himself when reflecting upon human frailty. Besides, Roy hadn't told him the whole truth. Greed had played a role, all right, but the real problem was urine. The hotel's hundreds of rooms were mostly locked, but every so often Roy would come upon one that wasn't. The suites boasted king-size beds with mountains of white pillows piled high on pristine white comforters that proved irresistible to Roy pretty much every single time. He knew it was dumb but just couldn't help himself. Unzipping, he'd arc his stream at the center of the mattress until a bright yellow puddle formed there, after which he felt empty and at peace. Why was leaving your mark so satisfying? That's what this whole business with Sully was about. Squaring things. Leaving your mark. Making sure people knew you'd been there. That you were just as alive as them.

Before abandoning Cora's vehicle, Roy checked himself out in the rearview mirror one last time. It was hard to see with just the dome light, but the swelling on the injured side of his face seemed to have gone down some, the imprint of the skillet a little less pronounced. What was left of his ear had stopped bleeding earlier in the afternoon, and the remaining cartilage was crusting over impressively, as if its intention were to grow a whole new ear. While he'd stand out in the daylight, in the dark he was unlikely to attract much attention. Sully's place was only a few blocks from the park's entrance, and if he ran into somebody walking over there he could pull Cora's Mets cap down over his eyes, maybe even cross the street.

What worried him more than being recognized and arrested was that he was down to his last three pain pills. He counted them again just to make sure. Not enough to get him through the fucking night. He suppressed the urge to swallow all three now, knowing that would be a mistake. Given his luck he'd fall asleep there, and when Sully came home and found him he'd hit him with another skillet and slice off the other ear. No, this was fucking crunch time, and he needed to show some discipline. He did need one pill, though, right this goddamn minute, to keep from howling like a dog at the moon.

He swallowed it dry, thinking of Cora. He swore he wasn't going to, but here he was doing it anyway. Damn, she'd gone down hard. Whoever owned that camp would need a whole new dock, and that was for true. His mistake—he saw it clearly now, like you always do when it's too late—was trying to explain to that cow what had to happen, that he had no choice in the matter. If he hadn't been fucked up, he'd have just hit her. Because when you came right down to it, why try to reason with any woman? Didn't really matter whether she was smart, like his mother-in-law, or dumb, like Cora. They were all incapable of seeing things from a man's point of view. Basically they wanted everything their own damn way. Still, he wished he hadn't hit Cora so hard. He hadn't meant to, or at least he didn't remember meaning to. It did piss him off how stupid she was, how she didn't even suspect why he was searching the shoreline for the perfect stone, not too heavy, not too light. "You need to find a flat one," she kept insisting, having apparently concluded that he got off on skipping rocks across the water. Even when he found what he wanted and explained what it was for, that one clean blow was what he was after, how he didn't want to punch her like he'd punched his mother-in-law over and over until she lost consciousness, no need for that, even then she just stared at him, like he was speaking a foreign language. "I don't understand," she whimpered. "Why do you have to hit me?"

"Because I can't trust you, girl."

"Why not?"

"Because I can't, that's all. Because as soon as I'm gone, you're gonna head back along that road and ask the first assholes you run into to borrow the phone so you can call the cops. And by the time I get back to town, they'll be waiting for me."

"I wouldn't do that, Roy. I swear I wouldn't."

He knew, though, that once he was gone she'd remember everything she'd done to help him and how he'd repaid her by making her hand over the keys to her shit-bucket and stranded her out here by herself with no food and night coming on.

"I'll do whatever you want, Roy, I swear," she pleaded. "I could just spend the night right here. You said yourself how nice it is in there. Then in the morning—"

"You won't do no such thing," he assured her. "You think you will, but five minutes after I'm gone, you'll be yelling for help and telling everybody about how I ditched you and can you use their fucking phone. Don't say you won't, either, because I ain't stupid."

"I won't, Roy, I promise."

"Don't promise, neither."

"I am promising, Roy." She was blubbering, just like he'd predicted, her lower lip quivering.

"No, we're gonna do this my way," he said, stepping toward her.

"Don't, Roy. Haven't I been nice to you all day? I said I was sorry about them clips. They didn't have the ones you wanted, I swear."

"This don't have nothing to do with that."

"I know I should've bought the Pringles like you said." She was crying in earnest now. "Next time—"

"There ain't no next time, girl. Get that through your head. After tonight I'm headed back downstate." Even if Janey's mother didn't die of the beating he gave her, he'd be there a good long while. If she did, maybe for good. "This right here is the last you'll see of me."

"I could come visit you," she pleaded. "I would, too."

Like that would be a fucking treat. "Stand still now," he said, but when he cocked his fist, she squealed and threw both arms up to protect herself. "You're just makin' it worse, Cora. Do like I say."

"Don't hit me, Roy. Please don't hit me." Her fat elbows still up in front of her face.

"This won't hurt but a minute," he promised. "It'll be like going to sleep. When you wake up it'll be like a hangover. I'll leave you one of my painkillers. Make you right as rain." He would do no such thing, of course. He didn't even have enough pills for himself. "Like I said: tomorrow morning you can hitch a ride back into town, and you can tell everybody what I done. What a bad guy I am. By then it won't matter."

"No, Roy. Please don't. I'm scared. What if you hurt me bad? What if I don't wake up?"

Well, that'd be good news, he thought but didn't say. Because really? To just go to sleep and not wake up? To be done with all of it? That wouldn't be such a bad deal, would it? He wouldn't mind that so much his own self, now that he thought about it. His night with Janey—God, how long ago that seemed—was the best life had to offer him, and that was in the shitter for good. Sure, there'd be satisfaction in crossing Sully's name off his list. He was definitely looking forward to that. But then what? The minutes and hours and days and months and years stretched out forever with nothing to fill them but Bullwhip's crazy tulip stories. Unless he'd died, in which case it'd be some other asshole who couldn't keep his mouth shut, who had to yak all the time because words, no matter how dumb and useless, were better than silence and the thoughts that filled *that* up. Of course Roy supposed it was possible that he had less time than he thought. Life was full of surprises, just like Gert said. The falling tree you didn't predict, the skillet you didn't see coming. Whatever. There was no point in dwelling on shit beyond your control. That included most of the shit out there in this world, and that was for true as well. Make the best plan you can, then see how it all works out. That's all Roy or anybody could do, all he *was* doing, not that he expected Cora to understand.

"Be still now," he told her. "Let's get this over with."

But the fucking woman refused to lower her arms, until finally he said, "Okay, I guess we'll do it your way, then."

"Really?" she said, suspicious.

"Yeah," he said, tossing the stone out into the lake. Only when she heard it splash did she lower her arms. God, was she stupid.

What he couldn't get out of his mind was the look of dumb gratitude on her face. Or who knew? Maybe it was love. Or something with no name. Whatever it was, it was what he hated most and what allowed him to do what was necessary. Because of course he'd picked up two stones, not one, and the second, the heavier, perfectly round one, was still in his fist.

He felt bad, though, about hitting her so hard, about how hard she went down, ass first, reducing that dock to kindling, her fat butt in the water, her arms sticking straight up. No chance she could stand up whenever she came to. Nothing to do except shout her head off until somebody heard her. And the whole time she'd be thinking it was because of the clips and the Pringles. He'd told her it wasn't, but that was the thing with women. You were better off saving your breath. He thought about the waitress at that diner he and his father had stopped by that time, the one who'd given him a look like his whole pitiful life was visible to her. He wondered what had happened to her. Nothing good, he hoped.

Motion

A FTER LEAVING CLIVE JR. at the Sans Souci, Sully dropped Rub off at the trailer with bowls of food and fresh water and spent the rest of the afternoon making the rounds of places where a man like Roy Purdy might surface, but no one had seen him. Somebody reported spotting the Cora woman's car at the reservoir, so he drove out there, went up and down the dirt parking lot and didn't see it. He stopped in at Gert's twice more, but he swore neither Roy nor Cora had shown up. Over the course of the afternoon it had come home to Sully that his search might be an empty gesture, the sort of thing a man does to convince himself that doing anything at all, even the wrong thing, is preferable to doing nothing. Staying in motion was easier than sitting vigil at the hospital, rotating in and out of Ruth's room with her daughter and granddaughter and husband, staring at her ruined face, waiting for her to open her swollen eyes, fearing she wouldn't ever again.

So by early evening, exhausted and with nothing to show for his efforts, Sully reluctantly concluded there was nothing further to be done, at least not by him. If Roy and that woman were still in the area, they'd eventually surface. If they'd fled, her car would soon give them away. When he passed the county home for the third time that day, it occurred to him that maybe he should do something difficult. See if the path of maximum resistance yielded different results than the more familiar path of least.

"Are you family?" the woman at reception wanted to know when Sully told her who he was there to see.

"Not exactly," he told her. "We used to be married, though."

She was squinting at her computer screen now. "It says here that her husband is deceased." She peered at him over the rims of her glasses, as if to inquire whether he was claiming to be dead.

"That's her second husband, Ralph," he explained. "I'm Donald Sullivan."

"Sullivan," she repeated. "There's a Peter Sullivan on her visitor list. Also a William."

"Our son," he said. "And grandson."

"But no Donald."

"I understand. There wouldn't be."

"But you want to see her."

Well, not really, but he didn't contradict her.

She returned to her screen. "Do you understand that your ex-wife is nonresponsive?"

Still?

"By which I mean she doesn't recognize anyone."

Promise?

"And even if she did recognize you, she no longer has the power of speech. You won't be able to converse."

Well, we never could. "I understand," he told her.

The woman studied him carefully. "I'm not sure I'm comfortable with this."

That makes two of us.

BEFORE GRANTING HIM permission to see his ex-wife, the nurse on the dementia wing prepared Sully for what—rather than who—he would find. The person he'd come to see wasn't really here anymore, she informed him. Today had been one of her good days, actually, but that just meant he was unlikely to witness the agitation and, often, anger that characterized the latter stages of her illness. He might glimpse in the odd physical gesture some vestige of the woman he'd been married to, though anything beyond that would be his imagination at work. She was no longer capable of eating solid food, didn't even understand what food was for and was as content to chew on a wristwatch as a carrot. He wasn't to give her anything to eat or drink, as swallowing no longer came naturally, and she might gag.

The volunteer who showed Sully to Vera's room couldn't have been over seventeen. "I'll wait out here in the hall," she said.

When the door swung shut behind him and Sully saw the mummy-like, slack-jawed creature that once had been Vera, he nearly lost his nerve. His ex-wife had been situated in her wheelchair so she could look out the window at the central courtyard, where several picnic tables formed a circle around a concrete fountain, which happened to be dry. Was it always? Sully wondered. Was water a danger in this place? "Hello, old girl," he said, his voice sounding strange, unnatural, like someone speaking in a room without furniture. Her eyes flickered in his direction when he pulled up the chair, then quickly returned to some unfocused middle distance. Beneath her thin housecoat, Sully could tell, little remained but skin and bones. When it entered his mind that this was the same woman who'd been his lover when they were both young, he quickly banished the thought, feeling embarrassed, indeed unclean, that it should have occurred to him even fleetingly. Most alarming was her hair, which Vera had always permed to a fare-thee-well, not a strand out of place. Now it looked natural, real hair at last, and yet wholly unnatural for her.

"I just came by to see if you were still mad at me," he said. That was what he'd been dreading, of course—that Vera's resentment, nurtured over the long span of years, might persist after every other aspect of her personality had faded away, but he saw now that he'd been fearing the wrong thing. Had she been furious with him, at least she would've been Vera. "You must be pretty tired of all this," he said, looking around the spare, institutionally impersonal room, this most house-proud of women. Though it wasn't her surroundings that he meant so much as existence itself. "I know I would be."

Her expression didn't change.

Then a door on the far side of the courtyard opened, and a small child burst forth, a girl, soon trailed by a young woman who had to be her mother. Vera's eyes registered the movement but with nothing akin to cognition or pleasure. A moment later the grandmother, clearly the genetic baseline for the other two generations, appeared in the open doorway. Somewhere inside, Sully suspected, was the great-grandmother all three were visiting.

Not knowing what to do with his hands, he shoved them into his pockets and felt Will's stopwatch, which he took out and studied. "This look familiar?" he said, holding it out in front of Vera. "Remember that Thanksgiving?"

Peter, who'd come with his then-still-intact family, had invited Sully for dinner but neglected to tell Vera, never dreaming that he'd actually show up. Everybody in the house was quarreling: Peter and his wife, Vera and Ralph, Will and Wacker, his little brother. Sully had shown up just as the shit started hitting the fan. Will had actually climbed out the bathroom window, stowing away in the back of his truck. After beating his own hasty retreat, Sully found him under a tarp hiding from his feuding parents and little brother, the source of his terror. That was the night Sully'd been inspired to give him the stopwatch so he could time himself being brave.

Outside, in the courtyard, it took the mother two trips around the fountain to capture the squealing little girl and return with her to the grandmother, who gathered up the wriggling child, and then all three went back inside, leaving Sully alone with a woman who wasn't there. When the fist in his chest clenched, he closed his eyes against the discomfort until it loosened.

"Here's something you might get a kick out of," Sully said, returning the watch to his pocket. For some reason he was determined to talk to Vera as if she were actually there. "Turns out I've got this heart problem. Don't laugh. I *do* have one. I only know because it's fritzed."

Had she really been present, Vera no doubt would have observed that it never had worked properly, a criticism that Sully could accept as a given.

"I've got a while yet," he told her. "A year or two, they say, but they're full of shit. Could be any day, is what it feels like. They want to put this thing in my chest. A defibrillator. They claim it would keep me going awhile longer, assuming I don't die on the table. The question that stumps them is why. I can't work. These days I just mostly get in the way. So what's the point?"

This time when he glanced over at her he got the very distinct impression the ward nurse had warned him about, the sense that an interior light had come on. A second later, though, it was extinguished again, and all that remained was the physical husk.

"Got you stumped, too, huh?" The shadows in the courtyard were lengthening. "Don't worry," he told her, "I'll figure it out. Meanwhile, what do you say we sit here a minute, just you and me. I don't think we ever did that, did we? Just sit anywhere quietly?"

He awoke to a light touch on his wrist, and for a fraction of a second he was sure it was Vera, though of course it was the girl from the hallway coming to tell him that visiting hours were over. Like last call in a bar, he thought. You don't have to go home, but you can't stay here.

SATURDAY NIGHT and once again the Horse was hopping, but the stool next to Carl Roebuck was vacant for Sully to climb aboard. "You're in a good mood," Sully said, once his friend swiveled to face him.

"I bet you could figure out why, if you put your mind to it."

Sully was about to say he had no fucking clue why a man so far up Shit's Creek would be in such good spirits, then he realized that he did. "Congratulations. You're not going to show me, I hope."

"It's not hard right this second," Carl admitted. "In a million years you wouldn't guess who gave it to me."

"Give me a hint," Sully demanded. "Man or woman?"

"Audrey Hepburn. Fully clothed."

"I told you porn wasn't the answer."

"Audrey Hepburn," Carl repeated, his voice full of wonder. "Hey, you think she ever did any porno?"

Sully just looked at him.

"Okay, Katharine, then," Carl said. "Either one. Pick any Hepburn." When Sully declined to answer, he grew serious. "I'm sorry," he said. "I just heard about Ruth."

That had been the worst part of Sully's day, actually. Everywhere he'd gone people kept telling him how sorry they were, as if they were married, which yet again brought home to him how profoundly he'd intruded into her family. Could he blame Ruth for thinking the time had come for him to move along?

Birdie set a beer in front of him and said it was on the house. "They find that asshole yet?"

"Not as of half an hour ago," Sully told her. There'd been a pay phone in the lobby of the county home, so he'd made a couple calls. One to the police station—learning that Roy Purdy was still at large—and the other to the hospital, where the intensive-care nurse informed him that Ruth's condition was unchanged. Yes, her husband and daughter and granddaughter were there. He'd been thinking about going over, but decided instead to make them a gift of his absence.

"The way I heard it," Birdie said, "he'd have killed her if you hadn't showed up." Clearly, she was trying to make him feel better, so Sully didn't object. Nor did he point out the obvious—that he'd saved Ruth's life only if she did manage to survive.

One of the waitresses came over and handed him a folded note that read, in a surprisingly elegant hand: *I win this bet.* Leaning back on his stool, Sully peered into the dining area and saw Bootsie Squeers all dolled up, waving at him with a smug grin. The tree limb, of course. He'd forgotten, just as she'd known he would. He didn't immediately recognize the man across the table from her. Did Rub own a sport coat? A shirt with a collar? Shoes that weren't work boots? "I'll take their check," he told Birdie.

Carl had followed his gaze. "That," he said, once they were turned back around, "is one homely woman."

"Aw, be nice," Sully said.

"I *was* being nice."

"Did it ever occur to you," Sully asked, "that in your next life you might be an unattractive woman?"

"Or an insect?" Birdie offered helpfully, passing by.

"Hey, that's one of the books they tried to get me to read in college," Carl called after her. "Where the guy wakes up convinced he's a cockroach?"

"Guess who I ran into this afternoon," Sully said when Birdie was out of earshot. "Clive Jr."

"You're shitting me. Here in Bath?"

"Claims he flew in for the middle-school dedication."

"From where?"

"Someplace out west."

"How did he seem?"

Broken. Unhappy. Haunted. Though at the beginning he'd tried hard to appear otherwise. Oh, sure, he admitted, things had been a little tough, but eventually he'd landed on his feet. He was married, happily, to a woman named Gale, whom he was sorry his mother never had a chance to meet. He'd done some other things for a while, but was finally back in banking, starting out at a small branch office until his work there had been noticed. Now he was at regional headquarters, in charge of special projects. The West was booming, he informed Sully. People living in backwaters like Bath had no idea what the rest of the country was like. He understood now why the Ultimate Escape deal had collapsed. There were just far-better places for investors to invest. He explained all this to Sully with the air of someone who fully expected to be disbelieved, so when Sully said, "Good. I'm happy for you," he reacted as if Sully was being sarcastic, which wasn't the case. At least he didn't think it was.

"So," the junior Clive finally said, dropping the boosterism. "A stroke is what I heard."

He nodded. "A bunch of little ones, at first. Then—"

"God lowered the boom."

Sully couldn't help smiling, since this had been one of Miss Beryl's favorite expressions.

"No pain, then?"

"Not so far as I know. Not that she would've said anything."

"You looked after her?"

"I looked in on her, if that's what you mean." Every morning he'd poke his head in to see if she needed anything. Either that or she'd thump on the ceiling with her broom handle and he'd come down. Occasionally he let her talk him into drinking a cup of tea with her at the kitchen table, claiming, as always, to hate her beverage of choice. Some days he'd find her confused and know she'd suffered another ministroke, but she knew what they were and what to expect. She wasn't afraid, so far as Sully could tell. Just puzzled as to why God was taking his own sweet time.

"I don't suppose she talked much about me?"

"No," Sully told him. "Your name didn't come up." Which was true.

"She could be one tough lady," Clive said, sullen now. "Not that you'd know anything about that, being her favorite."

"Well," Sully said, "I liked her, too."

"That's the part I could never get. I mean, I can understand her being disappointed with me. I wasn't her kind of person, not really. Never was. But what made *you* so special?"

This, Sully realized, was the reason her son had returned to Bath after a decade elsewhere: to ask that very question. It wasn't affection or pride in his mother's being honored that had motivated his return, merely anger. And yes, of course, hurt.

"I heard about the house," he said. "I might've contested the will. I still could."

"No need," Sully assured him. "If you want the house, it's yours."

He seemed to consider this, but only for a moment. "Nah," he said. "What do I need with that old pile of sticks?"

"It's up to you."

"In fact," he said, his mood having shifted completely, "maybe I'll just catch an early flight back. I'd forgotten how much I hated this place."

"I'm sure Gale will be glad to see you," Sully told him.

The look of puzzlement on the man's face was there only for an instant, but Sully caught it and understood that there was no wife. How much of the rest of it was bullshit was impossible to tell.

WHEN THE SQUEERSES FINISHED their meal, they stopped by the bar. "Look at you two," Sully said, rotating on his stool. Bootsie, unless he was mistaken, was actually wearing makeup, and her usually stringy hair looked shampooed and curled. Carl was right, she was no beauty, even when dressed up for a date, but there was something brave about the effort she'd put into looking her best for an evening out at the Horse, of all places, with her husband, of all people.

"You didn't have to do that, Sully," she told him.

She was right, too, now that he thought about it. He'd given Rub money to take her out the night before, which meant that he'd paid for the meal twice.

"Hey, rubberhead," Carl said, "how'd you like a job tomorrow and Monday?"

"Tomorrow's a fuh-fuh-fuh—"

"Fuckin' holiday?" Sully guessed.

"Fuckin' holiday," Rub confirmed. "So's muh-muh-muh—"

"Monday?"

"It's all double time," Carl said.

Rub looked at Sully.

"Tell him to show you the money first," Sully advised.

"Show me the fuh-fuh-fuh—"

"Fuckin' money," Sully finished, grinning at Carl.

He swallowed hard, met Sully's eye. "I might need to borrow that," he said, and Sully calculated what this exchange had cost him.

"We'll work something out," he told him.

"Yeah?" Carl said, with an arched eyebrow. "It's a two-man job."

"I know," Sully said. Then, to Rub, who'd broken into a wide grin: "How about I swing by and pick you up? We can haul off that branch, then head over to the mill."

"What tuh-tuh-tuh—"

"Six-thirty. Be ready."

"I'm always ready," Rub protested. "It's you that's always—"

"I know," Sully told him. "But tomorrow I'll be on time."

"Does this mean—?"

Sully knew what Rub meant to ask—whether they'd be going back to work together again—and cut him off. "I don't know what it means," he said. "Just be ready. We'll see how it goes."

"There's one thing, though," he told Carl once the Squeerses were gone. "All I can give you is Sunday and Monday."

His friend nodded, waiting.

"Tuesday I've got to go down to the Albany VA for"—he tapped his chest—"a procedure." He hadn't intended to say that. Hadn't really even decided to do the operation until that moment. Somehow, confiding his condition to Vera had led him to say so.

Carl was nodding. "We've all been wondering when you'd come clean."

"Never was my plan," Sully admitted. "I wasn't even going to let them do it, but then I figured what the fuck."

Carl was grinning now. "Well, it's good you reasoned it through so completely. You really think you can work tomorrow?"

"I guess we'll find out. Lately I have a bad day, then a couple good ones. Today's been a bitch, so tomorrow ought to be better. Even if I feel like shit, I should be able to sit on a backhoe."

And anyway, why not give it a whirl. During the course of the day something in him had pivoted. The promise he'd just made to Carl—to work something out—was vague and unenforceable, though in Sully's experience a man's character required him to make good on such deals. And it made a lot more sense than his earlier promise to Janey—that he'd find Roy and hurt him—a pledge he clearly wasn't going to make good on. So tomorrow he and Rub would descend into whatever vile, poisonous shit was oozing up from beneath that concrete floor at Carl's mill. There he'd listen to his friend's litany of wishes: that they'd stopped for a big ole jelly donut, instead of coming straight to work, that Hattie's wasn't closed so they'd have someplace to go for lunch, that he and Sully didn't always get the crap jobs, that Sully hadn't gone and renamed his dog Rub. When he was all wished out, Sully would tell him again to wish in one hand and shit in the other, then let him know which filled up first. Things were just the way they were, as they'd always been and always would be, and really—here was the important point—this life wasn't all *that* bad, was it? When they knocked off at the end of the day, they'd be welcome at the Horse, even if they did smell like Mother Teresa's pussy. And once there, whether or not he had an appetite himself, Sully would spring for the big ole cheeseburger Rub had been wishing for all afternoon, maybe get him to call Bootsie and invite her to join them, because when Sully was gone, he was going to need somebody to listen to him. He wasn't sure Bootsie was the right person for that job, but there didn't seem to be anybody else. And maybe, now that Sully thought about it, the time had come to let the dog go back to being Reggie again. He could do that much.

"If you don't mind, I'm going to make this an early night," he told Carl, pushing the dregs of his second beer away. Whatever he'd come to the Horse for, he seemed to have gotten it. If he went to bed early and got a decent night's sleep, he could be at the hospital before dawn and maybe steal a few moments alone with Ruth while the others slept. If he didn't go home now, Jocko would show up and buy a round, and later someone would suggest a poker game, and on the way home, two or three short hours before dawn, he'd be forced to admit he was the kind of man who could enjoy himself while a woman whose love had saved him more than once lay in a coma.

"Go," Carl said. "But first I'd like your opinion about something."

"What's that?"

"Rub and Bootsie."

"Yeah?"

"You think they'll have sex when they get home?"

"Jesus," Sully said, shaking his head. "You are *such* a sick fuck." Though he'd wondered the same thing himself.

"I don't know who I feel sorrier for," Carl said.

THERE IT SAT.

Next to the Dumpster, the yellow-and-purple beater that hadn't been there three hours earlier.

Sully'd been only a block from home when he thought to check the parking lot out back of the Sans Souci one last time. Now, feeling the fist in his chest clench painfully, he almost wished he hadn't. Grabbing the tire iron from the dash, he got out but left the truck running, its high beams trained on the back of the hotel. Then he blasted the horn for a full five seconds.

"Roy Purdy!" he shouted as the sound died away, causing the fist to clench again, harder this time, his wreck of a heart sending him an urgent, unambiguous message. *Cease. Desist.* "You might as well come on out."

When there was no response, he took out Will's stopwatch and depressed its tiny stem. "You got one minute!"

Fine, then, he thought when the minute hand had completed its revolution. He'd drive into town, report the vehicle's location and let Raymer and his crew handle it. Noticing that one of the beater's rear tires was missing its rubber valve cap, he used the edge of the tire iron to let the air out.

"The cops'll be along shortly," he called when the tire was completely flat. "And that's for true."

By the time he returned to Upper Main Street, though, the fist in his chest had become an anvil on top of it, and he knew he'd never make it down to the station. He'd have to call instead from Peter's flat. If he could make it that far.

Pulling up at the curb in front of Miss Beryl's, he turned off the engine, but then, unable to catch his breath, he just sat there. *Two years, but probably one?* Two *hours,* but probably one, was more like it. The truth he'd been unwilling to face all day was simplicity itself: he was finished. Back at the Horse he'd somehow managed to convince himself that his choice was between keeping his promise to Janey and helping Carl out of his jam, though he now realized this was an illusion, a fiction. The anvil sitting on his chest was the only reality.

Get out of the truck, old man, he told himself when he was able to draw at least a little oxygen into his lungs. *You can manage that much.* After that, the short walk up the drive and then three small steps onto the back porch. Make one call to the station, then another to 911 for an ambulance. Not because it would save him, but so nobody he cared about would have to find him. He thought about Rub, who'd need to be let out of the trailer soon. After the 911 call, if he had strength and breath enough, he'd telephone the Horse and get Carl to do that.

Move, he told himself, because he was still in the truck, still thinking about what needed to be done instead of doing it. Perhaps for the first time in his life thinking was easier, less painful, than doing. One more reason to believe the end was near.

He'd made it halfway up the drive when Miss Beryl's long-ago question popped into his head, unbidden as always. *Does it ever trouble you that you haven't done more with the life God gave you?* Even now he couldn't say for sure. Was it supposed to? Had he been wrong to take such pleasure in always doing things the hard way? And to banish self-doubt and regret before they could take root? Had it been selfish of him to make sure that his destination at the end of the day was a barstool among men who, like himself, had chosen to be faithful to what they took to be their own natures, when instead they might have been faithful to their families or to convention or even to their own early promise?

Not often, he'd told Miss Beryl. *Now and then.*

She'd immediately registered the change in him when he returned from overseas, no doubt sensing that his newfound ability to distance Sully from Sully would become his great skill in life. He'd always been bullheaded, of course, but the war had taught him to move forward, and as he saw it this meant putting one foot in front of the other, to keep going when other men stopped, to grind it out.

Except that now, almost to the back door of his son's flat, everything tilted, and he was on his knees on the hard ground, and a moment later there was gravel under his chin.

So, he thought. This was how it ended, how it had to end. The day had finally come when putting one foot in front of the other was simply fucking impossible, when the forward motion he'd depended on his entire life failed him and he it. *On your feet, Soldier,* he commanded himself, but his body was all done taking orders. The entire world, it seemed, was now reduced to silence and pain, the latter intense, the former unendurable. With the last of his strength he took out his grandson's stopwatch. The ticking, when he depressed the stem, was loud and strong, a comfort, though it was also, he realized, the sound of time running out.

Footsteps approached, but Sully didn't hear them.

Normal

B Y THE TIME he finished the last of the hospital's paperwork, signing all the necessary documents left-handed, with an untalented child's scrawl, it was going on midnight. Thanks to a megadose of antibiotics, Raymer's rationality, or what remained of it, had returned, and with it his normal depression. Hard to believe, but six short hours earlier, at Gert's, he hadn't had a care in the world, didn't give a tiny little shit about anything. He might need to have his right hand amputated? So what? Even Jerome—wild eyed and completely off the rails—pointing that gun at him had failed to focus his mind. The idea that he might actually pull the trigger, sending both Raymer and vile, sneaky, manipulative Dougie into oblivion, had felt more liberating than terrifying. Freed from reason, he'd been free of cares, whereas now, reason restored, item number one on his agenda was putting the town of Bath and its myriad humiliations in his rearview mirror.

Before he could do that, however, he had to rent a truck and a hitch for his car, buy cardboard boxes and packing materials, clear out his office at the station, then pack up his few possessions at the Arms. Could all that be accomplished in a single day? Was packing and taping boxes even a job he could manage with one hand? The wound of his ruined one, cleaned and freshly wrapped with gauze, throbbing mercilessly despite the prescription painkillers, now resembled a club. Would he be able to hire help on such short notice? Apart from his determination not to spend another night in the Morrison Arms, there was no real hurry about leaving. It wasn't like he'd be heading anywhere in particular. Where were fools supposed to go? Was there someplace known for welcoming them, where he might blend in with others of his ilk? A place inhabited by middle-aged men who found it impossible to put their deceased wives' infidelities behind them? Who fell in love again in the manner of teenage boys, too self-conscious and clueless to figure out whether their affections were returned? Was there such a place anywhere in the world?

When he was finally discharged, a woman was waiting for him in the hallway. She looked to be in her fifties, had short brown hair and was dressed in slacks and a tweed jacket. "I was hoping I might catch you before you left," she said. "We can talk in my office." Her nameplate read DR. PAMELA QADRY.

"Do we know each other?" he said, taking the chair she offered.

"No," she said, "but Jerome Bond is my patient."

"Oh," he said. So a shrink, then.

Poor Jerome. Raymer knew from Charice, of course, that he was prone to panic attacks, though he never would've believed that a functioning human being could come as completely unglued as Jerome had done over the last twenty-four hours. Since the keying of the 'Stang he'd become all but unrecognizable. In the ambulance he'd curled up into a fetal position and refused to look at Raymer, preferring to talk to the EMTs. "Do you even know what it's like to love somebody?" he blubbered to the one trying to take his vital signs. "I mean *really* love somebody? Do you even know what love *is*?"

Raymer, barely coherent himself, his fever raging, the pain in his hand so intense that it bordered on a religious experience, had been assigned his own EMT, a no-nonsense young woman who kept snapping her fingers in front of his face and saying, "Eyes on me, Mr. Man. None of that over there is our business."

Which had given Raymer a fit of the giggles. "Actually, it is," he whispered. "That's my wife he's talking about."

"Is he going to be okay?" he asked this Qadry woman now.

"We'll get to Jerome in a minute," she said, "but first tell me about your hand." Like every other woman he knew, she evidently could tell just by looking at him exactly what he didn't want to talk about.

"I had a small . . . abrasion. It became infected. Resulting in blood poisoning." He crossed his arms in order to slip the hand out of sight. Maybe if the woman couldn't see it, she'd lose interest.

"Why didn't you get it treated sooner?"

"I didn't have a chance to."

She let that lie just hang in the air, her eyes on him, until he looked down. "I hear you did a lot of damage, digging at it. Do you have an idea why you did that? Hurting yourself so badly?"

"At first it itched," he explained. "I don't think I was even aware I was scratching it."

"How does it feel now?"

"It hurts like hell."

"Do you think you'll start scratching it again?"

"No," he said. In fact, the idea made him feel faint. "But about Jerome?"

She didn't answer immediately, just kept studying him as if he were a human riddle. "Mr. Bond suffers from an acute anxiety disorder," she said finally. "Lately it's gotten worse. He's been sedated and is in no immediate danger, but he's not a well man. Is something wrong?"

Raymer realized he was frowning. "It's just . . . I don't know. Should you be telling me this?"

"Shouldn't I be?"

"Isn't it sort of . . . confidential?"

"I was under the impression you already knew."

"His sister, Charice"—he looked down, flushing again—"works for me. She's worried about him."

"How about you, Chief Raymer? Are you worried about him?"

"Sure."

"I ask because he believes you hate him."

"Well," Raymer sighed. "I kind of do. He was having an affair with my wife."

"And when did you discover this?"

"This afternoon."

"He says you've been tormenting him for weeks. Trying to get him to confess to the affair."

"Tormenting him how?"

"Calling him in the middle of the night."

"I can't remember the last time I called Jerome." Only when she gave him an odd look did it occur to him that the statement could yield more than one interpretation. "Not counting today, I mean."

"He claims you know exactly when he falls asleep. And you call him then."

"How could I know when he falls asleep?"

"He says you've installed secret cameras in his condo."

"Really?"

"When he leaves, you sneak in and go through his things. Pick them up and put them back in the wrong places."

"And you believe this?"

"*He* believes it."

"How do I get in?"

"Through the garage."

Raymer was about to say this was crazy when he remembered he'd done precisely this earlier in the afternoon. Seeing the garage door open just as he pulled up at the curb, he'd assumed Jerome had set it in motion, but now, in light of all that transpired there, he knew better. Using the sharp edge of the remote to dig at his wound, Raymer himself, albeit unwittingly (Dougie, the sneaky little prick, somehow taking over crucial functions), had been the one making the demonic door go up and down. Had some part of him suspected Jerome of being Becka's boyfriend before today? *Well played,* Dougie had said when Jerome finally confessed. Was it possible he actually *had* been tormenting him for weeks without knowing it, as this woman was suggesting? Or had Jerome come untethered all on his own, a victim of grief and conscience?

"No, I don't think I did anything like that," he told Dr. Qadry.

"You don't *think* you did?"

"Normally, I'm not a cruel person," he explained. Could the same be said for Dougie, though? After all, that asshole instinctively intuited the worst in everyone. "Though it's true . . ."

"Yes?"

"That lately I haven't been . . . well."

"Would you like to tell me about it?"

He considered the offer, but not for long. "No," he told her. "I don't think I would."

She nodded, apparently not surprised. "You mentioned Mr. Bond's sister? Charice? Would you like to talk about her?"

She'd followed the ambulance in her car, pulling into the emergency room lot just as he and Jerome were being wheeled inside. Raymer remembered wondering which of them she'd stay with, thinking that her decision would tell him everything he needed to know. As it had. When Jerome's gurney was wheeled off in one direction, his own in another, their eyes had locked for a brief moment, then she went after her brother.

Could there be any doubt she'd known all along? Her behavior over the last few weeks, at first so puzzling, was at last beginning to make sense. How she'd tried convincing him that the garage remote didn't mean anything, arguing that it wouldn't prove anything, that even if he could find a door it would open, it would prove nothing. At every turn, he now realized, she'd tried to get him to abandon his search for Becka's lover. She'd made it appear as if his own mental health was her primary concern. For his own good, it was time to move on. But it was her brother she'd been trying to protect. It was Jerome's fragile grip on sanity, *his* emotional well-being, not Raymer's, that worried her. Much as he hated to admit it, Dougie—asshole though he was—had been onto Charice from the start, and Raymer would've been smart to heed his warnings.

The question that plagued him now was, besides Charice, how many other people knew that Becka and Jerome had been lovers? Two? Two hundred? Had the whole town been laughing behind his back? For the longest time he'd been asking himself, *Who? Who? Who?* As if the man's identity would satisfy all his need to know. But in fact, knowing *who* had provided no relief at all, only more questions. Beyond *Who,* there was *How long,* not to mention *How* and *When?* Had they met at Adfinitum one of those nights when Becka went there with her theater friends? Had Jerome come over and reintroduced himself as Raymer's best man? Or had she recognized him, a tall, elegant black man sitting alone at the bar, and invited him to join them? How many times did they meet like this before it became clear to others in the group that they were a couple? Did they leave together in the 'Stang or, for the sake of appearances, separately? How frequently did she use that garage remote to slip unseen into Jerome's condo?

Almost as disconcerting was this: what did it say about Raymer that he never once suspected Jerome? "Damn, Dougie, you're marrying *up*!" had been the first words out of his mouth when Raymer had introduced them. Was it because they were friends that Raymer hadn't suspected, or because Jerome was black? How were you supposed to tell? Most people seemed to agree that it was impossible to be certain what was in someone else's heart, but surely that didn't apply to one's own. Or was it even *more* true of one's own?

"I thought Charice and I were friends," he told Dr. Qadry. "I even thought . . ."

"What?"

"It doesn't matter."

"And now you think you aren't friends?"

He shrugged.

"Maybe you're wrong."

"But probably not." She'd followed Jerome's gurney, not his.

"Okay, I can see how uncomfortable this is making you," she said, and he took this as permission to rise. "It was good of you to spare me a few minutes. I hope you won't try to communicate further with Mr. Bond."

She stood as well, offering her right hand, then remembered and, embarrassed, held out her left. "Failure of imagination," she apologized. "Amazing how often it comes down to that."

At the door it occurred to Raymer that there was one thing he wanted to ask. "Have you ever treated anybody who'd been struck by lightning?"

She blinked, then shook her head. It pleased him to see her so completely wrong-footed. "Why?"

"I just wonder what something like that would do. What effect it would have?"

"Well," she said, "human beings are mostly water and electrical impulses. A sudden surge like that, even if it didn't . . . fry you?"

"Yeah?"

"Well, there's nowhere in the body the current wouldn't go."

"Do you think it could put something inside you that wasn't already there?"

"Like what?"

"Like thoughts that aren't yours?"

"Doubtful."

He nodded. "What about afterward? Would things go back to normal, eventually?"

He was surprised to see how seriously the woman was regarding him. "You'll have to let me know," she said.

LEAVING THE HOSPITAL, Raymer heard a metronomic banging sound coming from the parking lot but paid it no mind. A cab was idling out front, so he got in and gave the driver Jerome's address. Once he fetched his car, he'd drive back to Bath, check in to one of the interstate motels and catch a few hours' sleep. In the morning, semi-rested, he'd decide how to proceed. The longer he thought about it, the more inclined he was to just leave everything and make a clean getaway. If there was such a thing.

"Hold on a minute," he said as the driver put the taxi in gear. Because standing in the middle of the parking lot, directly beneath a streetlamp, was a man Raymer recognized, even from behind, as Gus Moynihan. He was leaning forward, with his elbows on the roof of his car and his forehead resting on the frame. Only when he got closer was Raymer able to make out what he was using to make the banging sound: Alice's phone. "Gus?" he said, causing him to straighten up guiltily.

"Doug," he said, quickly putting the handset behind his back. "What are you doing here?" Even in the poor light Raymer could see that his eyes were red and puffy. Raymer held up his bandaged hand. "Oh," he said, "right."

Had the mayor been thinking clearly, he would've asked why, for such a complaint, Raymer hadn't been treated in Bath, but he obviously wasn't tracking. Something bad must've happened, bad enough to make him forget that Raymer had stood him up for all those interviews on the evening news.

"Gus," he said, "is Alice okay?"

"Yes, she's fine," he said, forcing a smile, but it soon crumpled. "No, that's a lie, actually. She's not fine. Alice . . . has never been fine."

"What happened?"

"She took some pills."

"I'm sorry. Is she—"

"She'll live. They pumped her stomach in Bath. Unfortunately, there's no mental health unit there," he laughed bitterly. "Yet another amenity Schuyler Springs offers that we don't. Anyway, she's resting. That's what they say, right? Resting comfortably? Words in lieu of truth. As if a mind like hers could ever rest." He shook his head and looked off into the distance. "Tomorrow she'll be admitted to the state mental hospital in Utica. The last time she was there I promised her she'd never have to go back."

"Maybe they'll be able to—"

"Yeah, but Doug? The thing is, I thought *I* could help her. I mean, wasn't that the whole idea? Me, helping? The man she was with before . . ." He let the thought trail off. "I thought I could do a better job, but instead I ended up making everything worse."

"How is it your fault if Alice is sick?"

Instead of answering, he took the handset out from behind his back and stared at it. Then, without warning, he hit himself in the forehead with it. Hard. Then twice more before Raymer, caught off guard, could yank it away from him. One of the blows, Raymer saw, had cut through his eyebrow, which now bled freely.

"Don't you see?" he said. "I took it away from her. I told her all those imaginary conversations were making her sick. That if she didn't want to go back to Utica, she had to give it to me."

"And you think that's why she swallowed those pills?"

He didn't answer, just stared at his bloody hands. "I'm bleeding," he said. "Good."

"Hold still," Raymer told him. "Tilt your head back. That's a deep wound, Gus. You need stitches."

"Better yet," he said. "You know what my problem is? In a nutshell? I always think I can fix things. The whole town of Bath. Turns out I'm the one in need of repair." He nodded at the phone. "Can I have that back?"

"Not if you're going to hit yourself again."

"I won't," he promised. "I'll go back inside and leave it on her bedside table. They say she'll sleep until morning, but if she wakes up in the middle of the night it'll be there for her."

Raymer reluctantly handed it over.

"Here's what I'd like to know. Why did I do such a thing? Why did I take it from her. Actually, I think I know. It made me angry that when she got scared and the world made no sense, it was never me she came to."

"I'm not sure I follow," Raymer allowed.

"It was like she knew I didn't have what she needed. To her, talking to someone who didn't even exist, on a phone that wasn't even connected, gave her more comfort than I ever did. I think maybe that's what I couldn't bear."

"You want to know what I think?" Raymer said, astonishing himself that he not only had an opinion but also wanted to share it.

"I would, actually," Gus told him, weeping openly now. "Especially if you think better of me than I do of myself. I'd really like to hear that. Do you think you could say something along those lines and make me believe it?"

What Raymer had intended to say, and what over the course of the last forty-eight hours he was coming to understand, was that it was a shame, indeed a crying shame, though probably not a crime, to be unequal to the most important tasks you're given. That was true of just about everyone Raymer knew, including himself. All his life, it seemed to him, he'd come up short, but his shortcomings were not, he hoped, criminal. And who knew? Maybe telling Gus something like that would be helpful. On the other hand, he seemed to want something else entirely, and Raymer found he could deliver that as well. "In the end I think things are going to work out," he said. "I think Alice loves you more than you know, and I think you love her. I think this time the

Utica doctors will know what to do. There'll be a new medication to try, or there'll be somebody new on staff who understands. I think that in no time she'll be back here with you. I also think it's possible for us to be better people tomorrow than we are today."

He had no idea, of course, whether any of these things were true, in whole or in part. Still, what possible good could come of believing otherwise?

HE WAS ON the interstate, halfway back to Bath, when he noticed an orange glow on the horizon and then, between the trees, what looked like the tip of a tiny flame. His first thought, given last night's weird atmospheric disturbances, was that this, despite the star-filled sky, must be yet another. Turning on the police band, he learned there was in fact a fire on Upper Main Street in Bath.

Unlike houses, trailers didn't take long to burn, and by the time Raymer arrived, there wasn't much left of Sully's. The fire department had managed to keep the flames from leaping to Miss Beryl's house, though the clapboards were scorched black right up to the eaves. About the only thing recognizable in the trailer's smoking rubble was the commode Raymer had fallen asleep on early that morning, waiting for Sully to return home.

Mark Diamond, the fire chief, noticed him and came over. "There's a body," he said.

Raymer nodded, because of course there would be. "Has the coroner been notified?"

"Expected momentarily."

"No other injuries?"

Diamond shook his head. "The son lives downstairs, but according to the neighbors he's away. Carl Roebuck rents the upstairs flat, but he isn't home, either." He frowned then. "Somebody said you resigned."

"I did."

"Over this new plan I keep hearing about? To merge our services with Schuyler's?"

"No. Nothing to do with that." His attention kept returning to the smoking ruin of Sully's trailer. Feeling a sudden, unanticipated surge of emotion for a man who, until today, had only been a thorn in his side. "I was with him last night," he told Diamond. "We were never friends, but I asked him for a favor. A pretty big one, actually. And damned if he didn't pitch in."

"That's Sully, all right," Diamond sadly agreed. "Lately, though, he had the look."

"Of what?"

"The one people get when they're not long for this world."

It was true. Out at Hilldale, Raymer's focus had been elsewhere, but he remembered how pale Sully'd looked on the backhoe, how much trouble he'd had climbing onto it and then down again.

"Gotta go," Diamond said. One of his crew was calling to him. "One other thing? Even though you resigned? One of the neighbors said he heard voices in the driveway not long before the fire started, and when we arrived one of my guys thought he smelled accelerant. I've asked for a canine unit."

That jogged Raymer's memory. "Any sign of his dog?"

"In the burn? No. No canine remains. Just the one human skeleton."

"You're sure?"

"Be pretty hard to miss."

Walking back up the driveway, Raymer kicked something solid that felt like a stone but sounded metallic. It took him a moment to find it in the dark. A stopwatch. Sully's? There'd been one on the kitchen table that morning, he remembered, and Sully'd put it in his pocket when they left. Had he accidentally dropped it when he got back home and came up the drive? No, it was too heavy. In the night's stillness he'd have heard it hit the gravel. Maybe he couldn't spot it in the dark and figured he'd look again in the morning. Possible, but again Raymer doubted it. It was supposed to rain again later that night. He wouldn't have left it lying there on the ground, not when he had a flashlight in the truck.

The crowd had begun to disperse by the time the coroner arrived. He and Diamond, their shoes covered with plastic, were standing in the middle of the burned trailer, studying the body's charred remains. "Raymer," said the coroner. "I heard you resigned."

He ignored this. "Can you guess the victim's height?" he asked. "Based on . . . that?"

"I'll be able to tell you within an inch or two tomorrow," he said. "Right now, I'd be guessing."

"Okay, so guess," he said. Diamond seemed puzzled by all this.

The man cocked his head. "Five-seven? Five-eight?"

"Guess again," Diamond said. "Sully was a good six feet."

Raymer's radio barked static. "Chief?" the night dispatcher said. "You there?"

"Yup."

"That yellow-and-purple vehicle we've been looking for finally turned up. Parked out back of the Sans Souci. We figure Roy Purdy must be holed up inside."

"Not possible," Raymer told him.

"Why not?"

From where Raymer stood, just outside the shell of the trailer, he could make out a blackened human foot. "Because then he'd be in two places at once."

HE COULD HEAR the dog barking from the foot of the steep drive. The husband's big flatbed was parked at the top. What the hell was the man's name? Suddenly it was there: Zack. Cutting his lights, Raymer pulled up and parked behind the truck. There were lights on in the house, which suggested that despite the lateness of the hour and the circumstances, somebody was awake in there. Ruth, his wife, was in critical condition at the hospital, so it was probably Zack, the man he'd come to arrest. There could be someone else, though. They had a granddaughter who sometimes stayed with them, but he guessed she'd be at the hospital, too, along with her mother. Raymer hoped so. He didn't want to have to cuff the man in front of his loved ones. Getting out of the car, he thought about double-checking his .38 to make sure it was loaded and the safety was on, then decided not to bother. He wouldn't be able to grip it with his bandaged right hand, and it would be useless in his left.

He paused to do a quick inventory of the truck bed, noting a big red gas can. Even in the moonlight he could see gas had sloshed out of its mouth recently. Only a small amount was left in the bottom. The barking seemed to be coming not from the house but the enormous shed out back, the scorched, mangled roof looking like it had been struck by lightning. The sight of this conspicuous damage caused Raymer to swallow hard. Why hadn't he himself been reduced to cinders? A padlock was dangling, open, from the latch, and as soon as he opened the shed's door, Sully's little dog came bounding out, squealing with delight. Did he recognize Raymer from the cemetery that morning, or did he just love people? Amazing that the animal could be in such high spirits given his condition, one eye swollen shut, the fur on his muzzle singed and matted with blood. Taken together with his half-chewed-off dick, he made a grisly spectacle. "You look like you had a rough night," Raymer told him, and the dog yipped enthusiastically, as if a little empathy was all he needed to be happy.

A light came on over the back door then, as well as a floodlight attached to the peak of the shed, illuminating the entire yard. A moment later a man in a sleeveless T-shirt came out and stood on the porch, scratching his enormous belly thoughtfully with his left hand. Raymer had seen the man around town and marveled at the thatch of unruly cowlick that was his distinguishing feature, pretty unusual on anybody but a kid. His right wrist and forearm were awkwardly wrapped in gauze and masking tape. "I been expecting you," he said, his voice carrying in the darkness.

"You know why I'm here, then?" Raymer said, approaching the house, the little mutt doing joyous laps around him. He half expected Dougie to advise him on how to proceed, but not a peep. Maybe he was gone for good. That's certainly what it felt like standing here, quite some distance from the nearest neighbor, with a very large man who'd already killed one man tonight: like he was on his own. "That looks painful," he said, staring at his bandaged forearm and wondering how badly it was burned.

"It is," Zack admitted. "Serves me right, I guess."

"How'd you know he was in Sully's trailer?" Raymer said. "Your son-in-law."

"I didn't," he said. "I went there to tell Sully she was gonna make it.

My wife. She was in a coma, and they kept tellin' us she might not wake up, but then she did."

Raymer, like everybody else in Bath, had heard about Sully's long affair with Ruth and also that her husband knew all about it. Apparently the fact they'd been sharing her didn't preclude the possibility of friendship and might even, weirdly, have been its source. Would Raymer and Jerome have arrived at some similar arrangement if Becka had lived? If she'd been killed in a car wreck years later, long after they all knew where they stood with one another, would Raymer's first thought have been to inform Jerome, since he'd loved her, too? "But when you got to the trailer, Sully wasn't there."

"There weren't no lights on," Zack told him, "but I heard this little guy whimperin' inside, and when I knocked I heard somebody stirrin' in there. I figured it wasn't Sully. He'd've come to the door. But this guy sounded hurt, so I went in."

"The door was unlocked?"

The man chuckled. "Sully never locked a door in his life. Most of the time he wouldn't even think to close 'em."

"And you found him inside. Your son-in-law."

He nodded. "I turned on a light, and there he was in the doorway, rubbing his eyes like he just woke up. He said, 'This ain't working out like I planned.' I asked him what he'd planned and he said, 'You're supposed to be Sully.' We just stood there lookin' at each other for a minute. Then I said, 'Aren't you gonna ask how she is?' And he said, 'How *who* is?' That was when I seen he was holdin' that hammer."

He showed Raymer his left elbow, which he must've used to block the blow, now ballooned up to the size of a knee.

"You don't have to talk to me," Raymer said. "In fact, you probably shouldn't, not without a lawyer. You know your rights?"

He shrugged. "I watch TV." He listened patiently while Raymer recited the Miranda, resuming his story only when that was over. "He got the one blow in, but that was it. Roy ain't much of a fighter. He likes to punch women. Kick poor defenseless animals. But a big guy like me? I just picked him up and tossed him. The back of his head hit the edge of the counter and that was that. He just laid there, not movin'."

"An accident, then."

"I never meant to kill him, if that's what you mean."

He seemed to understand, though, that a jury might not want to play ball, given his strong motive for vengeance.

"I probably can't really say that, though," he admitted, scratching his belly again. "'Cause maybe I did. When I grabbed him, I was thinkin' about what he just said—'How *who* is?'—like he'd already forgot about what he done to Ruth. Plus all those times he hit our Janey. So maybe I tossed him harder than I had to. Before tonight, I never wanted to hurt nobody. I like to get along with people, mostly."

"Why burn the trailer?"

Zack rested a hand on his cowlick, holding it down for a minute, though it popped right back up again when he dropped his hand. "He must've found Sully's gas can out in the garage, since it was sittin' right there on the kitchen table with a box of matches. I figure he must've planned to hit Sully with the hammer when he came in, then burn the place. Make it look like an accident."

"So you thought you'd do the same thing?"

He appeared to consider the possibility, as if he no longer had access to his earlier intention and the best he could offer was an educated guess. "You ever kill anybody?" he said, pointing at Raymer's gun, the butt of it peeking out from his jacket.

"No," Raymer said. "Never."

"You don't think normal afterwards," he said. "It's all different. Most of the time I can figure out what to do. It might not be what you'd do, but I kind of know what's right for me."

Raymer nodded.

"Kill somebody and it's like . . . you can't figure out what comes next, 'cause you ain't you anymore. You can't really even remember who you were. All there is is what you just did. That's the best I can explain it. I just did what he was plannin' to do."

"How'd you manage to burn yourself?"

"That was this guy's fault," he said, pointing at the dog, who'd tired of doing circles and figure eights and plopped down on his stomach midway between them, as if he couldn't decide which one was more likely to issue a command. "Roy'd locked him in the bathroom, and I kind of forgot about him. I'd just struck the match when I heard him whine, and I must've just stood there with it lit, because when I looked down my sleeve was on fire. Must've spilled some gas on it. Anyway, I got the shirt off, but when I dropped it, the whole place went up." He squatted in front of the dog, who rose and licked the man's left hand. "I just grabbed you and got us out of there before we both burned up, didn't I?"

Raymer couldn't think of anything else to ask except the obvious. "You aren't going to give any trouble, are you?"

"Me? No."

This he believed. "Well, let's stop at the hospital and get that arm looked at. But tomorrow you'll have to come down to the station."

Zack nodded. "You think they'll believe me about what happened? That it was an accident?"

"Well, I do."

"What'll they do to me?"

"That I can't tell you," Raymer admitted. "You picked the right man to kill, though."

"That's what I got to get straight in my head," he said. "From now on I'm gonna be somebody that killed somebody else."

Raymer couldn't help feeling sorry for the guy. He didn't look like he'd be getting used to that idea anytime soon.

Cured

U P," said the older nurse, yanking back Sully's bedclothes. He'd been warned this was coming, just a few minutes ago, he thought, but the clock said three-thirty, so they'd let him sleep for an hour. Mighty big of them.

"Have a heart, lady," he told her. "Four hours ago I was dead." Not exactly true, but close enough. "A life-threatening cardiac event" was how they were describing what happened in the driveway, one he wouldn't have survived if Mrs. St. Peter, one of the elderly Upper Main Street widows that he'd ferried to doctor and hairdresser appointments, hadn't called the police station to report a Peeping Tom, which she did at least once a week. An officer named Miller had been sent to her house, right across the street from Miss Beryl's, and he'd seen Sully stagger up the driveway like a drunk and then collapse. The protocol would have been to call for an ambulance, but Miller apparently saw an opportunity for heroism and dragged him out to the street, stuffed him into the back of his cruiser and raced him to the hospital, siren blaring, quite possibly saving his life in the process.

"Okay," the nurse said when he'd managed to swing his legs over the side of the bed. "So far, so good. Catch your breath a minute."

His breathing, actually, was pretty good. The best it had been in months. They'd told him at the VA that if he didn't die on the table he'd feel a lot better immediately, but he'd forgotten what a lot better felt like, when oxygen really penetrated his lungs. "Does my doctor know you're treating me like this?"

"Any dizziness?"

"No."

"Feel like you might faint?"

"No."

"Okay, then, on your feet, mister."

Up he went. Wobbly for a second, then steady. The older nurse at his left elbow, the younger at his right. "I feel this draft," he told them.

"That's because you're bare-assed," the boss lady told him.

"I thought that might be it," he said.

When he went to touch his chest, she said, "Don't," and swatted his hand away.

"What'd they put in there, a hockey puck?"

"It feels bigger than it really is. You'll forget it's even there."

"When?"

"Let's walk."

"Where?"

"Down the hall. Then back. You think you can make it?"

"I think we should go dancing, you and me."

"Where?"

"Wherever you want. But first you have to give me back my pants."

"How do you feel?"

Good. Good was how he felt. Which was strange in itself. "What ward are we on?"

"Intensive care. They'll move you to a regular room tomorrow."

"I have a friend who might be on this ward. Her name's Ruth?"

"Came in in a coma?"

The past tense stopped him.

"She woke up," the nurse told him. "She's going to make it."

"How far is her room?"

She pointed to the end of the corridor. "Can you make it that far?"

"Let's go."

SITTING IN THE CHAIR at Ruth's bedside, he woke up with her gaze on him and rain pattering against the window behind him. The wall clock said four-thirty, so he'd dozed there for half an hour. She'd been asleep when they arrived, but Sully talked the nurses into letting him wait there for a while. He must've nodded off as soon as they left.

If anything, Ruth looked worse than she did yesterday. The swelling in her lower face had spread right up to her hairline, the bruising more vivid. But the eye that seemed glued shut the day before had partially opened. Most important, unlike Vera earlier that evening, Ruth was really there, present in her badly damaged body, actually in the room with him. He'd promised the nurse that he wouldn't try to get to his feet without help, but now he did so without too much effort. Though there was discomfort in his chest where they'd inserted the internal defibrillator, it was nothing like the agony of the last few days. Leaning on the raised railing of the bed with one hand, he took Ruth's with the other.

"Okay, you win," he said. "We'll go to Aruba."

She started to smile, but he could see the pain in her eyes. No more jokes, then.

"How about us two going down for the count at the same time, huh?"

She blinked once, slow and deliberate. *Yeah, how about that?*

"Janey and Tina were here all day. Zack, too."

Another long blink.

"I'm sorry I've been so ...," he began, then stopped. "I'm sorry I made you worry about me. They wanted to do this down at the VA weeks ago," he said, laying a hand on his chest.

Yes.

"You're out of the woods, too. You know that, right?"

Yes. She knew.

"Maybe while we're here they'll fix everything. Make us young again."

Her head moved to the side ever so slightly.

"You don't want to be young again? Me neither. Make do with being alive, I guess."

Yes.

He wanted to, he realized. Live, that is. For a while longer, anyway. For the last month or so he'd been wondering if maybe he'd lost his taste for it, but apparently not. Rub would have to muck out the basement of the old mill by himself, but he'd manage. So would Carl, at least until Sully could get back on his feet.

"Well," said a voice behind him. "Look who's up and disobeying orders."

The older nurse was standing in the doorway. "Uh-oh," he told Ruth. "The gig is up. This one's going to throw me under the bus for sure."

Small pressure from Ruth's hand. Small, but not imaginary. Then they both let go.

A middle-aged man was leaning against the door to Sully's room when the two nurses escorted him there, and it took Sully a moment to recognize his son. "You're back," he said. "I wasn't expecting you until Tuesday."

"Keep moving," the older nurse prodded, "before you fall over." She looked at Peter. "Is he always like this?"

"Stubborn, you mean? Ornery? Cantankerous? Impossible?"

When the nurses had Sully tucked back into bed and they were alone, Peter said, "I can't leave you alone for two minutes, can I."

Sully ignored this. "I've got a job for you. I'd do it myself, but it could be a couple days before they let me go back to work."

Peter was grinning at him.

"What?"

"Nothing."

"You know where Rub lives?"

"Did he move?"

"Pick him up at seven. You know how to operate a backhoe?"

"Better than you."

"Yeah?"

"In my sleep."

"What?" Sully asked, because Peter was still grinning at him.

"I missed you, too," he said.

"Good," Sully told him, pleased to hear it. "I wasn't sure you would."

He closed his eyes, took a deep breath. The oxygen, bless it, ran right through him. "How'd you know where I was?" it occurred to him to wonder, opening his eyes again when Peter didn't respond.

The room was dark. Apparently he'd slept. Had he imagined the conversation with his son? No, he decided, it had been real. There was a hint of gray in the eastern sky. Another day, he thought. Sunday, in fact, and him around to see it. Imagine that.

IT HAD BEGUN to rain. Not violently, like the night before, but steadily, another drenching. Unless Raymer missed his guess, more of Hill would slalom into Dale by morning, Bath's dead slip-sliding, in clear violation of their unspoken covenant, into the terrain of the living.

He parked behind the station and let himself in the back door. He would be inside just long enough to lock his gun and badge and SUV keys in the large bottom drawer of his desk so he wouldn't have to come in tomorrow. He was turning the bolt when he heard a sound, and there, standing in the doorway, was Charice, her eyes swollen from crying. Tears for Jerome, of course, Raymer thought bitterly.

"There's some things I need to say before you sneak off," she told him, tossing his gym bag, which he'd left in her car the night before, onto the sofa.

Sneak off, he thought, hearing in that phrase a judgment. Well, he *was* sneaking off, wasn't he, so maybe he deserved it. He motioned to a chair. "There's no need to apologize—"

"Good," she said, sitting down, "because I'm not."

Raymer sat across from her, his desk and so much more between them. Charice, who was seldom at a loss for words, was silent so long that he began to wonder if she'd changed her mind and decided she had nothing to tell him after all.

"The first thing you have to understand," she said at long last, "is that from the time we were little I've kept Jerome's secrets. After our parents died, it was him and me against the world, you know? He was my protector. I was an adult before it finally occurred to me that I was protecting *him* more than he was *me.*"

"When did you learn? About him and Becka?" In other words, for how many days, weeks and months had she sided with her brother when she might've sided with him?

"I knew from the start," she told him, with unmistakable defiance. "He couldn't wait to tell me. Like I said, him and me against the world. That's the next thing you need to understand. Jerome? For him, this was no fling. It was love."

Raymer didn't doubt it, since his words were still ringing in his ears. *We were so in love . . . You have no idea . . . Do you even know what it's like to love somebody . . . I mean* really *love somebody . . . Do you even know what love is?* And of course that single word on the florist's card: *Always.* This had been seared into his brain much like the staple had been into his palm.

"He'd had a lot of girlfriends," she continued, "but love was a completely new experience—and it was complicated by this crazy idea he had."

"Which was?"

"He believed she'd cured him."

"Of what?"

"Of everything. Of being Jerome. All his obsessions and anxieties? Gone. He didn't need to perform his rituals anymore. The counting, touching, reciting, sanitizing. He might not act like it, but—deep down?—Jerome's the most anxious, insecure man you've ever met."

No, Raymer thought. *I am. By far.*

"You probably think he wanted me to move here so he could look after me, right? Not true. Whenever he has one of his panic attacks, I'm the only one who can help. Before I packed it in down home, I had a life. I was engaged to be married."

"And you let that go?"

"Did I have a choice?"

Of course you did, Raymer thought, but he couldn't help being moved by the fact that she thought she didn't.

She chuckled mirthlessly, shaking her head. "That James Bond stuff? 'The name is Bond' "—she was doing her brother's voice now, and it was spooky how well she nailed it—" 'Jerome Bond.' He did that as much for himself as for other people, the poor guy. But then just about everything he does is for other people."

"And Becka cured him?"

"That's what he believed."

"And what do *you* believe?"

She shrugged. "A man who has to clean the bathroom twice a day his whole adult life suddenly doesn't have to? The change was pretty dramatic. He kept saying, 'For the first time in my life, I feel . . . *well,* as in *not ill.* When I'm with her I feel safe.' I told him how crazy that sounded. I mean, here he was, six-six in his socks, strong as a bull, a pro at martial arts. And Becka was maybe five-eight? A hundred and twenty pounds? *She* made *him* feel safe? But you couldn't talk to him. He felt what he felt. When she was around, he wasn't tied up in his usual knots."

"That's exactly how she made me feel," Raymer admitted.

"We fought, Jerome and me. For the first time in our lives. You wouldn't believe how we fought."

"Why?"

"Lots of reasons," she said, causing Raymer to wonder if he might be one of them. It would've been nice to think he'd meant that much to her, at least. "I wasn't a big fan of Becka's."

"Really?" he said. "Why not?" Because everybody seemed to love her.

"Because Becka was all about Becka," she said, her expression now hard. Raymer started to object, but she didn't let him. "Didn't you ever notice how she always charmed people one at a time?"

Her custom, at a party or restaurant, of culling one person from the group, of getting him to turn his back on someone else, of enticing him to follow her into the kitchen or out onto the patio, where it would be just the two of them? Yes, of course. Who knew this habit better than Raymer? Hadn't it stoked the jealousy that was always present in the back of his mind? Though, really, he'd reason with himself, was there anything so wrong about making every one of the people she singled out feel special?

"Remember," Charice was saying, "how important it was for her to be able to touch people? How if you moved just out of physical range, something happened behind her eyes? It was almost like she couldn't be sure you were still you."

The night of that hateful dinner, every time Raymer looked down that table, his wife was placing a lovely hand on old Barton's mottled one. Here again, though, he'd blamed himself, assuming that he must've disappointed her somehow, or in a thousand ways, and made her ravenous for the company of other, more interesting people.

"That was her great talent. Making everybody love her. She couldn't help herself. She was as compulsive about that as Jerome had been about cleaning his bathroom. Men, women, old, young? None of that really mattered to her. It was seduction, yes, but I don't think it had much to do with sex. It was about adoration. The more obsessively people loved her, the more alive she felt. Jerome, being Jerome, was the mother lode."

Not *the* mother lode, Raymer thought. Because before Jerome there'd been Douglas Raymer. Not to mention poor Alice Moynihan, who used to stake out their town house, waiting for Raymer to leave in the morning so she'd have Becka all to herself. And it was Becka, to this day, she was talking to on her phone, Becka that her husband had taken away from her when he demanded she surrender that handset.

"I warned Jerome the day would come when she'd replace him just like she was replacing you."

"But he didn't believe you."

Her eyes had filled. "He said I was just jealous of his happiness. Because if they were together, then I'd be alone. He told me to go on back home. He didn't need me anymore. So much for him and me against the world."

"Did you ever think about telling me?" Which of course was a less pathetic version of the question he really wanted to ask: *So you're saying I didn't factor in at all?*

"You haven't been listening. I always keep Jerome's secrets," she said, her features hardening again. "Besides, he was going to tell you himself."

"When?"

"The day she died, actually. The plan had been for him to pick Becka up at your place, then drive down to the station. She was going to wait in the car while Jerome came in and told you they were going away together."

"But I went home early."

"You must've beat him there by fifteen or twenty minutes, because when he turned onto your street the ambulance was out front, along with two or three cruisers."

"What did he do?"

"What do you think? He called me."

"And you said?"

"What *could* I say? I told him to go back home. To let me handle things. By the time I got there, he was like what you saw today."

Raymer tried to square these revelations with his own memories of that awful day and those that followed, but it was all a dreamlike haze. Until now, Jerome's absence during that period hadn't really registered as significant, just a vague recollection that he hadn't been around for a while. He'd had more important things to worry himself sick about.

"So just like that, he needed you again."

"He took a leave of absence. We told people he was down in North Carolina finishing up his master's, but in fact he was in a facility in Albany trying to put himself back together. I visited him there on weekends and days off."

"And he got better?"

"More like the old Jerome," she said, "which was hardly *better*. With Becka gone, all his obsessions returned with a vengeance. But yeah, we patched things up between us. Things got back to being almost normal. Not that anybody else would call it normal. Still, I was proud of him. Inside he was still a mess, but at least he could function again. You finally seemed to be coming out of your funk, too, and I was thinking maybe we'd all dodged a bullet. But then you had to get ahold of that garage-door remote. I never should've told Jerome about that. Overnight he was batshit again. Imagining you knew." She met his gaze now. "Imagining I told you."

"Why would he think you'd do that? You always kept his secrets."

"Well, he knew I . . ."

"Knew you what?" Raymer said, his heart suddenly in his throat.

"Doesn't matter," she said, getting to her feet.

When he, dispirited, rose as well, she seemed to really take in his massively bandaged hand. "Will it heal right?" she said. At Jerome's she'd caught a glimpse of the grotesque excavation he'd made of his palm.

"There's evidently some nerve damage. They say I dug right through, almost. Speaking of batshit."

He expected her to chide him, but she didn't. "I read about this guy once?" she said. "He had an itch on his scalp, and he scratched straight through his skull and into his brain."

"That's supposed to make me feel better?" he said. "That you've heard of somebody dumber than me?"

She ignored this. They were standing there facing each other, the desk still in between them. "And this other guy," she continued, "had the hiccups for a whole year. Tried everything but just couldn't get rid of them. Finally he couldn't take it anymore and jumped off the Golden Gate Bridge. Which kills just about everybody, but somehow he survived. And guess what?"

"He still had the hiccups?"

She offered him a sad smile. "See, that right there is what we need to work on. No, the hiccups were gone. Turns out, jumping off the Golden Gate's a hundred percent effective as a cure for hiccups."

Feeling a smile on his own face, Raymer allowed himself to imagine what it would be like to spend the rest of his life with this woman, having conversations like this all the time. Now that he thought about it, every single conversation they'd ever had, even the ones that were exercises in pure exasperation, always left him feeling less alone. What would happen, he wondered, if he came out from behind the desk? "What *we* need to work on?" he said. "We? As in—"

"Us."

"There's an us?"

"If you want."

"I do," Raymer said, at once aware and not really caring very much that these same words had, when last uttered, caused him no end of grief.

"A couple things we'd have to agree on first," she told him.

"Like?"

"Like you'd have to figure out how to forgive Jerome. He's my brother."

"I think I can do that." In fact, he was pretty sure he already had.

"I'd ask you to forgive me, too, if I'd done anything wrong, but I didn't—unless you'd say keeping Jerome's secret was wrong. Is that something you'd count?"

"Not if you don't."

"And you'd have to let me out from behind my desk. Allow me to do the job I was trained for."

"Sorry, I can't do that," he said. And when she again narrowed her eyes dangerously, he added, "You forget. I'm not your boss anymore. I resigned."

From her hip pocket she took what was left of the resignation letter he'd given to Gus yesterday afternoon, now torn in quarters, and tossed the scraps on his blotter.

"Okay, then," he said.

"And speaking of coming out from behind desks . . ."

She met him halfway, with only the wastebasket between them now. She leaned toward him and he toward her. Suddenly, just as their lips were about to touch, an arc of static electricity leaped from Raymer's lips to Charice's, causing both to take a step away. "Whoa!" they said in unison, vigorously rubbing their lips with the backs of their hands. For a moment they just looked at each other, amazed. The office was carpeted, but still. "What the hell was *that*?" she said.

Dougie, Raymer thought, saying goodbye, leaving as he'd arrived on an electrical current. A fairly insane thought, sure, though just maybe . . .

Their second attempt was more successful. "Whoa," each said again, this time for a different reason.

"Actually," he said, "I've got one stipulation myself."

"What's that?"

"You have to come with me to the middle school tomorrow morning." Because if he was staying—and he most definitely was—in a matter of hours he'd be standing on the stage of his old middle-school auditorium talking to a couple hundred people about his eighth-grade English teacher. While still a scary idea, for some reason it inspired somewhat less than the usual full-blown terror. After all, within the last twenty-four hours he'd been struck by lightning and handled a deadly coral snake, events that cast public speaking in a whole new light. He wouldn't be brilliant, he knew, but he'd be no worse than Reverend Tunic, and at least he would be wearing pants. And, unlike Tunic, he'd stick to the truth. He'd tell folks about all the books Miss Beryl had given him as a boy. How he'd hidden them in his closet so his mother wouldn't think he'd stolen the damn things. He'd tell his audience that Miss Beryl had held a far-better opinion of him than he had of himself, and how as a boy that good opinion had frightened him, because he could see no rational basis for it. Further, he'd explain how the old woman had kept scribbling *Who is this Douglas Raymer?* in the margins of his essays. And how she'd remained in his margins down through the years, like a good teacher will. He would tell them these things because he'd meant for years to thank this dear woman and never gotten around to it.

THEY AGREED he shouldn't check in to a hotel for just a couple hours, as he'd planned to do, because that was silly. On the other hand, Charice informed him, accompanying him to the Moribund Arms was absolutely out of the question. It was her firm intention never to set foot in that place except to arrest somebody. No, they'd go to her place and take her car, which was parked out front. Next week Raymer would trade in his piece-of-shit Jetta for a vehicle more befitting a chief of police. Just not a Mustang.

Outside, the rain had stopped. When they got to her vehicle, Charice remembered something. "Wait here," she said, and as Raymer did so, it occurred to him that waiting for a woman who'd forgotten something was one of life's underrated pleasures. How many times had he and Becka been about to go somewhere when she had to go back for something she'd left on the kitchen table? An annoying habit, yes, yet how wonderful it was when she reappeared, how sweet the knowledge that she wasn't gone for good. Until the day she really was gone. And now it was every bit as wonderful when Charice reappeared, even though what she had in her hand was the ceramic cobra.

"What are you doing with that?" he said.

"Taking it back home, of course."

He arched an eyebrow at her. "Back home?"

"I bought it for Jerome, thinking it'd make him less scared of real snakes, but all it did was freak him out. Why? Does it scare you, too?"

"No, but you do."

Not really, of course. She might be full of surprises, but he'd basically been right to trust her, he reflected, tossing his gym bag into the back and sliding into the passenger seat. In truth, Raymer had always been attracted to women who were a step or two ahead of him, though naturally that was most of them. The snake, now lying stiffly on top of his bag, did make him curious, though, as to what else she might've lied about. Whether, for instance, she even had a butterfly tattoo.

Play your cards right for once, Dougie advised, *and you can find out.*

"What?" Charice said. "Did you say something?"

"I started to say that I think maybe I'm in love with you," he told her, which was, like the world itself, both a lie and the truth.

"That's the other thing we gotta work on," she told him. "That *maybe.*"

Acknowledgments

When a writer gets to be my age, the list of people he's indebted to is almost as long as the book itself. Many thanks to the usual suspects, acknowledged in all or most of my previous books. Barbara, Emily and Kate continue to make all things possible. Nat, Judith, Adia and Joel (my agents) could not have been more steadfast in their faith over the long decades. Gary, Sonny, Gabby? Along with everybody else at Knopf and Vintage, you continue to make me look better, smarter and more talented than I am, and I know you'd make me younger, taller and better-looking if you could.

As to this particular book, the following helped plug some of the more obvious holes in my knowledge: Judy Andersen, Tim Hall, Peter Tranchell, Bob Wilkins, Greg Gottung, Jim Gottung, Bill Lundgren and Carol Wolff.